RUTHLESS LITTLE GAMES

SIN CITY MAFIA
BOOK TWO

LANE HART

COPYRIGHT

Cover Photo of Marshall by Wander Aguilar Photography
Cover Design by Wingfield Designs

TRIGGER WARNING

THIS STORY CONTAINS THE FOLLOWING:

GRAPHIC SEX SCENES
PHYSICAL ASSAULT
HEAVY PROFANITY
BREEDING KINK
MANIPULATION
PROSTITUTION
KNIFE PLAY
WHIPPING
STALKING
STABBING

SYNOPSIS

My older sister ran away from home to avoid being forced into an arranged marriage with the mafia family blamed for her mother's death. Now that burden has fallen on me.

Eighteen and sheltered, my life has only ever revolved around the familiar comfort of the tennis court. I've always been shielded from the brutal realities of my father's world, protected from his enemies. Enemies like Lochlan Dunne, who my father now wants as an ally.

Lochlan is a ruthless businessman everyone fears. His family's wealth was built on the flesh trade. One he has been rumored to frequently enjoy, making us complete opposites. I'm so inexperienced that just being alone in the same room with the gorgeous tyrant terrifies me.

My terror only turns him on. In fact, Lochlan can't even wait until our wedding night to claim my innocence in the most ruthless way.

I love provoking him and hate how badly I want to surrender to him, but I can't risk falling for a man who'll only hurt me. That's why I give him an ultimatum before we say our vows: be faithful to me or I'll never share his bed or my body with him again.

Lochlan is too stubborn to cave to anyone's demands. However, the longer I refuse him, the more desperate he becomes to have me.

Teasing and taunting him during our tumultuous honeymoon period is all fun and games until someone in his inner circle tries to kill me.

1

Lochlan Dunne

B orn and raised in the city that never sleeps, I never had trouble getting any shuteye until recently.

My family's wealthy—has always been—so immense that it never occurred to me that anything could ever come along and wipe it out.

Then some motherfucker blew up my casino, killing twenty-two people and injuring more than a dozen others. They were innocent people with their whole fucking lives in front of them. People who came to support a fucking charity for starving children. I bet none of them were murderers.

Pulling up the footage from the security camera on my phone, I rewatch for the hundredth time the event room the day before the explosion, searching for the culprit.

Since that day, I've been left wondering: Why the fuck did I escape death the day it didn't just come knocking on my door, but busting that bitch down? And why do I feel emptier and more alone

1

in the world than ever before after getting a lucky as shit second chance? Shouldn't I be a changed man who wants to be better? Because I don't. If anything, I have an urge to be worse now that I may lose every penny of the Dunne family's wealth. If my father knew the legacy that he left to me was on the brink of being wiped out, he would probably crawl out of his grave and drag me back down to hell with him.

I hate that I still care about that bastard's opinion, even though he's been dead for three wonderful years.

He loved to remind me that I would never have what it takes to run his empire. The only reason he left everything to me is because my younger half-brother is an even bigger fuck up.

I will literally do anything to avoid admitting that asshole was right about me. But with each day, I doubt myself a little more.

There's a relentless black void inside of me that no amount of alcohol or debauchery can fill lately. I think it expands a little more with every shot I take, and each mediocre fuck I grit my teeth to endure. I should probably give up both vices before that emptiness swallows me up, sending me to an early grave. Twenty-six is probably too young to ruin a liver, though. That shit could take another decade at least.

Sex is still good for the rush of power it gives me, and a few seconds of oblivion, which is better than none. Afterward, I always need a strong drink to wash down the lingering flavor of bitter gold-digger. The worst are the ones who can't play the part of being ravaged by a savage worth a shit because they're too busy faking orgasms while deciding how to spend my dollar bills.

I've had to fake a few of my own Os recently. Lack of sleep and too many shots will do that to a man. Honestly, the sex lately isn't worth the effort or aggravation. I don't even know why I bother.

Putting my phone away since there is still no answer to my burning question, I stare out the window of the second-story office building in a daze, watching cars speed by on the early Vegas morning, racing to whatever hellhole they're headed to. The heat is already insufferable, especially in my custom-made, Italian, three-piece suit. My white dress shirt is soaked through the pits with sweat, which means I'll need another shower and change of clothes before lunch. A third before I eat dinner alone and then head out to the bar...

Fuck me. Maybe I'm already living in hell and am too goddamn stupid to realize it.

It's time to change shit up.

Tonight, to hell with it. I'm not going out. I'll go for a swim at the estate and then try to get a couple hours of sleep before I crash and burn out completely.

Finally, my attorney, Larry Warwick, slips into the conference room. The old man has been practicing law longer than I've been alive. "Sorry to keep you waiting. How's the recovery?"

"I'm fine," I assure him. A concussion and a few bruised ribs aren't worth mentioning. And rather than waste time on more bull-shit small talk, I decide to get right to the point of this meeting. "What's going on with the lawsuits?" I ask him.

With a wince, Warwick's shrewd eyes behind thick lenses briefly land on the Bowen knot tattooed on the right side of my face before he tells me, "I think I can get the ten most determined plaintiffs down to five hundred million."

"Down to...are you fucking kidding me?" I ask lurching to my feet. I knew I was going to have to take one hell of a hit, but goddamn.

Warwick cringes away, but still says, "Take your anger out on me if you want, but it won't change the fact that ten celebrities are dead, Lochlan, and everyone blames you. Their lawyers want fifty million each. That doesn't include the total for the other twelve deceased. Then there's the long-term care for the thirteen who were badly injured, and a half dozen traumatized employees. The liability for this type of tragedy adds up fast. So far, they won't even give me an offer because they're so certain they'll win at trial."

"Then we'll go to trial," I tell him.

3

Warwick is shaking his gray head before I finish speaking. "You really don't want to do that. They've got a strong case. If you go to trial, and put this before a sympathetic jury, you'll not only look like an even bigger asshole, but you will be bankrupted," he explains.

Bankrupted?

"Fuck."

"I wish I had better news, but you need to understand what's at risk for skimping on your security."

"Jesus." I scrub my calloused hand down my face and retake my seat, wishing this shit was all a bad dream and hating that he's right. I could've had better security in place, metal detectors, bomb-sniffing dogs, and whatever else to prevent this shit from happening, but I didn't.

Warwick leans back in his chair, more relaxed now that I'm seated. His clasped fingers rest on his rounded stomach. "If we go to trial, I'll need another retainer and an expense fund. My fees won't be cheap."

"So my options are what? Lose nearly everything with a potential settlement or go to trial with a high risk of losing every single penny?"

"Yes." He nods slowly as he stares at the thick file on the conference table as if in thought. "There are a few things you could do to help lower the amount of the damages."

"Like what?"

"You'll have to keep your public image squeaky clean from now until the trial."

"You think I'm capable of squeaky clean?" I mutter. While Warwick wouldn't bend any rule for fear of losing his law license, he's not stupid. He knows where my family's wealth comes from, and it's not from selling Girl Scout cookies. My girls sell something even more addictive—pussy. Not just pussy, but fantasies, the dirtier the better. Whatever it is that gets you off, at the right price of course. And there's a big ass, walk-in safe at my estate that houses all the dirty deeds of the most prominent businessmen and politicians, not just in the state but the entire country.

Peering at me over the top of his glasses, Warwick says, "I mean you'll need to lay low, get some good PR to combat the bad boy pimp image."

"I own the biggest brothel empire in the world, how exactly do you propose I clean up my image?"

The first thing I did when my father died, and I inherited his money, was to build a casino. I needed something that was my own, something separate from the goddamn whore houses.

The old man shrugs his shoulders under his suit jacket. "You could take a wife."

"Take a wife?" I grit out through my clenched teeth. "Are you fucking kidding me right now? How will tying myself to a woman who spends all my money help the situation?"

"A good woman can make even the worst man want to be better."

"That's the thing. I don't want to be better for some woman."

Sighing, he says, "A jury will be less inclined to bankrupt you if you have a wife and family to support."

"A wife and...wow." I scrape my fingers over my raspy jaw, feeling like I've been blindsided. Having a beautiful trophy wife on my arm is no big deal. I can handle a wife if she's hot, obedient, and the union is also beneficial to me, like marrying my rival Dante Salvato's oldest daughter. But becoming a father is not something I've given any thought to whatsoever.

"Other than working on your image, identifying who planted the bomb could take some of the heat off you during the trial. The police still don't have any leads, do they?"

"No. They never fingered anyone as the bomber. Kozlov or Petrov were no doubt the ones who paid for the assassination attempt, but there's no proof. And neither of them have been seen or heard from in months." I'm sure Dante made certain they will never be seen or heard from again.

"Which means you're left holding the bag of shit. Or in this case, holding all the body bags of those poor souls who died."

"Fuck." Running my fingers through my short hair, I tell

Warwick, "I was supposed to marry a rival's daughter, as a peace offering between us. But it's been on hold for months now."

I've known for a while now that Dante Salvato's daughter Madison ran away. Fucking fled the city, probably the state, just to avoid having to marry me. And the bastard has been lying to me about it this whole time.

"Find the bomber, take a wife, pretend you're using your second chance at life to fall madly in love." The bastard gives me an impossible to-do list like any of that shit is going to be easy. "The media will eat it up if you look more like a family man than a ruthless pimp, and we can show the jury you were also a victim if you can find who tried to kill you."

He keeps saying *take a wife* like it's that easy to pluck one out of the sky. And god knows I want to find the person responsible to make them pay.

"I'll see what I can do," I tell my attorney.

"Good. And hire a reputable PR person. They'll cost less by the hour than my firm. Which reminds me, I'll need another two million to bill my time and expenses against preparing for trial," he says, not even bothering to get up from his chair to show me out.

"You'll have your money by the end of the day," I promise him as I start to the door.

"Great." My hand is on the doorknob when he adds, "One other thing."

"What?" I ask him over my shoulder.

"Try to keep your brother out of trouble. The next DWI he gets could end with someone else in a body bag."

"I'll try," I respond with a heavy sigh.

My half-brother is a twenty-one-year-old walking disaster. I've lost count of how many times he's been arrested for assaults or wrecking the newest sports car I bought him. Flynn probably would've benefited from a little more of my father's tough love before he died. Now he's a spoiled little prick, which is another headache I don't need.

~

Later that night, while I'm lying in bed wide awake, I think over Warwick's advice. But what else is new? I haven't had a good night's sleep since before the bombing.

I checked in with all three of my PIs today, and nobody had any new leads on finding Madison Salvato or any evidence to help identify the bomber. None of the security videos show when exactly the bomb was planted and not a shred of DNA survived the blast. And Madison, well, she could be anywhere in the fucking world.

I keep wondering when the hell Dante Salvato will finally grow a pair and tell me the truth about his missing daughter. An alliance with him could be even more important now that he's taken over all the businesses of the dead Russian, Petrov. He's twice as powerful and rich as he was when we first talked about me marrying his oldest daughter.

His oldest daughter of three.

That means there are two other girls who could potentially take her place, solving my problem of avoiding a gold-digger. Salvato is a hell of a lot richer than I am, so his offspring won't be after my money when they stand to inherit part of his.

The only question is whether or not the other two daughters are of legal age yet.

Rather than put this kind of request in writing, I call up Owen, my cousin, best friend, and second-in-command. He answers even though it's three a.m.

"Yeah, boss?"

"I need you to find me someone in Salvato's household staff that will cough up intel for cash."

"Alright. Like what kind of intel?"

"I want details on his daughters. Photos. Schedules. Hobbies. Social lives. Anything and everything they can give me, and I want it within the next twenty-four hours."

"Loch, man, that doesn't give me much time to work with here.

You know most of the staff will be too scared to give up anything about Salvato's kids."

"Get it done. There has to be someone who sees those girls every day. Even if Salvato has them locked in their rooms, I bet he pays someone to clean them. Find a housekeeper and pay them whatever it takes to get me details."

"I'll see what I can do," he agrees with a sigh. "But why exactly —"

I cut him off. "I'll tell you when you need to know." He may be my best friend, but I don't answer to anyone or owe him any explanations.

Besides, I don't want to say it, to get my hopes up, if the girls are still children. Or too ugly to fuck, even with a bag on their head.

If I have to be stuck with a woman for the rest of my life, then they need to be fucking hot. I don't exactly have a type. All I need is a pretty face with a nice rack and enough ass for me to grab. The bigger the ass, the better it jiggles when I slap it.

Which leads me to a potential problem with an arranged marriage—if Dante Salvato finds out I only fuck women if they're restrained and completely at my mercy, there's no way in hell he'll give me one of his daughters.

2

Lochlan

Five months later...

L ately, I've been turning down all social invitations and staying
home, even on weekends, to try and improve my public image
in the community as Warwick suggested. He's not the only reason,
though. There's so much on the line right now that it's impossible to
party it up and pretend like nothing's wrong.

I go to work, deal with the required bullshit, then come home to
the sprawling family estate.

Not that we were ever a family.

My father claimed my mother only cared about his money, so he
wanted nothing to do with her after I was born. She left the state

before I started school. I don't see her more than once every three or four years, whenever she needs something.

Flynn and I may only be five years apart, but our father didn't find out he had another bastard until he was fifteen and I was twenty. We didn't grow up together and never really got along. I was too busy trying to be the perfect son while he did everything under the sun to piss the old man off in an attempt to gain a minute of his undivided attention.

His ploy worked for the first year or so, until our father decided to throw him out on his ass. Since his mother was even less maternal than mine, I was the one who paid for his apartment and gave him spending money that he blew on drugs. He never had to spend a penny on women since he's a Dunne and could visit any brothel he wanted. And since he always had drugs, the ladies love him.

Since our father died and left me everything, I've tried to make up for our old man's favoritism by giving Flynn whatever money and shit he wanted. After all, there was plenty of it to go around. I haven't told him much about the upcoming trial yet, or that the well may be drying up soon. I keep hoping he'll straighten up, stop fucking off, but lately he keeps doing shit to land his ass in a jail cell.

I'm the one he calls whenever he's in trouble, which is why I'm not surprised to see a younger, slimmer version of myself strolling up beside the pool in baggy jeans and an oversized rock tee. The drug use has always made him thinner, sickly looking, which is why he wears loose clothing. I've paid for ninety-days of rehab twice, which obviously didn't take.

I finish out my lap before acknowledging him. The physical activity has been good for burning off nervous energy lately, even if I sometimes push myself so hard for so long I can barely pull myself out of the pool at the end of the night.

"What have you done now?" I mutter. After wiping the water from my face, I clutch the side of the wall, waiting to hear about his latest disaster and how it's someone else's fault.

"Nothing," he grumbles, coming to a stop above me.

"Then how much money do you need?"

His golden eyes narrow before he says, "If you would just give me half of what's mine, I wouldn't have to keep coming to you for a handout."

"No," I say for the millionth time. "You would blow it all. And there may not be much of it soon."

That statement causes him to frown. "Bullshit."

"It's the truth. You know I'm being sued by all the bombing victim's families. My attorney said the odds of convincing a jury not to take every penny I have are low."

"But...why?"

"People fucking died!" I remind him. "They died in my casino because I didn't have enough security measures in place to know there was a goddamn bomb in the room!"

"What about insurance?" he asks.

I bark out a sarcastic laugh before dunking my head under the water. When I resurface, I tell him, "Insurance only covers the cost of repairing the structural damage and some medical bills due to the collapse. It doesn't pay a dime to anyone killed by a terrorist attack."

"Well, fuck," Flynn huffs, scuffing the bottom of his shoe over the concrete and raising it as if imagining kicking someone's ass.

"I have to find out who planted the bomb to shoulder some of the blame," I explain to him. "And even if I do, I could still end up losing the casino and brothels. Apparently my 'image' doesn't help me..."

"I bet it was one of the guests, a suicide bomber."

"Doubtful. If it was some sort of statement behind the bomb, they would've made sure to flaunt it before killing themselves and everyone else."

"Whatever," Flynn says with a huff. "Will you at least give me money for groceries?"

"Groceries? You mean actual food?"

"Yeah, food."

"I thought you were living off pills lately," I remark. "If I don't see a receipt afterward, it'll be the last cash I give you."

"Could I borrow one of your cars?"

"Fuck, no."

"Why not?"

"Because you've wrecked three and lost your goddamn driver's license for a year!"

"I won't get pulled over."

"No. You can Uber your ass around or walk."

"How about a car and a paid driver?"

"How about you fuck off before I kick your ass?" I grumble right before my phone begins ringing from a nearby chair.

"Answer that for me," I tell Flynn.

"I'm not your bitch," he says but he still starts walking over to grab it, probably just to be nosy.

I quickly pull myself out of the pool and grab a towel from the warming bin to dry off my face, ears, and hands. "Who is it?" I ask as I walk back toward him.

"Screen says 'Salvato.'" He holds it out to me and I grin at the sight. "Hell, yes." Taking the device from him, I answer and put it up to my ear. "Salvato. About fucking time you stopped avoiding me. Guess you finally opened the wedding invitation."

The wedding invitation I sent to him with Sophie's name on it nearly five months ago, but he ignored it. I guess he's heard from our mutual acquaintances that they've recently been notified to save the date of June first and witness our nuptials. The ones that Dante has been disregarding, like he thought I wasn't serious.

I slump into the pool chair while he roars in my ear. "You're out of your fucking mind if you think I'm going to let you marry my baby girl."

It took a few weeks to find someone who even knew Salvato was hiding daughters in his penthouse. Then a few more to find the right price to convince a housekeeper to cough up the information on the girls. The innocent-looking Snow White is the perfect princess to play the part of my sweet little wife, just like my attorney wanted to help improve my perverted brothel pimp image.

The fact that she's young and hopefully inexperienced is just a nice bonus.

"Didn't your baby girl just turn eighteen? I thought it was kind of me to send the save the date notices out after she legally became an adult."

Flynn takes a seat in the chair next to me with a heavy exhale, making it clear he's not leaving until I hand over some cash. The little bastard needs to get over himself. This is the call I've been waiting months for.

"How did you...you're not getting anywhere near Sophie!" Oh, he's definitely pissed that I not only know her name but also her birthday. Now he knows he's got a rat on his property who has been squealing all his secrets to me.

"You've been lying to me for months, Salvato. Months! Madison ran away last summer, and you can't find her, can you?"

"I've got people in every state looking for her. I'm sure Madison will turn up soon. You just need to be patient a little longer."

I loathe people giving me orders more than anything else in this world.

"Fuck you, Salvato. I told you last summer that you had six months to set the engagement dinner and you ignored me. Consider these extra four months of peace between us my wedding present to you. But don't you fucking dare confuse my continued patience as weakness. I'm tired of waiting. Time's up. You have two other daughters for me to marry. I chose Sophie."

"That's not going to happen."

"It is. Sophie will marry me on June first, or I'll share your secret."

There's a long pause, then he says, "What secret?"

"That Madison is out in the big, wide world, alone and vulnerable. It would be a shame if someone who hates you found her first, wouldn't it?"

"You son of a bitch!"

With the trial date approaching at the end of the year, Warwick is even more insistent that I need to start playing the role of a doting husband with a young new wife, so that maybe the jury won't rape me for all I'm worth.

"Shall I go send out a press release to the media so it'll make the ten o'clock news? I have Madison's photo ready to go," I threaten him.

"Don't you dare," he seethes.

"Do we have a deal or not, Salvato?"

A growl of frustration is his initial response. "Why Sophie?"

"Why not Sophie?"

"Cass is older. She's a beautiful girl–"

"I don't want the redhead."

"Who the fuck told you about them?" he snaps, furious that I know so much about his girls.

"My sources are confidential," I reply. "Now, I want to meet my bride tomorrow night. Are you going to let me see her, or do you want to put your oldest daughter in danger?"

Just because the girl looked gorgeous in the photos and videos I've been getting regularly from one of the housekeepers for five months, I've still been desperate to see her face-to-face. I've had eyes on the Salvato's casino the entire time, ready to approach her at a moment's notice, but she hasn't ever been spotted leaving.

"I'm not going to force Sophie to marry you," he warns me.

"No? While I do usually enjoy gags and handcuffs, they would likely ruin the wedding photos. It certainly wouldn't be appropriate to show off those pictures to the grandkids," I remark.

Hopefully, if I make light about my kinks, Salvato will think I'm being sarcastic and won't take the rumors seriously. And as for the idea of grandkids, starting a family, well, ever since I saw the photo of Snow White with mile-long legs running around in her short tennis skirt, I've had a growing desire to see her pussy overflowing with my cum. I want my seed dripping and sticky on the insides of her thighs because she's tied to my bed, and I refuse to let her remove a drop of it. "Give me ten minutes alone with Sophie and then it's her choice." My voice is noticeably deeper after those dirty thoughts. I'll do whatever it takes in those ten minutes to get a yes out of Snow White.

"You'll give up and walk away if Sophie says no?"

"She won't say no."

"That's awfully cocky of you. Do you really think she'll find you so irresistible that she won't be able to refuse you?" Salvato obviously doesn't know how ruthless I can be to get what I want. Fucking his innocent-looking daughter, trying to knock her up, will be a nice distraction from the shitstorm I'm dealing with. And I'll save my final demand for Dante for later.

"I'm coming to see her tomorrow night at nine. You want my contacts, right?"

"Fine. I'll give you ten minutes with Sophie. But you have to meet and consider Cass as well."

"Oh, and Dante, it's time to update your will."

"Don't fucking push your luck, Dunne."

"So, you'll leave a drug empire to one of your daughters, then? We both know you'll never put that burden on one of them, so draw up the fucking papers by June first."

"You know there will be a clause that if I'm assassinated, you won't ever see a dime."

"But you'll leave something to Sophie, right? My soon-to-be wife," I remark.

"Fuck you, Dunne."

"See you tomorrow night," I reply before cutting him off.

Hell, yes. I wasn't sure if Dante would even consider making me his heir, since he has three children. But no father would want his innocent girls knee deep in gangster shit.

"What was that about?" Flynn asks.

"You heard for yourself. I'm getting married. Don't make any plans on June first."

"You're marrying that fucker's daughter?"

"Yes."

"Why? He's a sleezy asshole. And he didn't sound too thrilled about the idea."

"He's just bitching, but I know he'll agree. He needs my connections if he wants to keep his fentanyl business thriving. I bet he's wishing he didn't need my contacts, but knows how much cash he's losing from being stubborn this long."

"Why does he need your connections?"

"To get law enforcement, feds, DAs, judges, etcetera to look the other way while he traffics product in and out of the state. I have blackmail on dozens getting spanked, fucked, or being sucked off. The sorts of videos these men would die before letting their families see them at their worst."

"That's what you keep in the safe? Blackmail?"

Ignoring his question because I don't want him snooping around, I say, "How much money will it take to get rid of you?"

3

Sophie Salvato

My life is like one endless loop of sleeping, eating, and tennis. I live and breathe for the sport. For eight or nine hours a day, I'm either doing cardio, drills, practice matches, or conditioning. The nights are for recovery, and thinking about how I could play better the next day.

And it's all for nothing.

I'll never go pro because I'm not that good, which is fine. Winning isn't why I spend my days running around on the court. I endure the heat and exhaustion just because I love the sport. If there's a racquet in one hand and a can of balls in the other, I'm happy. It's fun to play against my trainer, Betsy, even though she usually kicks my ass. But I have just as much fun on my own chasing down 80 mph balls being shot out of the tennis ball machine. It's just easier to enjoy the sport when there's no competition. Betsy doesn't understand. Her world revolves around being the best. She plays to win, is paid by my father to teach me to be better, while I play to... just play.

Sometimes I wish I had more ambitions, a few friends, a like-minded tennis partner maybe, but what's the point? Wanting things only leads me down a road of disappointment because my overprotective father doesn't like for me to leave the penthouse or be around anyone other than our family or his guards.

It's safer this way. That's what he says.

What I can't tell him is that I'm tired of always playing it safe; that a little danger in my boring world sounds...enticing. Exciting.

If I told my father I long to throw myself in harm's way just to know what it feels like to be alive, he would probably lock me up in a mental institution.

It's not that I'm suicidal or anything. I don't *wish* for pain or death. I only want to do more than merely survive. I want to be brave, to be dangled over a cliff or the roof of the penthouse by my ankles and trust that the person holding me could easily drop me, but probably won't. The fear of not knowing for certain what the future holds would make my heart race out of my chest and my lower belly to tighten...

Maybe there's something wrong with me if I want to go looking for trouble when everything in my life is perfect and safe.

Well, everything except for the fact that I grew up without a mother because she died from complications of bringing me into the world.

My father raised me and my sisters on his own. There was never a motherly figure around, not until a few months ago, when he met Vanessa and married her.

I guess I could ask my stepmother if my cravings for danger are unusual. She probably wouldn't tell my father. Not unless she thought I needed immediate psychiatric care...

I probably ought to just keep those thoughts to myself in case I am a freak.

When my phone buzzes across my desk just before dinner, I pick it up to read the text from my father telling me to come to his office ASAP. I momentarily panic, wondering if he's figured out a way to spy on my innermost thoughts. If anyone could do it, it would be the ruthless mafia king I call Daddy.

But no, our father probably hasn't tapped into any psychic abilities. And since I don't keep a diary, he will never know about the messed-up thoughts in my head.

I still hurry down the two flights of stairs to the first floor, knowing better than to keep him waiting. Cass and I nearly run into each other, heading in opposite directions in the hallway. My sister and I don't look anything alike since we had different mothers. Her long hair is the color of blood, her eyes a light green, and skin ivory, while I have our father's jet-black hair and deep blue eyes. I thought since we look so similar, I would be his favorite, but he doesn't seem to give any of us much notice. Well, at least he didn't before Madison ran away. Now she's all he thinks about.

"What's going on? What does Daddy want?" I ask her in a whisper since she was obviously storming out of our father's office.

"Take a guess," she huffs.

"He found Madison?"

She rolls her eyes. "No, the little bitch is yet to be found, which means someone has to step in and play bride to the Irish gangster." Reaching a hand up to pat the top of my head like I'm a dog, she says, "I flat out refused to be stuck with him, so congrats. Pack your bags, little sis. You're getting hitched."

I shake my head, sending my long black ponytail flying in denial of her claim while shoving her hand off my head.

Marry some man I've never met? "No. That's...no." This better be Cass's idea of a prank. Our father is a ruthless mobster, sure, but he wouldn't make me marry anyone, especially right now. I just turned eighteen!

"Good luck," Cass says with a sarcastic smile. She forcefully bumps her shoulder into mine while walking away.

When the office door opens again a few moments later, I'm still standing in the same spot, frozen with fear. My father's six feet plus frame is in his usual business suit, and he fills the doorframe. His stern face is blank, other than a tick in his cheek.

"Hey, baby girl. Come on in so we can talk."

Following him into his two-story office and library, I blurt out, "Cass just...I don't really have to marry someone, do I?"

I stare at my father as he comes to a stop beside Vanessa who is so petite, she looks like a child next to him. Despite her small stature, the sweet-looking blonde has never been cowed by Daddy like everyone else in the world. I envy her for her courage to go toe-to-toe with him and never back down.

Glancing between them both, I wait for them to assure me it isn't true, that Cass is just messing with me.

Finally, Vanessa glares up at my dad's face and says, "Of course, he's not going to make you marry anyone. He's just going to ask nicely. Right, Dante?"

"Right," he agrees. He slips his hands into his front pants pockets as if this is a casual discussion about what we should have for dessert tonight instead of the rest of my life. "You have every right to refuse..."

"Good." I sigh in relief, and my father instantly winces.

"If you refuse, Lochlan could retaliate by starting shit that gets people killed."

"Dante!" Vanessa exclaims, slapping a small palm on his chest. "You can't guilt her into marrying him!"

"I'm being honest with her, butterfly. Yes, it's her decision, just like it was going to be Madison's. But Sophie should know the consequences of refusing him. Not to mention that since you don't want Cole to be part of this world, someone has to take over for me when I die. As much as I hate it, he may be the best choice."

Whoa, what? He wanted Vanessa's son to take over his drug trafficking empire? I can't say I'm surprised that Vanessa objected to that idea. She's spent her entire life trying to keep Cole away from her mafia family.

"Wait, so who will take over?" I ask.

"Lochlan Dunne. I haven't made a final decision yet. He's still on thin fucking ice, but he'll keep pushing until I agree. He knows my business is fucked if I don't get some dirt on some feds."

"What do you mean?" I can't help but wonder.

Sighing, my father says, "An alliance between our two families could benefit us both, present a united front that nobody would want to fuck with either of us. I also need some of his...business connections. Now that Lochlan knows Madison ran away and I've been lying to him about it, we have two choices, have a wedding, or have a vendetta with each other that won't end well."

So, a wedding or a mafia war? One ends with me being handed over to a thug, and the other ends in bloodshed.

Just like Cass, I want to say hell no, to turn around, walk away and forget this idiotic conversation about marrying a man I've never met.

But at the same time...I've never been strong enough to refuse my father's demands. Besides, what if my rejection ends with my father getting killed? He lives a dangerous life as it is, constantly worried about threats to us, to Vanessa. Someone has to worry about him. If I could do something to help him avoid a war, then I should. I want to be a good daughter. Not to mention that this is probably the longest my father and I have had a conversation without my sisters in years.

An unknown future with a stranger is bound to be more exciting than my current one. I think I would agree based on that selfish desire alone. Being someone's wife, having the sole attention of a doting husband could be nice too.

I'm about to tell my father I'll do it when he says, "Before you give me a final answer, Lochlan is insisting on...meeting you." He grits out the last two words as if he doesn't like the idea of us being in the same room together, leaving me so damn confused.

"So, you don't want me to meet him, but you'll let him marry me?" I ask for clarification.

Vanessa grins up at my dad's scowling face. "Yes, Dante. Answer

Sophie's question. Why would you let your daughter marry someone you don't feel comfortable with her meeting?"

"Because if I know Lochlan, he'll do something he shouldn't, then call off the wedding just to be a dick."

Do something he shouldn't? Like what? I start to ask but decide I don't really want to know. I would rather be surprised. Not knowing exactly what my future holds is exhilarating.

"So, you want Sophie to marry a man you don't trust?"

Now my dad growls down at his new wife. My new stepmother. It's still weird to have Vanessa living with us. In all my eighteen years we've never had a motherly figure around. Or any woman for that matter. While Cass doesn't like Vanessa, I think she's nice. And she's been good for our dad. He's happy. Happier than I've ever seen him before, as if their marriage was some sort of magic spell that tamed his wild ways. Over the years, I heard the rumors about him from the staff and guards, all the partying and endless women before Vanessa came along. Maybe marriage isn't all bad. Especially if the man I'm going to marry is dangerous enough that my dad is worried about leaving me alone with him during our first encounter.

"I'll meet him," I agree on a ragged breath. My heart is already galloping in my chest, nervous and excited to get to dive headfirst into the unknown.

"You will?" my dad says, his black eyebrows raised in surprise as if he fully expected me to flat out refuse like Cass did. That's one of the differences between me and my older sisters. They obviously lack the freak gene that makes me even more curious about the man they both ran away from as fast as possible to avoid at all costs.

Cass and Madison were strong enough to refuse our father. Cass did so to his face while Madison ran away to avoid his wrath.

Rather than admit my morbid curiosity, I just give him a nod.

"Great. Thank you, Sophie. I'll set it up as soon as possible."

"Good," I agree, maybe a little too quickly. "I mean, I want to hurry up and get it over with, you know?"

"Of course," Vanessa agrees, giving me a supportive smile. "Just remember that nobody is forcing you to do any of this, okay sweetie?"

I bite my bottom lip to stop myself from pointing out that I don't actually have a choice. For this instance at least, I think I prefer it that way.

4

Lochlan

What kind of asshole demands that a man hand over his sweet, probably innocent, teenage daughter so he can tie her up, and ruin her?

Me. I'm the asshole.

Not that I'm going to tell Dante Salvato the depraved things I'm planning for Sophie. I'm sure he has a few guesses, which is why he looks like he's chewing on a roofing nail when he opens his penthouse door to let me come inside, jaw ticking.

Oh, if I were a glutton for punishment or a swift death, I could spin all kinds of innuendo here to make him even more uncomfortable. As it is, nothing is set in stone yet, and this is just a meeting to try to finalize our deal—a yes from his daughter and him that I'll inherit his businesses.

"Dante, stop glowering at the man and introduce us," a small blonde woman says from behind the tall bastard.

Sighing like it costs him deeply, Dante finally says, "Lochlan, meet my wife, Vanessa. Vanessa this is Lochlan Dunne."

"Nice to meet you." The petite blonde steps in front of him to offer me a handshake and a smile. No wonder Dante gave up his playboy ways. She's beautiful and warm, wearing a casual white and green floral dress that's short enough to be cockteasing. Still, she's nothing like the sluts he used to fuck around with before. "Although," she adds, "it would be nicer to meet you if you would call this wedding mess off."

Well, then.

When I turn to Dante, he shrugs his shoulders under his suit jacket as if to say he doesn't have any control over his woman's mouth.

"I'm not calling this wedding mess off," I assure them both.

Hell, this might be the only chance I have to marry a woman who isn't a literal gold-digging whore. After growing up in a world that revolved around fucking, I'm pretty sure I'm incapable of loving anyone. I sure as shit don't have a heart. In my entire life there's never been any strings or attachments to women. A warm, sexy body strung up or tied down is all it takes to get me to the next day, week, or recently, five months, however often I need to fuck. Sex has always been a simple transaction. A give and take that's fair—a few minutes of pleasure for a handful of cash. The kinky shit I require costs more, but it's usually worth it. Not that I've indulged in any of that in months because of one fucking girl...

"Now, are you going to let me meet my bride?" I ask Salvato before he can delay this any longer.

"Ten minutes alone with each of them," Dante says.

"I don't need ten minutes with each. You know I've already made my decision. Or was the wedding invitation with her name on it unclear?"

"I insist you meet both," he grits out.

"You still think I'll change my mind?" I huff in annoyance, which is met with silence. "Fine. I'll meet the redhead first if it makes you feel better. But our deal is your youngest. You owe me, Salvato. The bride you promised me ran the fuck off, and you've been lying to me for fucking months. I was starting to think you no longer needed my considerable connections to make your life easier."

Owning brothels and women for hire, I have dirt on a lot of powerful, horny men. In exchange for not ruining their lives, they do me favors. Salvato wants those favors as well to help him traffic in his fentanyl.

"Sophie's too young," Dante says as he stabs his fingers through the front of his black hair to give it a tug. "Hell, all three of my daughters are too young, but at least Cass is tough enough to call you on your bullshit and kick your ass if you hurt her. Sophie is...shy and softer. Innocent even..."

"That's exactly why I want her." I don't bother denying it. The two of us both know it. There's something irresistible about being the first to debauch his sweet, inexperienced little girl. Maybe it's knowing that she'll never forget being ruined by a ruthless asshole like me.

"Please," Salvato growls through clenched teeth. It's a word I doubt the man says often. "Meet Cass. Consider her instead. Or at least give Sophie a few years..."

"I'll agree to the first concession. The second is a hell no. Now stop delaying and let's get this over with."

Sighing again, he leads the way down a hallway, and to his expansive, formal office. "I'll send Cass in first."

"In here? No."

"What?" he snaps at me with a scowl on his face like he's thinking of drawing the gun from the shoulder holster peeking out from under his suit jacket.

"You think I don't know there are cameras all over this office?" I ask, spinning in a circle as if I could find them all. "My conversation is between me and the girls only. I'll talk to them in their bedrooms."

"Hell, no."

This son of a bitch...

Taking a deep breath, I button the front of my suit, and go for his jugular. "Are you forgetting that I have you by the balls?"

"I should end you right fucking here and now," Dante growls.

"We can be allies, Salvato. Give me this. Let me meet my bride and put this shit behind us. You still need my connections to grease palms to keep the fentanyl flowing, right? The sort of blackmail I have on people is invaluable. You only get to use it when we're family," I remind him. "And I swear I can keep my dick in my pants for ten minutes. I'm not a fiend."

"Yes, you are," he says staring me down, knowing I have him. "But fine. Ten minutes, and I'll be right outside the door. Don't make me regret this."

He finally turns on his heel, stalking past his frowning wife, and leading me up two-flights of stairs.

He opens the first door without knocking, so I walk in and shut it behind me. I'm not at all surprised to be standing in Red's bedroom first. Although, it looks more like a dojo with a red mat on the floor, a hanging bag, and dumbbell weights strewn over the floor like booby-traps. There's a jump rope draped over a chair, a few scattered water bottles, and a shit ton of mirrors.

"Get out!" She scrambles up from her chaise lounge like she was caught off guard.

"Nice to meet you too, Red."

Based on her black yoga pants and white sports bra covering her lean but muscular body, she obviously spends a lot of time doing physical activity. She arches one crimson eyebrow at me when we're facing each other less than five feet apart. "How original. Who the hell are you?"

"See, I knew you and I would never work out. You're too...difficult." I trail my fingers over the top of the messy dresser, picking up a hair tie.

"Stop touching my shit."

Tossing the hair accessory back down, I turn away from the dresser. Moving deeper into the room, I inhale deeply, taking in more of that oh so familiar scent. "You've been a busy girl. It reeks of sex and rubbers in here."

She scoffs then huffs, "Screw you!" Which is not exactly a denial.

"Don't worry. I won't tell Daddy you're not an innocent little virgin. Although, I do wonder what he'll do when he catches whoever it is you're screwing in here in secret. Killing them swiftly would be letting the poor bastard off easy."

Her eyes widen, anger completely fading. "Please...please don't tell him." Again, the word please doesn't come easy to the Salvato family, apparently. "I'll...I'll do anything."

"Anything, huh?" I lift an eyebrow, even more confident that this girl is not wife material when she nods. Her eyes skim down the front of my body, lingering on the front of my pants. "You gonna get on your knees to keep me from sharing your secret?"

She lifts one shoulder. "If that's what it takes..."

Jesus. I bet the little slut rubs her ass on every man she meets.

"Forget it. I won't rat you out," I assure her before she actually drops to the floor. Even if she did, well, I've grown bored of desperate whores. "I've seen all I need to see."

"What does that mean?"

"It means that I haven't changed my mind about you. I still prefer Snow White."

"She's a child!" the girl exclaims, then takes a deep breath to steel herself, crossing her arms over her chest. "Is that why you want her? You have some sort of sick pedo fetish?"

Ah, so Red is jealous of her little sister.

"She's legal, and only a year younger than you, right?" I remind her on the way back to the door. "And, Red? Green isn't a good color on you. It clashes with your hair."

5

Sophie

When my bedroom door opens without a knock, I spin around in my computer chair to find...a man entering and closing the door behind him. He turns to face me, his gaze starting at my feet and working their way up my bare legs, over my skirt and top to my chest, then finally my face. And I can't deny that I spend a few seconds of the extended silence studying the snug fit of his dark suit pants over his thick thighs and the tattoos wrapped around his neck and both of his arms. At least as much as I can see from the rolled-up sleeves of his white button-down.

He looks rich and dangerous like my father. Younger yet more intimidating though, since I know my father won't ever hurt me. This man looks like he would, and he would enjoy it. I'm too scared to move, and I've never been happier.

The sight of his tongue wetting his lips has me repeating the move since my mouth is suddenly bone dry.

31

"Who—" I start but he interrupts me.

"You...you are a beauty, Snow White." His voice is the deep, growly kind of a long-term smoker or someone who shouts at people a lot. Maybe both.

I was expecting something crass, not a compliment.

"Ah, thank you?" Maybe he's being sarcastic. I'm a sweaty mess, cooling off in my tennis outfit before I grab a shower. Strands of my black hair are falling from my ponytail. I'm in desperate need of soap, water, and lots of deodorant, but his compliment, ironic or not, automatically makes me less self-conscious. My spine even straightens a little.

The stranger stalks toward me, and I debate whether or not to stand up. Before I manage to rise to my bare feet he's there, towering above me. His much larger tattooed hands cover my own on the arm rests, and his touch is freezing cold on my overheated skin. I recoil, but there's nowhere to go. His face is so close to mine that I can see the specks of gold in his green eyes and scent cherries and tobacco on his breath as he gawks at me. He isn't unattractive, just sort of scary thanks to his angular face and the black Celtic knot tattoo beside his right eye.

"Tell me something, princess. Are you really a virgin or is that a pretty lie you tell Daddy, too?"

Ah, why is this intimidating man in my room asking me if I'm a virgin? There's no way in hell my father would've let a random guy sneak up to the third floor, which means...this has to be *him*.

Lochlan Dunne.

The man my father wants me to marry.

I think he might be the type to throw me over the ledge, but it could be fun to find out.

"Answer my question," he demands.

"I've never..." My face flushes in a rush of heat so fast I feel dizzy. I spent too much time in the brutal Vegas sun today.

"Never what? You've never been fucked?" He stares at my

mouth while asking that highly personal question and dropping the f-bomb.

I shake my head, swinging my ponytail from side to side until I can force the words from my mouth. "I've never even been near any men before."

"Good. Keep it that way." Now his face lowers to my white tennis skirt that doesn't quite reach my knees. "My dick is going to be the first one inside your tight virgin pussy."

His statement is so presumptuous I nearly scoff. The only reason I don't is because I'm not sure what he would do to me. On second thought, I like that unknown, and part of me wants to wipe some of the arrogance off his face.

"I-I don't *have* to marry you." Unfortunately, the stammer doesn't make my words sound very confident. "Just because Cass refused you, and I'm all that's left, I can still say no."

There's a flash of confusion in his eyes before he blinks it away. When I try to pull my arms out from underneath his, he tightens his grip, pinching them against the chair arms.

"Is that what you think?"

I lift my chin a millimeter higher to try and appear more assertive than I sound. "Yes."

His right hand leaves mine for a heartbeat and then I see a flash of silver. A long, sharp blade shoots out threateningly from what I realize is a knife. With a flick of his wrist, the pointed end of his knife is suddenly aiming toward the lap of my skirt. The tip slams down right between my thighs that I manage to part just in time, so that the blade thankfully imbeds into the cushion of the leather seat and not my flesh. My jaw falls open in disbelief looking between the weapon and the man, but no sound comes out. What is wrong with this guy? Is he insane? He nearly stabbed me! Did he want to hurt me?

Of course, he did.

And it's probably my fault for pushing him.

Do I regret it? Definitely not, even if I can't think over the pounding heartbeat in my ears.

33

Keeping hold of the knife handle, he steps up into the space between my legs, using his knees to force mine to open wider. His left hand still covering mine on the chair arm tightens to hold it in place. I'm completely at his mercy, which is scary and exciting all at the same time.

"How about now, princess? Still think you can refuse me?" His eyes are filled with the promise of pain if I reject him. Since I think I may have bitten off more than I can chew, I shake my head, unable to speak as he holds me in the crude position, stealing all the air in the vicinity.

In my head, I wanted to say the opposite. Other parts of my body are overheating and heavy, wishing I had refused for an entirely different reason—to push him further, to see what he would do if I deny him.

"Final answer, are you going to be my wife?" His eyes narrow at me as if he knows my inner turmoil.

"Yes," I reply, even though I'm still unsure what I'm agreeing to.

"Good girl," he says with a smug grin that makes me melt a little in the chair. Lifting the knife to free it, he retracts the blade and flips it over so the cool steel of the handle brushes my bare inner thigh, making me gasp. He grins wider, watching my face while slowly moving the knife higher and higher, heading for the part of me that no one has ever touched before.

I self-consciously try to close my legs, but he still has them pried apart with his bigger, heavier ones.

"When you're my wife, you'll spread your thighs for me when I tell you to. And if you don't, I'll do it myself. Nothing is going to keep me from your pussy once it's mine."

He drags the handle over the crotch of my panties, making me gasp again at the same time the fabric becomes damp. The touch is light as a feather, but I've never felt anything as acutely as that hard hilt of his knife. I hold completely still, afraid to breathe.

"So, tell me, princess, are you going to be a good girl who gives it up to me or a naughty girl who makes me take what's mine?"

"Naughty." The word flies out of my mouth before I can stop it. I'm not even sure where it came from. I've always been the good girl, but for him, I let him see that secret, dirty part of me that wants bad things that it shouldn't.

Smirking, he says, "That's the right answer."

Withdrawing the knife hilt from between my legs, Lochlan straightens to his full height. As soon as he takes a step back, I snap my legs together while he slips the knife back into his front pants pocket.

"Keep those legs closed just like that for everyone but me, Sophie."

Hearing him say my name sends a shiver down my spine. His words sound like a threat. Like there would be consequences if I disobey his command.

Before I can blink, he turns and strolls out of my room without another word, leaving me burning up, confused, and ashamed of myself for wishing he had done more than just graze my wet panties with his knife.

After he's gone, I can't stop replaying how his gravelly voice said my name, as if he already knows me.

Maybe he does, because I've barely even thought about having sex with anyone before tonight. It just seems sort of dirty and gross to be completely naked and sharing bodily fluids with someone else.

But now? Now Lochlan has me wondering if there's a lot more to sex than what I had assumed. And I'm almost certain he would be more than happy to constantly dangle me over the edge of the cliff.

6

Lochlan

"How did it go?" Salvato asks as soon as I walk out of Sophie's bedroom, shutting the door behind me.

"Fine."

"Fine?"

"Yeah, Dante. It was fine. She said yes."

"She did?" he mutters in surprise.

"I told you she would," I remind him. "Now, I'll show myself out," I say as I push past him to escape his third-degree torture interrogation and get the hell out of this penthouse.

It's not that I feel guilty for running my knife over his daughter's virgin pussy. It's just that if I don't leave now, I may not be able to resist popping her sweet cherry right here and now. He gave me ten minutes, but I bet I could be coming inside of her cunt within four. I don't even remember being more turned on than I was in that damn room. I don't know if it's the fact that she's so young and innocent or what, but goddamn I want to bury myself in her frozen, terrified body, to hear her scream for me while I make her mine. Mine, no longer Daddy's little girl.

Jesus. Going without sex for too long does make men go insane. Or maybe that's just the effect Sophie had on me.

I don't know what I expected Snow White to be like in person, but she exceeded all my expectations.

Hell, I would marry her for her tennis skirts alone. The fact that she's possibly the first woman to ever flinch away from me, makes my dick harder than steel.

Most women, or at least the ones who are drawn to me, can't wait to try and get their hands on me. They rub their asses on my dick or shove their tits in my face before I even know their names. But they know mine. I fucking hate when they say shit like, "How do you want it, daddy?" or "Give it to me good, big daddy."

They call me daddy because that's all they're looking for, someone to bankroll their entire lives, buy them whatever they want whenever they want it, and all it costs them is their soul. That's the cost of fucking someone for money. I know that for a fact. If they get my ring on their finger, it's even better than hitting the jackpot or winning the lottery because they'll never run out of cash. Or so they think. I wonder how many will still want me when I'm broke.

Not that I care. I'm so fucking sick of women dropping to their knees for me for their own selfish reasons. That kind of desperation is just pathetic. Before I became celibate, I don't know the last time I came without having to close my eyes and pretend I'm somewhere else, fucking someone else, to get off. The fact that I know all those women just want me to hurry up and finish so they can finally get off their knees or out from under me, only adds to the pressure.

I'm not their big daddy coming down their throats, I'm just a big fat payday.

But with Sophie...everything will be different. And I can't fucking wait.

Sophie

When there's a knock on my door a few minutes after Lochlan leaves, I nearly jump out of my seat, still lost in thoughts of Lochlan and his prodding knife.

"So, you told him yes?" my father asks when he walks right in before I can reach the door on shaky legs.

His gaze scans over me as if looking for injuries. Thankfully he doesn't notice the tiny hole within a pleat in the front of my skirt.

"Sophie?" he asks again when I don't respond. "What's the verdict on Lochlan?"

He's beautiful in an intense sort of way, like seeing a lion in the wild and wanting to get a closer look even though you know it's a bad idea. Oh, and I like that he scares the shit out of me.

But my father isn't asking if I think Lochlan is handsome or dangerous. Those things are pretty obvious. He wants to know if, based on a short, heart pounding conversation with him, I will agree to spend the rest of my life with an untamable lion.

I know I could say no. That my father would put a bullet in that tattoo on the side of the man's face before making me marry him. And yet...I don't want him to do that.

Lochlan is a mob boss like my dad, with people who would want revenge for his death.

Besides, I don't *want* to say no. The rest of my life is a long damn time, and yet I know that life with Lochlan won't be as boring as it would be without him. Having someone like Lochlan be as obsessed and protective of me as my father is over Vanessa is all I need to be happy. I just want to be loved like that, have that sort of passion with someone.

"I'll do it," I agree. "I'll marry him."

My dad's shoulders sink as if in relief that he won't have to kill the man or take on his entire crew. "You can take as much time as you want. I don't give a shit what Lochlan says about wanting a wedding by June first. He can wait."

"No." After his threatening display, I don't think Lochlan is a very patient man. "June first is fine."

"Really? This June? That's only three weeks away."

"I know. It's fine."

"Okay, then. If this is what you want?"

I nod, afraid that if I open my mouth, I'll admit to my father what he did with the knife between my legs and that I liked it.

Walking over to me, my father folds me into his arms, hugging me tight. "Whatever you need before June or after, just ask and it's yours. Thank you for agreeing to do this for us."

For us. Not for myself but for my family, for my dad's business interests.

I hug him back but don't respond. I don't tell him about what Lochlan said to me, or about what he plans to do to me. My dad probably expects as much anyway. I'm going to be the man's wife, which means he'll have certain expectations of me in the bedroom. Obligations I'll be expected to fulfill.

And I don't have the slightest idea where to even start.

Not that I think I'll have to do much when Lochlan seems to be so...dominating.

I need comfort food to help me wrap my mind around what I've just agreed to. So, when my dad leaves my room, I take a cold shower, then go to the kitchen to find a snack and quench my lingering thirst.

"I can't believe you caved," Cass says when she finds me in the kitchen guzzling my second glass of ice-cold water to try to cool myself down. "Actually, yes, I can believe it. Perfect Sophie does whatever she's told like a good little girl."

At least marrying Lochlan means I get to leave the penthouse and get away from Cass's constant attitude.

I ignore Cass, and she doesn't say anything while I wash an apple in the sink, then pull a knife out of the drawer. It's impossible not to think about Lochlan's knife while I begin peeling the green skin.

When I'm cutting the apple into slices, Cass grabs one from my plate and chomps down on it without asking. "At least Lochlan is kind of hot." Taking another slice, she smiles when she adds, "He practically begged me to blow him tonight."

"What?" The knife slips from my hand, clanging onto the countertop.

"Blow him. You know, suck his dick? God, you're so naïve." She rolls her eyes. "He didn't try anything with you? I'm not really surprised, since you're more inexperienced than a Catholic nun."

God, I'm so stupid.

Did I actually think a man like Lochlan would only touch *me* between my legs? He obviously did the same sort of taunting with Cass too.

And unlike me, like a normal, sane person, she rejected him.

"Did you know Lochlan owns a bunch of brothels? You're basically marrying a pimp, Soph." I shake my head, still unable to get over him prodding me with a knife after he may have done something with her. "I bet he fucks all those women whenever he wants. Make sure he wraps his dick up with you. You don't want to catch any diseases."

If Lochlan has been with women who have sex with men professionally then...well, I'm going to be a huge disappointment to him. While being afraid of him is exciting, knowing I'm probably going to be unsatisfactory to him in bed just makes me so nervous I want to puke.

"Congrats, sis, you're going to lose your virginity to a mafia pimp and it's going to hurt like hell."

"How do you know it will hurt?" I blurt out.

"Everyone knows the first time is painful. And I seriously doubt Lochlan Dunne will ever care if you're in pain. I heard he gets off on that sort of demented shit." While I hate hearing her say all that, it's exactly what I thought too.

"What am I going to do? How do I..." I trail off as I try not to panic.

"Do you want my advice?"

"Yes." It's rare for Cass to actually want to help me.

"If I were you, I'd find someone else to get the worst part over with before he repeatedly bangs your brains out on your wedding night," Cass suggests.

"Bang my...wait. What do you mean find someone else?" I ask.

She steals another slice of apple, chews it up while making me wait, then says with a smirk, "The whole point of a bachelorette party is to fuck other people before saying your vows."

"It is?"

"It's the last chance you get to experiment with other men."

Is that true? It's not like I know anything about bachelorette parties other than the casino has tons of them and bachelor parties almost every night. I had no idea it was some sort of sex fest.

"Like Daddy would ever let me have a bachelorette party."

"Sure, he will. Since you're stuck marrying the bastard to help keep his drug business running, he'll give you anything you want."

"Anything I want? Even a night like that?"

"Yep. You could be as wild as you wanted from now until the wedding."

"What about the guards?"

Cass rolls her eyes. "There will always be guards, but I guarantee that none of the guards or Daddy would stop you from doing whatever you want before you get married."

It's stupid to think about having sex with a random stranger, but it would be nice to have some sort of experience before my wedding night. A night where it will apparently hurt like hell when Lochlan repeatedly bangs my brains out. Any experience has to be better than none with a man who sleeps with professionals.

I bet Lochlan would be pissed if I let someone else take my virginity since he was adamant that he would be my first. And how exactly would he punish me for ignoring his order to keep my legs closed for everyone but him? Would he even care? Is he like my father and just expects everyone to do what he says?

I thought the way he treated me was different, that I was special. That the intense, at first sight meeting between us was unique since I had never felt it before. But apparently, that was just my naïve, lack of experience.

And if I'm not anything special to him then why should I give a shit what he wants?

Just because I have to marry him doesn't mean I have to obey him like I'm his dog or a child. After our first encounter, I bet Lochlan thinks I will make the perfect little subservient wife because I froze at the mere sight of his intimidating presence.

So, tell me, princess, are you going to be a good girl who gives it up to me or a naughty girl who makes me take what's mine?

I've always been the good girl. The obedient daughter. But for some reason, when Lochlan asked me that question, I told him "bad" even though he had a knife handle pressed against the crotch of my panties.

And surprisingly enough, he told me that was the right answer.

So maybe he doesn't expect me to be an obedient wife after all. Maybe he wants me to fight him, to refuse him, as if it's some sort of game he enjoys playing because everyone else in the world obeys his every word.

I want to play with him, even if I don't have the slightest clue what the rules are and know I won't ever win.

7

Sophie

The very next day, Vanessa and I go shopping to pick out a wedding dress. *My* wedding dress. Well, it's not just us. We're surrounded by guards who at least aren't allowed in the changing area of the boutique.

While the sales lady is pulling a few dresses in my size for me to try on, I ask a quiet, sulking Vanessa, "Do men like my father, like Lochlan, enjoy a challenge?"

"What sort of challenge?" she asks.

"Just...any sort of challenge." I can't exactly come right out and ask her if I should deny Lochlan my virginity or anything else he wants from me just to see if it excites him even more.

Vanessa tilts her head to the side in thought. "Yes. I think powerful men like those two are so ambitious that they want to earn their success. If a goal is too easy to obtain, they would get bored. At

least your father would. I have no clue what makes Lochlan tick."
She says his name like a curse.

"You don't approve of me marrying Lochlan?"

"I don't know much about Lochlan. What I don't approve of is
Dante twisting your arm to get you to agree to this wedding. You
should have the option of growing up, dating men, finding someone
you love and *want* to marry, not be handed over to a dangerous man
your father chose for you to help his business."

My stomach tightens at the word "dangerous."

"Madison wouldn't have ever married him," I admit to her. "Even
before she ran away, she was adamant about wanting to go off on her
own, to do all those things you mentioned. It's the same with Cass.
She hates being told what to do, and will refuse any order for the hell
of it. So that only leaves me."

"There has to be some other way for Lochlan and Dante to
become trusted allies than a wedding, though." She blows out a
breath that sends strands of her long, light blonde hair flying out of
her face. "I was once in your shoes, not given a choice."

"You married someone before my dad?" I ask in surprise.

"No. I was..." She cringes. "Dante will probably kill me for
telling you this, but I was supposed to marry your father when I
turned eighteen."

"Holy shit! What...how..." I can't close my gaping mouth.
Vanessa and my dad were supposed to get married decades ago?

"You know who my father is. Was," she goes on to explain. "He
made a deal with Dante's father without asking either of us. Dante
flat out refused to marry me. He would've had to wait two years since
I was only sixteen, but he said no. My father got pissed and put out a
hit on him. I ran away from home like Madison did right after that,
which may have been what saved Dante's life. My father was intent
on killing him for the insult of his rejection."

"So, you ran away and got pregnant with Cole after my dad's
rejection?"

"Yes. The reason I told you about all that was so that you would know that your father once refused an arranged marriage. He would let you out of this one, Sophie. All you have to do is say the word."

Pacing back and forth in front of the row of dressing room doors, I think over everything Vanessa just told me while chewing on my bottom lip.

My mind is blown.

Her and my father were supposed to marry each other when they were younger. She could've been my mother. Except, well, I wouldn't be me if I had a different mother. But they didn't go through with the wedding. Instead, Vanessa struggled alone as a single mother raising her son for twenty years, constantly looking over her shoulder, waiting for her father to track her down. And my dad ended up having me and my sisters with three different women. Women I don't think he ever loved. He felt responsible for them, like he feels responsible for us, but that's probably it.

And yet...after everything the two of them went through, Vanessa came back to work for my dad for whatever reason.

"So, about, what? Twenty-one years later you somehow still ended up married to my father? But this time it was a decision that the two of you both made voluntarily because you loved each other?"

"Yes."

"Hmm." It feels like a small weight has been lifted off my chest. While I was willing to marry Lochlan for the fear of the unknown if nothing else, finding out about my dad and Vanessa's history gives me...hope that I won't regret my decision to leap without looking just for the thrill of it. Smiling at my stepmother, I say, "Thank you for telling me, Vanessa."

"Does that mean you want to take more time to think this marriage over?"

"No."

"No?"

"Your story did the opposite of convincing me to back out of the wedding."

"What?" she exclaims as she gets to her feet. Since I'm about six

47

inches taller than her, she has to look up at me to ask, "How is that possible?"

"You and my dad belonged together. It was fate."

Her confused scowl softens at that comment. "Fate. That's what Dante said too. We were destined to be together."

"Exactly! Don't you get it, Vanessa? The universe wanted you two to fall in love and spend the rest of your lives together. You were meant to be, even if it took you both two decades to stop fighting it."

Pointing all that out just has her frowning even harder at me. "Just because it worked out for us in the future doesn't mean that it will for you and Lochlan. You two are so different."

"But it could work. The chance of being happy with him is fifty-fifty. The same as any other marriage. Some couples who get married have known each other for years, yet half end up divorced, right?"

"I guess so..." she trails off. Studying my face she says, "So you're really all in on this, marrying a man you only just met for ten minutes?"

"I don't want to wait twenty years to end up in the same place. Lochlan may not even be alive in twenty years. You're lucky my dad was still around."

"Wow," Vanessa mutters. "I didn't even think about it that way, but you're right. If something had happened to Dante...I could've spent the rest of my life alone, without falling in love, and that would've been awful."

"Alright," the sales lady says when she pushes a rack toward us full of dresses on hangers. "Are we ready to start trying these on?"

"Yes," I answer confidently.

Maybe it's naïve to think that I could find love in an arranged marriage like my dad and Vanessa, but at least I now have a little more hope. It's possible that I can find the kind of happiness they have together, not just an exciting adventure.

That doesn't mean I want to cancel the idea of a bachelorette party. I could just as easily meet the man of my dreams that night, prompting me to call off the wedding before the ceremony. Doubtful, but either way, I don't want my first time to be with a much older, much more experienced man who wields knives to get whatever he wants. I want to be confident when I'm naked with him for the first time.

My virginity isn't his to have. It's mine. I get to decide who I want to give it to for the first time.

More than likely, it will be Lochlan on our wedding night. I'm not sure if I could have sex with a stranger, but I'm still excited to consider giving it a try. After all, Lochlan's a stranger too and I was instantly attracted to him. I'm expected to have sex with him as soon as we say a few vows. And yes, I wanted him to push his knife in me so I think I might like when he puts something else inside me...

Even more fun is thinking about the man's reaction to disobeying his command because I wanted some experience. Will he punish me? I think I want him to, and I think he would enjoy it as well.

But how the hell would I know for sure? Any experience is better than none. Before I even consider experimenting, I need information. Lots of it.

That's why, after we've picked a beautiful satin dress and are finished having lunch at a local cafe, I ask Vanessa, "Will you tell me everything I need to know about sex?"

"Oh, lord," she whispers, like it matters if the guards standing at our backs overhear us. They hear everything. "I'm not...I appreciate you feeling comfortable enough to ask me about *that*, but I just don't know if your father would want me talking to you about sex."

"Who else is there for me to talk to about it?" I ask her. "Cass? You know she's as clueless as I am on the subject. And if my father thinks I'm old enough to be marrying a man, then surely, I'm old enough to have a conversation with you about sex. At least what to expect, that sort of thing."

"You're right. And Dante doesn't need to know about this conversation. He's never told you anything about sex?"

"Yes, he told me not to have it with anyone until I was married."

"Right," she says, wringing her hands in her lap. "So, where would you like to start? How much do you know? Have you ever read any erotica or watched any pornography?"

"Ew, no. Why would I want to see two strangers have sex?"

Smiling, she says, "Okay, so I guess we should start at the beginning?"

"Yes. And I know technically how a woman gets pregnant, that a man's sperm fertilizes her egg during ovulation, but sex wise, how does all of that work?"

"Oh, well, every time a man has sex, he will ejaculate at the conclusion in the form of a thick, milky substance called semen. The semen contains sperm which, when inserted into a woman's vagina will try to make its way to the fallopian tubes. Fertile women release an egg each month from their ovary, and if the sperm reaches the egg and fertilizes it without dying, then that could be the beginning of pregnancy. The fertilized egg still has to travel to the uterus and implant where it will grow and develop. If the egg doesn't get fertilized or implanted, then she has her period about two weeks later."

I try to process all that information. "So, if I don't want to get pregnant, then I need to keep his semen out of me, down there?"

"Yes. You're young. There's no reason for you to be in a hurry to get pregnant."

"I never want to be a mother," I assure her.

"Right. Well, make sure you tell Lochlan, so he'll respect your decision and use protection."

"Protection?"

"He'll need to wear a condom during sex to catch the semen unless you go on birth control pills or some other type of prevention."

"Is it easy to get pregnant or does it require multiple times? It sounds like a complicated process."

"The more times you have sex the higher the probability, especially around the time of ovulation. But even once could be enough if the timing happens to be right."

"Okay. And the actual sex part," I start. "What will Lochlan expect me to do? Will it hurt? Cass says it will hurt like hell."

"The first time could be uncomfortable for you, but it will be better if he takes things slow to help get you in the mood."

"Get me in the mood?"

Vanessa's face flushes red. "Ah, if he makes sure you're turned on enough that it doesn't hurt."

I don't really know what that means, but I don't ask her to elaborate since she seems embarrassed talking about it.

"And as far as what he'll expect for sex, well, that's sort of an individual preference or a decision you make together. There are different sexual positions."

"How many?"

"Several."

"Could you describe them, please?"

"Okay. Well, his...penis may enter you when he's on top of you, or behind you. You could be on top of him. Whatever feels good. And there are other types of sex that doesn't involve his penis penetrating you."

"Oh?"

"Hands or fingers touching those areas can feel good for men and women. As well as, um, mouths."

"Mouths?" Yuck. "Never mind." Who would put their mouth on someone else's private parts? I don't ask that question in case I'm weird for not wanting to do that. "So, sex is over when the man's semen is released?"

"Uh-huh." Vanessa takes a big gulp of her glass of water. "Most people call that an orgasm or 'coming.' The slang term of the substance itself is usually called cum, C-U-M."

"Okay. When he finishes coming, the sex is over? How long does it take for that to happen? What do I do during it? Just lie there?"

"So, let's back up a bit. A man isn't the only one who can have an orgasm during sex. Women can too. In fact, your...pleasure should be his priority every time."

"My pleasure? So, it doesn't hurt every time?"

"No, definitely not. It can feel good for women too."

"That's a relief."

"And sex is over whenever you both either come or you decide to stop. Your body will know what to do during the act to increase the pleasure."

"It will?"

"Yes. You just do what feels good."

"Okay. And afterward?"

"After sex you'll hopefully, um, cuddle."

"Cuddle?"

"Yes. That's when you just enjoy each other's company, the intimacy and closeness. After sex, if you have an orgasm, your body is filled with happy endorphins that make you feel good and relaxed."

"Oh," I say, wondering what that's like, the intimacy with someone else. I get plenty of happy endorphins from tennis, though. "But like, what if I'm bad at it?"

"You can't be bad at cuddling."

"No, I mean the sex part. Lochlan has probably been with tons of women. He's going to have so much experience while I have zero. I've never even seen a naked man before."

Vanessa nods. "I can understand why being with him could be intimidating, but you shouldn't be self-conscious about sex. You'll learn as you go, and believe it or not, some men are very turned on by virgins."

I recall vividly that Lochlan demanded I lose my virginity to him. "Why?"

"They like to be the first to, well, you know, go there."

Oh, yeah, I'm pretty sure Lochlan is one of those men. But, after the first time, if he's the one who takes my virginity, then what? Will he lose interest in me?

"Also," Vanessa adds, "if he has so much experience, then hopefully that will make him a good lover. Let him show you a good time and teach you what he likes. If you ask, I bet he would love to tell you."

"How often will he be expecting it? You know, for us to have sex?"

"Ah, that varies from couple to couple. When you both want to, it could be several times a day or a week. It's up to you. Just remember that, okay? Any and every part of sex is always your decision, not just his. It may not seem like it, but you will have all the power."

"I will?" I ask in disbelief.

"Yes, you will. You should always be the one to agree on when and how, Sophie. Don't go along with things you don't like just to make him happy."

"Okay," I agree, wondering if it will really be that easy to deny Lochlan. I highly doubt it. And I can't wait to find out.

"And if he ever does anything you don't want to do, or if he hurts you, promise me you'll tell me or your father."

"You think he'll hurt me?" Again, there's that excited jolt surging through my body at the idea. Definitely something wrong with me.

With a heavy sigh, Vanessa says, "I hope he won't, Sophie. I hope he cares for you and treats you like a queen, because that is how you deserve to always be treated."

Her words make me feel ashamed of those dark thoughts I've had, the ones Lochlan elicited to. So, I keep them to myself, and hope that if I ignore them long enough, they'll eventually go away.

And when we get home, I know what I'll be doing for the rest of the night—homework. I need to study up on the parts of human anatomy that I know the least about.

8

Lochlan

The past three weeks I've spent on more phone calls than I can count with Dante or his no-non-sense wife making wedding arrangements. Never with Sophie though. Dante refused to give me his daughter's phone number yet, which is fucking ridiculous.

And while I wouldn't have minded talking to her, teasing her, I didn't push the issue. There's always the chance that I could talk her out of the wedding if I run my mouth to her. We're too close to the finish line to fuck it up.

Still, I'm more fucking thrilled than I care to admit about being able to see her tonight during our engagement dinner at Dante's casino. He flat out refused to have the wedding or even dinner tonight at my estate or casino after the bombing. And I don't blame him.

Some people have a rehearsal and dinner the night before the wedding, but this is more of an engagement party for the two families since I don't need to practice standing, and I doubt Sophie needs practice walking down an aisle.

As for family, well, Owen and Flynn are my only blood relatives. I brought them both along with a handful of guards. When we reach the door of a smaller-sized ballroom, I warn them both to behave. "Watch your mouths and don't screw this up for me."

"Got it," Owen says with a wink before he walks off to the bar.

When Flynn starts to follow him, I grab his elbow to pull him to a stop. "Go easy on the booze. There's too much on the line for you to get drunk and act a fool in front of Salvato's daughters."

"I'm cool," he says, even though his brown eyes are bloodshot. At least he showered and put on a button down and slacks tonight rather than insist on coming along in his usual ratty clothes.

"Sure you are," I mutter.

"Go find your child bride and get off my dick," he huffs before pulling his arm out of his grip.

Speaking of my virginal Snow White, I finally spot her across the room talking to Dante's wife. Since her entire back is bare other than her long, flowing black waves, I begin to wonder how much of the front of her body is covered. But then she turns, revealing the entirety of the white pleated halter-top dress. The hem brushes midway up her thighs, and the material is so sheer it would be see-through, if not for the second layer underneath. And goddamn, her black strappy high-heel sandals accentuate her long, toned legs, adding three inches of height. I had no idea she was so damn tall since she was sitting down the other night. And in the still photos the housekeeper provided, I was too captivated by her short tennis skirts to notice she's nearly six feet tall with heels.

When she sees me, her eyes do a sweep up and down my entire suit twice before they reach my face. Her cheeks redden when she realizes I caught her checking me out. She turns back to her step-mother who gives her a gentle shove in my direction as I begin to approach. Sophie doesn't budge, as if she's hesitant to speak to me.

She's a sexy deer in headlights, rightly afraid of what's coming for her, but unable to run.

"Hi, Vanessa."

"Lochlan," Dante's wife replies. "Everything is all set for tomorrow."

"Great, thank you for your help," I tell her. Then the three of us stand silently until Vanessa eventually murmurs, "I should go find Dante," and wanders off.

"Hello again, princess," I say once we're alone.

"Hello, Lochlan." Damn, I love the way she says my name. Her voice is quiet, a little shaky too, because she's scared of me. I shouldn't want her to be, and yet, here we are.

"Are you ready for tomorrow?"

"Yes."

"That doesn't sound very confident. You're not thinking about running, are you? Because it would be a shame if I had to hunt you down." At that comment, her big blue eyes widen. "But I would, you know. If you run, I will find you, drag you back here, and spank your gorgeous ass until you can't bear to sit down."

The blush spreading across her cheeks and even her button nose instantly makes my dick hard. God, I love how easy it is to get a reaction from the little virgin.

And fuck, I can't wait to spend the next few weeks teaching her every sexual position under the sun. Knowing I'll be her first everything turns me on like nothing else. She'll be mine. Only mine. For the rest of her life.

Unless...unless that's changed in the past three weeks. If Sophie got a wild hair up her ass about sowing oats or some shit before tying the knot, I will lose my goddamn mind.

Slipping my arm around her waist, I lean in close so the front of our bodies brush against each other. I'm big enough to block her from anyone's view as my palm slides down her bare back, lower so I can cup her sweet ass. Her gasp of surprise, a reminder of her innocence, has me barely holding in a groan. My fingertips slip lower until I find the skin along the back of her smooth thigh.

"You are still keeping your legs closed for me, aren't you Sophie?" I ask with my lips hovering over her ear. We're close enough that I inhale her lavender and rose scent, searching for any hint that a man's been rubbing against her recently. There's no aftershave smell or masculine bodywash, just her sweet smelling bodywash or shampoo. "Sophie?" I ask when she doesn't answer me.

I don't even realize how tense I am waiting for her response until she nods, and I finally am able to exhale.

"Good girl."

Unwilling to stop touching her just yet, I sweep my fingertips up along the curve of her ass cheek. It's noticeably bare because she must be wearing a thong. I'm so jealous of the material that I can't help but use my middle finger to seek out that thin strip of fabric...

"Lochlan!" Sophie exclaims and jerks toward me. Her palms press against my chest when I continue to rub along that string wedged in the crack of her ass. Huh, even though I make her nervous, she still came toward me rather than jerking away, out of my reach. She wants my hands on her ass, even if she's scared of me. And that is hot as hell.

"I can't wait to devour every inch of you tomorrow night," I tell her. Then I pull the string back and let it go, popping her flesh, making her squeak. "Especially this ass."

"Almost time to eat," Dante says from behind us by way of greeting.

"Damn right it is," I agree when I reluctantly remove my hand from underneath his daughter's dress, at least until I get her to her seat at the table.

Sophie

. . .

Lochlan's words repeat in my head during dinner while everyone makes polite conversation. I don't say much. I'm too busy replaying his greeting, remembering how it felt when he was touching the string of my panties, and trying to ignore his tattooed left hand that's constantly rubbing my thigh underneath the tablecloth.

As expected, he's adamant that I keep my legs closed for anyone but him. And while I told myself that I wouldn't obey him, it's not as easy to refuse him as I thought it would be. Not when he's so intimidatingly close, touching me, stealing my breath and my defiance.

At this rate, he'll have me begging so fast it won't even be a challenge. He'll take my virginity, then get bored and move on to someone else once I'm no longer a timid innocent girl for him to torment.

Like tonight, he relentlessly teases me for the next forty-five minutes of dinner, making me think his fingers are going to move higher up my thigh. The entire meal, he eats with his right hand while making chitchat with everyone around us, while his left hand softly strokes my skin. Never moving an inch higher, only remaining in that same spot, his thumb constantly rubbing circles.

The room grows warmer with each passing second until I'm certain I'm going to combust from overheating. I'm burning up and all my muscles are all tense from waiting, wanting him to touch me again like he did with his knife. For the first time in my life, I can feel my pulse throbbing between my tightly clenched thighs.

I should stop him, stand up and leave the table or push his hand away. Especially with my dad sitting near Lochlan at the head of the table. But I desperately *want* Lochlan's hand to move higher *because* it's wrong. The anticipation of if or when may kill me. When his fingers snuck up the back of my dress and rubbed my thong earlier in front of the entire room, I thought I was going to melt into a puddle of mortification. My panties got so wet I was afraid he would feel the moisture seeping from them. Now, I'm past caring, I just want him to

59

touch me. The plan of mine to refuse him, to be a challenge for the mob boss, seems incredibly ridiculous now. His harsh grip on my leg is too possessive, too threatening to even try to defy.

By the time dessert comes, my hand is trembling as I lift the first spoonful of bourbon glazed cheesecake to my mouth. Right when the delicious dessert hits my tongue, it happens.

"*Mmm!*" My moan is thankfully muffled around the cheesecake when Lochlan's fingertips graze the crotch of my panties. His touch is even more intense than the brief poke of his knife.

And thanks to my outburst, our family members all sitting at the long table stop talking to turn to look at me. My face is on fire. My makeup is going to start dripping down my face any second.

Does Lochlan move his fingers even when all eyes are on me? Yes, but he doesn't remove them from under my dress. No, he rubs me through my panties with three digits, up and down, up, and down, causing happy little tingles to spread through my limbs. Is that my clitoris he's touching?

"The cheesecake is amazing, isn't it? Great choice, Sophie," Vanessa says to break the silence and I nod my head.

"It looks delicious," my father agrees just before Lochlan's fingers press against my panties harder, causing me to gasp at the rush of liquid heat filling them once more.

"I know I can't get enough," the bastard says to my father as he casually eats with his right hand while his left is still up my skirt. If anything, the embarrassing dampness he has to feel by now has him rubbing me faster, harder. "I could eat *this* all night."

His words barely register in my ears. There's an unfamiliar, growing ache in my lower belly. Not a bad ache, but a good ache, like when I think about dangling over a ledge. My fingernails dig into the tablecloth while my right hand somehow continues to clutch my spoon. I'm unable to move, my thigh muscles squeezing together so tightly around Lochlan's hand that they're shaking. God, I can barely even breathe normally. I'm basically panting at this fancy table surrounded by people. I turn my head, my eyes locking with

Lochlan's. His half-grin is smug, his green eyes dancing as if he's enjoying my discomfort.

I think...I think I'm enjoying it too. In fact, it feels good. Really good, embarrassing as it is to have him touch me down there in front of my father during a meal.

"You can't stop now, princess," Lochlan leans over to whisper in my ear before he shoves his spoon between my parted lips. I have no choice but to swallow the bite of cheesecake down with a whimper as the sensation intensifies.

But then suddenly Lochlan's fingers slow, going back to the barely brushing tease as if he's now focused on eating his fucking dessert.

He's playing with me, tormenting me on purpose. Is this what our marriage is going to be like? Me trying to gain the upper hand but never succeeding because his hand feels too good between my legs?

I hate myself for blurting out the word, "Please." I'm not entirely sure why I need Lochlan to keep going. I just...do. I drop my arm under the tablecloth to cover his hand with my own, pushing his digits back to my sex, to that fun spot. My clitoris or clit, whatever the heck it is, I want more.

Turning his face to me, he licks his lips and quietly says, "Please what, Sophie?"

"More, please."

I can feel my father's curious dark eyes on us, but I refuse to glance in his direction. Of course, what I'm saying doesn't make any sense. I have almost an entire slice of cheesecake on my plate and I'm asking Lochlan, a man I'm just meeting for the second time, for his serving.

As soon as I say please, though, I forget everything else because Lochlan's fingers resume their stroking with a vengeance. He covers my gasp by shoveling more of his cheesecake into my mouth. My eyes slam shut as I savor the taste and his teasing fingers at the same time. My thighs clench tighter. It's all so overwhelming...

"Ah!" I gasp loudly before biting down on my bottom lip to keep quiet. I erupt in a wave of blissful shudders that travel throughout my lower body. I'm torn apart and put back together within seconds as everyone around us keeps eating.

Only Lochlan is staring at me now, his greenish-gold eyes dark with hunger. His fingertips continue to move slowly, gently, drawing out the twitches of pleasure until they're sadly over and I'm left way too sensitive.

God. That was...that was...

Was that an orgasm?

Holy shit.

I've never touched myself down there like that before. And now that it's over...I'm sort of sad. I don't think my limbs have ever been so limp and relaxed. There's no tension at all in my whole body for once. Vanessa was right about those happy endorphins.

Is that what it feels like having sex too? If so, I can't wait to try it now. Cass said the first time would hurt but after that small taste...I think it could be fun.

Lochlan pulls his hand away from me. Mine is still clutching it tightly without me realizing it. Before I understand his intention, his hand slips from underneath mine to grab the top to drag it over to his lap. He presses my palm down onto the crotch of his pants where there's a rock hard bulge. He molds my fingers around the length of what I finally realize is his long, thick penis. It suddenly twitches, causing me to jerk my hand away so hard and fast that the top of my hand hits the underside of the table, rattling all the dishes.

Again, all eyes turn to us as Lochlan covers his mouth with his fist when he laughs, attempting to turn his chuckle into a cough.

"Hit my damn knee," he explains it away to everyone who is waiting for an explanation.

I'm absolutely mortified. I barely touched his penis, and it scared me. Lochlan laughed at me. He thinks I'm a silly, inexperienced child. And he's right. I am inexperienced, but I'm no longer a little girl.

Tonight, I'm going out with Vanessa and Cass for my bachelorette party, where I now plan to touch a man without flinching away.

My father kept me from men and dating my entire life, but he's agreed to give us a night of freedom. Just one before I likely will go from being a captive in one home to another.

Nobody even cares what I want. Not that I even know what that is either. All I know is that I don't want Lochlan to use me, to take my virginity, and then toss me aside when I'm no longer a toy he wants to play with.

I want my future husband to love me, to only want to be with me. I don't want to be treated like a child anymore.

There's only one way to find out if my innocence is the only reason Lochlan wants to marry me.

If I'm not a virgin tomorrow at our wedding, maybe he'll call it off.

Sex probably isn't that big of a deal anyway. I'll be safe, use protection, and it'll probably be over and done in no time.

9

Lochlan

Making Sophie come while having dinner with her family, her father sitting a few feet away, was one of the hottest things I've ever done. The sounds she made, before they were muffled by dessert or her biting her bottom lip made me so damn hard.

While I wasn't expecting her to jerk me off under the table, I wanted her to feel how much I liked having my fingers between her damp thighs. Her reaction to the twitch my cock gave when she squeezed it was priceless. I shouldn't have laughed, but I couldn't help it. I fucking love how innocent my Snow White is when it comes to sex. And I can't wait to show her everything she's been missing.

I can't wait until tomorrow night when Sophie becomes my wife, and I can finally have her in all the ways I've been fantasizing about for months, ever since I saw her photos for the first time. Knowing that she's likely terrified of being alone in a bedroom with me, much-less naked and at my mercy, only turns me on even more.

Unfortunately, there's a very real chance that she could change her mind, come to her senses, and refuse to walk down the aisle tomorrow on the rooftop gazebo.

Sophie agreed with my choice of the outdoor ceremony on the second-story balcony of the local chapel with no more than thirty guests for the ceremony. The fewer people there is the less likely another unfortunate incident will occur. God knows Dante and I both have countless enemies for a public event like this. I hope he's as prepared as I am.

Before I could ask him about it at our dinner, though, Flynn knocked over his glass of champagne all over Cass who of course had a conniption. I got my brother out of there before he could fuck things up even more.

Instead of taking me home, though, Owen insisted they had a surprise for me.

I never enjoy their surprises, so I knew I wouldn't like this one either.

Taking me to a bachelor party held at one of my brothels was the last place I wanted to be tonight.

If Dante finds out I fucked around on his daughter the night before the wedding, he would probably castrate me. That's why I head outside with a cherry cigar in my mouth and my guards following behind to call him up even though it's nearly midnight to coordinate our security protocols.

"Lochlan," Dante answers after the first ring, as if he was holding his phone, expecting a call. "What can I do for you at this hour? Have you come to your senses, and changed your mind?"

"No. I just wanted to make sure all bases are covered for the balcony tomorrow. I'm going to have a few of my guards lurking in nearby building windows, so tell yours not to shoot them. I'll make sure they all wear a white Bowen knot patch on their chests." Everyone, including Dante, knows that the Celtic symbol of love and loyalty is mine alone in this city.

"Fine," Dante replies. "Even though I'll have my own snipers keeping an eye on things."

"You can never have enough security," I mutter.

"No, you can't," he agrees since we both nearly died in the casino bombing.

"How will my guards be able to tell your men from potential enemies?" I ask.

"Vanessa has dressed the whole security team in black suits with gold ties so even they will match the theme. My wife is always thinking ahead."

"Good. I'll inform my men."

"Is there anything else you wanted?" Dante asks tersely.

"I suppose it's too much to ask to speak to my bride?"

"Yes, it is, but..." he trails off, leaving me hanging.

"But what?" I snap.

"But Sophie's not here anyway."

"What? It's almost midnight. Where the fuck is she?"

Dante's heavy sigh tells me I'm not going to like the answer. "Cass said Sophie wanted a bachelorette party, so I let them go out tonight after dinner with Vanessa."

"Out? Out where?" I demand. "Where is she, Dante?" I'm already gesturing to the guards to bring the car around.

"Where Sophie goes isn't your concern until after tomorrow's ceremony," the asshole replies. "The wedding you rushed her into even though she's still too young for this shit."

He's stalling, making me want to rip his head off. "Goddamm it, Dante, tell me where they fucking went!" When he doesn't respond after several seconds, I lay into him. "If another man touches her, I swear to god, I'll eventually find him, gut him, and make her watch the entire time."

"She deserves one night of freedom before you take it from her.

God knows I never gave her any either. Do you think I like the idea of my wife being out late with my daughters in some club?"

"Where. Is. She?" My teeth are clenched so tightly, I can barely speak.

"Sorry, Lochlan. I'm not supposed to interfere tonight, so neither can you."

"Are you fucking kidding me?" I explode. "Do you really want Sophie fucking some stranger she just met tonight instead of me?"

"She's my baby girl, I don't *want* her fucking anyone!" he yells right back at me. "And if you tell me you don't want to marry her if she's not a virgin in the morning, then you're a goddamn hypocrite."

"That's not..." Fuck. The sudden throbbing in my head is making it impossible to think. I have to find her, that's all I know. "Look, Salvato, I just need one good thing in my life right now. One perfect, innocent thing like her because I don't know the last time I had either of those, if I've ever had them. And I sure as fuck don't want her getting knocked up with some man's kid or catching a disease the night before she becomes mine."

Dante sighs again, even heavier than before. "They were going to Caesar's Palace, that's all Vanessa would tell me. Cass somehow managed to manipulate the guards into not reporting a thing to me tonight unless it was life or death, so I don't know if they're still there or went somewhere else."

"Thank you," I tell him before ending the call. At least I have a destination. There are ten bars and lounges in Caesar's, but only one nightclub.

~

Sophie

I've never seen so many people in my life. The Omnia club in Caesar's Palace was amazing, but the music was so loud I couldn't hear a thing. I was afraid of getting lost in the sea of dancing bodies, so we decided to go next door to a club called Chemistry that's smaller and has live bands. There are still plenty of people, plenty of nice-looking men, but it's less crowded, and the music isn't rattling the windows.

"Let's find a seat," Vanessa says as we take our drinks from the bar to the table in the corner. Cass and I aren't old enough to have any alcohol, so we are only allowed to have soda. Vanessa refused to bend on that issue, even though we have wine most nights at dinner. She said that even if we were of legal drinking age, it's smart to stay sober around strange men.

Which of course made me want to drink even more, for the thrill of not being smart for one night.

"So, what do you girls want to do tonight while you're free?" Vanessa looks between us, giving us the option to decide once we're seated. "Dance some then go to a show?"

"Sophie wants to get fucked."

"Cass!" Vanessa exclaims.

"It's true, right Soph?" my sister asks with a single red eyebrow raised.

"Sophie? Is that really what you want?" Vanessa asks quietly, as if she doesn't approve.

"I don't know. It's just...nothing has ever really been my decision. It could be nice to choose this one thing for myself." And not have my soon-to-be-husband laugh at me when I can't even touch his penis without flinching. If he even still wants to marry me once I tell him I'm no longer innocent.

"Well, as your stepmother, I should try to change your mind. Tell you that waiting for a man you love is best. But since you don't love the man you're marrying tomorrow, and barely know him, I guess..." She cringes, her nose wrinkling. "I sowed some wild oats of my own, which is how I ended up pregnant at sixteen. I don't have a right to tell you not to do it. Just promise to be super careful and safe?"

"See?" Cass turns to me and slurps her soda through the red straw. "Even Vanessa thinks you should whore it up tonight."

"I didn't say that!" Vanessa scoffs. "And if your dad finds out..."

"He won't," Cass says confidently. "The guards confirmed that we've got a longer leash tonight. They won't interfere with anything we do or report back to Daddy unless someone is dying."

"And what about you, Cass? Do you plan on whoring it up?" I can't resist teasing my sister.

"No."

Liar. She answered that question way too fast.

"Well, how about instead of starting the night with casual sex, we just go dance?" Vanessa suggests.

"Sounds good," I agree.

"Fine," Cass says. "It'll give us a chance to survey our surroundings, find the hottest guys."

I thought that I would look stupid throwing my arms in the air and swaying my hips like everyone else when I've never done it before, but there are so many people crowding around us that I think I blend right in.

And while I was trying to figure out how to even start a conversation when approaching a man, we were quickly surrounded by several who were friendly, smelled so good, and were young and attractive enough.

None of them had tattoos, at least none on their face or hands, which was a little disappointing. Although, I'm not entirely sure why. Maybe because I would like to dance with someone more like Lochlan to gain some insight into a bad boy.

"Back up, buddy! I'm married to the mafia king of Vegas," I hear Vanessa shouting to one of the guys while holding up her drink in her left hand to flash her rose gold wedding band.

Keeping our drinks in our hand was another suggestion from

Vanessa. She said someone could still slip something in it, so we should keep a close eye on it at all times.

I wish someone would slip me something to make me brave enough to lose my virginity tonight. Or at the very least, get a little experience in touching a man's penis.

"I like your dress," the blond guy dancing behind me says with his lips against my ear. "It's very sexy."

"Thank you," I reply with a smile over my shoulder at the compliment. It's the same white dress I wore to dinner. Lochlan seemed to like it too.

The stranger grabs my hips to spin me around so I'm facing him but doesn't let go.

"What's your name?" he asks, again, leaning close enough for his bristly cheek to brush mine so I can hear him over the music.

"Sophie. Yours?"

"Austin."

"Austin?" I repeat. "Like the city?"

"Just like the city," he agrees with a smile.

We talk about ourselves in short sentences that are practically screamed in each other's ears. Austin goes to college in California, is a marketing major, and came to Vegas for the weekend with some friends in his fraternity.

I tell him I live in Vegas, like to play tennis, but don't mention that I'm supposed to be getting married tomorrow. After tonight, maybe I won't be. I honestly don't know what I want. I'm so confused, and my head is all over the place. This is all too much, too fast. What the hell was I thinking? Just because I was lonely and bored, I agreed to marry a stranger with a teasing knife?

Austin sips from his drink while we dance, an amber liquid.

"Want to try it?" he asks when he notices me eyeing the glass.

"I'm only eighteen," I admit.

"I won't tell the Alcoholic Beverage Control police, if you won't," he says with a smirk. "Open up!"

It takes me a second to realize he means to give me a sip, so with a quick glance to make sure Vanessa isn't looking, I obey his command, parting my lips and letting him pour the liquid into my mouth. Not just one sip, but the entire rest of the glass. The bitter taste burns my tongue, and all the way down my throat, making me shiver. Even my nose feels scalded.

"Not a fan of Fireball?" Austin asks with a chuckle.

"It's okay," I lie.

"Then how about a refill?"

~

Ten minutes later, another glass of Fireball, and everything Austin says is hilarious. It's also funny that I keep sliding off my stool at the bar.

"I think I'm drunk!" I say before I spot Vanessa coming toward us. "Shh, don't tell my stepmom."

Austin mimes zipping his smirking lips and throwing away the key.

"Hey, Soph. You doing okay over here?"

"Yes." I blink at her a few times until my vision clears. "Perfectly fine."

"Okay. Good." She glances between me and Austin. "I'm going to sit out a song or two. You know where to find me," she adds, pointing toward the table in the corner.

"Got it. Thanks," I tell her cheerfully.

Once she walks away, Austin grabs a thick strand of my hair. Wrapping it around his fist he pulls my face to his. "You came to a club with your stepmother?"

"Yes. She's cool. I don't have many friends," I admit, which is a lie. I have zero.

"I'll be your friend," Austin says before his lips slant over mine. When he pulls way, he says, "Mmm. You taste like cinnamon."

"It's the drink," I assure him.

"I know. How about another?" I may be tipsy, but it sounds like

72

he's enthusiastically encouraging me to drink, knowing I'm underage. The liquor is so much stronger than the wine I've had at dinner.

I look to the bartender who is an older guy. I expect him to ask for my ID, but he just winks at me, as if he knows my age and is letting it slide.

"I think I have to go to the bathroom," I say to try and put a little space between me and Austin and to clear my fuzzy head.

The frat boy hops off his stool and holds out his hand for mine. "I can show you where it is, if you want?"

"Ah, sure," I agree, even though I think I remember seeing a pink neon sign near the door that said "Restrooms."

Still, I can't be too careful in a place packed with strangers.

I slide off the stool and have to grab Austin's upper arm to keep from stumbling. "Sorry."

"No worries. Let's get you to the bathroom," he says as he grips my elbow and steers me through the crowd.

I was right. There is a sign near the front door. Seeing the familiar faces of our two guards, I wave at them.

One takes a step forward, but the other throws his arm out to stop him.

"You know those men?" Austin asks, slowing his steps down once we're down the much quieter, empty hallway.

"Oh, yeah. They're our guards, but they're only here to observe, not interfere tonight."

"Observe, huh? That sounds kind of hot."

"Does it?" I ask in confusion.

Instead of answering me with words, Austin presses his lips to mine again. This time, he shoves his tongue into my mouth and there's a lot of saliva. Like a gross amount. He doesn't stop so I let him keep kissing me while walking me backward. Back, back, back, until we're in a small dark room with a flickering glow from a television.

I put my palms on Austin's stomach, pushing him away so I can glance around. "This isn't the bathroom," I remark. There's a desk and chair, a refrigerator and microwave. Then a loveseat, raggedy and torn chocolate leather positioned in front of a television mounted on the wall. It's on but there's no sound coming from it, so the room is way too quiet after just being in the noisy club.

"It's the employee's break room," Austin explains as he takes a step back. "Don't worry. They'll all be busy for the next few hours."

When I drag my heavy eyes back to him, I notice his hands are on the front of his pants, unbuckling his belt, then unbuttoning.

"This isn't the bathroom," I repeat again.

"No, it's not," Austin agrees before he's pressing me to the wall at my back and kissing me again.

I must be drunk because only when I feel his bulge do I recall Lochlan's, and realize his intentions.

So, I guess I'm about to lose my virginity, just like I wanted.

In a ratty employee breakroom of a nightclub.

With a man I just met who doesn't make me nervous or set my heart racing like Lochlan.

My knees go weak, causing me to wobble to the right. Austin instantly grabs my waist to steady me then laughs. "You are already hammered. I better get you on the sofa before you pass out."

The sofa? No, I don't want to sit on that sofa. It looks like it's well used, and if I had to guess, probably not from just sitting, but from sleezy hookups like this every night.

"How did you...how did you know this room was here?" I ask when I grab his hands to shove them off me.

"The bartender told me. He rents it out, actually. Better than fucking in a bathroom stall, right?"

He rented out this weird little room to fuck me in it? When? How? I can't seem to form any of those questions. And even if I could, Austin's lips are on mine again. His hands are back on my waist, sliding around to my ass that he squeezes in both hands and groans into my mouth.

I think I've made a huge mistake.

This doesn't feel right. It just feels...gross. Not exciting at all, just disgusting, like Austin had this planned all along as if he was so certain I was going to want to have sex with him.

A loud bang causes us both to startle apart, and the much-appreciated inches between our bodies become feet when Austin turns around.

"Get the fuck away from her," a deep voice growls from the dark doorway before it slams shut again.

My eyes can't focus, so I can't tell which one of the guards has thankfully interrupted, but I don't care. I just want to kiss them for their perfect timing. Maybe I could lose my virginity to him.

As the man moves closer to the glow of the muted television, I finally see his face. His furious face with tattoos climbing up his neck, and fisted, tattooed hands by the sides of his wrinkled suit. Every inch of him is promising violence. Beautiful, savage, violence.

He's not one of the guards.

"Lochlan?" God, I'm so drunk. Does too much alcohol cause hallucinations because there's no way he's here. He can't be. It's a big city and I'm in a shady backroom in a small nightclub.

"You've got three seconds to disappear if you want to walk out of this room alive."

Wow. That sounded like a threat Lochlan would make. And back up. Shit. It is him.

"Yo, man. I've got the room for the next hour, so you should mind your own business and get the fuck out."

Uh-oh. That was the absolute last thing he should've said to Lochlan. I don't think anyone ever gives him orders.

As if that wasn't bad enough, he gestures with both hands to his half-opened pants.

Neither Austin nor Lochlan say another word before Lochlan's fist slams into his face. The force of the blow knocks the guy sideways, where he drops to the floor, clutching his jaw.

But Lochlan isn't finished hurting the other man. It's like he goes into a blind rage, smashing his dress shoe into Austin's face with a loud crunch of bone. Then he starts kicking him in the stomach before bending over him to land punch after punch until blood runs down his forehead and nose. That's about the time Austin's entire body goes limp. I'm not even sure if he's still breathing. He won't be for much longer.

"Stop! You're going to kill him!" I shout at Lochlan.

The punches finally stop, if only momentarily. When Lochlan straightens to his full height again, he lifts his snarling face to mine. His eyes are still dark and murderous. "I warned him I would kill him. He should've fucking listened."

Yes, he did warn him. Even I remember that in my drunken haze.

Lochlan's gaze scans every inch of me, my white dress, my bare legs, then he wipes his bleeding knuckles on his pants leg and says confidently, "You've been drinking."

"Just a little." It was a little for me. That's all it took for me to get, what was it Austin called it? Hammered.

"You're only eight-fucking-teen!" he yells as if I don't know my own age. "Where did he touch you?"

"What?"

"Where. Did. He. Touch. You?"

"Nowhere. He didn't. He didn't touch me," I rush to assure him. "How did you...what are you even doing here?"

"I came to stop you from making a goddamn mistake. What the fuck were you thinking, Sophie?" he asks, sounding like my father.

And of course he had to barge in here tonight to stop me from having sex. He's adamant that he's going to be the one who takes my virginity. No one else is allowed to have it, despite the fact that it's *my* body. Even though I didn't want it to be Austin, I still want it to be my decision. It's the only thing Lochlan wants from me, and I hate it. Hate him. Nothing in my life has ever been my decision.

"It's none of your business what I do tonight with him or anyone else," I remind him since we're not married yet. He's free to back out now if he wants.

"You're wrong about that."

I guess he's made it his business to beat the shit out of any man I go near, which is one hell of a deterrent unfortunately.

"Well, you...you're overreacting."

Lochlan rolls his broad shoulders back, then his neck, cracking it so loudly I can hear it. "Where did he touch you, Sophie?"

"I told you, nowhere."

"You're lying. His fucking dick was practically hanging out of his pants!" His face suddenly goes from enraged to...something else. It's just blank as he looks at Austin's undone pants then me. "Has he already fucked you?"

I shake my head. "No." *Thank god. Or thank Lochlan for interrupting.* Not that I'll tell him that.

There's obvious relief on Lochlan's face. I knew it. I knew that my virginity was all he cared about.

"Where did his hands touch your body, Sophie?" he repeats slowly. "Either you can tell me the truth, or I'll cut off every limb and his dick to cover all the bases." His glare warns me that I better not lie to him again or I'll regret it because he would do exactly what he promised.

"Just my waist and, um, my...bottom. My butt."

"*Fuuuck, man,*" Austin groans, sounding groggy, as if he just woke up. He plants his palms on the floor to try to push himself up, but only manages to lift his head.

"He touched your ass?" Lochlan's eyes lower to my waist and his jaw tightens as if he's imagining the man's hands palming my backside. His jaw ticks as if the thought is enough to make him furious.

"He-he just sort of grabbed it for a second." I try my best to downplay it.

"He grabbed your ass?" he repeats again. "After he got you drunk. Underage and drunk?"

I nod, and swallow around the sudden knot in my throat because not only is the murderous look back in his eyes, but it's also got an edge of a need for brutal, painful murder. "Yes, but I'm not drunk."

Lochlan reaches into his pocket, then there's a flash of silver in his palm. His thumb engages the mechanism that makes the sharp blade jut out of the end. Spinning it around, he angles the point downward, and crouches to slam it straight through the top of Austin's hand.

I don't scream but Austin does, a moment before his entire body goes limp again.

The wound is bad, blood seeping from it, but it's thankfully over. At least I thought it was over until Lochlan leaves the knife sticking up from the top of the man's hand and stands all the way up. His dress shoe stomps down onto the handle, shoving the knife through bone, all the way to the cement floor. It's a horrible crunching, scraping noise I never want to hear again.

"Jesus, Lochlan! That's enough!" I scream at him, unable to look away even though my stomach is rolling with nausea.

There's a hole in this man's hand, and all he did was talk to me, share his drinks with me, and take me into this room like I wanted. Or at least I thought that's what I wanted.

"Are you sure you want me to stop?" Lochlan looks over at me, his foot still propped on the handle. "Because if I'm not hurting him, I'm going to be punishing you."

"Then hurt me instead!" I blurt out.

He chuckles darkly. "You don't know what you're asking for, princess."

"Hurt me instead," I repeat. "*Please.*"

Lochlan stares at me for a long silent second. "Well, since you said please...." Lowering his foot to the floor, Lochlan leaves the knife jutting out of the bleeding hand when he stalks toward me.

I back up as far as I can go, which is only about two steps until my back hits the wall.

Seeing his busted, bloody knuckles, I expect him to hit me. Slap me. I have no idea what he intends to do to me as my punishment. How did I ever think I could refuse this violent man anything? Whatever he wants from me he'll take, and there's nothing I can do to stop him.

As exciting as that is, I'm terrified for another reason. Tonight could be the last time he wants anything from me.

Grabbing my chin roughly, Lochlan holds it tightly, his eyes lowered to my lips before his thumb swipes over the bottom one hard. "Did you kiss him?"

I nod since I can't move my lower jaw to speak.

The murderous glint in his green eyes returns with a vengeance, making my breath catch and my heart pound even faster against my ribcage.

"Are you scared of me, Sophie?" he asks.

"Yes," I answer honestly.

"Good," he replies before he leans forward, his teeth nipping at my bottom lip. I hiss at the sting, then Lochlan's tongue is sliding along the ache, shoving into my mouth like he owns it. The second our tongues collide for the first time, a frenzy begins. They can't seem to stop meeting. His grip on my chin directs my lips where he wants them. We can't seem to get close enough either. Lochlan's bigger heavier body flattens me to the wall. I barely have room for my lungs to expand, but I don't mind. I like his weight pressing into me like he can't get close enough.

Kissing Austin wasn't anything like kissing Lochlan. He's addictive. I want more, and I want it now.

As if he heard my request, Lochlan's hand slides up the back of my thigh. When he grabs a rough handful of my ass possessively with a growl, liquid heat floods my panties.

Wow. That *definitely* didn't happen with that other guy whose name I can't seem to recall. What's-his-name's touch felt wrong, while Lochlan's...I just want more. I want him to keep touching me. Everywhere. Just like under the table earlier tonight.

His fingers find the string of my thong, ripping my panties down to my thighs with an impatient roar. A second later his palm is back on my bottom, his long fingers running through the dampness from behind. The most embarrassing whimper escapes me.

"Fuck, you're dripping wet," Lochlan grumbles against my lips. I still don't know if that's a good thing or not until one of his fingers easily slides inside of me. I cry out in surprise as I go up on my toes. My hands fly out to clutch the lapels of his jacket to brace myself. Without the added moisture the invasion would've hurt, but thanks to it...well, it's still strange to be penetrated in such an intimate way, over and over again. Not bad, just different.

"So damn tight. I've never had a virgin pussy," Lochlan informs me as he tilts my head to kiss my neck. I knew that was his only draw to me. I should've known that he wouldn't have ever been with a virgin since he has sex with prostitutes. "You wanted to get fucked tonight after coming for me earlier? Is that why you came here dressed like a little slut begging for a dick?"

"I...I'm not..." It's impossible to form a coherent thought with how he's touching me and kissing down my throat. A second finger joins the first, both thrusting deep inside of me. My own fingers grip the front of Lochlan's suit jacket tighter.

"Were you going to let him fuck you?" When I don't respond, his face appears in front of me. "Answer me, Sophie!"

"M-maybe. I don't...I don't know." A third finger filling me makes it hard to think.

Lochlan's tongue darts out, licking a line down the other side of my neck. At the spot where my shoulder meets my neck, Lochlan's teeth sink into my skin for a second before he lifts his face to mine.

"In that case, I better pop your cherry before you give it to someone else. You're good and ready now, aren't you?"

A whimper escapes my lips when he removes his fingers from me to tug my panties the rest of the way down my legs to my ankles. When he stands up to his full height again, he says, "Kick your panties off."

I lift one heel to discard the fabric, then the other.

"Good girl. Now lift up your dress."

"What?"

His jaw clenches as he stares at the short hem of my dress. "Lift your dress, Sophie. Show me your virgin pussy. I want to see how perfect it looks before I ruin it."

I glance back to the door to the lounge that I don't think is locked, down at the man still unconscious on the ground. Lochlan slams a palm against the wall beside my head to get my attention. He tilts my chin up to look at him. "Lift your dress. Now, Sophie."

I release his suit to lower my hands, hiking up the tight material, baring myself to the cool air and the mad man in front of me.

While staring down at the apex of my thighs, Lochlan releases my jaw to shove his fingers between my legs and begins to rub me again. Both of my hands shoot out to wrap around his unmovable, tattooed arm, to stop him or urge him on, I'm not sure.

No, that's a lie.

I'm already addicted to how he can make me feel after one orgasm. As his fingertips move against my bare flesh, I can't help but squirm and gasp at the return of the tingling sensation.

The back of my head falls limply against the wall, causing Lochlan to smile smugly at me like he did the first time.

My thighs tighten, holding his hand hostage. His touch feels good. So good. And I don't want him to ever stop. With each passing second his groping gets even better until there's that familiar growing pressure in my lower belly.

Two of his long fingers push inside of me again, and combined with his thumb rubbing me...well, I'm in awe of how good it feels when my inner walls clench around his thrusting digits. I thought sex would only hurt, not feel so...*wow*. I've only ever had tampons inside of me, and they were dry and uncomfortable. Lochlan's fingers are completely different.

My breathing grows more rapid the longer he keeps it up, like I've been playing tennis for hours when I'm only standing against the wall getting harassed by my soon-to-be-husband.

Not that it's a bad thing. No, it's a good kind of harassment. Seeing him so upset because another man kissed me and touched me shouldn't make me happy, but it does. I'm a horrible person. The poor guy's hand is destroyed, and yet I can't find it in me to feel all that bad for him.

I'm still holding onto Lochlan's arm to help keep myself upright when he starts to pull away. I dig my fingernails into his arms to stop him.

"Say it, Sophie."

Knowing exactly what he wants to hear, I give it to him. "Please," I whisper.

"I like hearing you beg, princess. Especially when you do it in front of Daddy while I'm fingering you so good under the dining table. Now, say it again."

Since his thumb continues teasing my clitoris, that spot that feels so good, I oblige. "Please, Lochlan."

"Say, 'please make me come again, Lochlan.'"

"Please...please make me...make me come again, Lochlan."

"I'll let you come this time. But the next time you beg to get off, you're going to have to use that pretty mouth of yours to convince me first."

It takes me longer than it should to realize he's not talking about speaking words but using my mouth to...pleasure him.

And right now, with the warm, tight sensation building inside of me, I would drop to my knees and take him in my mouth if it meant he would keep going. I didn't get it when Vanessa talked about oral sex. Now I do.

I cry out when three of his thick fingers suddenly penetrate me again while his thumb rubs that sensitive spot in circles. The muscles in my thighs tense as the room darkens. My jaw falls open on a silent scream as my entire body shudders. I grasp Lochlan's arm tighter to ride out the jolts of pleasure making my hips buck. I vaguely hear myself chanting the word "yes" over and over again. The pleasure is...even more intense than the first time.

After it's over, Lochlan's lips press against my neck, making me shiver. "Oh, princess. Did I give you your first orgasm tonight in front of Daddy?" When I don't respond, Lochlan removes his fingers from between my legs. Still, I hold on to his arm. His face appears in front of me, eyes intense. "Sophie, have you ever come before tonight?"

I shake my head no, unable to speak yet.

"Good," he says. Leaning forward his lips press more kisses to my neck. "I love that you're already greedy for more. But now it's my turn."

That wakes me up. Does he want me to touch his dick again? Will he laugh again if I flinch? Is he going to tell me to get on my knees?

I watch as Lochlan undoes his pants, whipping out his long, hard penis from its depths. He grips it tightly in his fist, stroking up and down as I watch in a trance. He's so big, thicker than his three fingers for sure. There's no way he'll fit all of that inside of me.

"You've never seen a cock before either, have you?" Lochlan asks. I shake my head again since the man on the ground never pulled his out. "Fuck, that shouldn't be so damn hot."

I don't have a chance to respond before he releases himself to grab the backs of my bare thighs, reminding me my dress is still hiked up to my waist. Before I can tug the material down, he hefts me off my feet until we're face to face, pinning my back to the wall. My hands shoot out, grabbing onto his wide shoulders for balance. But with the tight grip he has on me, I'm not going to fall. Lochlan is in complete control of my body when he pries my thighs apart as wide as they'll go. Only then do I realize his intention. I feel stupid that it took me so long.

"I told you my dick was going to be the first one inside of you," he says as he reaches between us and rubs me. That's not his fingers this time, but his...

"*Oh!*" I scream as he invades me, his impossibly large cock forcing its way into a tight space that refuses to allow him entry.

I feel the vibrations of Lochlan's masculine groan deep within my own chest. Then, somehow, he shoves even deeper inside of me.

God, Cass was right. It's...uncomfortable. My eyes squeeze shut, teeth gritting together when he pulls back giving me a momentary reprieve, only to thrust his hardness up into me again and again, harder, deeper each time.

"Look at me, princess."

My throat is raw and burning as moisture fills my eyes, so I ignore him. If I open my eyes, the tears will fall. He won't care that I'm terrified, nervous, hurting, or that I'm crying.

"Look at me!" This time he roars it loud enough that I flinch and comply. I have to blink away the wetness until his face is no longer blurry in front of mine. "Watch me while I fuck you, Sophie. I don't want you to forget my face, or whose cock is claiming your virginity tonight. The only cock you'll ever have. Do you hear me? Answer me."

"Y-yes."

Leaning forward, the flat of his tongue sweeps up one of my cheeks then the other while pumping inside of me faster.

"You begged me to hurt you, remember? I told you I would punish you if I wasn't punishing him. Regretting that decision now, aren't you?"

My teeth clench tighter as he slams up inside of me as far as he can go. "Yes."

"Louder, princess."

"Yes!" I shout.

My voice breaks on a sob, making me hate myself for getting emotional. I'm just furious at him for being so callous. He just licked up my tears while ripping me apart!

"I've wanted this tight ass pussy since the first day I was in your bedroom," he tells me what I already knew. He never wanted me, just my innocence. "I should've taken you then and there, saved the frat boy a hole through his hand."

I glance over to find Austin not only awake but watching us through swollen eyes, the knife still sticking up out of his hand. He's either too terrified or too injured to move, and it's my fault. No. It's Lochlan's.

"I-I hate you," I stammer through a sob, not sure if I'm talking to Austin or Lochlan. Maybe both.

Lochlan chuckles, as if he's enjoying my discomfort, his fingers digging even tighter into my ass cheeks while slamming into me so deep my teeth chatter. "That a girl. Show me some backbone while I'm balls deep inside your virgin pussy. Fight me if it makes you feel better while you go for your first ride on my cock. Pretend like you didn't want to get fucked like a little slut tonight." His words hurt almost as much as his dick.

I hear the break room door open, and without turning around or even looking in the direction, Lochlan bellows, "Get the fuck out!"

I don't see who it was who walked in on us before the door shuts again. Lochlan pumps into me harder, faster, making me wince with each thrust, wondering how long I'll have to endure this. Dangling over a cliff by your ankles isn't a fun kind of scary excitement. It just fucking hurts.

When another tear rolls down my cheek, Lochlan says, "Cry all you want, princess, but I'm not stopping until my cum is dripping down your thighs."

His cum? His release. Lochlan's not wearing a condom, which means...I could get pregnant. Pregnant at eighteen by a mobster who only wanted one thing from me.

10

Lochlan

S ophie is so innocent it blows my goddamn mind. My dick has never been in anyone so tight, so perfect, making me fight for every fucking inch. I would've already blown my load if not for her tears and agonized whimpers. I thought for sure that once she started crying, she would beg me to stop, to go easier on her. But she didn't. And now it's a race to the finish listening to her muffled cries while I take her, and the bastard who tried to take advantage of her bleeds on the floor.

I couldn't help myself. I wanted her. Needed her tonight, before another asshole came along and took what was mine.

Sophie's the best fuck of my life, and I never want it to end.

More tears and maybe I can hold off just a little longer to stay buried in her snug wet cunt.

She was soaking wet after that fucker pawed all over her. Kissed her. He stole that first from me, and I made him pay. Her too. I should've kissed her earlier at dinner, before or after I fingered her under the table. Now it's too fucking late.

"Cry all you want, princess, but I'm not stopping until my cum is dripping down your thighs," I warn her.

The words are even a shock to my own ears. I don't want kids anytime soon, and yet...here I am, unable to pull out to finish because, fuck if I know. This first time I just need to fill Sophie's pussy with my release. Mark her. Claim her. Whether or not she's on birth control doesn't even matter to me.

The beautiful girl is no longer flinching in pain. No, now she looks...pissed off. I told her to fight me, and yet, I'm still shocked as shit when both of her small hands lift from my shoulders...to wrap around my throat, squeezing.

I freeze in place when she touches my skin for the first time, her fingernails digging into my neck. Staring down at her face, I wonder what the tipping point was for her. What did I say to flip her switch from docile virgin to hard-ass mafia princess? Ah, I bet she doesn't like the idea of me putting my kid inside of her so soon.

Too fucking bad.

Tomorrow she'll be my wife, and one day I *will* get her pregnant. Probably more than once. Unless I let her kill me right here, right now just so I can finish inside of her.

It's been years since I've allowed a woman to put her hands on my bare skin without my permission. And nobody has ever fucking tried to choke me while we were fucking.

But I don't mind Sophie's fingernails digging into my flesh deeper. In fact, I find it hilarious to know that some part of the sweet virgin wants to hurt me back.

Chuckling, I tell her, "Do it, princess. Squeeze harder and see what happens." Some of the fire in her ruthless blue eyes dims, but she doesn't stop. "You think you can kill me? I don't. Still, I guess I better take you from behind next time."

"Next...next time?" she asks softly.

From the back is my preferred position even when a woman's

restrained. It's less personal, and easier to forget who I'm inside if I can't see their face. I've never had the desire to look at the face of the women I fucked before. But with Sophie, I want to watch her expression go from surprised, to anguished, to pissed-off, witnessing every single reaction while my dick's buried inside of her sexy little body.

Since I don't like the thought of not seeing her beautiful face each time I take her, I tell her, "I'll just have to tie you down to keep your hands off my throat when I fuck you tomorrow night."

Her pretty pink lips part on a gasp at the same time her pussy clenches around my shaft, making me groan. "Oh, Sophie. You dirty girl. You like the idea of being my unwilling captive, letting me take what I want, when I want it when you're my wife?"

I resume fucking her against the wall, this time a little slower, watching her fury soften as if she's starting to savor the slide of my cock thanks to the mention of being restrained by me. Her pussy softens too, making it easier to fill her up with each stroke. I make sure her clit grinds against my pelvis on the next thrust. Her eyes drift closed as a surprised moan escapes her sensuous mouth. It's followed by another on the next thrust. The fingers digging into my neck shift to the sides of my face, urging my mouth back toward hers. Yeah, that's not going to work because I don't take orders.

"You're just full of surprises," I murmur against her lips. "But since you're not going to try and choke me out, put your hands above your head right fucking now."

Her eyes fly open at that command. Curiosity and arousal swirls in their blue depths. "Hands up. Now, Sophie."

She slowly complies while her gaze remains locked on mine. I grip both of her wrists with one of my hands to stretch her arms high up above her head on the wall. The move arches her back, shoving her small but perky tits into my face. I'm unable to resist swiping my tongue over the swell of her breasts revealed by the top of her dress. Her legs tighten around my waist, ankles finally locking, as if she wants to keep them there now. And when I suckle and nip her breasts, her pussy tightens around my cock.

"Come for me again," I lift my face from her cleavage to order her. She winces when I slam deep, eager to get myself off, so I keep still for her for a moment. "There's pleasure in the pain. You like that don't you? A little pain with the pleasure? Your soaking wet pussy seems to enjoy it."

She nods her head in agreement, so I grasp her wrists tighter, tight enough to leave bruises on them. Sophie's front teeth bite down on her bottom lip as she leans her head back against the wall, watching me. Waiting for me to move again. Wanting me to keep fucking her, even if it hurts. She may be innocent and inexperienced, but the girl likes it rough, which is fucking perfect for me.

"Say it," I demand, wanting to hear the words from her mouth. "If you want me to keep going, say it."

Releasing her bottom lip from her teeth, she licks her lips...then she rolls her body from chest to ass, bearing down on my dick like a goddamn sex goddess, nearly setting me off.

"I-I like it when you hurt me," Sophie replies softly, as if she's embarrassed to admit it.

Her words shouldn't make my dick swell even more, but they do. She asked for it tonight, begged me to hurt her instead of the asshole on the ground.

I never cared if I hurt a woman I was fucking before. But now, I want to hurt Sophie and I want her to get off on the pain with me. Her needs come before my own. I'm not racing to the finish line like usual. No, I want to drag this out, make it good for her.

She's a virgin who should remember her first time with me. I want her to enjoy my dick so much she begs for it every day and night after we say our vows.

Another roll of her body, followed by a whispered, "Please, Lochlan," and I fucking lose it.

My lips slam over hers, my tongue shoving inside. She whimpers into my mouth when I bottom out, hitting that magical spot.

"That's it, princess. Give it up to me, only me. Your pussy might hurt now, but it's going to miss my cock filling it, claiming it," I tell her between eager tongue thrusts. It's like I can't keep my mouth off hers. I want to be inside of her every which way I can. And I can't wait to get my tongue in her sweet pussy. "I promise I'll lick it better tomorrow before I fuck you again."

Sophie lifts her head to put her lips back on mine to shut me up. I love invading her mouth and her pussy at the same time, flattening her smaller, softer body to the wall with my bigger frame as I thrust upward and slam her down on my dick. I take her harder, faster until we're panting into each other's mouth. Her pussy pulses, pulling me in deeper. With a mewl that turns me inside out, her entire body trembles against mine and I erupt.

We come together, like a give and take, a push and pull, feeding off the other for so long I'm not certain my legs will keep holding us up. Her cunt drains every single drop from me, like her womb is greedy for my cum.

All too soon, though, the tremors ease up for both of us. The final jerk rips a growl of disappointment that it's over from me that I bury in her neck.

Already I want more. I want to take Sophie home with me tonight, to tie her to my bed and stay buried inside of her for hours.

Soon.

Tomorrow we'll be married, her pussy will heal enough to take my cock again, and I can have her whenever I fucking want her.

11

Sophie

Lochlan said *the next time,* and it was such a relief that I relaxed, allowing him inside me, even welcomed the pain because it means he still wants me, still wants to marry me.

The man still intimidates and overwhelms me but in a good way. He may not be kind or gentle, but nobody has ever made me feel like this—like the center of their world and nothing else matters.

Being with him, it's like I'm someone else. Someone sexy and experienced. Not a child but a grown woman who made a man lose control.

At least it felt like Lochlan lost control with me. Maybe sex is always like that for him. At least he didn't laugh at me if I did something wrong...

As my body cools, my doubts and insecurities begin to grow. Did he mean what he said? Maybe I misunderstood.

Lochlan's face is buried in my neck, his teeth nipping at my throat as we both catch our breath, my arms still restrained above my head.

"You still want to marry me tomorrow?" I ask and he pulls back to look at my face, a single eyebrow raised in question. "Even if I'm not a virgin?"

Now he releases my wrists and takes a step back. I'm actually sad to be rid of his penis when the weight and girth slips out of me.

"Your father and I have a deal," he says while reaching down to tug the hem of my dress back down where it belongs. I assume that means yes. "Fucking you a day earlier doesn't change that. It's after midnight, so we'll be married later today," he adds. "Not that Salvato needs to know..."

Taking himself in his hand, he fists himself to put his dick back in his pants and freezes. Lifting his long, slightly less rigid penis, he examines every inch of it in the dim light before scowling at me. "You didn't bleed."

"Wh-what?"

"Was it all just an act?" he asks while finally tucking himself away, fixing up his pants.

I have no clue what he's talking about so I can't begin to form a response.

"Why did you lie to me about being a fucking virgin?"

"I am a virgin. I mean, I was," I reply in confusion. I try to tug the bottom of my dress lower as the sticky mess he made begins to leak from me, and I'm still not wearing any panties. His cum that's full of sperm that could get me pregnant. That's what he left behind. Lots of it. The throbbing ache between my legs is yet another confirmation that I'm no longer a virgin.

"Stop lying to me."

He actually thinks I'm lying about being a virgin? What the hell?

"I'm not lying. Why would I lie about that?"

"You tell me."

Scoffing, I admit, "I thought that was all you wanted from me. Do you think I *want* to be the inexperienced virgin marrying a man who owns a bunch of brothels?"

"How do you know about my brothels? Did Dante tell you?"

"No. Cass told me. It's true, isn't it?" I ask, feeling more confident in standing up to him now that we've had sex. I know I'm not his equal yet, and probably never will be. But at least I'm no longer an innocent girl. Don't I at least deserve to know how my husband earns a living? It can't be that big of a secret.

"Yes, it's true," he replies. "My family has owned brothels world-wide for three generations."

"Do you fuck them?" It's not the first time I've used the f-word, but it's the first in front of Lochlan. He arches his eyebrow again as if he's surprised I said it or asked the question.

"Do you really want to know?"

"Yes."

"Then, yes. I've fucked some of them in the past."

"And in the future?"

Now he smirks. "Is my little wife getting jealous? One ride on my cock, and you think you own it now?"

Of course, I'm jealous of those women who know what to do to make men happy because they've done it so many times. They know what to do to make Lochlan happy, which is knowledge I currently don't have. And once we're married, I don't want his dick going anywhere near another woman again. My husband should only want me, especially if he demands to be the first and only one who gets inside my body.

"If you sleep with any of them after tomorrow, then I don't want you to ever touch me again." I'm not sure why I tell him that. Must be the jealousy combined with my self-consciousness, along with the throbbing ache and mess he caused between my thighs.

Lochlan's jaw ticks like my dad's does when he's pissed. "That's quite the ultimatum, princess. Nobody tells me what I can or can't do. Especially not my little liar of a wife."

Wow. If he still thinks I'm lying and refuses to do that one thing for me then screw him. Or better yet, I won't let him screw me again. I should've insisted he not sleep around with anyone else before I let him take my virginity. Would he have even stopped if I told him to? Guess I'll never know.

He talked about his plans for "next time" as if he was already looking forward to it. So, I remind him.

"Until you agree to my ultimatum, you can forget tying me down or whatever else tomorrow night."

"Did you forget my warning that nothing will stop me from spreading your legs whenever I want?"

My lower belly clenches at the reminder of his threat.

So, tell me, princess, are you going to be a good girl who gives it up to me or a naughty girl who makes me take what's mine?

Lochlan wants a challenge. Needs it to keep his interest. He even said so himself when I gave him my answer to his question. He doesn't want me to be a good, obedient girl. He wants me to refuse him. To make him work for it.

Like tonight.

He somehow found me, interrupted me with another guy, and stabbed a man because he was jealous or possessive of me, of someone else having my innocence. He can call me a liar all he wants, but it doesn't change the truth.

He said he still wants me. I think...I think I want him too despite the pain he inflicted. So, I'll play along with his cruel game, waiting him out until he either agrees to be loyal to me, or takes what's his again.

"You-you should prepare a separate bedroom because I won't be sleeping in your bed."

"Done."

Lochlan agrees quicker than I expected. Or hoped.

I thought he might cave, but maybe sex with me wasn't that great for him. He got what he wanted most from me, even if he now thinks I lied about it. He said he'll still marry me, because of the agreement with my father, but then what happens?

"You'll have your own bed until you come crawling into mine. Now go home, Sophie. Get ready for tomorrow. I've got a bachelor party at the brothel to get back to," he says before he turns around and walks out the door without a second glance at me or the man he injured.

His sudden abandonment after taking my virginity, for calling me a liar, his adamant refusal to be faithful, admitting he's going back to his bachelor party at a fucking brothel, it's all too overwhelming.

A quick peek at the floor and I find Austin wide eyed or as wide as his swollen eyes can go, watching me. He slowly eases his phone from his jean pocket with his uninjured hand.

Thankfully, he wasn't my first, but he got a front-row seat to the show thanks to Lochlan.

"Could you..." He jerks his chin toward his hand, the shaking knife jutting out of it.

"You...you want me to pull it out?" I ask in surprise. "Are you sure? You'll bleed even worse."

"I just...I can't look at it another second. Please."

I take a step toward him, and stagger. My legs are so wobbly I can barely walk in my heels, and it has nothing to do with the alcohol. Lochlan managed to burn it all out of my system using lust.

Slowly, I bend down and yank the knife free, the same silver knife Lochlan teased me with the first night I met him in my bedroom.

"Thank you," the guy says before he's clambering up off the floor and out the door clutching his bleeding appendage to his chest.

I pick up my panties from where Lochlan had me toss them aside, then use them to clean between my legs, then the bloody knife. It's gross but it's all I have to work with since there are no towels lying around. Once the blade is as clean as I can get it without water, I retract it. Clenching it in my fist, I toss my ruined panties in the garbage. The knife could come in handy someday, possibly against my ruthless husband. A gun would be too obvious, but the knife I can easily hide. I do it now, tucking it down into the front of my strapless bra. Then, I finally head back out to the club searching for Vanessa and Cass. Only Vanessa is at the table in the corner.

"Hey, where have you been?" she asks, looking concerned.

"Bathroom. And now I'm ready to go home."

Her brow furrows as she studies my face. "Already? Did something happen with that guy at the bar?"

"No. I'm just tired. Nervous about tomorrow."

"Are you sure that you're okay, Soph?"

"Yes," I lie. If I tell Vanessa about Lochlan showing up, she'll tell my father, and he might kill Lochlan for, what? Fingering me under the table? Fucking me the night before the wedding? Taking my virginity a few hours early? Making me come three times tonight? Doubtful.

"If you're ready, then let's find Cass and we'll head back."

"Okay. Thank you."

Her eyes are searching the room for Cass when I blurt out, "Would you leave my dad if he slept with someone else?"

Vanessa's green gaze snap to mine. "Wha-huh?"

"If Dante cheated on you, would you stay with him?"

"I...I would be very hurt if Dante was with another woman. So hurt that, well, I may not be able to forgive him or stay with him. Not because I don't believe in second chances, but because I know that if a man betrays your trust once then he'll most likely do it again and again." She shakes her head. "I don't want to be in a relationship like that again. I definitely wouldn't have married your father if I didn't think he would be faithful to me. That's all I have, though. Faith in him to not hurt me. Why do you ask?"

"Just wondering what to expect after tomorrow."

"You're worried Lochlan won't be faithful to you?"

"Do you think he will be?"

"I don't know, Sophie. I've barely spoken to the man, so I haven't been able to get a feel for him. If he does, then I hope you know that it's not your fault. Some men are just born to roam, never settling down. And if you're ever unhappy, Dante would gladly help you leave him. He can find another heir."

I really hope she's right.

Wait. Did she say heir? How could I forget that my father wants to have Lochlan take over his businesses for him? That's probably the reason why he picked him for Madison to marry.

I guess his choice could've been worse. It's just, Lochlan is so... frustrating. Confusing. Addictive. I like the way he makes me feel excited and alive for the first time in my life. But those feelings are only one-sided. Will probably only ever be one-sided. I'm not sure if he will ever love me.

Our marriage is part of a deal with my dad for an alliance. I'm nothing but an object for him to use when he wants.

Or at least that's what he thinks I am.

I can't help but wonder how far he would go if I continue to refuse him. Of course, I wouldn't actually kill him. I have no clue what I was thinking when I put my hands around his throat. I just felt so...powerless and needed to do something, anything because I was angry when I realized he hadn't used protection and may not want to marry me after we finished.

Then when he mentioned a next time, tying me up to keep me from choking him again, my body melted for him. Especially after he pinned my wrists above my head. It was like a switch was flipped inside of me. His thrusts began to feel good. I forgot what I was upset about, as if being a pregnant teenager was no longer a big deal as long as I was being held down by him. Taken. Restrained. Trapped.

I liked it too much when he dominated me.

I wish I didn't.

Now I feel...ashamed of letting him have complete control over me. It's wrong to like that. To want it. To want someone like Lochlan who only wants to hurt me.

Which is why I'm not going to let him lay a finger on me again. Not unless he loves me, and I'm the only one he touches.

12

Lochlan

After last night's disaster, I'm not even sure why I'm surprised when I'm standing at the gazebo waiting for my bride. Even my slack brother, who passed out in a bed of whores around sunrise, managed to make it on time for once and is waiting next to me.

Ten long-ass minutes past when the ceremony was supposed to start, I decide to go downstairs to drag her ass up here if necessary.

On the first-floor landing of the chapel, I find my bride's sister in a long, golden gown, Dante in his black tux with a gold tie, and his wife Vanessa wearing a black and gold dress as if she's only half supportive, half in mourning for her stepdaughter being betrothed to me.

"Where's Sophie?" I ask them.

"She wanted a few minutes alone," Dante explains. "She's not ready yet."

Not ready for the wedding? Not ready for marriage? Not ready to belong to me? He doesn't elaborate and I'm not sure I want him to.

"If she's not out here in five fucking minutes..." I start but Dante interrupts.

"Then you'll marry Cass instead."

I blink at him, waiting for the punchline because he must be making a fucking joke. When he remains stone faced, I force out a single word. "What?"

"I'm not forcing Sophie down the aisle, not when our agreement was one of my daughters, and Cass is ready and willing."

"Oh, I know *she* is ready and willing," I mutter, eyeing the curves she proudly displays in her snug dress, including the slit up to her hip. The girl is practically begging for dick more viciously than most whores I've met. And I bet she would love a chance to steal the show to throw this in her sister's face afterward.

There's no fucking way I'm marrying anyone but Sophie today.

"I'll go get her," I tell her family, stalking down the hallways in search of her room before Dante can try to stop me.

Was this his plan all along? Wait until his youngest had a second of doubt to spring the desperate daughter on me? He doesn't know that I made Sophie mine last night. That I fucked her without a condom. I'm not about to tell him those things, or walk away from Sophie, even if she is a dirty little liar.

Fuck all that.

I'll convince Snow White to marry me today one way or another.

I open several doors of drunken groomsmen and even half-dressed bridesmaids getting ready for other weddings in the chapel before I finally find Sophie standing alone in front of a mirror.

"You're supposed to be walking down the aisle right now, princess," I tell her when I slip into the bridal suite and shut the door behind me.

She's stunning in her white satin dress, her black hair pinned up with a veil streaming down her open back. It's hard to believe that she's about to be mine. That is, if I can convince her to come up to the roof and say the vows.

I know full well that I don't deserve someone so beautiful and perfect. I shouldn't tell her that, though. Admitting that her beauty alone could bring me to my knees isn't smart. Still, I can't resist telling her the partial truth. "You look gorgeous."

"Thanks." That one word when her eyes meet mine in the mirrored reflection is so icy, the temperature in the room drops fifty degrees.

"Cold feet?" She's obviously still upset with me from last night, stabbing a man for touching her, refusing her ultimatum. And yet she's wearing the dress. All that's left is to get her upstairs to the gazebo.

She turns away from the mirror but doesn't face me, like she doesn't want to look at me. "Did you fuck any whores last night after you took my virginity? More than one?"

When I don't answer because I'm still not convinced that I was her first, she finally turns to face me, blue eyes blazing in anger, assuming silence is a confession. "You're a disgusting bastard."

Oh, yeah, she's definitely still pissed. And it takes all my restraint to not flinch at her accurate, yet still infuriating, insult.

"It doesn't matter who I fucked or not last night because your ass is still going upstairs and saying those fucking vows." When she doesn't respond, just paces away from me, I take an unconscious step toward her before catching myself.

Rather than convincing her, I'm only succeeding in driving her further away.

Fuck. Maybe I shouldn't have lost my temper last night. Even if I wasn't her first, I was rough. There's no doubt about that. "Are you sore?" I ask her to try and change the subject.

"Yes."

I'm not sure why I'm surprised that she's sore or angry at me for how hard I took her. I couldn't sleep last night, unable to forget how amazing it felt fucking her, and thinking about her assertion that she wouldn't let me touch her again unless I swore not to fuck anyone else. She's not even giving me the benefit of the doubt before the ceremony. There's not an ounce of trust in those incensed sapphire eyes of hers and I hate it.

Telling her I don't want anyone else would never be enough. She'll have to learn to trust me, or this marriage will never work.

And if she doesn't trust me, she won't let me inside of her snug cunt again. Virgin or not, she was unbelievably tight compared to the women I've been with. I'm trying hard not to think about my Disney princess with another man before me, the man I stabbed on the floor possibly if she was lying. Even if I wasn't her first, I still want her again. More than I should.

While I've always known sex can be used as a weapon, today I intend to utilize it, giving Sophie a taste of how good I get her off on my tongue whenever she wants. I may not be capable of love, but if I can convince her to meet me halfway on the loyalty issue, trade her honesty for my own, then we can both enjoy ourselves in this marriage.

"Are you going to marry me or not?"

"I don't know yet," she finally admits.

While I hate that she's having doubts, I'm still confident when I tell her, "I bet I can get a yes out of you in the next five minutes."

"How? By threatening me?"

"Come sit down." I point to the velvet armchair, wondering how big of a stain we'll leave on it.

"What?"

"Sit down so I can lick your pussy better, and then we can get this show on the road."

She shakes her head so hard I'm surprised hairpins don't go flying. "No."

"That wasn't a request. Now sit down and spread your legs, Sophie. You're not leaving this room until I taste you. And if you refuse to marry me, your father will have me marry Cass instead."

"What?" The appalled look on her perfect face is one that likely matched my own.

"You heard me. Sit. Down."

She looks from me to the door, thinking it through. I brace myself for her to tell me to get the fuck out and go marry Cass, that she doesn't give two shits.

Instead, she asks quietly, "Are you going to at least lock the door this time?"

That's when I know I have her. Sophie doesn't want me to marry Cass any more than I want to be trapped with her scheming sister.

"No."

"No? What if someone walks in again?"

I barely remember being interrupted last night. I was too busy to care. She will be too soon enough.

"Then you better hurry up and sit down so I can get you off before anyone comes to check on us. But honestly, I don't give a shit who sees me licking what's mine."

She opens her mouth as if to disagree or make a comment, but wisely closes it again before she reluctantly obeys. As soon as she lowers her ass down, I drop to my knees in front of her, pushing up the layers of skirts under her dress to get to the part I'm desperate to bury myself inside of again. But right now, this is about convincing Sophie. Only Sophie. I need her docile and obedient again. A screaming orgasm should do the trick. After all, it worked last night.

A pair of white satin panties that match her dress cover her pussy. I grab the front and yank them down her legs, over her heels to get them off and out of the way. Only once they're gone do I look at what they covered.

Her smooth pink pussy looks so delectable I press my face to it, inhaling her scent before swiping the tip of my tongue over her clit. Sophie's hips jerks in surprise, her hands clinging to the arms of the chair. I don't even have to tell her to keep her hands off my throat, because she apparently has no interest in laying a finger on a disgusting bastard like me right now. Not that I give a shit. I'm used to women not wanting to touch me. It's why I prefer restraints like the ones I had installed on my bed this morning.

Hiking Sophie's knees up over my shoulders, I spread her thighs wide then repeat the tongue flick over and over again. Each and every time she squirms. Several times she gasps. Finally, she throws her head back and mewls in that same sexy way as last night. She slumps bonelessly, deeper into her chair, all the tension in her body quickly melting away.

I lap up her flood of arousal, prodding her cunt with my tongue, flicking it back and forth.

"Oh! *Oh god!*" she exclaims.

"You like that?" I look up at her face to ask between teasing licks.

When she lifts her head, her eyes are heavy lidded, cheeks flushed blood red. My Snow White is beyond stunning now, whatever that may be. "It's...it's okay," she stammers.

"I didn't know Disney princesses could lie so easily," I remark, rubbing the pad of my thumb over her clit. "If it's just okay then shall I stop?"

"No!"

Chuckling, I tell her, "That's what I thought," before I get back to work, drawing out her pleasure with the tip of my tongue on her sensitive little button until she's whimpering with need. Both of her palms are now cupping the back of my head, pressing my face to her pussy, no longer caring about how disgusting I am.

Hell, she probably doesn't even realize her fingers have a death grip on my hair. She's past the point of self-consciousness, right on the brink of a release. Desperate for it.

I pause long enough to ask her again, "Are you going to marry me?"

She tries to push my face back to her cunt. "Don't stop!"

"Answer me first."

"Yes. Yes!" she shouts while lifting her hips off the seat of the chair, begging me to keep going. "Please, Lochlan!"

Once I have the answer I wanted, I finally take mercy on her, focusing the tip of my tongue on attacking her swollen clit.

"I'm...I'm...*oh, fuck!*" Hearing her swear in the heat of passion is hilarious since she looks so sweet and innocent. But I don't have a chance to laugh for long, too busy drawing out her orgasm, wringing every twitch and gasping moan I can get out of her until she stops shuddering.

Sophie's a fucking mess. She's breathing heavily with her once-perfect hair in disarray. Her skirts, all four layers of tulle, are nearly piled up in her face, leaving her glistening pussy exposed. Her blue eyes are shuttered, glassy and unfocused, face flushed bright pink.

I want her so fucking bad my balls may burst, but if I touch her again, I'll have to fuck her when she's already sore. It's all I can do to get to my feet, and back away from her instead of ravaging her. Tonight. I'll have her again tonight in my bed after making her my wife. She'll be so desperate for my tongue again that she'll forget all about her little ultimatum.

"Don't take too long recovering, princess. There's a roof full of people waiting on us."

"Why?" she asks just as I turn to leave. I barely hear her over the sounds of rustling fabric.

Glancing over my shoulder, I find her fighting with the skirt layers, anxiously covering herself.

"Why what? Why did I eat your pussy? Because you were pissed, and I needed to convince you to marry me." It's not a complete lie. She did need to relax before she thought too hard about what she's about to do and fled like her older sister. Also, I want her addicted to coming for me because I want her in my bed every night.

"No. Why do you still want to marry me? You got what you wanted."

Got what I wanted? What the hell does that mean? I have no clue, and Sophie wouldn't believe me if I told her I haven't thought of anyone but her since the first time I saw a photo of her months ago. So, I lie. Sort of. Every word is true, it's just not the whole truth.

"Because your sister ran away to get out of marrying me, and I didn't want to go to war with your father."

"I'm just a pawn to keep both of you from killing each other. And by marrying me, you'll inherit all of Dante's...business dealings when he dies?"

Holy fucking shit.

Dante actually caved and put me in his will? I wasn't sure if he would or not, even if I am the obvious choice to take over when he's dead. None of his three daughters could handle his empire. Hell, one is still missing. And the girls shouldn't have to deal with that burden, to have all the blood on their hands it takes to be a ruthless gangster.

Rather than admit that this is all news to me, I just tell her, "Yes."

With Dante making me his heir, it's like an answer to an unspoken prayer. I've got an army of lawyers coming after me, threatening to take everything I have in the civil trial.

For the first time in nearly a year, the air moves in and out of my lungs a little easier.

"But what's to stop you from murdering my father tomorrow?" Sophie asks softly.

"I guess he just has to trust me, and trust that I'll put a kid in you before he's dead."

"What?"

"Our son or daughter will be Dante's grandchild, so eventually, he'll still be leaving his empire to his blood."

She shakes her head, face paling. "Is that why...last night you didn't use protection?"

"Exactly. Figured I may as well get a head start."

"No. Nobody said I had to get pregnant. That...that is not happening!" All the calm from her recent orgasm is gone. She's back to being angry again.

"It may have already happened last night, Sophie," I tell her before I walk out the door.

Somehow, I know she'll still follow me upstairs and meet me at that fucking gazebo, even if she's furious with me. If for no other reason than to avoid disappointing Daddy or letting her redheaded sister steal her thunder.

But I get the feeling that she's not going to be the docile little wife I assumed she would be.

Which is perfectly fine with me.

Too many women in my life have pretended to be eager to do anything to please me. I much prefer Sophie outright hating me then faking to like me for a second.

After all, she may have hated me last night, but she still let me fuck her. Let me lick her pussy just now even though she was furious I came inside of her and won't promise not to fuck around on her.

It may take a little time, but eventually, I will break her again. Getting there will be half the fun.

Every woman has a price, I just have to figure out what it will take to buy Sophie.

But then again, she's a spoiled rich girl. What if her price is higher than I can afford?

13

Sophie

M y father and Lochlan expect me to get pregnant, to have kids? Why didn't anyone tell me that before now? Why didn't Vanessa? Does she know and kept it from me?

There's no way I got pregnant from last night. And to be safe, I'm not letting Lochlan's dick anywhere near me again unless he keeps it away from other women and puts a condom on it.

His tongue maybe...

No. I don't want any other part of him either.

What he just did wasn't unselfishly done. He wanted me meek, compliant. He knew an orgasm would have that effect on me to make sure I walked down the aisle like a good little girl. God, he even made me scream the word "yes" agreeing to marry him. He laughed at me yet again, which was even more embarrassing than last night when I jerked my hand away from his dick.

I've just stood up and slipped my panties back into place when the door opens again. My hands fight with the layers of tulle to get them down.

"Daddy wants to know if you're going to marry him or if I need to," Cass huffs in annoyance from the doorway, before frowning even harder than usual at me.

"Since when did you change your mind about marrying Lochlan?"

Cass doesn't answer. She just wrinkles her nose and asks, "What happened to your hair?"

Reaching up, I feel the veil has shifted to the left, so I hurry over to the mirror to try to fix it.

"Oh my god. Did he just come in here and fuck you?"

"No," I answer coolly. "He did that last night."

"Last night?" she exclaims while I remove and redo a few pins. It's sort of fun catching her off-guard.

"Yes."

"So, what happened when he was in here just now?"

"He got on his knees," I say since I'm not entirely sure what to call that thing he did to me with his tongue. Oral sex? All I know is I loved every second and now my panties are soaking wet. When he told me to sit down, I should've refused because now I won't be able to stop thinking about his tongue...

"He made you get on your knees?"

Turning to face my sister, I say, "No, he got on his. I haven't... done that yet."

And I'm not going to.

"Wow," Cass whispers, sounding surprised? Impressed? I can't ever tell with her. "You've already pussy-whipped him. I'm surprised."

She thinks I've pussy whipped Lochlan Dunne? As in I have some sort of power over him? Maybe Vanessa was right, and I have more power than I realized when it comes to sex.

"He...he also fingered me under the table last night at dinner," I admit, figuring that's the correct way to describe what he did.

Now Cass grins. "No shit? I knew the cheesecake wasn't that damn good."

"I'm not letting him touch me again, though," I admit, standing up a little straighter.

"Yeah, right. You're about to marry him."

"He didn't use a condom last night." Confessing that to her feels good. I need to vent to someone, even if she won't give a shit. "And he wouldn't agree to stop fucking other women once we're married."

"Jesus. He wants you barefoot and pregnant, stat."

"What?"

"He's trying to lock you down. Once you have his kid in you, you'll never be able to break free of him."

"Never?"

I assumed he only wanted my virginity last night, then couldn't understand why he still wanted to marry me. He wants me to be the mother of his child, not just for my father's money, but so I can never break free of him?

"Never. Even after the kid is grown, you'll both be in his or her life."

"But I don't want to have kids."

Is that the only way Lochlan will want to keep me—if I give him kids?

"Then you should take a morning-after pill."

"A what?"

"The pharmacy has a pill you can take if the condom breaks, or the man forgets or whatever. It's not one hundred percent effective, but it can stop most pregnancies from occurring if you take it right after."

"How do you know about a 'morning after' pill?" I can't help but ask.

"Everyone knows about it. Some women carry them around all the time, just in case."

"Could you get me one?"

"No."

"Cass..."

"Not because I don't want to, but Daddy will find out from the guards and think I'm fucking someone. Ask Vanessa to get you one or go get it yourself."

"If Vanessa gets one, he'll still find out."

"True. You could ask your husband, but he's not going to want you to take it. In fact, he could lose his shit if you do."

"Lose his shit?"

"If you don't think he won't hurt you, sis, then you're ridiculously naïve. Daddy may keep us locked away for our safety, but some men hit women or worse."

I don't know what the "worse" is and really don't want to find out. "It was just one time, so I'm probably not going to get pregnant." If I did get pregnant, would Lochlan give up other women then? Doubtful.

"Where did you do it at?"

"Against a wall."

"Ow. Losing your virginity against a wall must have hurt like a motherfucker. But I meant where, what location?"

"It did hurt. And we were in an employee break room at that club. After Lochlan beat up the man I was with, he stabbed his knife through his hand, then he kissed me roughly and we...did it."

"Whoa. He stabbed a guy? Why?"

"The guy kissed me, and he grabbed my ass before Lochlan interrupted."

"How was it?" she asks with a grin.

"Hard and painful at first, but it got better toward the end. His tongue felt so much better... Still, neither of those things are going to happen again until he refuses to stop sleeping around with other women. His prostitutes."

Cass tilts her head, studying me. "Does he have a pet name for you?"

"What sort of pet name? He likes telling me what to do. Sometimes I think he wants me to act like an obedient dog, while other times I think he would prefer if I disobeyed him..."

"No, I mean, you know how Daddy has always called Vanessa *butterfly?*"

"Yes. And?"

"Does Lochlan call you Sophie?"

Thinking it over, I tell her, "He doesn't use my name unless he's angry. Most of the time he calls me princess."

"*Princess?* Oh, he's got it bad."

"Got what bad?"

"Nothing. Are you going to go marry him or not? If he's that damn good with his tongue, then I'll definitely marry him."

Is she kidding? If I don't marry Lochlan, would he really marry Cass instead? I thought she was adamant that she wouldn't, but I don't want to find out. The thought of Lochlan with her makes my stomach clench into a knot.

"No, I'll marry him," I blurt out in a rush. "Did you know he's going to be Daddy's heir?"

"What?" she whispers, her face frozen. "Are you serious?"

"Yes. I guess he doesn't think we're capable of handling it."

"That's bullshit," Cass mutters. "If Lochlan's marrying you to get his hands on Daddy's money and power, then his tongue isn't worth it."

To hear her say that...is that what she actually thinks or is she trying to convince me to back out of the wedding so she can swoop in to be Lochlan's wife instead?

My head tells me to let her have him.

But my heart, for whatever reason, aches at the thought of seeing her and him together. Along with another body part that's aching and wants him for some stupid reason...

Blowing out a breath, I ask her, "Is my hair fixed?"

"So, you're going to do this? You're going to marry him even though he only wants Daddy's money?"

"Yes."

"And will keep screwing hookers?"

"I won't let him touch me again until he stops."

"That's never going to happen," she says confidently. "Maybe he'll let you watch."

"Watch what?" I ask before I realize what she meant. "I don't want to watch him with other women!"

"Then you're going to need some leverage."

"Leverage?"

"If you get pregnant with his kid, you could have the upper hand."

"I don't want to be a mother."

"Expecting a man to be faithful is unreasonable," Cass grumbles.

"Daddy's faithful to Vanessa."

"For now."

"He loves her. He wouldn't ever cheat on her."

"And you think Lochlan Dunne will fall in love with you?" she asks with a bark of laughter. "If so, you're delusional."

"Why are you such a bitch?" I ask her.

"Right, I'm a bitch and you're Daddy's little angel. You do everything Daddy says, so let's get on with it. We both know you were never going to back out. You're so pathetic you'll do anything for his attention, even pretend to have cold feet so Daddy and Lochlan would come running."

"I'll do anything for attention?" I scoff. "You're the one walking around with your boobs hanging out of your dress for attention. I agreed to this marriage to avoid a war, but you were too selfish to do that."

"Yes, you're such a selfless saint."

"Ugh, let's just get this over with," I huff before leading the way out of the suite.

Near the stairs leading to the roof, my dad and Vanessa are waiting for us.

"Ready?" my father asks.

I grit my teeth and nod before taking his offered forearm, even though I'm furious with him. This marriage is more for him and Lochlan than for me. I'm just supposed to be a broodmare. Madison knew that, it's why she ran away to wherever the hell she went.

And why am I sort of glad she left so I get the chance to be his? I'm a horrible sister. There's definitely something wrong with me if I still crave Lochlan's depravity even knowing he doesn't care about me, and probably never will.

"I'll go take my seat," Vanessa says with a sigh. "Then Cass will come out first. That's when the quartet will play the wedding march for Sophie."

"See you out there, butterfly." My father kisses Vanessa's cheek before she climbs the stairs, the love between them so obvious it's nearly palpable in the air. That's what marriage is supposed to be, being with someone you love for the rest of your life.

"Told you," Cass murmurs before she shoves a bouquet of black and gold flowers into my hands. She takes her own smaller bouquet and climbs the stairs.

When she's gone, I turn to my dad and say, "You slept with a lot of women, so how did you know you loved Vanessa?"

"How did I know I loved her?" he repeats, staring up the stairs as if he's longing to be with her already.

"Yes, why did you give up other women for her and not...not for anyone else?" I don't mention my mother by name, or Cass's, or Madison's.

"Vanessa was...a challenge that I didn't know I needed. She made me earn her love, prove myself to be worthy of her. I wasn't sure I would ever convince her, but eventually I did."

"She didn't give in right away, so you had to chase her?" Will being a challenge, withholding sex from Lochlan eventually lead to him loving me? Doubtful. It'll probably make him cheat on me even more, but it's the only card I have left to play once we're married.

"Right. And I guess I knew Vanessa was the one when I realized I didn't want to live without her, that I would do whatever it would take to keep her, to make her happy. There's nothing that could come between us, no argument that would ever break us apart."

"What if Lochlan doesn't ever love me like that?" He's so cruel and callous, I don't know if he's capable of loving anyone other than himself, money, and power.

"Then we'll do what we have to do…"

What does that mean? I don't let myself dwell on that question or any other. If we keep them waiting too long, Cass may throw herself at Lochlan. I can't even stand the thought of that.

My father leads the way up the stairs, and then it's happening.

On the rooftop, powerful and rich people I don't know sit on two sides of an aisle that leads to a gazebo covered in flowers where Lochlan is waiting. With the sun setting in the background, it looks so romantic. Too bad it's all a lie. This wedding is nothing but a business arrangement. A business arrangement with sex and the potential for an heir as added bonuses.

The kind of love like my dad and Vanessa have seems so rare that I doubt I'll ever experience it. Lochlan just wants a big inheritance of money and power when my father dies. I could see the greed in his eyes when we discussed it earlier. I really hope he doesn't try to kill him to take it, that this stupid wedding will be enough to avoid any violence.

Once my dad and I reach the steps up to the gazebo, he kisses my forehead, then sits down in the front row next to Vanessa.

An older male officiant I've never met before speaks words I barely hear. He talks about love and unity or whatever else while I can't stop thinking about the embarrassing dampness between my legs. Why didn't I go to the bathroom to clean up first? Now my panties are ruined, and I have to either wear them for hours or take them off and go without.

The orgasm feels like a taunt now. A way to convince me to do this, to throw me off balance, to make me look stupid and foolish for squirming so desperately for his wriggling tongue. I hate that he had that sort of power over me even momentarily.

My entire life I've been timid and weak, mostly ignored by my sisters and our father. I'm the perfect bride for a dominant gangster to manipulate, bending me to his will, whatever that may be.

I'm no longer a child, and I don't want to be bent by anyone anymore.

I stop thinking about my impotence and damp panties long enough to repeat what the officiant says, although there wasn't much to it before I had to say, "I do."

Only when the officiant says, "Do you have rings to exchange?" do I snap out of my frozen stupor.

Rings? I was supposed to get Lochlan a ring? How embarrassing.

I finally look at his face and then back at Vanessa since she planned pretty much everything, soliciting my choices here and there when decisions needed to be made. I don't remember her ever mentioning rings.

Before I can ask, Cass leans over and holds up a thick silver band in front of my face. "Here."

Why did she have Lochlan's ring? Was she seriously that close to marrying him if I hadn't come out of the dressing room? I don't understand her at all lately.

"Sophie, place the ring on Lochlan's finger," the officiant instructs, so I do it one-handed since I'm still holding flowers. It gets stuck at the knuckle, so Lochlan shoves it the rest of the way. "Good. Now, repeat after me: I give you this ring as a sign of our love and commitment to each other."

The officiant looks to me expectantly and I blurt out, "No."

In this moment, I actually have a little power. The marriage doesn't become official unless I say all the stupid words. Nobody can force me to say them. It feels...nice to be in control of something for once.

"Excuse me?" the officiant whispers, glancing between me and Lochlan.

"Those words are lies. I won't say them." My spine straightens as

I grow more confident in my new assertiveness. I refuse to stand up here and lie to make my father or Lochlan happy.

Lochlan clears his throat and cuts me a look as if he's annoyed. I know the feeling. Finally, he explains to the officiant, "Could you please revise the wording for my young bride who I barely know?"

"But..."

"We don't love each other, and he's refused to be committed to me," I enlighten the man, more confident in my stance to not cave.

"Oh," the officiant replies, his forehead now full of creases. "How about: With this ring, I promise to support you, care for you, and stand alongside you for all of our days?"

That I agree to say, with a small edit. "With this ring, I promise to support you, care for you, and stand alongside you."

"For all of our days," the officiant whispers.

Ignoring him, I tell Lochlan, "Your turn."

He arches an eyebrow at me for a long silent moment, as if in surprise or to try and warn me to behave. I don't cower or speak the words, so eventually, he reaches into his tux's inner pocket, but he doesn't pull out a ring.

"Instead of a diamond engagement ring, I bought you a tennis bracelet." He holds up the sparkling piece that is blindingly beautiful in the rays of the sunset.

"Oh, my goodness," the officiant mutters. "I've never seen so many diamonds..."

"Do you want it or not?" Lochlan asks me.

I don't want anything from him at the moment other than a morning-after pill.

But the bracelet is too gorgeous to refuse.

I don't wear much jewelry since I'm usually in the gym or on the court and have never been into it like my sisters. Usually I prefer fancy clothes to diamonds, but I want this bracelet.

I hold up my wrist to let Lochlan fasten the closure, right over the bruises he left on my wrist last night. I'll wear the beautiful diamonds for myself not for him.

It weighs a ton, which will take some getting used to. It's stunning, even if it feels like a dog collar of sorts.

Now Lochlan holds up a thin, plain white gold wedding band and takes my left hand to slide it on my finger.

"Oh, right," the officiant says. "Lochlan, repeat after me: With this ring, I promise to support you, care for you, and stand alongside you..." He trails off since I didn't say the rest so he's not sure if Lochlan will or not.

But of course, Lochlan makes his own edits. "With this ring, I promise to support you, cherish you, and protect you through whatever may come, for all of our days."

Cherish and protect? If I had to bet, my father probably required him to say those things. And I guess he would say "all of our days" since it could be a while before my father dies, unless he kills him first.

"Now, it is my honor to pronounce Lochlan and Sophie husband and wife. You may kiss your bride."

Kiss him? Now? In front of everyone, including my father when I'm so furious I could scream?

Not to mention the frenzy that happened last night as soon as our lips met. That would be a bad idea in public, just like sex against the wall of a breakroom was a horrible idea. I refuse to go down that road with Lochlan again, especially here!

Not to mention the fact that I can't look at Lochlan's mouth without remembering where it was just a few minutes ago. His smirk says he knows exactly what I'm thinking about. He'll never let me forget pressing his face to that part of my body.

When Lochlan leans forward, I allow a brush of his lips on mine before I take a step back. Or at least I try to.

The bastard grabs both sides of my head, holding me captive while his lips not only caress mine, but his tongue forces its way into my mouth. The instant, heated reaction it causes throughout my body pisses me off, especially the lower regions. I don't want to want him. But god, I do. I want him relieving the ache between my thighs with his fingers, tongue, or big cock...

Then I remember him not using protection, calling me a liar when I told him I was a virgin, refusing to commit to only me, reminding me I'm his second choice because my sister ran away. All that, along with the power and money he'll inherit from my father one day helps to instantly cool the rising heat.

No more sex. If I refuse him long enough, maybe he'll eventually give up and send me back home since Cass is right. He'll never love me or give up other women.

When Lochlan stops kissing me, he speaks quietly into my ear as our guests clap and cheer for us. "What's the matter, princess? You don't like tasting your pussy on my tongue?"

I'm not sure who is more shocked by his words, me or the officiant who suddenly turns away, breaking into a coughing fit. No words come out of my mouth since I didn't even think about the... flavor until he mentioned it. I was too annoyed with my reaction to his kiss that I didn't even notice how he tasted.

I don't have a chance to respond before people come up and start congratulating us.

My dad is one of the first. In fact, he grabs my elbow to drag me away from Lochlan. "What's wrong? Did Lochlan do something? Did he hurt you? I saw you...flinch away from him but it didn't deter him."

"Did you actually ask me what's wrong? I just married a man who will never love me, who I don't want to touch me, and definitely don't want to have kids with. Why would I want him to kiss me?"

Why indeed? It's a conundrum I can't seem to figure out myself, which is even more infuriating. Are orgasms from him really worth my dignity? Definitely not.

"Sophie...I'm sorry I put you in this position," my father says. "But it's done now. Just—can you try to give Lochlan a chance? If he hurts you, I'll kill him. If you're still miserable after a few weeks, you can come home and get an annulment. It'll be like it never happened."

"I can come home whenever I want? You would really let me do that?" That's what my father meant when he said, *Then we'll do what we have to do?* He'll kill Lochlan, or let me leave him?

"This marriage isn't the end of your life," he goes on to say. "I hope it's the beginning. But if not, I don't want you to be miserable."

First, my father gives me to Lochlan, but now he says that he'll gladly yank me away like it's a game. Like my life is a game to him. I have to play along when required, without knowing the rules or having any say in them.

"I hate you both," I tell him honestly when actually I hate myself more. Yes, I could've backed out, Cass would've taken my spot, and it would've been her kissing Lochlan just now. Would he have given her the diamond tennis bracelet too?

"It's too late to complain here and now, isn't it?" my father grits out, looking as pissed as I am. I shouldn't have said I hate him. I don't. I'm just so confused. "The best I can do is offer you a way out if it's not what you expected."

"What about making him your heir?" I ask.

My father shrugs as if it's not important. "If you're no longer married to him, then I'll find someone else to take over for me."

"Good."

Cass said I needed leverage, and this one is so much better than her stupid suggestion that I get pregnant.

14

Lochlan

I can't fucking believe it.

Salvato is already filling Sophie's head with annulment bullshit, threatening to remove me as his heir, when we haven't even been married for ten goddamn seconds.

And Sophie...is she just telling him she doesn't want me to touch her because she's pissed at him, or does she actually mean it?

Either way, I interrupt the father daughter argument, taking Sophie's other elbow, wondering if we're going to have a tug-of-war fight over her. "The photographer is ready to take some pictures."

"Great." She shrugs out of both of our holds to walk away.

I turn to follow her, but Dante's hand clasps my shoulder, turning me around. "She's my baby girl. You better be good to her. Worship her and *only* her."

"Oh, I worshiped your baby girl real good right before the ceremony," I say while swiping my thumb over my lips that still taste like Sophie's pussy.

Salvato's face turns crimson, no doubt his blood pressure is going sky high. If I'm lucky, maybe he'll stroke out here and now before he removes me as his heir.

Fucker deserves it.

If you're no longer married to him, then I'll find someone else to take over for me. That's what Salvato told Sophie. I should've known better than to get my hopes up that I may not lose everything my father and his father built. It was too easy to be real.

His fingers are halfway to curling around my throat when I jump back, and Vanessa pops up between us.

"You two better behave or I'll throw you both off this roof!" she warns, pressing a palm to Salvato's chest to make him take a step backward.

"Listen to your wife, while I go worship mine," I reply with a smirk before walking away. I hear his indignant growl following me.

"If she tells me she's not happy..." he calls out.

I lift my hand to wave him off without looking back. "Yeah, I heard you."

The bastard never intended for this to be a real marriage. He let his daughter marry me just to appease me temporarily, to try and use my connections that he needs for his fentanyl trafficking. Maybe try me out as his heir. I knew he would change his mind, if he was ever serious about it to begin with.

The only thing I can do is to try and smooth things over with Sophie, to convince her not to walk away from me before this marriage even begins. Whatever it takes, I have to try because I refuse to be penniless and at anyone else's mercy ever again.

I have no clue where the shy, innocent Disney princess who was so terrified of me went? Was her innocence all just an act this entire time? Now that I think about it, what could she possibly get out of agreeing to marry me other than to oblige Salvato's request?

It never occurred to me how one-sided our marriage was until now. There's nothing I can offer her that her Daddy can't except orgasms.

Following Sophie back to the raised stairs of the gazebo where the photographer is waiting, I grab her hand to halt her steps. I'd give anything to keep her moaning underneath me like she was earlier all day and night.

She tries to jerk away, out of my grip, as if that much direct contact with me is too much to ask of her.

Filthy. Disgusting. That's how this perfect little princess sees me. And she's right. I'm not sure why I'm even surprised by her rejection.

I clinch my fingers tighter around hers. She allowed a lot more than my hand on her last night and this morning, enjoyed coming on my filthy, disgusting tongue, fingers, and cock.

Giving up on getting her hand back, she glares at me over her shoulder. "What do you want?"

Shit. She's even colder than before.

"What's wrong, princess? You should be happy since Daddy just gave you an out."

She scoffs and rolls her eyes, looking her age, reminding me she's still a spoiled, fickle teenager.

"Seriously, Sophie. A few minutes ago, you were...melting for me. And now you won't even look at me. You fucking flinched when I kissed you in front of everyone after we've done a helluva lot more than that. What changed?"

"I want a morning-after pill."

"Not happening. I would rather be shot in the dick."

Which is a damn surprising instantaneous reaction to her demand for a pill to prevent a possible pregnancy of my baby. I tell myself it's because a kid would ensure she stays married to me, that I remain Dante's heir.

And how the hell does Sophie know about that fucking pill? She must have confided in her sister that I fucked her bareback last night. Goddamn Cass must have told her all about the fucking pill that Red probably wishes she had.

"That shot can be arranged," Sophie remarks with a quick glance down to my crotch. Then, her face grows more serious. "Why can't I have one?"

"You're not getting rid of me that easy," I tell her. "Don't even think about asking someone else to buy you one either. If I find out you've taken one, I'll shove my fingers down your throat until you barf it up."

Sophie's nose wrinkles, but I know she trusts that I'll do just that. "You're disgusting. I'm not going to have your spawn or *ever* let you fuck me again."

Wow. I've heard sex happens less often after marriage, but this is ridiculous. After she came on my tongue and said the vows, I thought we were good, that she had forgiven me, and she was getting past her abhorrence to having my hands on her, but I guess not.

I've been looking forward to getting this ceremony done so I could tie her up in my bed, lick her again, and fuck her tight pussy until we have to leave tomorrow for our honeymoon. Not that there's any reason to fly thousands of miles when I'm not going to let her out of bed.

She may still be sore, but I could eat her pussy until she's so slick it'll only feel good when she takes my cock again. If that doesn't convince her then I don't know what the fuck will. All I know is that I need her in my bed.

Winding my arms around her waist, I pull her backside flush against the front of my body so she can feel how badly I want her. I've been achingly hard for her since her thighs nearly crushed my head when she came for me. Only her. Pressing my lips to her ear, I say, "You don't really mean that, do you Sophie? The second time won't hurt as bad. My tongue will have your pussy so wet my cock will slide right inside."

I've never been rejected before, so I refuse to admit defeat yet. There has to be something I can do to convince her...

Spinning around in my arms to face me, her gorgeous face is twisted into a scowl. "You took my virginity against a wall at a nightclub last night and didn't use a condom! There are bruises on my wrists!" She says this loud enough that the officiant's coughing fit resumes and the photographer clears his throat while glancing away.

"What about it?" I ask with a grin as I recall every little detail of her squirming around on my cock like she loved and hated it at the same time.

Virgins bleed and there was nothing but cum coating my dick, mine and her own. I do think it hurt for her to take all of me so hard and fast, but that's nothing new with the size of my cock.

"And you've been with prostitutes! I don't want your filthy dick anywhere near me again."

Hearing her insult me again pisses me the fuck off. "How about my filthy tongue?" I ask. "You seemed to love it earlier. You were fucking begging for more."

If I could just get her in the cuffs and go down on her, I bet she would let me inside of her again. I'd make her come over and over again on my tongue until she couldn't refuse me.

The photographer clears his throat again then says. "I'll give you two a minute."

"No," I huff since the photo is the proof my attorney says the public needs to prove that I'm no longer just a rich fucking pimp. Now I'm a filthy fucking husband too. But Sophie overrules me, telling the photographer, "Thank you. That's enough pictures. I don't need any more reminders of today." Then she just walks the fuck off as I stare after her.

Are all wives so fussy and difficult? Or is my teenage bride just acting like a brat? She's nothing like the scared little girl I met that first night.

"Should we get some photos of you alone?" the photographer asks.

I lift my middle finger in response before stalking off to find a stiff drink. Hopefully, the PR guy can just use a photo from the ceremony.

~

I'm on my second glass of scotch, wishing I had a cigar or, even better, a joint, when my brother wanders up next to me. He's so smashed he has to grip the bar to stay upright.

"He's cut off," I snap at the bartender who gives me a nod. "You better not cause a scene," I warn Flynn.

"What's it matter now?" he asks, slurring his words. "Weddings done. Still can't believe you married into the sleazy Salvato family."

"Watch your fucking mouth," I warn him under my breath.

"Already kissin' father-in-law's ass? Pathetic."

The drunk bastard thinks I'm pathetic for creating this alliance? Asshole. He has no clue what's at stake, which is why I tell him, "If I don't fuck up this marriage with Sophie, Salvato is going to make me his heir."

My brother blinks his brown eyes at me, as if suddenly sobering up. "No shit? Everything? The properties and all the F trade too?" he asks, referring to fentanyl trafficking and I give a quick nod. "Forget kissin' his ass; go suck that man's dick!"

"Shut the fuck up," I growl at him. Grabbing his tie, I pull him staggering over to one of my guards and shove him away. "Get him home and make sure he stays there."

"Yes, sir."

"Asshole!" Flynn shouts as I walk back to the bar, and he's taken downstairs.

"Everything okay?" Owen comes over to ask me while throwing back my third drink.

"Flynn just being Flynn," I tell him with a sigh. "And my wife doesn't want me to touch her."

"Seriously? Little virgin scared of the snake or what? Don't let her see it all long and hard before popping her cherry..."

"No. It's not that." I don't bother telling him I had her last night when she may or may not have been a virgin.

"Then why not? It's your wedding night. You're entitled to hit that at least once tonight. And for those diamonds on her wrist and the new tennis court, she owes you like a lifetime of blowjobs."

"Unfortunately, Sophie doesn't agree with that sentiment. And fuck you, now I'm not going to be able to stop thinking about putting her on her knees."

"You know where to go if she won't open wide."

How ironic is it that the woman I want more than anything hates me? For years, women I don't want have been throwing themselves at me, begging me to fuck them.

And while Sophie may have begged for my tongue earlier, I think it's going to be a while before I hear her pleas for any part of me to touch her again.

~

Sophie

The reception thankfully didn't last very long. I ate standing up, rather than sit beside my husband at another table. And I didn't feel like dancing in my uncomfortable heels. Lochlan left me alone after his refusal to get me a morning-after pill. He seemed content to throw back drink after drink at the bar while scowling at me from the other side of the rooftop.

With the heavy diamond bracelet on my wrist, and the wedding band surrounding my finger, it's all starting to feel a little too...real.

I should've listened to Vanessa. Only a child would think there could actually be love and a happily ever after with a man like Lochlan.

I'm angry at everyone except my stepmother, though, when I'm corralled into an SUV and taken away to Lochlan's estate. My father, Cass, Lochlan, it's like they're all on the same team, and now I'm on my own, walking into a house I've never been inside before. Everything is changing, and I hate it.

Lochlan's home is...enormous. Past the walled, gated entrance, it's three stories tall with manicured hedges, palm trees, so much open land surrounding it, and not a neighbor within sight. It's the opposite of where I grew up overlooking the busy city from the casino's penthouse.

Inside it's all pristine whites and creams, elegant with tall columns, marble floors and high archways.

"You can get a tour tomorrow. I'll show you to your room," Lochlan says shortly, sounding irritated. We slip past his door guards to climb the staircase to the third floor then down a long, carpeted hallway. "It's right next to mine to make it easier for you to find it when you change your mind."

"I won't," I reply without hesitation. "Although, I might be inclined to reconsider if you give me a morning-after pill and agree to use protection."

"No," he replies instantly without even slowing down his steps.

"Why not?" I spent the entire reception trying to come up with an offer he might accept.

"Because if I wanted to prevent a pregnancy, I would've pulled out or finished in a condom instead of letting your tight pussy milk me dry."

Pulled out? I'm not sure what he means by that, but it looks like Cass was right. He won't give me a pill or let anyone here buy me one either. He threatened to make me vomit if he finds out I took one.

"Your body did exactly what it was made for when it came for me and greedily drained all the cum from my dick."

Remembering the way my walls clenched repeatedly around his shaft, how good it felt when he pumped inside of me while pinning my wrists above my head, causes a throbbing between my legs.

I hate that I enjoyed that part, and that I crave more of it.
Bastard.

All his experience is good for something at least. He knows how to make me feel stupidly good, even if it only lasts a few seconds.

"The separate room you demanded." Lochlan opens the door at the end of the hallway for me to enter first. I step inside...and see the huge, inviting bed with a thick fluffy sky-blue comforter with navy flowers and birds covering it. It would be a very bad idea to be alone with Lochlan in a room with a bed. So, I shut the door behind me before he steps a foot inside, then turn the lock for good measure.

"Really, Sophie?" Lochlan calls out through the door. "You think one measly little lock would keep me out if I really wanted in?"

Then come and get me, husband. Take what's yours, is what the stupidly horny part of my mind yells, but I drown it out with a threat.

Leaning my back and head against the structure, I warn him. "Come in my room without an invitation and I'll stab you in the dick!"

"Stab me with what exactly? A hairpin?"

Reaching down into my strapless bra, I pull the knife free. The one that went through a man's hand. I had to wash someone's blood off of it, which was gross. "I think your knife would hurt more."

There's a long silence, followed by, "You have my knife? The one I used last night?"

"Yes, I do."

"And you're going to stab me in the dick with it if I come in there?"

"Exactly."

"What the hell happened to you, princess? Where's the scared fawn who trembled at the sight of me?"

Flicking the switch to eject the blade, I press my finger to the pointy tip. Then I tell a small lie. "I would rather have your knife inside of me than any of your body parts."

"Fine, that can be arranged. But I want to be the one who wields it," he replies like the bastard he is. And I don't know why there's a smile stretched across my face. Maybe because I feel safe to taunt him with the barrier between us.

"I would rather do it myself."

"That's a lie, princess. You and I both know it. And the next time I fuck you, I promise it won't hurt. The only reason I didn't lick you first last night was because I *wanted* to hurt you. I had to punish you for being a little slut."

My jaw gapes at his insult.

And that was my punishment? Withholding his tongue trick from me before shoving his dick into the snug space to steal my virginity?

I close my eyes and try to imagine what sex with Lochlan would've been like if he had got on his knees last night like he did this morning before penetrating me. While he did give me an orgasm with his fingers before the sex, I wasn't nearly as slippery down there as I got from his mouth. The slide of him moving in and out would've been much easier.

"Should I cancel our honeymoon since you refuse to share a bed with me?" Lochlan asks, interrupting the mental redo of losing my virginity.

"Yes."

"Dante, well, Vanessa, thought you would like Anguilla. We would have a beach resort to ourselves..."

"No, thanks."

"You don't want to go to Anguilla?"

"No."

"Do you have any idea how many women would love for me to take them on a luxury vacation or buy them eighteen fucking five-carat diamonds?"

"Then why didn't you marry one of them?" I yell through the door, then I lift my wrist to count for myself. Eighteen diamonds. Huh. It probably cost him a fortune.

Lochlan grumbles something I can't make out before, "Good-night, my pain in the ass wife."

A nearby door slams shut, making me jump against mine.

He's not happy with me. Which means it's only a matter of time before he'll either toss me out on the curb in front of the Royal Palace or...he'll *take what's his.*

I shouldn't want to be his. Not when I know it will never happen. He won't give up other women for me.

While I hate him for that, once he's gone into his room, I feel so... lonely and abandoned. Tonight, I could be sleeping in a bed with Lochlan instead of a strange one alone in a strange room of a strange house.

Sinking down to the floor in a pool of my dress skirts I bury my face in my hands and let the tears fall. I have no clue what to do with myself tonight, tomorrow, or next week. Keeping my distance from Lochlan is going to be harder than I thought, so I need to find something to keep myself busy.

That is, if he even lets me leave my room.

I've traded one prison for another, all because my father asked me to for a business deal. I thought it would be exhilarating to marry the ruthless businessman.

I wish I had known that no amount of excitement fills the emptiness, and that Lochlan may not be capable of ever loving anyone.

15

Lochlan

Sophie didn't come to my room last night. Not that I expected her to. Maybe I hoped she would change her mind once I left her alone, but she didn't.

Her line has been drawn in the sand. I'm not allowed to touch her. Not unless...what the hell is it she wants from me? A pill and a promise to be faithful to her when there's a fucking timer counting down the seconds on this stick of dynamite of a marriage.

If Dante backs out of our deal, there will be hell to pay. He'll wish that bomb at the casino would've taken him out when I'm finished with him.

Him and his infuriating daughters.

The frustration left over from not spending my wedding night inside of my wife led to a four-a.m. run, followed by another hour in the gym. I think the guards hate my insomnia more than I do since two of them go wherever I go.

The rest of the morning I spent reading Lena and Toni the riot act about what will happen to them if they allow Sophie to endure even a scratch on their watch.

I started the search for formidable female guards as soon as Sophie agreed to marry me. After three weeks of rigorous background checks and field testing, I picked the two I think will best protect my wife during the day whenever I'm not around.

While my male guards all know I would string them up by their balls if they looked at my wife wrong, I refuse to allow any of them to be alone with Sophie. Hell, I wouldn't even trust Owen with her, and I trust him with my life.

I've had breakfast and am reading through messages on my phone, the article arranged by the PR firm announcing my and Sophie's nuptials, when my new bride finally comes slinking down from her room in search of food. She walks right past the dining room before backing up to eye the buffet laid out on the table, her eyes skipping right over me.

"Help yourself," I tell her when she just stands there in the doorway. Her black leggings and snug white tank top look so good hugging her curves that they should be illegal. Her eyes are puffy and red like she's been crying either this morning or last night. Already homesick? Regretting her decision? I don't like not knowing when and why she cried. I prefer when her tears are caused by me fucking her too hard.

Goddamm it. I have got to stop thinking about fucking her.

Her palm covers her wrist as if she hadn't expected to run into me while wearing her bracelet, and she doesn't want me to notice it. It's impossible to miss so much bling that the reflection of light alone could probably create solar power.

"Did all of your belongings make it to your room?" I ask, rather than making a smug remark about how she likes the jewelry I bought her, or demand to know the list of shit that made her cry.

"Yes," she answers as she comes over and picks up a plate to start filling it. "How did they get here before us last night?"

"Dante and I arranged for his staff and my own to pack it up and move it while we were getting ready for the ceremony."

"What if I had backed out?" she asks, sneaking a quick glance at me before it returns to the fruit tray.

"Then they would've moved your shit back to Dante's last night." My words are clipped, remnants of irritation from having my dick throb all day and night for my wife's pussy, without getting any fucking relief.

Trying to ignore those desires, I ask Sophie, "Did you sleep well?"

"I guess. Hard to fall asleep in a new place."

"You would've slept better in my bed," I promise her. "I would've made you come so many times you would've passed right out."

I wait for her cheeks to redden, or for her to respond to my claim. Instead, Sophie takes a seat at the other head of the table, as far from me as possible, and asks, "What are my rules?"

"Your rules?"

"Yes." She pops a grape into her mouth, then another. "Where can I go and when? Who can I see? That sort of thing."

"You want rules?"

"I don't *want* them, but I know there must be some."

"Like your father had rules to keep you in the penthouse to ensure your safety?"

"Yes."

I hadn't yet thought of any rules. The guards I gave orders to—don't let her get hurt or killed, don't let anyone lay a finger on her.

Leaning back in my chair, I watch Sophie eat her breakfast, all prim and proper-like as I think it over, trying to come up with ideas that are of course, to my advantage.

"Fine. Here are my rules—we have breakfast together every morning and dinner together every night when I'm in town. You're on your own for lunch."

"Okay."

"There will be some events I must attend, and, as my wife, you'll go with me and smile for the cameras."

"Like what kind of events?"

"Parties, fundraisers, networking. That sort of shit."

She nods her head in agreement, and when I don't add any others, she asks, "Do I have to stay in my room unless we're eating or attending an event?" she asks softly.

"Stay in your room? What? No. You may go anywhere you want whenever you feel like it."

"Without guards?"

"Hell, no. You'll be meeting Lena and Toni soon. They go where you go during the day, every day if I'm not with you."

She looks up at me now. "Female guards?"

"Trust me, these women are just as tough as any man."

"I don't doubt that. I just...I'm surprised my father never hired female guards for me and my sisters."

"So am I. Anyway, where you go, they go here on the property or out in public."

"You mean, I can just leave?"

"Yes, if your guards are with you. At least four on any public outings, which means there may be two males, but I don't mind since Toni and Lena won't let them near you. Which brings me to the next rule..."

Sophie's shoulders slump, as if she's expecting the worst is yet to come.

"You will not touch or be touched by any man other than me."

She blinks her big blue eyes at me as if she's thinking about calling me a fucking hypocrite.

"And you will not touch yourself without my permission either," I add after her comment last night that she would rather fuck herself with *my* knife. She kept *my* knife, which shocked the shit out of me. I had been so fucked up in the club that I hadn't thought to retrieve it from that asshole's hand before leaving the breakroom. It's the only gift my mother has ever given me, so I don't tend to misplace it.

Now Sophie's eyes widen in surprise. "Excuse me?"

"You heard me. Keep your hands off *my* pussy unless I give you my permission to touch yourself. If I do, I'll also provide the toys."

"Toys?"

"Vibrators, dildos, bullets, those sorts of things. You will only use them with my permission, and I'll be the one controlling them."

"What do you mean you'll be the one controlling them? You're not coming in my room."

"I won't have to. They have remotes or apps to turn them on and off, increase the speeds."

"But...how would you know if I...touch myself?"

"There are cameras being installed in your room later today." That brilliant idea just came to me, a way I can see her when she cries. "And there will be one in your bathroom as well." Seeing her naked in a shower may be the only time I get a look at every inch of her sexy body. "Don't worry, though, the toilet closet will continue to remain private. Never had those kinks and never will."

Both of her palms slap the table on either side of her plate. "You can't be serious! Even my father didn't watch me in my room and definitely not in my bathroom!"

"You're mine now, Sophie. That sweet little body of yours belongs to me, and since you're living in my house, I will look at it whenever the hell I want."

"I can't believe this. I didn't agree to be watched by a pervert in my own room!"

"This pervert will be watching you wherever you go inside or outside the house as well."

"I don't have to put up with this, with you."

"Oh, but you do, Sophie. At least until you bleed." As soon as I overheard Salvato telling her she could leave me whenever she wanted, that he would find another successor, I knew I would need something to hold her here. To keep up the public image that I'm a lovesick husband, even if it's only temporarily, as well as inherit

141

Salvato's empire. I doubt it'll be enough time to convince her to stay for long, but it's better than her walking out right now.

"What do you mean until I bleed?"

"After the other night, there's a chance you're carrying my child. Which means I'm not letting you walk away from me until I know for certain. If you still want to try to get an annulment after that, then I can't stop you." She would probably have to get a divorce after that long, and since we've had sex, but I don't bother bringing that shit up. Maybe I could work out some sort of separation agreement to keep us technically married a little longer.

"My father wouldn't give a shit if I'm pregnant or not. He would let me come home right now."

"Is that what you think?" I ask her. "Because I don't. I think Dante Salvato would never be foolish enough to destroy our alliance in less than twenty-four hours because of a teenager's tantrum, especially if there's a chance you have our heir growing inside of you."

"There wouldn't even be a chance if you had worn a condom or let me have a morning-after pill, you fucking asshole!"

"I expect better insults than that, princess." She slouches in her chair, ignoring her food, sulking like the teenager she is. "Finish eating so we can go meet your shadows. They'll show you around the property, get you settled in. And I will see you at seven o'clock tonight for dinner."

"What if I don't want to have dinner with you? Or breakfast?"

"Then I'll find some way to punish you until you change your mind. Isn't that what your father would do?" I ask her. "If you want to act like a child, then I'll treat you like one."

"You think I'm a child because I'm upset that you didn't even ask me if I wanted to be a mother first? If anyone is childish, it's you for that and for calling me a liar when I told you I was a virgin! And you're the one who practically had a foot-stomping temper tantrum when I asked you to stop playing with your whores."

"I don't play with whores; I fuck them."

"You're disgusting." Those two words are filled with buckets of venom, sharper than any knife I've wielded. They spear through me like the girl knows exactly where to hit to bring me to my knees. "If you gave me a disease or got me pregnant, I will make you fucking sorry."

"You already have," I assure her.

It's been years since I let fucking words get to me, since I allowed the duct tape holding what remains of my worthless soul to be pierced.

Sweet little Snow White managed to rip off a chunk in less than twenty-four hours together. Why am I surprised when all I've wanted to do since I saw her is ruin her? She's the closest thing to good and innocent that I've ever known in this world.

And she doesn't want any fucking thing to do with me.

"Finish eating your breakfast so I can be rid of you. Since we're not going on a honeymoon, I have business to handle," I snap at her. As intended, she flinches at my words. Daddy no doubt made her feel like he had better things to do than coddle her constantly, while she pined for a sliver of his attention.

"I'm finished," she mutters, getting to her feet.

"Great, let's go." I stand up and lead her down the hall of the first floor to my office. The two guards are still standing where I left them, waiting for us.

"Sophie, meet Lena and Toni. They're both highly skilled warriors. Lena is a military vet who kicks ass at hand-to-hand combat. She's also a sharpshooter that makes all the other guards jealous. Toni can choke out men twice her size in the cage and doesn't mind fighting dirty. I would trust them to keep you safe even while blindfolded."

"Being blindfolded was actually part of our performance test," the blonde who is taller than I am says with a grin. "I'm Lena and this is the second best in the business, Toni," she adds. Both women offer their palm out to Sophie who shakes them tentatively.

"It's nice to meet you," my wife says to them sweetly with a smile. Her venomous viper fangs are now carefully hidden behind

143

her elegant beauty that's blatantly obvious even in her casual attire.

That façade is why I thought she would be a docile doll who would always be terrified of me. I had no idea she could cut me open with only her words.

"Show her around and make sure she's at dinner by seven," I tell the women, talking about my ferocious little wife as if she's not there, just to piss her off before I walk out the door, out the house, to go find someone to bleed.

16

Sophie

Neither of the guards speak a word until the front door slams with Lochlan's abrupt departure.

I don't play with whores; I fuck them.

Dirty bastard.

And how dare he put up cameras in my personal space? When I'm naked in the shower? He's a disgusting pig, and now he's my husband.

"Shall we?" The tallest guard with a blonde ponytail and perfect posture, Lena, waves her arm toward the door. When I don't move, she adds, "Mr. Dunne wants us to give you a tour of the grounds."

"Right. Okay. Thank you."

The shorter, stockier brunette with a buzzcut and biceps bigger than my thighs, Toni, takes the lead with Lena right behind me. I'm used to being the center of a guard sandwich, although I do already feel safer with two women.

"We heard the bossman yelling at you," Lena says as soon as we're outside through the backdoor leading to a spacious patio deck. Her and Toni both don dark sunglasses, making me wish I had brought mine. "You shouldn't antagonize him."

"Antagonize...are you kidding? He's a psycho stalker! I'm married to a psychotic asshole who won't let me leave him and who insists on watching me every second of the day."

"Give him a chance," she says quietly, calmly like he's not going to be spying on her and Toni all day too. "He's actually pretty fair and generous for a mob boss. Although, rumors say he has been surly ever since the bombing."

"The what? Oh, the bombing at his casino. My father was there. He barely survived unscathed."

"*They* barely survived. I bet whoever planted the bomb wishes they hadn't. When Lochlan finds them, they'll be begging for a swift death that he'll never give them."

That brings me up short. Coming to a stop on the paved path I ask, "What do you mean they haven't found him? I thought the bombing was set up by Petrov who is dead."

"Oh, it was definitely Petrov's lacky who planted the bomb. Lochlan won't rest until he finds out who exactly it was and makes them pay the way your father made Petrov and Kozlov pay."

"They'll deserve every second of the torment too," Toni agrees, her first comment on our walk. "All those innocent lives lost...it's so fucked up."

"Toni was a huge Michael Avanti fan. You know, the action movie star? He died that night in the explosion."

"I'm sorry," I tell her.

"It's not like she knew him personally or anything," Lena remarks.

"Still, I'm sorry all those people died just because someone wanted to hurt my dad. And Lochlan."

The two guards are both silent and share a look between each other through their dark sunglasses.

"What?" I ask them.

"We're going to have to toughen you up, girly. You're a mafia queen now. There's no room for sweetness and light in this world."

"I know that. My father is..."

"Yes, we know Dante Salvato is your father," Lena interrupts. "And that he sheltered you and your sisters to keep you safe. Lochlan isn't going to keep you locked away. In fact, everything depends on you being seen on his arm, which means you need to put some steel in your spine."

Everything depends on me being seen on his arm? What's that about? Toni keeps walking so I continue following along.

"Not to mention all his little harlots who will want you dead," she adds.

Lena chuckles. "Death by the poison-tipped claws of a hooker. I wouldn't put it past them."

"You think...you think his prostitutes would hurt me?" I ask the two guards.

"Not physically, not when we're around," Lena says confidently. "That doesn't mean they won't try and tear you down with words or fill your head with bullshit. They all worship the ground Lochlan walks on."

"And his dick," Toni inserts.

"That too. You caught their white whale," Lena explains. "Even if they all knew there was never a chance of Lochlan putting a diamond ring on any of their fingers, or over a dozen on a single one of their wrists, they'll still be jealous as fuck that he married you. Try not to let them get to you. We're not allowed to hit them. Nobody will want to screw a woman who is black and blue."

"Well, there's probably someone out there with that sort of kink, but Lena is right," Toni replies. "We can't lay a hand on them unless they physically assault you. Then again, if we were to somehow blink and miss an assault, it's your word against theirs, and your word wins every single time."

I'm still thinking that comment over when I see a busy construction area roped off with yellow caution tape up ahead in the distance. Men and equipment are strewn around the familiar green sight.

"Ah, it looks like the court is almost done." Lena lifts her hand over her sunglass-covered eyes to block out the sun.

"Jeff said they just need to finish putting up the fencing and shade, so it should be ready for play later today," Toni interjects while leading us closer.

"A tennis court?" I squeak in disbelief.

"Yeah." Lena falls into step beside me. "You're an avid player, right? Lochlan did his research and hired some folks last week to do the install. He has a few trainers and pros lined up on your approved visitor list to come play with you whenever you say the word, including the one from before, Betsy something-or-another."

"He hired Betsy?"

"Yes, ma'am."

"And if I want to play or train, there will be someone on the courts, just like that?" I snap my fingers while still staring at the site.

"Yes."

"Lochlan was super pissed that the installation took a day longer than the company said it would take," Toni informs me.

"He built all this, just for me?"

"You're his wife." Lena says this simply as if it explains the trouble, the effort and money that had to go into the construction. "If you asked him for a piece of the moon, he would probably find some way to hop on a rocket to go fetch a chunk for you tomorrow."

"But...why?"

To convince my father he's making an effort with me, so he'll keep him as his successor?

"Why else does a man spoil his beautiful wife?" When I stare at Lena, waiting for her to answer her own question, she finally says, "For sex, of course."

"What? No," I sputter. I prefer the impressing my father option to that one. "I'm not...just because he built me a tennis court, I'm not going to have sex with him."

Nothing will change my mind about that until Lochlan agrees to use protection and stop screwing his prostitutes.

"Then hold out for something better," Toni suggests. "It's not like he's going to force you."

"Right. No reason to force me when he has so many willing women at his brothels," I grumble.

"Exactly," Toni unfortunately agrees. "Ready to see the indoor and outdoor pools?"

I nod, at a loss for words, following along behind my two guards when I remember what I needed to ask them.

"Will one of you buy me a morning-after pill?"

"Never heard of it," Toni instantly responds, which is most likely a lie.

"Sorry, girly. If the boss told you no, then we can't help you," Lena explains. "He would do worse than kill us if we helped stop you from conceiving his kid."

"Worse than kill you?" I repeat. "Why would either of you take this job and work for him if pissing him off could happen any second?"

"Lochlan pays us enough to love you like a sister," Toni explains. "Sure, there are risks, but it beats literally busting up my face to pay the bills."

"What did you do before you came to work for him?"

"Little bit of this and that," Toni replies. "I've been a bouncer, done some competitive weightlifting, and knocked some heads in MMA until I ran out of women to beat in my weight class. Most men were too big of pussies to fight me and lose."

"And you?" I ask Lena.

"United States Army Special Forces. I can't tell you more than that because it's classified."

Her rigid stance and perfect posture make sense now that I know she has military experience. Lochlan may have even mentioned it in the introduction, but I was still fuming mad at him, and only heard half of what he said.

"And Lochlan pays you enough to think of me like a sister?" I ask Lena.

"No. Like a daughter," she replies with a grin. "I get paid twice as much as Toni."

"Because of your service?"

"No, because if shit goes sideways with you, it's on her as my superior," Toni explains. "She calls the shots, gives me my orders."

Lena shrugs like it's no big deal. "I don't like taking orders from anyone who doesn't sign my paycheck, especially some idiot meathead on a power trip."

"The male guards are tough, sure, but they're not the brightest bulbs in the box," Toni tells me. "They all think with their dicks instead of their heads if given half a chance."

"Don't all men do that?" Lena asks.

"True enough." Toni and her fist bump each other in solidarity.

With my limited knowledge of men, or one man, I would have to agree with that statement.

All Lochlan seems to care about is sex and money.

17

Lochlan

I don't even make it half an hour riding in the back of the SUV to the city before I pull up the surveillance feed around the estate to see Sophie.

We should be on our honeymoon now, but I'm not taking her to a resort paradise until we're fucking. Seeing her strut around in a bikini would give me blue balls from hell unless she's putting out.

It's only a matter of time before she changes her mind.

Hopefully the tennis court will do the trick. I have to figure out a way to make her happy, to convince her to stay long enough for me to appease Salvato and get through the civil trial.

Speaking of bikinis, the guards are hard to miss so it doesn't take long for me to find them wandering around the indoor pool. Thankfully for my needy dick, Sophie doesn't decide to go for a swim during her tour.

The rest of my morning is spent getting up to speed on the casino renovations caused by the bombing. Instead of replacing the ball-room, I'm having an indoor butterfly garden, a memorial with fountains and shit that are supposed to make the scene of so much death serene. I don't know if it'll work, but the PR firm suggested it.

I don't have time to check on Sophie again until after a lunch meeting with business partners opening a new "escort service" in Berlin.

As soon as I'm alone in my office, though, I pull up the surveillance feed again. I find Snow White already on the newly finished tennis court, hitting the ball back and forth with her former trainer. And damn, she looks good in that short white skirt. It reminds me of the day we met, when I ran my knife under that cock-teasing outfit and made her gasp for the first time.

Thinking about that day in her room and remembering the feel of her tight wet pussy makes me rock hard. Even if she wasn't a virgin, it was the snuggest fit of my life. The girl hasn't had much sex before me, which is almost as good as being her first.

It's impossible for me to look away from her tenacity on the court. Even if she misses a rally, she does it with an all-out flourish, giving it everything she's got.

Seeing her bend over to pick up the ball or her water bottle offers a fine view, even if it's not an up-close shot.

Now I'm hard yet again, with no relief in sight, unless I take matters into my own hands. Everyone around me would likely benefit from me relieving some of the pent-up frustration. That's why I pop the button on my pants then lower my zipper to free my swollen dick. My pumping fist is a poor substitute for Sophie's sweet cunt, but it'll have to do for now.

I don't even remember the last time I had to use my own hand to get off. There has always been a line of willing women, ready to offer up their mouths, pussy, or ass to me at a moment's notice. Pros who know exactly what I like to make me come apart. Or at least what I used to like. Now the thought of any mouth or pussy other than Sophie's won't cut it. Not that I've had her mouth yet. I will one of these days. I need her pretty lips wrapped around my cock at least once before I die, or before she leaves me.

That last thought is almost enough to derail my orgasm, so I push the notion aside. Instead, I imagine Sophie hot and sweaty in her tennis outfit kneeling before me. I would wrap her long, silky black ponytail around my fist and use it to guide her mouth up and down my cock, then hold her head hostage until I finish coming down her throat.

I wonder if she's ever sucked a dick before. I would like to pretend she hasn't, that mine will be the first. That she would be drooling and choking on it when I fill her mouth with more cum than she can swallow.

"Oh, fuck!" I exclaim as I start pulsing in my hand thanks to that image in my head. The only thing that would be better than seeing Sophie's sweet, innocent-looking face covered in my cum is watching her stuff her hand in her skirt and panties, fingering herself at the same time I do it.

***

Sophie

I considered avoiding dinner with Lochlan, even after he had a tennis court built for me. But Lena and Toni urged me to shower and change by seven to avoid the fallout. Since they also told me that their day is over once I'm in for the night or left in Lochlan's charge, I conceded, knowing they were more than ready to get home after twelve hours watching over me.

Fully aware of the new cameras when I had to take a shower, I undressed in the toilet closet and kept a towel wrapped around my body until the shower glass was steamy enough to hide most of my nudity from view. Only then did I remove the towel when I stepped inside.

After my shower, I keep the towel on to go pick out my underwear, planning to take them to change in the walk-in closet which doesn't have cameras. In the top drawer of the dresser filled with all my panties and bras, I find a box that wasn't there this morning. A box that says, "Emergency Contraceptive."

Someone bought it for me, even knowing the cameras would see them. Was it Lena? Toni? Both of them?

What if it's a trick? Lochlan told me he would make me throw the pill up if he found out I took it. Would he also fire my new guards? Kill them?

I quickly shut the drawer, leaving the box where I found it while I think it over.

Part of me knows I should have quickly removed the pill, then swallowed it once I was in the changing room.

Now if I go back to the drawer, it might look suspicious if Lochlan is watching the security footage. I could take my pair of panties back and change them for a different pair.

Ultimately, I decide to wait until later, to think about my options during dinner.

Two place settings are laid out on the dining table, along with water and a glass of red wine. I take a big gulp of the wine while weighing my choices. Not to mention, I'll probably need the alcohol buzz to get through another meal with my perverted husband.

Speaking of the philandering devil, Lochlan strolls into the dining room right on time according to the antique grandfather clock, looking too damn good in his three-piece suit. He looks so...perfect as if he stepped out of a billboard advertising men's cologne. Except, unlike a beautiful model, he puts knives through men and fucks prostitutes.

"Did you have a good day?" Lochlan asks as soon as he sits down at the opposite head of the table. His mere appearance initiates the presentation of salads which was brought out by staff that I met in the kitchen earlier when I grabbed a quick lunch.

I study his face for any signs that he knows about the pill. He doesn't look any angrier than usual or suspicious.

"Sophie?" he says to get my attention, reminding me of his question.

"Yes, I did." There's a long pause, so I decide the polite thing would be to ask him the same question. "How was your day?"

"Fine."

He doesn't give me any other details, just continues to watch me intently. He's a beautiful savage, and I think he might kill whoever gave me the pill, if he hasn't already. And just like that, I make my decision. I won't take it. I won't risk anyone's life because I stupidly had unprotected sex with my heathen husband the night before we got married.

A tiny voice in my head is also relieved. While I don't want to be a mother, at least I know Lochlan would keep me forever if I am pregnant. Belonging to him is better than being alone. At least, I think it is.

I finally stop staring at him long enough to remember that if it weren't for his generosity, I wouldn't have spent the afternoon doing what I love most in the world. And since I don't plan on sleeping with him to show my appreciation, I decide to at least give him the words. "Thank you for putting in the tennis court for me."

"You're welcome." He frowns at my blue blouse with sheer sleeves. "I thought you might wear your tennis outfit to dinner."

"Why would I do that? It was sweaty and dirty."

"No reason," he says, but it sounds like there is obviously a reason. Whatever. If he wants me to know he'll tell me. I won't waste my time obsessing over his every look or comment trying to figure him out. If the person who gave me the pill has already been punished, there's nothing I can do about it now.

"I watched you playing earlier. Got so hard I had to rub one out."

Is he referring to... does "rub one out" mean what I think it does? While watching me play tennis?

Rather than encourage more details from him, I swallow another gulp of wine, then dig into my salad, starved after all the calories burned on the court.

"You seemed to have found workarounds for hiding your nakedness from me in the bathroom," Lochlan eventually remarks.

Lifting my wine glass, I swallow another sip, telling him, "You haven't earned the right to see me naked."

"You haven't earned that right either. But me? Eighteen diamonds, nearly one hundred carats, along with your own personal tennis court and staff aren't enough for me to earn it?"

I look at the bracelet shimmering under the chandelier, then him. "I didn't ask you for those things. Besides, you have plenty of money. You only went to the trouble of buying things for me to appease my father and try to bribe me to fuck you. So no, you haven't earned anything from me."

"What do I have to do to earn it, Sophie?" Lochlan asks. There's an edge to his voice, almost like he's desperate. Desperate for me? Doubtful when he has all sorts of other options.

"You can't buy me. And I've already told you what I wanted," I remind him just before a phone rings. It's Lochlan's since mine is in the bedroom. I forgot it and everything else once I saw the pill. The device is sitting on the table all lit up, and he doesn't hesitate to answer it even though we're eating dinner and are in the middle of a discussion.

"Let me guess, you want to talk to Sophie?" he says, which means it must be my father or Vanessa. "I don't fucking know why she didn't answer your call. Maybe because we were in the middle of dinner, and she doesn't appear to have her phone with her." With a sigh, he holds out the phone to me. I can't reach it without getting up and walking over to him.

Which I do, then snatch the device from his palm and put it up to my ear. "Hello?"

156

"Are you okay? When you didn't answer the phone..." my father's frantic voice asks.

"I'm fine. We're eating dinner."

"How was your day?"

"Fine." When he doesn't speak, waiting for me to say more, I give in and tell him, "Lochlan had a tennis court installed here so I played with Betsy this afternoon."

My father is silent for another long moment. "He built you a tennis court overnight?"

"No, it was just finished today."

"Huh." He makes the same noise Cass made when she asked me about his nickname for me. Not that he's used it recently.

"Is he...treating you well?"

"Yes. I have two female bodyguards who are nice." *And hopefully still breathing.*

"Why didn't I think of that?" he mutters. "I should hire some women for Cass."

"Maybe so," I agree.

"Okay, well, I'll let you get back to your dinner. Vanessa sends her love." My father doesn't sound like himself. Maybe he regrets forcing me into a marriage for a business deal. Or maybe he's still upset that I told him I hated him.

"Tell Vanessa I said hi and hopefully I'll see her soon." I lift my gaze to Lochlan's to see his reaction to that idea. His face remains blank. "And I'm sorry about what I said yesterday."

"I don't deserve your forgiveness," he says in response.

"Bye, Daddy."

"Love you, baby girl."

I don't return the words. Just because I apologized for saying I hate him it doesn't mean I'm not still mad at him for using me.

As soon as I end the call, I take the phone back to Lochlan and lay it on the table next to his plate. I don't want to accidentally see any incriminating messages of the murder or infidelity variety.

"Am I allowed to talk to my dad and family whenever I want?"

"Yes."

"Can I go see them?"

"Only to visit until we know for sure that you're not pregnant," he replies, giving me a pointed look. "When will that be?"

Ugh, he's asking me when I'm supposed to get my period? I can't believe we're talking about this at the dinner table. Is he bringing it up to see if I'll admit that I got the emergency contraceptive pill? Does it make periods come sooner?

"Sophie?"

"Hold on. I have to try and remember when the last one was," I huff. A moment later, I tell him the truth, "Maybe in two or three weeks."

"Maybe? You can't give me something more concrete than that?"

"No. Mine aren't ever regular."

"Why not?"

"My doctor seems to think the irregularity is due to my physical activity."

We eat the rest of our dinner without mentioning my menstrual cycle again, thankfully. Lochlan does ask me lots of questions about tennis, my instructors, how long I've been playing. I don't think anyone has ever shown so much interest in my boring life.

Before I ask to leave the table after dessert, a raspberry cheese-cake that was no doubt supposed to be a reminder of a different one, Lochlan says, "There's a fundraiser we have to go to on Thursday night. Formal wear. Be ready by eight."

"Okay," I agree. "And, um, thank you for hiring Lena and Toni. I like them." Trying to figure out a way to ask if they're alive without seeming obvious, I ask, "Will they be with me every day this week?"

"Yes. Every weekday and on weekends if necessary."

"Okay, good," I say with a sigh of relief. He would've told me if he had replaced one or both.

"Am I excused now?"

"Yes. But you don't have to ask my permission to leave the table."

"I don't?"

"No. I'm not your father," he mutters before he gets up and leaves the room before me.

∽

Over the next few days, I consider going home for a visit. The reason I don't is because my dad is probably busy, and Cass wouldn't care to see me. It would be nice to talk to Vanessa, but I'm afraid that once I'm back there in the familiar penthouse, I won't want to leave again.

And I'm afraid my father would just send me back until I know if I'm pregnant or not, just as Lochlan predicted.

For now, Lochlan owns me.

Unlike at the engagement dinner, or in the club's breakroom, he hasn't touched me. I told him I didn't want him to unless he gave up other women and used protection, which makes me wonder how he spends his days and nights, and with whom.

I didn't ask Lena or Toni about the pill since it's impossible to talk to them one-on-one. And since I decided not to take it, I try to pretend I never saw it.

But I did keep it. I pushed it over the back of the drawer and crushed it in the space that's unreachable unless the entire drawer is removed just in case I need it later.

18

Lochlan

"You look like shit," Owen remarks when he and Flynn waltz into my office at the hotel Thursday afternoon. "Your child bride still withholding pussy?" my brother asks.

"Yes," I mutter, tossing the tablet I've spent days clutching on the top of my desk. The tablet I was using to watch Sophie doing leg lifts in the gym. Those weren't nearly as fun as seeing her legs open and close over and over again on the abduction machine. Maybe fun is the wrong word. It was more like torture. "I don't know what else I can fucking do to get her in my bed. I had hoped the tennis court and bracelet would be enough to have her eagerly spread her legs for me."

"How ungrateful of her," Flynn remarks with a chuckle. "Maybe you should give up and get a divorce. Or an annulment."

"No. Not yet."

"Why not?" Owen asks.

"Because, I'm not ready to give up yet. Too much is at stake. I need the PR and I need Salvato to make me his successor in case I lose everything at trial." I hate to admit to myself that I am sort of enjoying the challenge of changing Sophie's mind. No woman has ever been worth putting in effort for before my young wife. I want her, and I want her to want me, even though she thinks I'm a dirty bastard.

Getting up from my desk, I go over to the mini bar to pour myself a scotch. After I drink half of it, I confess to them, "Sophie could be pregnant with my kid, which would probably seal the deal with Dante. We won't know for sure for a few weeks, and he's not getting my contacts until then."

"What?" Owen mutters.

"How is that possible if she won't let your dick anywhere near her?" Flynn asks.

"Because I fucked her the night before the wedding, against the wall in a club breakroom."

"You did what now?" Flynn takes one of the seats, followed by Owen who joins him. "You fucked her before the wedding ceremony?"

"You both know I left my so-called 'bachelor party' that night. I went looking for Sophie after Salvato confessed that she was having her own version of a bachelorette party. Well, I found her drunk and getting felt up by some asshole. I put him down, then yeah, I fucked her. She claims I took her virginity, but I think she's lying. She didn't bleed."

"Not all virgins bleed," Owen remarks.

"How do you know?"

"A dick isn't the only thing that can rip a cherry. Sophie's athletic, right? She probably uses tampons."

"Or she could've fucked a dildo," Flynn helpfully offers.

I consider those possibilities for a second. Why didn't I think of them before? Probably because I've never been near a virgin before. I feel a little sick, wondering if they're right, and that I was wrong for calling Sophie a liar, for being so callous her first time.

"So, you think maybe she was telling me the truth, and I was her first?"

"Maybe," Owen answers.

"Who knows, Loch," Flynn says. "Maybe you're right and she's a lying sack of shit."

"She did cry once I was inside her. And told me she hated me," I remember with a smirk. I don't tell them about her wrapping her small hands around my throat as if to kill me. They probably wouldn't find it as funny as I did. I knew she wouldn't do it, and I could've easily stopped her if she had really wanted to hurt me.

But if that was actually Sophie's first time, well, I probably shouldn't have fucked her against the wall or after she had been drinking. She seemed pretty coherent to me, though. I do seem to remember some sort of sofa in the break room. We could've done it there instead of the hard wall with me impaling her so abruptly. Hell, at the moment I would do her anywhere, any way, even standing on my head.

"You used a condom, though, right?" Owen asks.

"No."

"Well, that was stupid," Flynn remarks and Owen agrees.

"No shit. She despises me, and she's too young to be a mother. But at the same time, as much as Salvato would hate it, he would definitely want to share his empire with a grandchild, my son or daughter. Not to mention that whenever I think about putting my baby in Sophie, it makes me so fucking hard."

Shaking his head with a grin, Owen says, "You're never gonna wrap up if she ever lets you near her pussy again, are you?"

"No," I answer honestly. How can I go back to having a layer of rubber between me and that tight wet heaven? Never again. With only one little exception. "Not unless wrapping it up is the only way I can have her. She asked for a morning-after pill, and for me to promise not to fuck around with anyone behind her back, and I refused to agree to either. So right now, I'm more concerned with when she'll let me touch her again. We have the fundraiser tonight, a birthday memorial thing for Salvato's guard, the bombing victim who saved us. It'll be obvious to everyone who sees us together that Sophie doesn't want to be in the same room with me, much less in my bed."

At the rate I've been jerking off multiple times a day, I'm going to sprain my wrist. Even though my dick likes to remind me that Sophie doesn't have the only pussy in the world, I refuse to give in and fuck around with anyone else. Mostly because she's so certain I will. Also, there's no cunt that could compete with hers. Besides, if Sophie found out I cheated on her, it would send her running back to Daddy even faster.

I'm not promising to always be faithful to my wife like she demanded of me, though. Nobody gives me orders. And even if I did agree to her ultimatum, she wouldn't actually believe that I wasn't fucking around. At least not yet. She doesn't trust me as far as she can throw me. Not that I'm any better since I was so quick to assume she lied about her virginity.

"There will be plenty of beautiful women at the event tonight who could help you take the edge off," Owen suggests.

Flynn nods in agreement. "I have no doubt Shana will be there and be down for a quickie or a blowie."

"No," I immediately decline. "Not until I have my wife again."

The sooner the better. If I didn't knock her up the first time, then I want another shot at it before the window closes and she comes up not pregnant, then leaves me, taking Salvato's empire with her. If her period is two or three weeks away, that means I need to try and make some progress tonight.

And I won't have anything get in my way.

"You're not coming to the fundraiser tonight," I tell my brother.

"What? Why not?"

"Because you don't give a shit about raising money for anyone. And I don't want you to cause any scenes. The last thing I need right now is bad PR."

"Fuck you," he huffs before getting up and storming out.

"Really?" Owen asks once he's gone.

"He's a distraction I don't need tonight," I tell him as I rub my throbbing forehead. "You saw how he acted at the wedding and the dinner with Salvato. I don't want him running his mouth or stumbling into a champagne fountain."

"Yeah, he is a constant sort of chaos," Owen agrees. "See you there?"

"Yeah, I'll see you there. I have to get home and shower, make sure my wife is ready for our first outing as husband and wife."

Sophie

Since there's an event I have to attend with Lochlan tonight, I'm excused from having dinner with him so we can both get ready. I have a quick snack while several attendants do my hair and makeup, before a third helps me try on dresses from a rolling rack. We finally decide on a simple black floor-length gown with a slit up the front of my thigh. It reminds me of Cass's bridesmaid dress that she of course picked out herself. The off-the-shoulder cap sleeve crisscrosses with the neckline showing two teasing glimpses of skin just above my right breast and the side of the left one. It's elegant and classy, especially with the three-diamond drop earrings peeking out from the long, loose curls of my black hair. The earrings were another gift from Lochlan, as if I need any more diamonds. I can't help but notice that the tennis bracelet goes with everything, but especially my formal dress.

A pair of strappy heels give me a height boost I don't really need, making me close to six-feet tall. Still, when Lochlan meets me in the foyer, he has at least four or five more inches on me. He's even more intimidating in a tux than I remember from the wedding, probably because I was either in an orgasmic, blissed-out state after he licked me between the legs, or because I was too furious at him to pay attention.

If I had to bet, the hungry look in his green gaze makes me think he's remembering the former.

"You are absolutely stunning, princess," Lochlan says his eyes still taking in every inch of me, his tone softer than it's been all week when he finally uses that moniker again. "I want to lick my way right up that slit to taste your silky sweet one again."

Oh, yeah, he's definitely thinking about that thing he did with his tongue before the wedding ceremony.

And while I would love nothing more than to feel that good again, I'm certain his offer isn't manganous. No, Lochlan would expect his own pleasure in return, and I would be too blissed out afterward to stop him from crossing the line I swore to myself I wouldn't cross.

Not until he agrees to use protection and swears he won't seek his own pleasure in any other woman. Or pleasure anyone else.

Imagining Lochlan's tongue between one of his harlots' legs quickly extinguishes the inferno his words tried to start inside of me.

"I'd rather you keep your filthy tongue in your mouth," I tell him as coolly as I can manage, my fingers clutching my small purse tightly before I do something stupid like hike up my dress and show him my sexy lace thong that's now damp thanks to his offer. "Can we please get this over with before I get blisters on my feet?"

Lochlan blinks at me silently as if stunned, perhaps because he's not used to being rejected.

Finally, he sighs heavily and walks over to open the front door for me. A group of guards congregating in the driveway turn toward their boss.

"We're ready to leave. Is a car ready?" Lochlan asks them.

"Yes, sir," one of them responds instantly.

I hate to say it, but I miss Toni and Lena. While they may be assigned to me as part of their job, they're highly entertaining, always teasing each other, making jokes, and talking about how horrible men can be.

~

The short ride in the SUV takes us down the familiar road of the Vegas strip. While I rarely left the penthouse, it's impossible not to recognize the landmarks nearby.

"Where are we going?" I ask Lochlan.

"Salvato is hosting a fundraiser for the family of his deceased guard, so where do you think?" he replies blandly while staring down at his phone, the glow of the screen emphasizing his deep frown.

"We're going home," I blurt out when I see the resort sign lit up just ahead. That causes my husband's eyes to snap up.

"The Royal Palace is no longer your home. Don't even think about trying to stay tonight when it's time to go. You know the rules, so don't make me draw blood in your father's casino during a memorial event for a dead man."

Wow. I didn't even mean it like that, I was just excited to be going somewhere sort of familiar.

The security checkpoint at the front door is new, although I'm not surprised by it. Especially tonight when my father can't be too careful. It would be awful if there was another bomb during a fundraiser for a man killed in the last one.

We have to wait for all the guards to get approved through too since they're carrying concealed weapons. Then, Lochlan leads the way with his entourage surrounding us. He stalks through the resort as if he's more familiar with the place than I am. And he probably is. My father didn't like for me and my sisters to come down to the main floor unless there was some special event.

Which means, I've only been in the largest ballroom a handful of times. Tonight, it's decorated in a celestial theme, dark purples and blues, low light, giving it a sedate vibe, which I can understand for this occasion. The room is packed full of people. It's all a little over-whelming until I see two familiar faces.

"Sophie!" Vanessa shouts when she spots me and comes over, pulling my father along by his hand. She lets go of him to wrap me in a tight embrace, then my dad does the same. Vanessa's gown is a shimmering violet, matching his boutonniere, the only color on his black tux.

"It's good to see you, baby girl. How are you? You look...so grown up," he says as he eyes my dress. The tic in his jaw makes me think he wouldn't have let me leave the penthouse with the slit so high up to my thigh. At least Lochlan isn't that strict about what I can and can't wear.

"Salvato. Looks like a great turnout," my husband says to my father as the two shake hands briskly.

"It's the least I could do for Frank's family. I should've hosted a fundraiser for them sooner," Dante replies. When the two begin to talk, or argue, about their new business arrangements, Vanessa wraps her hands around my elbow. "Let's grab a drink and catch up while the men talk shop." She steers me over to grab a glass of champagne, offering me one before grabbing one for herself.

Taking a quick sip, she says, "You look gorgeous, Sophie. I barely recognized you. I don't think your own father did either."

"Thanks," I reply with a smile as I glance down at the gown. "It's not something I would've ever worn when I lived here."

She chuckles. "I imagine not if Dante had a say in it. Now, tell me the truth, how are you *really* doing with Lochlan?"

"I'm fine."

"Just fine? Is he good to you?" Lowering her voice she asks, "Has he...hurt you? Forced you to do anything you didn't want to do?"

"No, no. Nothing like that. He...he's left me alone in my own bedroom every night."

"Your own room? That's surprising," Vanessa remarks. I'm not sure if she means she's surprised he's left me alone or that I have my own room.

Disappointing is the word I would use instead. I swallow it down with a sip of bubbly.

It's not that I *want* to have sex with Lochlan again. At least not voluntarily. Despite my weak threat about cutting off his dick, if he came into my room one night and climbed on top of me, well, I wouldn't really have a choice but to let him take what he wanted, right?

Why hasn't the bastard done that yet?

And what's wrong with me that I want him to do that sort of thing?

"I figured Lochlan would manipulate you into sleeping in his bed, even if only for sleeping. That's what *some* men I know would do," Vanessa explains.

"Well, he hasn't," I assure her. "He also built a tennis court for me on his property."

"That was sweet of him," she agrees, although there's still a crease between her brow as if she's thinking the same thing as the guards—that the court comes with strings attached to it. It would be nice to actually get Vanessa's opinion on that.

"I don't owe him sex for the court, do I?"

Vanessa's jaw falls open then closes. "No. No, of course not, sweetie. You don't *owe* sex to anyone, ever. Don't let him make you feel that way either." She searches the crowd for him, her lips pursed as if she wants to give him a piece of her mind. We both find him surrounded by not one but four beautiful women of various shapes, sizes, and ethnicities. A kaleidoscope of sluts. No wonder there's such a smug grin on his handsome face. He knows he could have any or all of them whenever he wants. Probably all of them at the same time. "Wow, he's quite the ladies' man, isn't he?"

"Those are probably his whores."

"What?" Vanessa exclaims, her face turning back to me, emerald eyes wide in shock.

"I meant literally, as in his employees from the brothels. I bet he's slept with all of them. Maybe he still is…"

"Huh," my stepmother mutters as she turns back to stare at my husband being idolized from every direction. "Even so, it's rude of him to let them monopolize his time and attention like that in public, in front of you now that you're married. If Dante did that...well, he would find himself locked out of our bedroom tonight."

Shaking her head, her eyes flit around the ballroom again, before a slow smile spreads across her face. Gently grabbing my elbow again, she says, "Come with me. I have a wonderful idea." While we're maneuvering our way around the crowd of people to get to the other side of the room, she glances over her shoulder and says, "Cole is still here. He's out of school for the summer."

"Oh. Right." I'm not sure what her son has to do with anything, but a moment later we're standing in front of the tall, handsome blond college boy, and...Cass?

Both of her eyebrows raise when she examines my gown. "Wow. Look what the cat dragged in."

"I'm surprised Daddy let you come down here for this," I remark.

Her pale green eyes continue to take in my dress and heels, then my hair and diamond earrings. "Lochlan doesn't keep you on a tight leash? Surprising. How is married life?"

"Fine." I don't tell her how much I want to leave my philandering husband and come home, mostly because I don't want her to know I'm not happy with him. Cass relishes my misery.

Nodding her chin over near the door, she says, "Looks like your new husband is being swamped by sluts. Is the honeymoon already over?"

"We didn't have a honeymoon," I remark. "But he built me a tennis court on his estate."

"No shit?" Cole says with a chuckle. "He just...built you a court from scratch?"

"Yes."

"Cole," Vanessa says. "You've complained about how bored you are during the days here, maybe you could go play tennis with Sophie sometime soon."

Scowling at his mother, he asks, "Damn, Mom. Do you want me to die of heat stroke?"

"It's shaded," I add.

"See, it's shaded. And don't even try to pretend you don't have an amazing serve," his mother huffs.

"You're a tennis player?" I knew Vanessa played, but I didn't know her son did too.

"I taught him a thing or too," she replies proudly. "Right, hon?" When Cole doesn't respond she slips her arm around his waist and gives him a shove toward me.

"I guess I could get up early one morning..." he trails off, eyes now slits while glowering at his mother.

"Great! Cass, let's leave these two to discuss the details. I need your help schmoozing some rich assholes."

"But..." Cass starts as Vanessa takes her by the wrist and pulls her along behind her.

As they walk away, Vanessa calls over her shoulder, "Cole, do keep Sophie company until her husband returns. Dante would hate for her to be left all alone in a crowd."

"That's okay. His guards are..." I start, searching around for Lochlan's men. They're still standing near the entrance. By the time I turn back to Vanessa, her blonde head and Cass's red one have disappeared into the growing crowd.

Taking a deep breath, I gulp down another sip of champagne, then offer Cole a small smile. "I'm sorry you got stuck with me."

He gives me a dazzling smile back. "I don't mind. It's not like I know anyone here other than your family."

"Do you miss New York?"

"Yes," he says. "Vegas is too damn hot. But at least I don't have to work the entire summer to pay for tuition this year. You know, since my mom inherited everything from her father? She won't use a penny of Petrov's blood money, but she did set up a decent trust fund for me to pay for school and a little to live on, so I don't have to juggle a job and studying anymore."

"That's great," I agree, even if I can't relate to the struggle of not having endless money.

Cole is a talker, which is perfectly fine with me. I'm more than happy to listen to him talk about his friends back at school and future business plans since it keeps me distracted from glaring at my husband while he continues to flirt with his harlots.

19

Lochlan

I'm grateful that the ladies paid for tickets to help contribute to the fundraiser, to the family of the man who saved my life and Salvato's, but now they won't give me a moment's peace.

It's always something with them—in-fighting, thievery, overdoses.

To be honest, I didn't mind their rabid attention or the brush of tits against my arms. Let my beautiful wife see that even if she doesn't want me, there are plenty of gorgeous women who do. Not that I want any of them, but she doesn't know that.

And it worked. Within minutes of Sophie chatting with Dante's wife Vanessa, both women were glaring daggers at me.

During Silvia's extended rant about wanting to increase her number of vacation days but Mary, the madam, won't let her, I realize I haven't laid eyes on Sophie for a few minutes. I seek her out in the crowd. She's no longer near the table of champagne with Vanessa. In fact, I don't see her at all. I do another sweep of the room and finally spot her. Her back is turned to me, her long raven hair sweeping over the peeks of skin on the back of her dress. And then I see who she's talking to—a tall blonde bastard. One who is currently beaming at her from ear to ear with the kind of affection that makes we want to snap his neck.

Fuck me, I'm an idiot.

Trying to make Sophie jealous has backfired spectacularly, practically pushing my wife into the arms of another, younger, handsome man.

I push past Silvia who grumbles my name to try and call me back. Ignoring her, I stalk straight toward Sophie, shouldering past idiots who get in my way until I'm finally interrupting their conversation to ask blondie, "Who the fuck are you?"

"Don't talk to him like that," Sophie has the nerve to snap at me, like she's giving me orders now.

"I'll talk to anyone however I fucking want, *wife*."

Rolling her eyes at me, she shares a conspiratorial grin with blondie that has me seeing red, the color the bastard will bleed when I gut him. Sophie may still have my favorite knife, but I have others.

"Lochlan, this is Cole, Vanessa's son." Goddamm it, I hate the sweet way she says the asshole's name. She pauses after the introduction, tilting her head of softly flowing black curls. "I guess that makes him my stepbrother."

That label doesn't make me feel any better. If he's not blood related, then I have no doubt he'll still want to fuck what's mine.

Blondie holds out his palm toward me for a handshake, still grinning. "I was at your wedding, and we've actually met once before that."

"Have we?" I ask as I squeeze his palm to the point of pain.

"Ah, yeah," he replies. Jerking his hand from mine he shoves it in his tux pants pocket. I'm happy to see he's no longer smirking until he says, "It was the night of the celebrity poker game."

I blink at him, wishing I didn't recall anything from that night, but unfortunately, I doubt I'll ever forget a second, including my conversation with Dante in the hallway which likely saved my life. "Right. You were one of Dante's uninvited tagalongs I was trying to make accommodations for at the last minute."

"Right. Now I'm glad you didn't have a table ready for me and my friends," Cole remarks. "And since you're back, my job of keeping Sophie company is fulfilled."

"Yes, it is," I adamantly agree.

"See you Monday morning bright and early, Soph," he tells my wife, using a shortened version of her name like he knows her so well. His perfect Colgate smile is also back in place. Thankfully he wanders off so that I don't have to knock all of those perfect white teeth out of his mouth.

Wait. He'll *see* Sophie Monday morning?

"What the fuck was he talking about?" I ask her. "You're not going to see him Monday or any other day bright and fucking early."

"You didn't have to be such a dick to Cole," Sophie huffs. That's twice now that I've had to hear his name on her lips, which is fucking infuriating.

"Answer my question. *Now.*"

"He's coming over to play tennis with me."

"No."

"Yes!" she exclaims so loudly that several heads turn in our direction. "Yes, he is. Cole is the closest thing I have to a friend thanks to my father keeping me locked away."

Rather than continue to argue in public that blondie's not coming anywhere near her if I'm not around, I ask, "How well do you know your stepbrother, princess?"

She shrugs. "He came to visit Vanessa before she and my dad got married. Then we spent a few weeks together while everything was happening with that Petrov guy..."

"Weeks?"

"Yes, on a private island with Cass, Cole's friends, and a bunch of guards of course."

She spent weeks on an island with the frat boy?

"Did you fuck him?"

"What? No!" she scoffs before lowering her voice. "I told you I was a virgin until you, until that night in the club." Her cheeks flush red in anger. "How can you be jealous of Cole when you refuse to stop fucking other women?"

"You better remember my rule, Sophie. If you lay a hand on him or if he dares to even try to touch you, I will eviscerate him and make you watch."

"No, you won't," she replies confidently with her chin lifted. She's sexy as hell when she tries to act all tough. "Because Dante would kill you for hurting Vanessa's son."

"Try me," I grit out. "And every time you say his name, you earn another lick from me tonight. You're at five right now."

Her eyes widen in surprise before she glances away trying to cover it. "I told you earlier that I want you to keep your filthy tongue in your mouth."

"Oh, I'm not talking about licks of my tongue, princess."

"Then what..."

"You'll find out soon enough," I assure her. "For now, we need to speak to a reporter and take a photo. Then there's someone I want you to meet."

"Who?"

"Julia Townsend. This way." I grab her right wrist, the one without the diamond bracelet to pull her over. Like an insolent child, Sophie tries to dig her heels in, so I tug harder until we're headed to our destination. Ungrateful little brat.

I give a local reporter five minutes to ask me a few questions about the event, the gardens being built to replace the ruined section of the casino, and then, as hoped, he asks if his photographer can get a photo of me with my new wife.

"Smile," I whisper in her ear when I pull her to my side. "Unless you want me to lock you away like Dante."

"Always manipulation tactics with you two," she murmurs but then thankfully flashes a brilliant smile toward the photographer.

Once that's over, I place a hand on Sophie's lower back to guide her toward our next encounter.

"Mrs. Townsend," I say, interrupting the wealthy widow's conversation with an ancient-looking hag who probably can't hear a word she says anyway. "Good to see you here tonight."

"Of course," she replies with a smile, turning toward me and Sophie. "Always happy to help a good cause, especially local ones. And please, call me Julia."

Rather than reminisce about the bombing, I tell her, "Speaking of noble local causes, I would like you to meet my wife, Sophie, another tennis enthusiast."

"Is that right?" Julia beams. "Then it's a pleasure to meet you, Sophie."

"You too," she says softly.

"Julia is a prolific philanthropist, contributing to a long list of charities across the state, including her own, the Townsend Tennis Center."

"I just try to help where I can, do what my husband would've wanted to do himself if he were still here with us."

"You run a tennis charity?" Sophie asks when she catches on.

"Julia's foundation provides youth tennis programs to the community for free, and low-cost private lessons for adults. She even has indoor courts."

"Really?" Sophie's definitely more interested in the woman now. "Indoor tennis courts?"

"Since we primarily teach kids ages six to sixteen, the Vegas heat can become a bit extreme."

"No kidding," she agrees. "I love playing outside, but sometimes..."

"A little air conditioning while you play would be divine?" Julia finishes with a broad smile.

"Exactly."

"We're always looking for volunteers if you have any free time."

"All I have is free time," Sophie mutters.

"Then you should join us. If you're interested in making a career out of it, you can even earn your USPTA teaching certification after six-months full time or twelve months part-time."

"Oh, no. I'm not good enough to be professional tennis association certified."

"My wife is being modest," I interject. "She spends most days on the court, regardless of the heat, all for her simple joy of the sport."

Sophie's head tilts toward me. "How do you know that?"

"Because you aren't aggressive enough to become a hardcore competitor."

Now she frowns at me. "Is that another way of saying I'll never be a great player?"

"It wasn't a criticism," I assure her, and give Julia a smile of apology for having this argument in front of her. "I just meant that for you, there's more to tennis than winning. Am I wrong?"

"No," Sophie replies softly, her glare saying she's still cross with me for some damn reason. I'm not the one who was practically moaning someone else's name over and over again.

"Winning is great, but the kids and adults we teach just want to have a little fun and get some exercise," Julia tells us. "How about I give you my business card and you can reach out if you're interested?"

"Yes, please. Thank you," Sophie says as she accepts the card and stares down at it long after Julia hurries away as if to avoid getting caught in another one of our marital arguments.

The excitement in Sophie's blue eyes as she tucks the card away carefully in her purse makes me think she'll call first thing tomorrow morning.

While I want her to be happy, and to find fulfillment in her days while I'm busy, that doesn't mean I'm not still furious with her for making plans with another man.

In fact, I spend the rest of the night of idle chit-chat with donors thinking about when and where I'm going to punish my wife.

It's definitely going to be tonight. The parking lot here is out of the question since I have no doubt Salvato has every inch covered in security cameras. I guess that means I can either punish her in the SUV on the way home or wait until we're back at the estate. Either way we'll have an audience since I know Sophie won't step foot into my bedroom. With witnesses, at least I'll be less likely to snap and fuck her brains out afterward.

When I'm finished, she'll probably beg to go back home, but that's not going to happen. Guess I'll have to figure out a way to console her.

We're back in the SUV headed home when I realize belatedly that because I'm wearing a tux, I'll have to borrow someone else's belt.

"Wolfe, give me your belt."

That statement has Sophie's head whipping around from gazing out the dark window to facing me. She's been nearly silent since our conversation with Julia Townsend, and barely even looked in my direction.

"Yes, sir," my head guard says without hesitation from the passenger seat. He just unfastens the seatbelt, then unbuckles the belt to slide it through the loops. Folding it in half, he swivels around in his seat to hand it over to me.

"Thanks," I tell him, not bothering to mention that he won't be getting it back after I'm done with it. Now it's my trophy. Possibly the final thread snapping on my marriage. A psychologist may even point out that I'm intentionally trying to ruin our unhappy union with this type of behavior. Despite knowing that, I'm not the least bit deterred thanks to my seething anger.

When we pull up to the front of the estate, one of the guards opens Sophie's door. She climbs out of the SUV with me right behind her. I snatch up a handful of her thick curls in my fist to pull her feet to an abrupt stop.

"What..." she trails off when I halt her steps, dropping her clutch to the ground.

"You're not going inside yet, princess." Wrapping her long hair around my fist three times, I grab her waist with my other hand to shove her stumbling around in her heels to the front of the vehicle. When she's facing the front bumper, I press her face down on the still-warm hood.

"Lochlan!" she shouts while trying to stand up straight again.

I lean over to whisper in her ear. "Oh, good, you do remember your husband's name."

Curving the front of my body around the back of hers, I let her feel how long and hard I already am in anticipation of her punishment, even if my dick won't be getting any relief until I'm alone in the shower.

"What are you doing?" she asks, going completely still underneath me.

"Do you remember those licks I mentioned earlier?"

My wife's body goes slack now, the fight completely leaving her so that her upper body is draped over the hood like a blanket. "The ones for saying Cole's name?" she asks me quietly.

"Yes. And that makes six. Time to pay up."

While my right hand continues to apply pressure to keep her head on the hood. I toss the belt down beside her, so my left hand can reach down to start hiking up the back of her long black dress. There's more of the material than I expected. The only way to make it stay out of the way is to bunch it up and shove it under the front of her body I have pinned to the hood.

When Sophie lifts her face enough to turn her head from facing right, looking at the belt, to the left, I let her. She gasps at the sight of the guards who are quietly observing us. They're gathered by the front entrance of the house, lined up facing us about twenty feet away. Hands clasped behind their backs, they're all standing at attention, patiently waiting, as if the scene before them is all part of a day's work.

It's dark enough out here in the driveway that from the glow of the sidewalk lights they won't see much of my wife's body, just her long legs and the swell of her ass in profile as I finally reveal it.

Mostly, they're here to keep me from going too far. And with good reason. Seeing the black thong caressing the crack of her beautiful ass drowns out every thought in my head for a long moment.

It's a pale, gorgeous, unmarked ass, but not for much longer.

I replace my right hand wrapped in her hair to wind it around my left so I can pick up the belt in my dominant hand. Then, I tell my wife, "You're getting six licks of the belt for saying another man's name to me, over and over again. And don't worry, I'll keep count for you."

Unable to resist, I remove my index finger from the belt long enough to run it down the string separating her ass cheeks. "I love these panties by the way." When I reach the crotch she squirms again, either trying to get away or wanting more. I don't even know what to make about her dampness. Did they get wet for blondie? Assuming so, I haul the folded belt over my shoulder then bring it down hard, swatting her ass with it.

Sophie cries out even louder than the *whap* of leather slapping her flesh. The fact that her scream makes my dick harder is beyond fucked up.

"That's one," I tell her.

"Don't you–" She tries to push herself up off the hood just as I land the second and third blow in quick succession, counting them aloud.

After the fourth lash, she sobs, "I hate you!" then turns her face away from the front of the house. If she was referring to me or the guards who refuse to help her, I'm not sure which. Probably both.

"Only two more to go. Unless..." I lean over her again to whisper in her ear and rub my dick on her ass. "Unless you're going to cancel your tennis date with blondie, in which case, I'll stop right now."

I wait for her response, grinding my hardness against that lacy thong while she sniffles. I'm certain she's had enough...

"No."

"No?" I repeat, convinced I misheard her. She's crying, sobbing even, and yet she won't concede to stop the pain.

"You're going to regret that decision," I warn her.

Because of her defiance, I put more force into the fifth and sixth lashes, certain by her shriek and the jolt of her body following each of them that they hurt like hell and are sure to leave red welts that remain on her ass for days.

Good. She needs the reminder to watch her mouth.

I'm not sure who is panting harder afterwards, me or her. I toss the belt on the hood, not caring if the buckle scuffs the paint to press the front of my body over her backside, eliciting a whimper from her. The fabric of my tux pants brushing her sore bottom is probably hellish right now.

Pressing my lips to her damp cheek before lapping up her salty tears with a swipe of my tongue, I tell her, "You can go to bed now, princess. Sweet dreams."

I lift my weight off her and unwind her hair from my fist. I take two steps back to put space between us before I take out my cock and shove it where it's not wanted.

I assumed Sophie would pop right up and run inside. Instead, she doesn't move. Well, other than her shoulders and back quivering from her soft sobs. And I just stand there and watch, waiting for her to pull her shit together. I didn't hurt her that badly.

Did I?

Fuck.

I look toward the guards as if they could provide some insight. Barely even a blink among them.

Right. This is my fuck-up to fix with my wife, not theirs.

20

Sophie

H*e beat me.*
Lochlan actually beat me with his belt just for saying Cole's name. No, not even his belt. One of the guard's belts that they gladly handed over on the way home. Did the guard know what his boss planned to do with it? How he planned to hurt me with it?

At first I was stunned by the slap of leather. But then, I don't understand why, but for some reason, those six licks from the belt made me long for Lochlan's tongue and his fingers, but mostly his dick to follow. Instead, he just stopped and told me to go to bed.

What the hell is wrong with me?

The lines on my ass burn so badly I'm afraid to even move a muscle. I'm still trembling, tears streaming down my face, and yet, I'm mostly distraught that Lochlan got me all worked up and then just stopped, sending me off to bed alone. I wanted him to keep going.

Not with the belt.

Maybe with the belt?

I'm so damn confused. All I know is that when I felt him long and hard against my backside, I wanted him inside of me again. I wanted him to take me like this, bent over the hood of the SUV with my hair wrapped around his fist, and his guards watching, just because he could, which is so incredibly messed up.

"Sophie?" Lochlan says quietly. I shiver when he places a palm on my upper back while the other fists the belt on the hood, causing me to flinch away. Neither of those things halt him. He doesn't lift the belt again, but his fingers on my back gently stroke my skin through the crisscrossing of the dress. My dress that's still hiked up around my waist, the fabric bunched and shoved underneath my pelvis. The added pressure there just increases the throbbing ache between my thighs.

"Are you going to stay out here all night?" he grumbles, sounding like he's growing more frustrated with me. "Just to warn you, princess, if I have to carry you inside, it's going to be straight to my bed."

God, yes.

His palm moves lower, skipping over the bunched material to cup my left ass cheek. It took the least damage of the two. My right cheek is on fire while the left is mostly unharmed. Lochlan must know that since he continues groping it.

"Let's go, Sophie," my husband demands. He sadly withdraws his hand from my ass...only to swat at it lightly. There's enough force that my hips buck, pressing my pelvis into the bundle of my dress. An embarrassing whimper-like moan escapes my lips, causing Lochlan's hand to freeze a moment before he swats my flesh again.

"Ah!" I cry out a little louder. Again, and again, his large, warm palm spanks my bottom while I lie on the hood, melting in a needy puddle, producing the exact same sound over and over again. My fingernails try to dig into the slick paint of the vehicle desperate for something to hold on to. Desperate for my husband's big hand to move lower. I'm almost ready to beg for more when Lochan's fingers dip between my thighs. We both groan when he rubs the crotch of my panties.

"Drenched," he grits out. "You're so damn wet."

I'm unable to feel embarrassed or anything else because he's finally touching me where the pulsing ache is the strongest. When Lochan's fingers fall away, I sob in frustration ready to finish myself off with my own hand if necessary. Before I can lift it from the hood, my panties are tugged down my legs, and then his fingers are replaced with...his wet, flicking tongue.

"Oh, god!" I scream, pressing my forehead to the hood as he licks me frantically. He shoves a finger inside me, fucking me with it as if there's some race I'm unaware of for how fast he can make me come. Not that I mind. Fast is good. Fast is... "Oh! *Oh!* I'm...*Lochlan!*" My hips jerk and buck as my release slams into me, so intense it's nearly painful.

As the tremors slow, I feel Lochlan's lips on my right ass cheek, softly pressing kisses to what I have no doubt are the marks left from the belt.

When he finally stands up again, I hear his zipper go down, then the prod of the rounded tip of his dick seeking a way inside me.

"No," I tell him, surprised when he actually halts his progress.

"No?" he repeats.

"No."

"Why not?" he leans over me, his flesh pressing into my ass when he fists my hair again to lift my head to see my damp face "Are you going to get on your knees then?"

On my... "No."

He presses forward into the wetness between my thighs, groaning deep. "I'm aching, Sophie. I need to fuck my wife."

"You hurt me."

He's quiet for a moment before saying, "You fucking deserved it."

"So do you." I push my bottom back, making his cock slide along my damp slit. Now he growls his frustration in my ear as his grip tightens on my hair.

"Do that again," he orders, and I do because I enjoy teasing him.

"Fuck," Lochlan whispers. Burying his face against my neck, his breathing grows more rapid along my skin while taking himself in his hand to push against my entrance, stroking along my clit. "Let me inside of you."

I shake my head, incapable of words. Why is he even asking my permission? I thought by now he would've taken me...

"Goddamm it, Sophie!" he shouts his frustration right before his fist pumps faster and faster until his thick liquid joins the dampness between my thighs.

His cum.

I made him come in his hand outside of me, so close to where he wanted, but was denied entry. And I guess he didn't want me bad enough to just slam inside of me. Now, I'm glad since he wouldn't have used protection.

When he stops moving, just breathing heavily against my neck, I warn him, "If you ever touch me with a belt again, I'll choke you with it in your sleep."

His huff of a chuckle warms my cheek. "Ruthless, princess. You're fucking ruthless." Lifting his weight from me, he slaps the sore right side of my ass, zips up his pants, and then walks into the house, gravel crunching under his shoes as he leaves me sprawled half-naked on the hood.

21

Lochlan

The number of times I've rewatched and jerked off to the video surveillance of whipping Sophie after the fundraiser isn't healthy. I can't get enough of her mewling for me. The sound is addictive, and since I can't hear it live, the video is the best I can do.

Snow White somehow guilted me into going down on her as an apology, when I never fucking apologize for anything. I've tried to tell myself that I did it because I realized she was turned on from the belt whipping I gave her. Either way, I got on my knees for her yet again, and all I got in return was jerking off on her slick pussy lips.

Sure, the wetness between her legs felt better than my own hand, but it's not even close to what I needed. I thought for sure she was going to let me fuck her tight pussy, erupt inside her again, so I could see my cum drip down her thighs, all while the guards watched.

Why the addition of witnesses to the attempt at impregnating my wife was so hot, I'm not sure. I just want the world to know who she belongs to, that I'm the only one who gets to have that snug cunt or fill her up with my seed. Only me because I think she really was a goddamn virgin the night I fucked her.

No matter how badly I want her, how much I ache to claim her, Sophie refuses to let me inside of her.

Pervert. Bastard. You're disgusting.

She has no idea how right she is about all of those things she called me. If I wasn't certain Salvato would kill me as soon as she told him I fucked her after she refused me, I would've just shoved inside of her and taken what I wanted. What I would kill to have again.

The only way around that outcome would have been to slap my palm over her mouth before she could reject me.

And that would make me a bastard and ensure Sophie never let me near her again. And without her, I'll lose everything in the trial, and won't have a chance at being Salvato's successor.

Sophie's already warned me that if I hit her with a belt again, she would choke me to death with one in my sleep.

It's impossible to sleep with one eye open, what little I do sleep, which means, unless I keep a guard at my bedroom door all night, it's possible she could slip in and actually attempt to kill me.

She probably wouldn't go that far, but I won't put anything past Sophie once she puts her mind to it. I think she can be nearly as ruthless as I can when necessary.

I haven't forgotten her threat to also stab me in my dick if I step foot in her room. It's the only reason why I haven't gone looking for the knife my mother gave me. My wife has boundaries and I need to respect them. Some of them at least. Not going through her things is one of them I'll uphold.

Since the night of her spanking, there hasn't been a hint of Sophie fingering herself on the cameras, making me wonder if she doesn't think about it obsessively like I do, or if she's figured out some way to hide it from me.

Either way, my days and nights are spent being distracted by my infuriating wife.

The only good thing is that Warwick seemed happy enough with our photo op at the fundraiser. He's still trying to convince the plaintiff's counsel to try and settle before trial and told me to keep up the good publicity with my pretty new wife.

If Sophie goes to work with Julia Townsend's charity, it could certainly help my image as well.

And I have no doubt that she'll call the widow soon to join her cause.

Now if I could just find the fucking bomber to pin the catastrophe on them...

When my phone dings with a text message notification, I pause the replay on my tablet. Picking up the device, I read the short update from Lena bright and early Monday morning just as promised.

Her stepbrother has arrived on the court.

I quickly type back a response.

Keep a close eye on them. I'll be there shortly.

Sophie

I was both equally surprised that Cole not only showed up to play tennis with me Monday morning as we agreed, but that Lochlan didn't have the guards immediately send him away.

The day is already warming up by the time we finish our first match with me winning two out of three sets, trying to take it easy on my stepbrother who is rusty.

"Water break?" Cole suggests, swiping his forearm across his sweaty forehead.

"Yes, please," I easily agree.

Strolling over to the fence surrounding the court, I bend down and pick up my stainless-steel gallon water jug to take a big swig. I love it because it will stay cold for two whole days despite the temperature outdoors.

Following behind me, Cole clears his throat. "Ah, Sophie, I hope you don't take this the wrong way, like I'm perving on you or whatever, but what the hell happened to your ass?"

"What are you..."

Oh, shit.

I freeze with my jug halfway to my mouth for another sip when I realize what he's referring to. He must have seen some of the lower belt marks Lochlan made Thursday night when I bent over to pick up my water.

Glancing over my shoulder, I find Cole's head cocked to one side, still trying to see the marks. Spinning around to face him, and to remove the evidence of my punishment, I cut my eyes to Lena and Toni. Seeing their rapt attention on us, I wave innocently at them while whisper-yelling to him, "Stop looking at my ass! He'll see you on the surveillance cameras and he'll be furious."

"He being Lochlan?" Cole asks when he comes closer.

"Yes," I answer then offer him my jug of water since he only brought a small water bottle that he finished off the first fifteen minutes.

Cole takes the jug but doesn't drink from it, his brow still furrowed in thought. "Lochlan did that to you? With what? A belt?"

When he tries to slip around me to see it again, I walk backward until my back hits the fence, rattling it.

"Everything okay?" Lena calls out.

"Yep!" I assure her before turning back to my too-curious-for-his-own-good stepbrother. "You can't look at my ass, Cole!" As soon as his name leaves my mouth, I slap my palm over it. I have to be more careful. I'm not sure if the cameras are too far away to pick up audio or not. Or if Lochlan will punish me for saying another man's name even if he's not present. After all, that's what left me with the marks...

190

and turned into me coming on Lochlan's tongue then refusing to let him inside of me.

The reminder of how I denied him makes me smile when I lower my palm from my mouth again. Honestly, I didn't think Lochlan would stop. I wanted to push him, to see him lose control after I felt so vulnerable bent over the SUV in front of half a dozen guards. They saw and heard everything, including me moaning while he licked me. I made the powerful mob boss kneel in front of witnesses, which still feels like a win.

"Start explaining, Soph."

"Can we just pretend that you didn't see...that?"

Frowning harder, Cole says, "You just got married to him! If Lochlan is already beating you with a belt, then you should tell Dante."

"No. It's fine. I-I deserved it, apparently."

Cole's jaw drops open with a scoff that reminds me of his mother's. "I don't care what you did, Sophie. You don't deserve to be hit for it!"

"It's not a big deal. And trust me, he won't use a belt on me again."

"How can you be certain? Because he promised not to? There will most likely be a next time, and the violence could escalate. That's how abusers operate."

"Maybe so, but I warned Lochlan that I would choke him with a belt in his sleep if he ever touched me with one again."

Cole blinks at me silently for a long moment. "You did what now?"

"I threatened to kill him in his sleep. I think he knows I'll do it too. Or at least I would try..."

Cole laughs as if he thinks I'm joking or that I wouldn't dare.

"Let's just play. Drink up, then it's your serve," I tell him before heading back to my side of the court while he finally guzzles some water.

～

I'm not the least bit shocked when, about half an hour later, a group of men march toward the courts from the main house. My husband leads them from the front, looking flawless in his custom three-piece suit.

"Time for doubles?" Cole calls out. I can't help my wince from just thinking his damn name in the same vicinity as Lochlan.

But my husband's attention isn't on me; it's on Cole as the guards wait outside the fence and he strides through the gate.

I'll give my stepbrother credit; he doesn't look intimidated by Lochlan and his crew of waiting armed guards. Heck, he even walks right up to him. Maybe because Cole knows as well as I do that the fear of Dante's wrath will probably keep him unharmed. Guess we're about to find out.

"Why did you hit her with a fucking belt?" Cole asks while pointing his racquet toward me.

Oh, crap. I jog over to the two men, hoping to prevent him from pushing Lochlan too far.

I make it in time to hear Lochan's growled response. "Why were you looking at my wife's ass?"

"Her skirt is short, and the red welts stand out," Cole explains calmly.

Finally, Lochan looks at me. Even with his eyes covered by sunglasses, I know his gaze has lowered to the hem of my white pleated skirt. "Yes, it is a rather short skirt."

"Well?" Cole demands, refusing to let it go.

Lochlan's jaw ticks before he faces him again. "The marks on her ass are not your concern, blondie. They're between me and her."

"I think her father would want to know why you're beating his daughter, don't you?"

Without missing a beat, Lochlan says, "Do you think her father would also want to know how wet her pussy was after her whipping? Or how she screamed my name when I licked up every drop?"

Oh my god.

My cheeks go up in flames thanks to my embarrassment of him being so damn blunt after something so personal.

Cole clears his throat and glances away from Lochlan, thankfully not in my direction either. "No, I doubt Dante would want all of those details."

"It's all or nothing in this case. If I had to bet, I'm guessing Dante would've gouged your eyes out just for staring at his daughter's ass."

Sighing heavily, Cole's shoulders slump before he turns back to us. "You know what? I think the heat is starting to get to me. We'll continue this set another day, Soph?"

I nod my agreement, even though I'm not sure if he'll be allowed to step foot on the property again. "Sure thing. Thanks, Col-" I barely catch myself before I say his entire name. "Thanks for coming over," I say instead.

He smiles, and with a wave of his racquet, he walks out the gate and toward his own waiting SUV and guards, no doubt sent by my father. At least they all stayed far enough away, leaning against the vehicle so I wouldn't have to wonder if they were spying on me for my dad or not.

Facing my husband, I tell him through clenched teeth, "You didn't have to come home and run him off. I have Lena and Toni here watching over us every second."

"Maybe I just wanted to see your beautiful face in person, rather than on a grainy feed."

I knew it! He was watching us, and likely saw the whole exchange where Cole blatantly stared at my ass.

Holding my arm and racquet out, I tell him, "Well, now you've seen me and ran off my only friend. Mission complete."

"Hmm. You're more smug than usual today, princess." I can't be certain, but I would almost bet his eyes are narrowed behind his aviator glasses like he's studying my face.

I hate that I can't see his shielded eyes but that he can see mine since I prefer wearing a visor. It doesn't feel fair that I always have to look up at him either. It's like I'm always at a disadvantage when it comes to Lochlan. Still, I answer his question with the truth.

"I don't know what you're talking about." I'm not smug. He's the one who is always smirking at me.

"Oh, I think you do know. I think you enjoy making me jealous. Taunting me. Tempting me. Teasing me."

"Maybe I do." I don't bother to deny that I get immense joy from doing all those things. The only time it feels like I have the upper hand is when I'm manipulating Lochlan or rejecting him.

When he doesn't respond, just keeps staring at me behind the wall of reflective lenses, I turn away to go grab my water jug, making sure I bend over to give him a nice long look at my ass. "I'm done for the day too. Time for a shower."

Once I straighten and head for the gate, I see that Lochlan has finally removed his sunglasses, as if he wanted an unobstructed view of my backside. Or the damage he did to it.

"Yes, you are a very dirty girl," my husband remarks as he follows me off the court. "You know I won't be able to resist seeing you stand naked under the spray, watching the suds running down your tits to your stomach and down between your marked ass cheeks."

Of course I knew he would be watching me shower. It's the only chance he gets to see me nearly naked. I just hope the shower stall steams up enough to hide most of my body from his view. I bet the fog infuriates him. Knowing how frustrated he will be makes me even hotter than the hours spent playing tennis under the Vegas sun.

As if hearing my thoughts on the short walk back to the main house, Lochlan says from behind me, "How would you like to try one of my toys to alleviate that ache between your legs?"

Asshole.

I hate how he seems to always know when I'm turned on. But then again, it seems like just being around my husband makes me wet.

Knowing the cocky bastard is probably certain I'll refuse his offer out of self-consciousness, I glance over my shoulder to tell him, "Sure."

He grins like I've just made his day. "I'll have Lena bring a device to your room. Unless you need me to demonstrate how to use it?"

"Thanks, but I'm sure I can figure it out on my own," I reply sweetly.

22

Sophie

Twenty minutes later, I've finished my shower and dried my hair. I head to the bedroom with my towel still wrapped around my chest, and find a box with a bow tied on it waiting at the foot of the bed as promised.

Removing the lid, I stare down at the object...and don't have a fucking clue what I'm supposed to do with it.

There's a long, thick device that's shaped like a broken branch of a tree next to a tube of something that claims it's a type of jelly.

I'm too proud to ask Lena or Toni who are likely on their lunch break. No, if I ask them then Lochlan will find out, and I don't want to remind the prick that I'm clueless about anything to do with sex while he's beyond expert level.

Unhooking the towel, I let it fall to the floor, figuring it'll distract Lochlan while I consider the toy a little longer. The longer, thicker side obviously goes inside of me, and I assume that once it's all the way in, that will put the smaller, split antennas right against my clit.

The jelly though...I pick it up and see the description on the back that says it "compliments your body's natural lubrication." I figure that means it will help the device slide inside of me easier.

Except, I'm not sure if I put the lube in me with my fingers or put it on the toy.

Lying down on the bed with both items in my hands, I decide to slather the jelly on the part that goes up in me. I'm already soaking wet just thinking about Lochlan watching me right now.

I've never been so blatantly naked like this in my room before, but I'm hoping it'll even the playing field a little between us. He can see what he can't have while I try out the sex toy.

The dildo is heavy, as if there's more to it than just the shape. It must turn on and do...something. Vibrate I assume. I guess I'll find out if or when Lochlan decides to oblige since there are no buttons on it that I can find.

It meets more resistance and takes longer than I expect to get it inside of me. I close my eyes, try to forget I'm being watched, and think about the other night when I was bent over the hood of the SUV and Lochlan was licking me from front to back, then using the tip of his tongue on my clit. That's what really gets me going.

Gradually, it becomes easier to move the toy, to adjust to the fullness. There's no pain like the night Lochlan took my virginity. Not that it was all bad that night. Still, this is much more pleasant.

Once it's all the way inserted, the antennas brushing my clit, I glance up to the camera as if to ask him what now. While I'm definitely aroused, I don't think I'm anywhere close to coming. It's not nearly as fun when I'm putting things in my body. I prefer when...

With a gasp of surprise, I jolt into a sitting position when the damn thing suddenly begins buzzing inside me. Not just buzzing but...Oh. My. God.

The device starts thrusting all on its own without me guiding it. I collapse onto the pillow again, and my back arches. My free hand grips the bedding beside me to hold on. The tip is also swirling deep inside. And those antennas? Holy shit. They flicker faster than Lochlan's tongue, tickling me. There is so much happening at once that it's overwhelming, but in a good way.

Tipping my head back and closing my eyes again, I keep one hand on the device to make sure it stays where it is while I try to relax and enjoy the sensations that imitate the things Lochlan did that first night.

Not that it's the same.

Not even close.

How could the cold silicone toy ever compare to his big cock shoving inside of me so roughly, so urgently?

I bite down on my bottom lip as I edge closer and closer to a release, the pressure building in my core.

Remembering the way Lochlan pinned my wrists above my head, restraining me while he fucked me sends me over the cliff. I shatter apart from that memory.

My orgasm seems shorter, less intense than the ones Lochlan gives. Like a single sparkler compared to an entire fireworks show.

The lack of his molten release filling me up at the end is sadly missing too, even if I shouldn't have liked that part.

After the pleasure leaves me, I'm so sensitive I quickly withdraw the device and toss it down next to me on the mattress while I catch my breath. It keeps vibrating for several more minutes before finally turning off again.

Still, I don't lift my gaze to the camera. No, I just lie there recovering a little longer, trying not to think about how much better it would've been if it had been Lochlan's fingers, tongue, or cock inside of me instead.

While the orgasm was okay, now I just feel...lonely. I tell myself that I'm just sad that it's over.

Finally, I roll out of bed to get dressed in an oversized tee and cotton shorts in the closet. When I return to the bed, I pick up the toy and take it to the bathroom to wash it with soap and water, figuring that should be safe enough.

After drying it off with a towel, I start to return it to the box when it begins rattling in my hand so suddenly that I drop it on the bathroom floor.

Jackass.

I wait until the vibrating stops again before snatching it up. I only make it maybe two steps before he turns it on again. This time I swear it just thrusts itself out of my hand and jumps to the floor where it continues to flop around as if possessed.

While I watch it, waiting for him to make it stop again, I swear I can hear that asshole laughing at me through the walls. And I hate it so much when he laughs at my inexperience.

～

Lochlan

Catching Sophie off-guard when she's obviously uncomfortable handling the phallic sex toy is more hilarious than it should be.

The second time she drops it, a bark of laughter escapes me. As if hearing it, my wife glares up at the camera in the corner of the bathroom.

Once it's off, I don't press the button to turn it on again. Not until she's holding it over the box. This time when it jumps out of her hands, I'm certain I hear her shout, "Asshole!"

Laughter takes me over again. I can't even remember the last time I laughed so hard. Maybe I'm just in a good mood from jerking off watching Sophie masturbate naked. While I would rather have been inside of her, it was a much-needed release. At least I could watch the image of the toy on the phone screen mimic its current movements. I saw each and every thrust, decided when to make it go faster, vibrate harder, when it should flick her clit.

I can't deny I was jealous of the damn device going where I can't. In fact, if Sophie hadn't washed it off, I would've licked it clean just to get another taste of her.

Why does my wife have to be so damn stubborn?

I've never been jealous of anyone in my life and now there's a growing list—her blond stepbrother, a vibrator, and every man in every room who looks at what's mine.

At dinner, Sophie's cheeks are still glowing with a beautiful rosy color when she takes her seat, wearing a casual tee and shorts. I want to kiss those cheeks, but most of all, I want it to be my body part that gives her that just fucked flush.

"Have fun earlier?" I can't help but ask her.

"I'm sure you know that I did," she replies without lifting her eyes to me.

Ah, she's still embarrassed about playing with herself or revealing every inch of her naked body to me. Probably both. Before I can assure her there's nothing for her to be insecure about, Sophie says, "And now I know that I don't need a single part of *your* body to get off."

"What?" I ask in confusion.

"With the toy, I don't have to put up with your bad temper to get what I need."

Son of a bitch.

She would rather have the toy than me making her come?

No. There's no way. She's lying. Has to be. I don't buy for a second that she prefers a vibrating rubber cock to mine or my tongue.

"Too bad a vibrator can't spank you, restrain you, or finger you under the dinner table so your father can hear you moan when you come."

Now Sophie looks at me as if shocked that I know her body so well, all the little things that get her so hot. And hell yes, her cheeks flush a deeper shade of red.

"Those are a few of your favorite fetishes, aren't they princess?"

"I don't have enough experience to know what my fetishes are yet," she says. Then she asks, "What are your fetishes?"

If I told her the truth, that I constantly fantasize about taking her hard when she can't get away or stop me, I doubt she would ever let me touch her again. The restraints I installed in my bedroom were a stupid idea. Sophie's too innocent to want to be tied down and used that way. She probably dreams of romance and lovemaking in candlelight, not hardcore fucking like savage animals.

Avoiding her question, I simply tell her, "I'll text you a link to the app with the password so you can go buck wild with your new toy." If she would rather fuck the rubber cock, then...I give the hell up.

For half a second, it looks like disappointment on Sophie's face, disappointment that I won't be controlling the device. But it was probably just my imagination since she says, "Great, thanks. It is waterproof, right?"

"Yes."

Picturing her standing in the shower or lying in the bathtub using it, makes my dick dribble precum.

My obsession with Sophie and sex is definitely an unhealthy habit. Wanting her is a distraction I don't need when I have a bomber to find, a civil case to settle before trial, and an empire to inherit from her father.

23

Sophie

Lochlan and I have breakfast and dinner together each day, but that's the only time we see each other for an entire week after he gave me the vibrating toy. Not that I've used it again.

He may look annoyed with me, but that doesn't mean he doesn't still ask me a million questions about my day. Lochlan wants to hear every little detail, no matter how minor. I've been keeping myself busy at Julia Townsend's tennis center, so I have a few stories by each night. The facility is amazing with indoor and outdoor courts and so many amazing kids.

The first day I just observed, watching the other instructors teach classes, mostly helping with equipment. The second day I was allowed to offer constructive criticism to the children, give tips on improving their swings or serves. It was intimidating at first, wondering if my advice was helpful or not. The girls and boys actually listened to me intently, as if I held all the secrets to the game of tennis. And seeing them not only take my suggestions but implement them and improve make me feel like I had made a difference, even if it's only a small one.

"Time to pack it up!" Stacy, one of Julia's teachers calls out to the courts, ending the six- to eight-year-old class for the afternoon.

When I grab the rolling cart to start rounding up all the tennis balls to get ready for the next class, two little girls follow me around, helping with my collection.

"I hope I grow up to be tall like you, Miss Sophie," one of the girls remark. Nora, I think, is the redhead's name.

"Me too," her friend Ellie agrees, her ponytails swinging as she nods her head. "And as pretty as you. Do you have a boyfriend, Miss Sophie?"

"Ah, well, not really. But I do sort of have a husband."

"You're married!" the two girls squeal as I bend down to gather up tennis balls.

"Yes, I am."

"Did he give you this bracelet?" Nora asks, one small fingertip poking the stones. I probably shouldn't wear the tennis bracelet on the courts but it's too pretty to leave at home, and secure enough that it's not going to fall off. "Are those real diamonds?"

"Yes, he did, and they are," I tell her, holding out my wrists for her to see it closer.

"Wow. He must be super rich!" Ellie exclaims, making me laugh.

"Very rich," I agree. "He built me my own tennis court with a shade over it."

Ellie beams up at me. "He must really like you."

"I guess he has his reasons," I tell them, rather than try to explain to children that he's trying to buy what's between my legs and my father's blessing to be his heir.

"Ellie, Nora, your parents are here!" Stacy calls out.

"Will you be back next week to help me with my backhand?" Nora asks me.

"Absolutely," I agree. "See you both then." I wave goodbye to them then continue my circuit to collect all the scattered tennis balls along the walls.

"All done," I say when I take the cart back to the equipment station.

"Thanks, Sophie," Stacy says. "And don't worry, you won't be the ball girl forever."

"I don't mind," I assure her with a smile.

"You'll be teaching your own classes soon."

"Oh, I don't know about that."

"Why not? The students have had nothing but great things to say about you. They even listen when *you* offer them pointers. It's not always easy to get them to follow instructions. Most want to do things their way more than they want to listen to another adult telling them what to do all day."

"I don't blame them. They just want to come here to have fun, not be perfect little tennis prodigies."

"Fun is great, but for some a tennis scholarship may be the only way to escape poverty and actually get to go to college."

"Really?"

"Really. Not that we want them to eat, sleep, and breathe tennis. We just want those with talent and determination to let it take them as far as possible."

"I've never had to think about those sorts of things," I admit.

"Truth be told, me either," Stacy says with a smile. "We were lucky."

"Guess so," I agree. "Nora and Ellie think my husband must be super rich."

"They're adorable. And they're not wrong. The Dunne family have been major donors to the center since Julia first thought up the idea for it."

"Really?"

"Well, the donations are anonymous to the public, but there's always a paper trail that we see in the office."

"Why would they make anonymous donations?"

Stacy lifts an eyebrow. "Everyone knows how the Dunnes earned their wealth."

"Of course." A tennis center for children wouldn't want to have any association with a brothel empire. "How major are the Dunne family contributions?" I can't help but ask.

"Probably as much as that bracelet on your wrist."

"I don't have even the slightest idea how much it's worth," I tell her honestly. "A lot?"

"I bet that ice is worth about the same as this building we're standing in."

"Really?"

"Really. But we both know there are more important things than money."

"There are definitely some things money can't buy," I agree. And I would like to think that I'm one of them.

Why would Lochlan ever want to be with someone who can be bought for the right price like one of his whores?

Unless...that's all he's ever known—women who trade sex for cash and pretty things. He's never said much about his mother, which makes me wonder if she was only with his father for his mountains of money.

It's none of my business. And even if I asked, I doubt my husband would tell me anything about his life.

While Lochlan may tolerate having conversations with me during breakfast and dinner, all he really wants from me is my father's empire and sex.

Money, power, and sex is all he'll ever want.

And I refuse to be another one of his whores.

Lochlan

It's been a week since the afternoon I watched Sophie get herself off. Seven days since I saw her naked. The few times I've allowed myself to check in on her through the video surveillance she was fully clothed, never using the toy, much to my disappointment.

And while most men would love to be in my shoes, standing before two beautiful naked brawling blondes, I would rather be at home eating dinner with a woman who thinks I'm a disgusting bastard.

"Well, boss, what are you going to do about this bitch?" Dana asks. I've just heard both sides of the argument about why she and Tricia were in a hair-pulling fight trying to claw each other's eyes. Apparently, Dana took Tricia's regular client because she ran over on time with someone else. Dana shouldn't have tried to poach the man, but Tricia shouldn't have been late for an appointment. The red, bleeding marks on both their faces mean no shift tonight or for the next several ones, so I make my final decision. And I'm still wondering why the fuck I'm here.

"You're both fired. Pack your shit and get out tonight," I tell them which is met with swears and indignant scoffs. Turning to Mary, the house madam who is paid to run this place like a well-oiled cum machine, I ask her, "Why the fuck couldn't you handle this without involving me?"

"Because Tricia and Dana are our two highest earners," she explains while wringing her wrinkled hands as the two women begin to sob and shove each other again.

"Enough!" I yell at them. To Mary, I say, "So what if they are high earners? It's the third strike for both of them, so they're done."

"What will we tell their regulars?"

"I don't give a fuck what you tell them, and they won't either. Tell them to pick another girl on the house for the first fuck if they bitch. But either way, those two are done. There are rules, and they don't change for anyone. And the reason there are rules is so I don't have to come down here and get involved in shit. Do your job, Mary, or the next time I have to come down here, it'll be to find your replacement."

"Yes, sir. I'm so sorry. It won't happen again," she promises with glistening eyes.

"Now get them dressed and out of here."

Leaving the destroyed bedroom, I make it halfway down the stairs where Owen and the guards are waiting for me when my phone rings. I would probably have ignored a call from anyone other than Sophie's guards or Warwick.

"Yeah?" I answer.

"Hiring that PR firm is working. Marrying Snow White and taking her to the fundraiser helped like I told you it would," my attorney says, getting right to the point. I'm not surprised that he also thinks my wife looks like the Disney princess. "The lawyers have all agreed to sit down for a settlement conference with both of us a week from today."

"That's a good thing, right? Rather than take our chances at trial?"

"As good as it'll probably get if they're ready to sit down and talk numbers in person. They want us to come to them in LA, though."

"Fuck. Okay. Send me the information. I'll make flight arrangements for us," I agree.

"Great. And Lochlan? Don't get your hopes up. If I had to guess, we're still looking at a loss of three or four hundred million."

I can't even begin to wrap my head around that much of a loss after I end the call. And I don't want to right now.

In the lobby, I find Owen and Shana getting friendly, my brother nowhere to be found.

"Where's Flynn?" I ask them.

"Where do you think?" Owen chuckles, tipping his chin up toward the second-floor rooms.

"We're leaving. He can find a ride home," I tell him. "And I need you to book a plane for a week from today. Warwick will be sending over the details."

When I turn to walk out the door, Shana shouts, "Loch, wait!"

"What?" I bark at her.

"You weren't going to visit me before leaving?"

"No, I'm trying to get home to my *wife* for dinner," I remind her, even though I know she's well aware that I'm married now. "Owen is welcome to stay, though."

My second opens his mouth no doubt to agree to some fun, when Shana steps around him to strut up to me, close enough to touch but knowing better if she wants to keep her fucking hands. "While you're here, you may as well work off some of your...frustrations." She gives me a pout as if she actually gives a shit about my frustrations rather than my cash.

"What are you talking about?" I ask. Sure, I'm more high-strung than usual because I'm not getting laid, but it can't be that obvious that I have a terminal case of blue balls.

"Come on, Loch. There have been rumors," she says softly.

"Rumors?" I snap, glancing to Owen who shrugs his wide shoulders.

"Rumors that your arranged marriage was just a business arrangement, that your young wife still won't put out, and that you give her pleasure and get nothing in return."

"Who the fuck told you that? Did you tell her?" I ask Owen.

"Hell, no."

Yes, it may be the truth, but it's nobody's business. "Who then? Flynn? A guard from the estate? I'll teach them to mind their fucking business!"

"I don't remember who it was," Shana says while biting her bottom lip. "Several girls have heard it, actually. It seems like everyone knows. It must be hard for you to play the part of the intimidating bossman when you can't even get your wife on her knees, even after you bought all those diamonds for her..."

Grabbing Shana by her throat, I slam her back into the nearest wall. "Shut your fucking mouth."

"Easy, Loch," Owen tries to warn me as he approaches us. "You're down two girls tonight. No need to make it three."

"Do it," Shana whispers. "Take your anger out on me. I know exactly what you need."

"Oh, yeah? And what do I need?"

"My lips wrapped around your big cock while you fuck my mouth. You could tie me up how you like..."

"That sounds like more fun than burying a dead whore, right, Loch?" Owen asks.

It doesn't escape my notice that she said *how I like*, not *how she likes*, as if my kink is something to be tolerated or endured if it's required. The truth is that what Shana likes, or any other woman, has never mattered to me. Sex with them has always been about me and my selfish desires. What turns me on.

Unlike with Sophie.

I would do anything to find out what my wife needs, what it would take to finally get her into my bed.

While I think she enjoyed her spanking, I'm not stupid enough to take a belt to her again. She may look delicate and innocent but if she put her mind to it, I have no doubt that she would figure out how to choke me to death in my sleep just like she promised.

And if she found out that I fucked another woman tonight then that may be enough to push my princess over the crazy bitch ledge.

Just because I refuse to cross that line, doesn't mean I shouldn't indulge in some live-action porn while easing the ache.

"Do you by chance have a white tennis skirt?" I ask Shana when I release her throat.

24

Sophie

After cleaning up following my long day at the tennis center, I step into the dining room a few minutes after seven expecting to find a grumpy Lochlan waiting for me. But his seat at the head of the table is empty and there's not even a place setting for him.

"Lochlan just messaged me," Lena says when she comes in behind me. "He won't be able to make it home in time for dinner tonight."

"Oh," I say when I turn around to face her, ready to head back to my room. "Then I'll just wait until he's back to eat too. I'm not that hungry," I lie.

Lena winces. "He specifically said that you shouldn't wait for him."

"He doesn't want me to wait?"

With a few pokes of her finger on her phone she turns it around, showing me the screen and the exact message from Lochlan.

"Wow. So, he won't be home until late tonight? Where is he?" I didn't see that information on her text message.

"He didn't say."

"Right, but do you know where he's at or what he's doing?" When Lena doesn't answer me, her silence is answer enough. "The guards all communicate with each other throughout the day, so you do know where he's at, don't you?"

Lena doesn't say a word, so I look around her tall frame to ask Toni. "Will you tell me?"

Her eyes go from me to Lena who turns to face her, as if to intimidate her.

"I'm sorry, Sophie," Lena mutters.

"Yeah, sorry, Soph. He's the boss," Toni adds. "You know how it is."

Scoffing, I shake my head and glare at each in turn. "I can't believe you two! I thought we were..." I start to say friends, but Lena and Toni aren't my friends. They're paid by Lochlan to keep me safe. Their loyalty will always be to the man who pays their salaries.

And since I'm in such a bitchy mood, mad at them and my husband wherever the hell he is, I do something really shitty.

"Could one of you make sure the lights are turned on over the tennis court? I need to hit some balls for a few hours, probably until it's dark out."

"Now?" Lena asks at the same time Toni screeches, "It won't be dark for hours!"

"Oh, right. If I leave the house and Lochlan's not home, then you have to stay with me. I'm so sorry." I take a little pleasure in throwing back the worthless apology in their faces before I go get changed. "I hope neither of you had any plans tonight."

I do feel pretty wretched for making Toni and Lena work over tonight. I shouldn't take my anger at Lochlan out on them. It's just, I didn't want to be alone tonight, and I am a little pissed that after spending every day for nearly two weeks with them, I stupidly thought they liked being around me even if it was their job.

After years of being on my own at home, it felt nice to have company and easy conversations. The guards my father hired never spoke a word to me, probably because he forbade them. I'm glad because it meant I never forgot who they worked for and why they were there.

Honestly, there's no reason why Toni and Lena can't just ask two of the many guards positioned around the grounds to take over babysitting me so they can go home.

I even suggested it after about half an hour, but Lena informed me that it was Lochlan's rule that they stay, and she wouldn't break it.

Where the hell could that bastard be that they wouldn't tell me?

It's obviously not good wherever it is, or why else would they keep it from me?

Asshole.

Ever since the afternoon Lochlan gave me the vibrator, he's been distant. Well, even more distant than usual. He still asks about my day, but he hasn't tried to lay a hand on me, or any other object. Which my mostly healing ass appreciates. But still, I... miss him.

I miss his dirty mouth; the way his eyes eat me up like he wants a taste of me; how amazing it feels every single time he touches me.

It's stupid to want those sorts of things from him. If I'm not careful, I could easily lose myself in his magical tongue or talented fingers and end up having sex with him. No doubt it would be unprotected sex again, while he's still doing who knows what with his whores. There is no reason to increase the odds of pregnancy this month. Once was plenty. Once may have been all it took since my period still hasn't come yet.

Manipulative asshole.

I'm so consumed channeling my anger into hitting balls that I don't catch whatever it is that Lena calls out to me. All I know is that her and Toni are both suddenly running onto the court toward me, dodging balls.

"What—" I start to ask when Lena grabs me up and tosses me over her shoulder like I'm a sack of potatoes. I lose my tennis racket after it gets hung on the fence on the way off the court. "Hey! What the hell?" I ask before Lena shouts, "On your left!"

Her warning is followed by the *pop-pop-pop* of rapid gun fire.

"Wait!" Lena screams just before there's a loud *boom*.

The whole world seems to spin around me. My face and stomach hit the ground hard enough to knock the air from my lungs. The fact that Lena's considerable body weight is on top of me doesn't help my lack of oxygen.

I don't bother asking her what's going on or demand she move. The acrid scent of shit burning stings my nose and throat.

"Another drone incoming!" It sounds like Toni yells frantically from somewhere nearby.

A drone? The flying robot contraptions with a remote control? Why does she sound so concerned about one of those little things?

"What the fuck should I do here, Lena?" Her voice is closer, near panicked as she asks for her superior's advice.

"If it's going to blow anyway, then try to hit the damn thing before it gets any closer!"

There are more pops of gunfire, and this time I can feel the moment something crashes to the ground. Even with Lena's body draped over me I see the bright flare of flames emitting from where it exploded and feel the heat coming off of it on my face.

Lena shifts us both around so that the light isn't as bright or as hot just as Toni screams, "How many fucking more are there? Fuck! Lena, your hair is on fire!"

Oh, shit.

I try to escape her grip to help put out the fire, but the iron bars of her arms won't relent.

"I got it, I got it!" Toni announces, which I hope she means the fire is out of Lena's hair.

In the distance, I hear more booms and sirens.

"Finally, a little help! Looks like they got one at the gate," Toni informs us, sounding relieved. Then, "We need to move her inside. We're sitting ducks out here. I don't see any more for now."

"I'm not taking her inside where she could be burned alive or crushed by a collapse!" Lena argues. Neither of those things sound like fun, but I also know we can't just stay here in the middle of the yard either.

"Fine, then can we put her in a car and get the hell out of here?" Toni requests frantically.

"Yes! Text the group to have someone get a ride over here now!"

It's so weird to have them arguing about what to do with me without bothering to ask my opinion. Honestly, my mind is a complete blank right now. There are no good ideas. All I can think about is that maybe my father was right to keep me and my sisters locked away. If he had considered a drone attack like this, then I would've never been allowed to play tennis on the roof.

And if Lochlan had been home, would we have both been killed when the house burned down around us?

Just when things seem to be calming down, Toni yells, "*INCOMING!*"

25

Lochlan

Shana's ass and pussy may look great in a tennis skirt and no panties, but she's too...aggressive sucking Owen's dick.

Sure, he's enjoying himself. I have no doubt she'll have him coming so fast he'll embarrass himself. But it's not doing shit for me. My dick is still only semi-hard and still in my pants. I was hoping that the view from behind them, where I can't see Shana's face or, thankfully, Owen's dick, would allow me to pretend for a few minutes that it's sweet, innocent Sophie giving head instead.

Rather than putting myself in Owen's place, all I can think about is seeing my wife kneeling in her skirt before *him*, Owen gripping her ponytail and telling her to take his cock like a good little whore. It's fucking infuriating.

The knock on the bedroom door is a welcome distraction. At least for me. Shana and Owen don't hear it or don't care. I'm relieved I'll get to rip a new one in whoever is stupid enough to disturb us after I told them not to. Yelling is better than continuing to contemplate if Sophie has somehow managed to break my mind and my dick in a matter of weeks.

"What did I fucking say?" I growl when I unlock, and whip open the door.

I figured it would be one of the newer guards, not Wolfe who has been with me the longest and is in charge of my entire security team.

"I apologize, sir," he says before I notice he looks pale, like all the color has drained from his face.

"What's wrong?" I ask, knowing it must be serious if he came knocking. Life or death situations, that's the only reason he would interrupt.

"There's been an aerial attack on the estate."

At the word *attack,* a million thoughts crowd my mind. My heart is thundering in my chest, while my tie suddenly feels like it's strangling me. Reaching up to loosen the knot, I try to calm the panic so I can think rationally here.

"Was anyone hurt? Was Sophie..." I pull my phone from my pocket, but there are no messages, no calls.

"All I know right now is that the guards are all in a panic, shooting down relentless drones."

"Drones?"

At first, that doesn't sound serious. Someone attempting to spy on me at worst.

But then I recall the drones used in warzones, the kamikaze ones that carry bombs, self-destructing when they reach their target.

"Owen! Let's go," I call over my shoulder.

I take a step to leave but Wolfe doesn't budge to let me get past him. He even holds up his palms to stop me. "You should prepare yourself for the worst, sir." Wolfe is a pragmatist, never one to exaggerate or panic. It's not like him to think shit's gone all to hell. That his carefully constructed security measures guarding the estate are fucked.

"Why the worst?"

"Sophie was still out on the tennis court when I received the report."

I shake my head; I'm certain he's been misinformed. "Sophie doesn't go out to the court at night even though I had the lights installed."

"She did tonight," he replies. What he doesn't have to say is that she probably went back out because I didn't come home for dinner. I wasn't there.

"You...filthy...fucking...whore! *Fuck!*" Owen bellows from behind me, ignoring my order that we're leaving.

"Let's go," I say to Wolfe, refusing to wait for Owen to take his dick out of Shana's mouth or see if Flynn is finished having his fun. They can walk home for all I care.

On the jog down the stairs to the SUV, I feel like the biggest piece of shit. Of all the places, I'm here in this disgusting hellhole that reeks of cum, cheap perfume, and sweat when I should've been at home with Sophie.

And because I wasn't there, because I was frustrated with her constant rejection, I may never get to see her again.

No, she *has* to be okay. Toni and Lena are smart. They'll keep her safe while I can't.

Right now, I would give any-fucking-thing just to have a chance to see Sophie smiling and happy on the tennis court, doing the one thing I know she loves most in the world, even if she never speaks to me again for failing her.

I pull up Lena's contact and have the phone ringing in my ear before I climb in the SUV that's already running and waiting out front.

She answers on the fourth ring which is four too many. "She's safe. We got her off the property."

"Thank fuck," I mutter on a heavy sigh of relief.

"Here she is," she says, handing the phone to Sophie.

"Lochlan?" Her voice sounds shaky, scared, like the fragile girl I met that first night in her room who cowered before me. I hate that so fucking much. She may drive me insane, but I love the stronger, tougher Sophie who refuses to put up with my shit.

"Are you okay? Are you hurt?"

"No. I don't think so. Lena's hair caught on fire. God, I'm so sorry I made you stay over tonight." She's obviously talking to the guards now, apologizing to them, when I'm the one who should be saying I'm sorry.

In the background I hear Lena tell her, "Stop apologizing. If those things had dropped when you were inside the house, you may not have made it out alive, and then Lochlan would've disemboweled me with a rusty knife."

"She's not wrong," I tell Sophie. "I'm so sorry this happened, and that I wasn't there."

"Where are you? Why didn't you come home?" that soft, fragile voice asks.

I can't tell her the truth. If she knew, she would never believe I didn't touch anyone, and if I tell her I watched Owen get his dick sucked, she'll think the worst.

"I was in a business meeting," I say which isn't a complete lie. "Employees fucked up for the last time and had to be fired."

"Oh," she replies, and I can't tell if she believes my half-truth or not.

"Where are you?" I ask.

"We're on the way to the airport. Toni said it's the only place she could think of that wouldn't allow drones to swarm."

"Good. I'll meet you there in a few minutes, okay?"

"Okay."

There are a million things I want to say to her, but I don't know how. "See you soon," I tell her before forcing myself to end the call.

"Get me to the airport as fast as possible," I tell Wade who is driving. "Find out where they'll be waiting," I instruct Wolfe who is in the passenger seat.

"Yes, sir."

A half hour drive is cut down to twenty minutes thanks to Wade breaking every traffic law. It's still twenty minutes too long.

As we pull into the airport, I tell my men, "I'll grab Sophie and get her in here. Then I want you to just keep driving until I figure out where the fuck we're going to sleep tonight."

I can't think about anything right now other than seeing Sophie, wrapping her in my arms, and never letting her go again.

"Just up ahead," Wolfe points out the direction to Wade where one of our SUVs is sitting between other vehicles in the crowded lot, trying to blend in. He rolls the vehicle up behind them, and as if Wolfe told them the plan, Lena and Toni have Sophie out and hurrying toward us.

Throwing the door open, I sweep her into my arms. For once, she doesn't flinch or try to pull away. Sophie lets me hold her, and even winds her arms around my back squeezing me tight.

"Best to keep moving, boss," Lena says, ever the professional when I freeze.

"Thank you both," I tell the women before I release Sophie to guide her to the other vehicle. She climbs into the backseat with me quickly following behind. Wade is pulling away before my door shuts all the way. The jolt of acceleration makes Sophie gasp. Her fingers clutch my thigh in a death grip, as if I make her feel safe or she's at least reassured by my presence. Hell, maybe I was just the only thing to hold on to in the backseat.

When she doesn't relax her grip even once we're smoothly cruising down the highway, I realize how starved I've been for her touch. That I enjoy when she's touching me.

I usually don't allow it. It's always felt too fake and obligatory for the women I've been with. Sophie isn't like them, though. She's never casually laid a hand on me before now, and she would never do it because she wants something.

Feeling brave, I attempt to slip my arm around her back to pull her closer to my side.

Not only does she accept the embrace, but some of the tension also drains from her body as she relaxes against me, even letting the side of her head lean on my shoulder. I take a deep breath, inhaling the scent of her lavender and rose shampoo to remind my frazzled nerves that she's alive and unharmed by some miracle.

"It's okay. You're okay," I assure her, pressing a kiss to the top of her head.

My relief is short-lived when she shivers. I tilt the air conditioning vents above us so they're pointing away from her when I realize she's still in her sleeveless shirt and short tennis skirt. Slipping my arms out of the sleeves of my suit jacket, I drape it around the front of her body like a blanket.

"I'm so sorry this happened," I tell her again. "I had no idea..."

"Are we going back there?" she asks softly.

"No. Not tonight. I'll take you someplace safe," I promise her, even though I haven't figured out where yet.

My phone buzzes in my suit pocket. Sophie fishes it out and I hold my breath until I see whose name is on the screen when she offers it to me. I take it in my left so I can keep my right arm around her.

Thankfully, it's just Flynn.

"What?" I snap at him.

"You just fucking left us here!"

"There was an emergency. Get an Uber."

"An emergency?" he repeats.

"Sophie was attacked by exploding drones at the estate tonight."

"No shit? Is she okay?" I'm surprised that he even bothered to ask how she's doing. I eye her profile carefully, hoping I didn't overlook any internal injuries. But the color is coming back in her cheeks the longer I stare at her.

"Other than a few scratches, she's unharmed. Her guards got her off the grounds and we won't be going back there tonight."

"Yeah, don't blame you," he agrees. "Owen's getting us a ride."

"Good. I'll talk to you later," I tell him before ending the call.

As soon as I end the call, Sophie says, "You left him at the office?"

Thankfully, Flynn's loudmouth hadn't disclosed his location.

"I was in a hurry," I reply.

"Can I use your phone? I should call my dad," she says, making me go still.

"What? Why?" I ask. That's the last thing I want to do right now —deal with a furious, vengeful Italian mob boss who could very well take her from me for putting his daughter in danger.

"If he hears about it, he'll worry..."

"He won't hear," I assure her. "Trust me. It's best if we keep this quiet. If Dante found out I almost got you killed..."

Now her head turns to look at me, making me cringe at the sight of scrapes and dirt on her perfect face thanks to her near-death experience.

"I could've died, and you're worried about my father finding out and being pissed off?"

There's the fire-breathing Sophie I know and love.

Goddamn it.

I fucking love her.

That's what this immovable knot in my chest is that's been hurting for days. The knot that doubled in size when Wolfe told me she may be hurt or dead.

I barely know this girl, she's made no secret that she's repulsed by me, and yet, I've somehow fallen in love with her. I love the way she challenges me, drives me crazy, and leaves me always wanting more. Sophie's been mine since the second I saw her. Now I just have to convince her to stay with me.

"No, princess. I'm worried about you more than any fucking thing right now," I tell her softly as I push those thoughts away for now. "You're my responsibility, and I didn't protect you. If Dante finds out I fucked up, he'll probably kill me, and I'll deserve it."

She stares at me for a long moment. "Promise?" she asks, as if she doesn't believe me. I'm not sure which part she's skeptical about, that

Salvato will murder me or that I'm more worried about keeping her safe.

Both things are absolutely true.

"Promise."

Her shoulders slump, and she leans against my shoulder again. "Fine. I won't tell him either."

"Thank you." I kiss the top of her head again and wrap my jacket around her shoulders tighter. "Are you sure you're okay?"

"Just some bruises and scratches from being slammed to the ground."

"You'll be sore tomorrow."

"How do you know?"

"Because I survived a bombing a few months ago with your father the same way, with someone diving on top of me."

"Oh, right. I forgot."

Is it a coincidence someone tried to hurt Sophie with drone bombs on my property?

No, it can't be. Salvato said Kozlov and Petrov are dead. They were the ones responsible for the hotel bombing. But we never found out who planted the bomb. He couldn't get any names of them before he killed them either.

If that person is still out there, they could keep trying until they take me out. Or Sophie.

Was she the main target? Did they wait until she was outside in the open? The guards didn't mention any hits to the house itself.

The only reason anyone would want to hurt Sophie is to either push Salvato into killing me or to hurt me. Killing my wife would send me into a downward spiral while also making me look weak, incapable of handling shit. How can I protect my men, my business interests, if I can't even keep my new wife safe?

Possibly more than just my wife...

"Have you bled yet?" I ask her.

"No, I'm not bleeding. I told you; it's just bruises and maybe a few scrapes."

"No, Sophie." Reaching for her chin because I need to see her face again, I gently turn it toward me. "Have you bled this month?"

"That's none of your business." She tries to turn her head away, but I grip her chin tighter, holding steady.

"It is my business when you could be carrying my child, and you were hurt today."

"Your...oh. No. I haven't yet," she replies. "But I doubt one little time would get me pregnant."

"One little time?" I repeat as my gaze lowers to her lips, wanting to claim them so fucking badly. "I left a goddamn gallon of cum inside of you because it was the first time..." I stop myself since she doesn't need to know the rest of that sentence.

Of course, she won't let it go.

"First time what?" she asks.

I let her chin go, but she doesn't turn away from me, so I cave and tell her the truth. "The first time I fucked anyone since the wedding date was set. Since I chose you."

She turns even more of her body to face me while frowning so hard I want to kiss it away from her lips. "Chose me?" she repeats as if the words are foreign. "You mean the night you came to the house?"

"No. Since the day I sent Dante the wedding invitation with your name on it."

"Which was after we met?"

"It was in December, long before we met. *Months* before. Like five of them."

Fuck, I hate admitting it had been that long since I've fucked anyone, as if I was pussy-whipped before I even saw her in the flesh. That's probably why I lost it and snapped, taking her right there against the wall so rough the night in the club. I was horny, and I needed her more than anything. She was all I could think about for months. The thought of another man touching her was infuriating.

"I didn't agree to marry you until three weeks before the wedding, after Cass turned you down."

"Cass didn't turn me down."

"She didn't?"

"No. I never wanted her. I chose you before I even met you or your psycho sister."

"But...how?"

"Last year, once I heard Madison had run off, I gathered intel on all of you. As soon as I saw a photo of you in that tennis skirt, I knew I wanted you."

"But Cass told me that she refused to marry you."

"She never had the chance to refuse me. Ask Dante. I sent him a wedding invitation months ago with your name on it, then a similar one to all our powerful associates in the city. When he finally decided to acknowledge my claim, he insisted I meet Cass the night I came to see you. He wanted me to change my mind because he thought you were too young and innocent."

"Cass told me...did you ask her for a blowjob that night you met us?"

"Fuck, no." That little cunt told her I wanted her to blow me when she's the one who suggested it?

"She said you did."

"I figured out one of her secrets, and I think she would have sucked my dick to try to keep me quiet. I turned her down flat. Believe me or don't."

Sophie frowns harder as she thinks it over. "I...I believe you."

"Good, because every word is true." I rub my thumb over her bottom lip, wishing I could make her smile after such a shitty day. "While we're on the subject of truths, I believe you too, that the night in the club you were a virgin."

"I was. You were my first."

"Do you have any idea how fucking desperate I am for a second time?"

She shakes her head, either in refusal or because she doesn't care how much I want her. I thought I had made it pretty damn obvious that I needed her.

This is as close as she's let me get to her since the night I whipped her ass, and she just scared the shit out of me. That's why I can't help myself. I grab the side of her face to bring her parted lips to mine, plunging my tongue between them.

Sophie actually kisses me back, tongue and all. For only ten seconds before pulling away. Turning her face toward the other window, she swipes the back of her hand across her mouth. As if her rejection isn't bad enough, she has to go a step further to show her utter aversion to kissing me. I'm abhorrent to her. Dirty. But she still wants me. How do I know?

Because her fingers are not only still gripping my thigh, but they moved a few inches closer to my dick during our short kiss. Fuck, I actually want her small hand wrapped around me, stroking me.

"I know you want me, Sophie, so what the fuck is the problem here?"

"You...you refuse to be faithful to me, and yet you want to get me pregnant. That's the problem."

"I haven't been unfaithful. And I didn't say I would be when you asked because I knew you wouldn't believe me." The tension in her shoulders relaxes a hair, so I take that as a good sign. "I swear I haven't fucked anyone else in months, princess. I've been faithful to you since the second I saw your photo. You are the only woman I want."

Nothing. No response. Not even a twitch.

Until a few minutes later when she finally says, "I...missed you tonight."

She missed me. Sweeter words have never been spoken.

"Fuck, I missed you too," I assure her, pressing a kiss to the side of her neck. Then another when she tilts her head to the side, giving me access, and the green light to keep going. "So damn much."

When I add a stroke of my tongue to her flesh, she quietly moans. Her fingers on my thigh sink a little lower, inches away from touching where I've been aching. The attack tonight along with that constant ache has me feeling desperate for her.

"Now that the danger has passed, and you admitted that you missed me," I whisper, licking a line along the column of her neck up to her earlobe that I nip with my teeth. "Why don't you come sit on my cock like a good little wife."

Something between a laugh and a gasp escapes her. It's not a rejection, so I grab her waist to lift her onto my lap, her back to my chest. She doesn't fight the new position, even when I press her ass down on my hard bulge.

God, I couldn't get it all the way up watching a man receive an enthusiastic blowjob earlier, and now I'm ready to come from just having Sophie's ass barely graze my cock through layers of clothing. Underneath my suit coat still covering her, my palms roam up and down her sides, reassuring myself again that she's unharmed. Her elbows and knees are scuffed so I steer clear of them while my lips continue to brush along her neck.

When she relaxes fully, sinking back against my chest with her head falling back on my shoulder, I could almost cry.

Holding her tight, I chance skimming my fingers up over her ribs, then the swell of her breasts. Sophie arches her back, pushing her tits into my palms, urging me to keep touching them.

"Oh, princess. I knew you were a horny girl."

When my hands slip underneath her top to skim along her bare stomach, she tenses. "The guards..."

"Won't look or I'll stab their eyes out," I promise her.

I trust both men with my life and they're staring straight ahead at the road, not even thinking about sneaking a peek in the rearview mirror. With my jacket draped over her, they wouldn't see anything anyway. That's why I have no hesitation in letting my fingers skim under the tight waistband of her skirt. It's a snug fit I have to work for rather than just reaching under her skirt, but I eventually get my entire hand down inside the front of her panties. Her ragged gasp when my fingertips brush her clit, makes me impossibly harder.

"There's my sweet pussy. I've missed the taste of you flooding my tongue with your honey. The mewling sounds you made when you got off."

Sophie's arms both reach up above my head to grab my hair, bringing my mouth down to hers. I fucking devour her with my tongue while I finger her pussy. By now she knows my cock is trying to rip through my pants to get inside of her.

Before I can unzip them, Sophie's hips start bucking, chasing her release.

"Come for me, princess." I squeeze her breast harder, pinching her nipple between two fingers while rubbing her clit faster and deepening our kiss.

She whimpers into my mouth the same way she did that first night we fucked, letting me know she's close. Her thighs clench around my hand and then she's shuddering and panting.

I run my finger through her wetness, shoving it inside of her to feel her cunt clench around it until she finishes throbbing.

Only then do I pull my hand free. I have never undone my pants faster, needing to shove inside Sophie's tight heaven before I explode. I want to feel her pussy squeezing my cock the exact same way it did my finger. I don't take the time to even remove her panties, I just tug the crotch to the side to make room for my dick.

Sophie's hips jerk like my cock bit her, then she's sliding right out of my lap, down to the floorboard between my legs.

"What the hell are you doing?" I ask her. It becomes obvious when she turns around to face me and stares at my dick that's now eye-level with her face.

Goddamn it. She's not going to let me in her pussy.

And while I've wanted to fuck her mouth since the first time I saw it, want it so bad I had a woman put on her skirt and act it out with someone else, it's not what I need right now. Still, I'll take whatever I can get from her.

"What are you waiting for?" I snap when she hesitates. I'm an asshole for even letting her get on her scuffed knees after she was just attacked, but I'm a selfish prick.

"I don't know how…"

Gripping her ponytail, I pull her face forward at the same time I hold up my shaft until the head grazes her slightly parted lips. "Lick it."

The tip of her tongue darts out, swiping over my slit while her eyes stay locked on mine. God, it feels amazing. Every little thing she does is so fucking hot.

"Again," I order, my voice deepening as I urge her head forward. Another sweep of her tongue steals my breath. This girl makes me feel like a horny teenager who can't hold off for five seconds without coming. Since I don't want to finish before I even get inside her mouth, I tell her, "Open wide, princess."

She does, so I bring her head forward and shove the first few inches along her tongue. "Wrap those pretty lips around the crown and suck on it."

And fuck me, her cheeks hollow out, sucking me so good I instantly leak pre-cum. If Sophie notices, she doesn't seem to care. Her timid blue eyes just hold mine while she applies that warm, wet suction.

"Oh, fuck," I groan at the sight and feel of being in her pretty mouth. I lift my eyes to the front seat to make sure the guards aren't watching in the rearview. Wolfe can probably see us in the corner of his eye from the passenger seat, but he at least pretends he's looking forward, searching for drones or any other danger.

Not that the threat currently matters since the woman on her knees might be the death of me. If so, I'm glad I didn't die before having her mouth once. But I want more. I want her fingers wrapped around my cock stroking me. Only her fingers, her hand touches me like she's not doing it with the expectation of getting something from me in return.

"Give me your hand," I tell her. She lifts the right one from where it was resting on my thigh. I wrap her fingers around my shaft, then show her how to jerk me off. She doesn't let up on her suction even a little bit the entire time, and the combination feels fucking amazing.

"That's it, princess. Don't stop."

I want her playing with my balls at the same time, but she's a beginner and grabbing my dick is already wading into new territory, so I stick with the basics. Cupping her ponytail again, I tug her mouth forward, shoving more of my swollen dick down her throat.

When she gags, my eyes close on a groan and I swear the SUV swerves to the right. I open my eyes again finding hers glistening with tears. "You know I like your tears. I'll lick them away after I come down your throat," I promise her. "Now breathe through your nose and take what I fucking give you."

My next thrust has her making a garbled sound of distress and me swearing shit to the ceiling of the SUV. I force my eyes down to keep watching her and don't let up, earning those sounds again. Her fist tightens around my shaft, hurting me oh so good.

"This is what you wanted," I remind her since I could've been coming in her pussy right now if she hadn't slid down onto the floor-board. "If you're not going to let me fuck you...then you better get used...to having my cock shoved...all...*fuck me*...all the way down your throat," I tell her through my panting breaths.

Her wide blue eyes look panicked when I wrap my hand around her ponytail and thrust fast and deep until the sounds of her muffled heaving have me on edge. I don't need her to stroke me in her hand because I'm nearly balls deep in her mouth.

"Here it comes. Start swallowing, princess," I instruct her, holding her head still for the first jerk of my cock. "*FUCK!*" I yell as I explode with a tortured growl. My jaw nearly cracks from how tightly I clench it during the soul-shattering tremors of pleasure.

When I finally pull out of Sophie's mouth, her cheeks are damp, and her chin is covered in drool along with my thick, sticky release. The little brat smears her cheeks then her chin on my pants leg to dry them before climbing back onto the seat next to me.

And I was looking forward to licking her clean.

Sophie stares silently out the window as if nothing happened even though she's still breathing hard with her fists clenched on the lap of her white skirt. Fuck I love her tennis outfits. It's a fetish I never realized I had before I saw Sophie in one.

My only regret is that she's no longer cuddled up to me. And I guess she no longer needs my suit coat since it's still on the floorboard from when she slid out of my lap.

"Is my little wife angry at me now?" I can't help but ask with a satisfied smirk while fixing up my now stained pants.

"Are my hands around your throat?" she instantly replies without delay.

"I bet my guards would laugh their asses off if I told them you tried to choke me out the night I took your virginity."

Wade's perplexed gaze momentarily meets mine in the rearview.

"I should've kept squeezing and clawing."

Now Wolfe glances back at us too. He knows better than anyone that I don't allow anyone to touch my clothed body, much less dig fingernails into my bare skin. I should've realized that night that Snow White was an exception to all of my rules. I didn't even think before putting her hand on my bulge under the table when we were eating with her family either. I just wanted her to feel how hard I was for her before she jerked her hand away when my cock twitched, jostling the whole damn table.

God, I love how innocent she is, and how she constantly surprises me by doing the last thing I expect. Sometimes I think she wants me, like thirty seconds ago, even if the rest of the time she thinks I'm repulsive.

Still, there are moments she forgets. And her innocence is sexy as fuck.

When I chuckle at the memory of her juggling and dropping the dildo, Sophie calls me a dirty bastard under her breath. It's been a nice reprieve fooling around with her after the scare of the attack.

"You say the sweetest things, princess. Keep it up and you may melt my cold heart."

Now she crosses her arms over her chest. Oh yeah. She's definitely pissed at me for giving her more than she could handle for her first blowjob.

Shit. My dick was the first in her mouth, the first inside her body. I love being the first and only.

"I assume you won't be swayed to sleep in the same bed with me tonight?"

There's barely a second of silence before she responds. "Nope."

The fastest dismissal of my life. Maybe the only dismissal if I think about it, and she's the only woman I've ever wanted more than anything else in the world. Even though I now know that all the women in my past were fake as hell, Sophie's rejection still stings.

I reach over to pinch the side of her pleated skirt and she jerks her leg away. "You didn't get even a little wet from sucking my dick?"

"No."

"Liar. If you didn't enjoy being used like that you would've bit me, not sucked harder."

She scoffs because she knows I'm right. "I hate you."

"I hate that you hate me," I admit honestly, wishing a perfect girl like her could ever care for a dirty bastard like me. "But I sure do love when you cave and give it up to me like a good little slutty wife."

"I haven't caved. We're still not having sex."

"Didn't you know, princess? Men enjoy fucking a mouth more than anything. We're all selfish that way."

What I don't tell her is that she's the first person in eight years that I've allowed to touch my dick.

26

Sophie

I've never been as relieved as I was when I heard Lochlan's voice on the phone and saw his face in the airport parking lot. Being in his arms made me feel safe again.

So safe that I apparently couldn't keep my stupid mouth off of him. At least there's no pregnancy worries with that method.

And I hate that I was turned on having him use my mouth so callously, so forcefully like...like he owned it. I didn't know what the hell I was doing, which seemed to make him angry with me.

Seeing him come undone, turning into a panting, growling desperate man was fun. He always looks so perfect, polished in his suits, even when he's angry. But when he's coming, his head is thrown back, his handsome face is all scrunched in a snarl. With his slumping posture and lazy smirk after he came, he looks nothing like a professional businessman. Or a womanizing heathen. He just looked like...mine. My Lochlan that no one else, no other woman, gets to see, even if I know that's a lie. While he claimed he hasn't been with anyone in months, I find that very hard to believe. I hate that a part of me thinks it's the truth, and that it means more than it does.

Even though I had no clue what I was doing, Lochlan seemed to at least enjoy my hand and mouth enough to finish, which is all that matters.

The day Vanessa told me about oral sex, I never thought I would want to do it. Now it's maybe one of my favorite things. I want to do it again, try to do it better, making him come faster. Not that I plan to tell my husband any of that.

"Where are we going?" I ask after he finishes teasing me.

"I don't know." Lochlan sits up and straightens his vest and jacket, putting himself back together.

"You don't know where we're going?"

"Not yet. I haven't decided where would be the safest. You distracted me."

Right. The drone attack. It was nice to forget about that near death experience with Lena and Toni for a few minutes when I was on his lap and between his legs. What was even nicer was curling up to Lochlan's warm body heat. That must be the cuddling Vanessa mentioned.

We cuddled, and I told him I missed him before he kissed me.

He may have said it back, but I don't know if he really means it. If he had actually missed me, wanted to have dinner with me, then he would've figured out a way to get home.

"I'm hungry," I tell him.

"You didn't have dinner before you went out to the court?" he asks while reaching for my skirt pleat, running his finger along the inner hem.

"No. I didn't want to eat alone."

"Because you missed me?"

Rather than answer him, I roll my eyes and face the window again.

"We'll find some takeout, then a hotel tonight using an alias. When we get to the room, I could eat you out..."

Eat me out?

Oh.

That's what he calls the thing he does with his tongue? Eating me out?

"Takeout is fine with me," I reply, ignoring the whole oral issue even if I do enjoy his tongue. "And I want dessert."

"Cheesecake?" Lochlan asks, his finger now brushing my upper thigh instead of the skirt hem.

"Sure, if they have it. And two bedrooms for the hotel."

He heaves a heavy sigh followed by, "Of course."

After we grabbed dinner, we ate in the SUV that the guards drove for four hours, all the way to Laguna Beach before stopping for the night. The oceanfront, two-bedroom penthouse suite of the hotel Lochlan chose is romantic with a serene view after the chaotic night. It reminds me of home. My real home at the Royal Palace. I went right to sleep in my own bedroom, confident that Lochlan had our safety and security under control.

The next morning, I've just stepped out of the shower when there's a soft knock on the locked bedroom door.

Since my outfit from the day before was dirty, I throw on the hotel provided white robe, then tie the sash tight before answering it.

"Yes?" I ask when I open the door...and find Lochlan on the other side in army green athletic shorts, a white T-shirt, and sneakers. I've never seen him so dressed down before in so few clothes that I can't help but stare. Bare legs and arms full of big, corded muscles and so many tattoos. I want to examine and kiss every single one.

"Get dressed and let's go." My husband holds out a stack of white fabric to me, his own eyes dipping to where my robe criss-crosses.

"Go where?" I ask as I take the pile from him. Clothes. A new tennis skirt and sleeveless top, even underwear. I have no clue where he got them since I didn't bring anything with me, or how he knew my size.

"Don't you want to play tennis today?"

After the attack on the court last night, I can't say it was the first place I yearned to go this morning. I don't want to think about the thing I woke up yearning for requiring a cold shower.

"Sophie? You're not going to let what happened yesterday prevent you from doing what you love, are you?"

"No," I scoff when he makes me sound like the coward I am. "But we can't go home yet, can we? And if we do, the court is probably still fucked up."

I don't admit that I'm not feeling brave enough to return to the scene of the crime.

"The guards said the court took some damage. And it'll take a few extra days to replace the fencing with bulletproof glass around it.

"Bulletproof glass?" I repeat.

"It seemed like a necessary precaution. We could enclose it entirely, add air conditioning..."

"No. I like the outdoor court, with regular fencing."

"I'll think about it," Lochlan grumbles. "I reserved a court for us to use here until it's repaired."

"You reserved a tennis court here? For us? You and me? *You* play tennis?" I still haven't recovered from the sight of his muscled covered tattoos, and now he drops this bomb on me.

Bomb is probably not the most appropriate metaphor today.

"Yes, I play. And since your guards are still recovering, I'm your escort for the next few days."

"You?"

"Are you just going to stand there in nothing but a fucking robe repeating everything I say until I rip it off of you and take you against another wall? Or do you want to get dressed and go play tennis, princess?"

I swallow down the desire raised by him mentioning ripping things off and fucking me.

"I'll get dressed," I agree, even though I'm curious to see how long he would wait before he snapped.

Half an hour later, sweat is dripping off every inch of me from trying not to let my husband beat my ass in the last set. Playing against him is not as easy as I thought it would be.

"Game...set...match," I gasp triumphantly when he lunges to the right and just misses my volley.

"Damn," Lochlan huffs, bending at the waist to catch his breath. "No cardio competes with this fucking sport."

"You're actually...good," I remark as we both meet at the sideline bench to rest and gulp down water.

"Don't look so surprised," he says with a smirk. "Business dealings with the rich are made on golf courses and tennis courts in country clubs. My father made sure I had lessons in both so I wouldn't embarrass him." He chugs water, then pours it on the top of his head to let the clear liquid run in rivulets down his face mixing with his sweat. "Julia Townsend actually. I still prefer golf since it's mostly standing around and waiting. Tennis is more brutal on my lungs than I remember. Fucking cigars."

The next match I don't have a chance of winning, not when Lochlan peels off his shirt. Seeing his rippling chest and stomach muscles for the first time is too distracting. Especially the ones on his abdomen, where sweat drips down between the crevices of his six-pack.

"Like what you see, princess?" the arrogant bastard asks with a grin when I miss another volley.

"How well do you think you would play if I took off my shirt?" I snap back at him. It's so hot the thought of stripping off my top and

239

only wearing the new sports bra he bought me this morning is very appealing.

"Oh, we wouldn't be playing tennis anymore if you took off your shirt because I would have to put my mouth and hands on you."

Yes, that's the exact thing I want to do to him—get my hands and my mouth on every inch of his glistening skin.

"Too bad for you that's not going to happen," I reply before we continue our game.

~

When we take our next water break on the bench, Lochlan won't shut up about beating me. The close proximity of his half-naked body doesn't help my recent urge to touch and lick him. After all, he swore he hasn't been with anyone else. Would he use protection if I asked him to fuck me?

Lochlan doesn't seem to notice my rapt attention since he's not trying to seduce me at the moment. He's leaning his head back against the fence, catching his breath between sips from his nearly empty water bottle.

Instead of caving to my silly bodily cravings, I glance away before he catches me gawking at him and ask him, "What would you be doing right now if we weren't here?"

"Oh, I would probably be in a meeting with casino staff or running around putting out fires elsewhere." The elsewhere I know is the brothels. "Most likely the same things your father does each day."

"I don't really know what Dante does," I admit with a sigh. "He never told us anything."

"Trust me, you weren't missing much. It's boring paperwork and accounting shit usually." Rubbing his fingers over his perspiring temple, he says, "Or right now, shit with the lawsuit."

"What lawsuit?"

"The one from the casino bombing."

"Oh. Right." Staring out at the quiet, empty courts we've had to ourselves uninterrupted thanks to Lochlan's reservation, I tell him, "I'm sorry someone did something so awful because they wanted to hurt you or my father."

"We think they were aiming to take out both of us."

"Were you hurt badly?" I ask, unable to remember what happened to him months ago.

"Not really, just a few bruised ribs and a concussion that knocked me out. I got off easy. If I had been in that room..."

"Yeah," I say, knowing everyone in that event room died or was horribly injured.

"What pisses me off the most is that we still haven't been able to find who planted the bomb."

"You haven't?"

"No." Reaching for a towel, he mops up his face, then the back of his neck and chest. I force my gaze away for the third time. "The bomb apparently had a remote and was placed in one of the rolling bars the servers and bartenders brought in. We've tracked it back to the kitchen on surveillance, but not a single camera captured who snuck in and put the bomb underneath it or when. Only the usual employees were around it from the time it left the kitchen until it arrived in the event room the night before the poker tournament."

"So, it was an employee who planted the bomb?"

"No. Someone just got past our cameras..." he trails off, then twists his body to face me, his auburn brow furrowed. "Motherfucker. It *was* an employee. Jesus, Sophie. I think you're right. All these months, and I didn't see what was right in front of my fucking face."

"What do you mean?"

"I've been looking for a stranger on the surveillance videos from all over the hotel, someone who didn't belong in the kitchen or the casino because I couldn't fathom one of my employees doing something so heinous, killing all those people. The police interviewed all of them, looked into criminal histories, but they all checked out.

They must have missed something because there's no other explanation. Nobody was seen sneaking in or around the room. Everyone in the kitchen or in that room near the bar was either an employee or a guest. I doubt any of those celebrities would've blown themselves up."

"Then how will you figure out which employee is responsible?"

"That's a good question. I hate suspecting my own people. They've already been questioned by Vegas Metro PD. Torturing them probably would be a bit too extreme."

I nod my head in agreement before I get an idea. "What about the threat of torture?"

"What do you mean?"

"If you circulate the rumor that you're certain it was someone who works for you, and that you're going to be questioning them again one by one, then the person responsible may get nervous and try to run. Especially if word got out that the questioning was actually torture. I've heard some of our penthouse staff talking about how everyone fears my dad's guy Eli because of the rumors about things he's done to people. The grossest was that he removed a man's eyeball from the socket and then, he, um, they said he, you know, screwed it."

Lochlan laughs. "I happened to have heard that rumor as well. Is it true?"

Grasping the bottom of the bench on either side of me, I shrug. "No clue. But it's an effective deterrent either way."

"This idea of yours could work to send the rat scurrying. Salvato may even let me borrow Eli to really scare the shit out of them."

"You are supposed to be allies now that we're married. Wasn't that the whole point of it?"

"Fuck," Lochlan mutters as he gets to his feet to pace away then come back. Lifting his arms, he locks his hands behind his head, flexing his biceps in a way that makes me wish I had a camera to capture the image forever. I've never wanted to lick anything as much as I want to run my tongue up his abs, down to the cut V-muscles dipping into his shorts...

"He's going to be fucking furious with me."

"What?" I ask when he continues to pace and curse.

"I'm going to have to tell Salvato about the drones."

"Honesty is probably best before he finds out on his own."

Lochlan nods but doesn't lower his hands from his head as he stares off in the distance. "I'll reach out to him when we get home, finally give him the blackmail on my contacts to appease him."

"When are we going home?"

"Once the tennis court is repaired, and I come up with how to make sure an attack like that never fucking happens again."

"You're not psychic, Lochlan. You couldn't have known."

Now his arms drop to his sides. "No, but I could've been more prepared for an aerial assault. I should assign snipers to observe the sky from the rooftop like I did for the wedding."

He actually had snipers watching us during the wedding?

"A sharpshooter could safely hit any incoming drones before they get too close to the property. I'll figure out a way to keep you safe, Sophie. I don't want you to live in fear when we return home."

"I'll be fine," I assure him. "Do you think it was the same person who planted the bomb at the casino?"

"Possibly."

"Well, if I were you, I wouldn't tell anyone about the 'fake torture' if you decide to go through with it, not even the guards. Everyone should be considered a suspect for now."

"You're right," he agrees, fingers raking through his hair. "I fucking hate not knowing who I can trust, if it could be someone I consider more than an employee but a friend. One who betrayed me, tried to kill me, and murdered so many innocent people."

"I'm sorry you don't know who's loyal and who isn't. It kind of makes me glad I don't have friends or anyone I'm close to other than my family who isn't paid to be around me."

"Salvato really kept you that insulated from the rest of the world?"

"Yes."

He stares at me for a long moment, then says, "You can play tennis with Cole if you want. I won't run him off again if he's your... friend."

That concession makes me smile because I know he hates when Cole's around me, that he's jealous, when he shouldn't be. Cole is a cute, silly boy while Lochlan is a sexy, dangerous man. "Thank you."

"Although," he adds. I knew it was too good to be true. "I doubt Vanessa will let her son come back to our house after bombs were dropped on it."

"Dammit. Probably not. She was furious my dad took Cole to that poker tournament."

"At least he walked out unharmed."

"Yes, he was very lucky," I agree.

"So you seem to be enjoying your time at the tennis center," Lochlan says as if wanting to change the subject from my step-brother.

"I love working at the center. Thank you for introducing me to Julia. Her and Stacy think I should work toward my teaching certi-fication."

"Of course, you should. You're the best person to teach others tennis, especially children. I'm sure they realized that too."

"Why do you say that?" I narrow my eyes at him, wondering if he's just flattering me to try and get in my panties.

"You love tennis because it's fun, not to beat people. You let me win, didn't you?"

"I did not," I huff. Lochlan just stands there and stares at me waiting. "Fine, maybe I wasn't trying my hardest. If I win every set, nobody will want to play with me again."

"Let me guess—your evil redheaded sister taught you that life lesson?"

"Yes," I reply, surprised he figured it out so fast. "Cass is just as competitive as I am. And she has her own strengths and skills that I don't have in mixed martial arts. She has no problem kicking my ass on the mats, but god forbid she lose to me at tennis."

"I think we would've killed each other," my husband mutters with a chuckle. "Literally."

"I do too," I agree with a grin. "I think she could kick your ass. She trains with some of our guards."

"Ha, that's probably not all she does with the guards," it sounds like he murmurs, but my thoughts are on Toni and Lena. Poor Lena.

"I feel awful about making Lena and Toni work late last night," I admit to him. "And that Lena's hair caught on fire. If I had stayed inside..."

"Lena's hair will grow back," Lochlan says. "And those two are both well aware of the risks associated with this job. It's why I pay them three times what the other guards make."

"You pay them more than the other guards? More than your own guards?"

"Of course. Lena more than Toni. At least I can defend myself if it comes to it. You can't."

"You think I'm weak," I say in understanding.

"No, I think you're too precious to risk."

For a moment, his words wrap around me like a warm blanket. Until I consider them a little longer.

Getting to my feet to put distance between us, I state the obvious. "Precious to my father. He would kill you if anything happened to me."

"Sophie—"

"Ready for another match?" I ask.

"Yeah. Sure. Thanks for the talk, and the advice with my employees."

"It was nothing you wouldn't have thought of on your own," I reply before walking away to my side of the court. It's best to keep the net between us, to avoid getting too close to Lochlan.

If he had married Madison or Cass instead of me, he would

protect them the exact same way. It's all just part of an alliance with my father for him, getting Dante's agreement that Lochlan will be his heir. There's nothing more to it. And part of that agreement came with the added bonus of fucking me, taking my virginity, and using me however he wants.

I will not willingly get into his bed, no matter how badly I want him. Lochlan can keep trying, but it's not going to happen.

27

Lochlan

Sophie and I spent two days at the resort in Laguna Beach. Two days I thought she might come to my bed after spending our days playing together and bonding. But we both passed out exhausted in our separate rooms each night.

At least the repairs to the estate and court were finished quickly, as well as the implementation of the newly hired snipers. I let Lena supervise the hiring once she assured me she didn't need time off, just a haircut. She has a good eye for finding sharpshooters like herself as well as weeding out untrustworthy psychos, so I put her in charge of the assignment to recruit good people fast.

Sophie seemed on edge the ride home, like she was nervous about going back. But she didn't ask to stay longer at the resort when I told her we were leaving.

The two of us have only been home long enough for me to

shower and put on a suit when Wolfe appears in my open office doorway.

"You're still here?" I say in surprise since he and Wade were with us the entire time we were gone, taking turns monitoring the resort.

"I was on my way out when I heard you had a visitor at the front gate. Dante Salvato is here, and he's demanding to see Sophie."

"Fuck," I mutter. "That took less time than I thought it would." I probably should've answered one of his calls on the ride back. I just wasn't ready to have him chew me out for the same shit I'm still berating myself over. Or have him take Sophie from me.

"Show him in," I say with a sigh. "Then you should go home and get some rest."

"Yes, sir," he replies before he disappears.

Dante storms into my office in a whirl of fury.

"I was just about to call you to set up a meeting," I say when I get up from behind the desk to meet him halfway.

He doesn't lay hands on me, but I know he wants to when he gets in my face and snarls, "You son of a bitch! My daughter is nearly blown to smithereens, and you didn't bother to tell me?"

"I was going to tell you. We were laying low and just got back home today. And Sophie is absolutely fine."

"That's not the fucking point and you know it!"

Glancing down, I straighten the sleeves of my suit coat and button the front to give him a moment to calm down.

"Look, Dante, I understand that you're upset. I figured you would overreact, and that it wouldn't help Sophie any. I assumed that the next thing you would say is that you're taking her home with you."

"Damn right I am, before you get her killed!"

It takes a great deal of restraint not to wince. He's right, she could've been killed, and I fucking hate myself for putting her in danger, for not stopping the attack, just like I couldn't stop the one at the casino.

"Answer one question for me first."

"What?" he snaps.

"What would you have done if Sophie was attacked by drones while on your rooftop court?"

"The guards would've shot them down!"

"Right. And when shooting them down makes them explode over her head, raining down fiery debris then what? There was no good solution at the time. Yes, I was stupid to not think about an aerial attack, and I hate that my oversight nearly cost Sophie her life, along with her guards lives. They did their job, though, and protected her. Now the situation is being remedied."

"Remedied how?"

"Snipers on the rooftops at all times. They can shoot down any flying objects before they cross the property lines."

"Snipers?"

"Yes. Until I can get my hands on some kind of anti-air defense missiles. That shit isn't as easy to obtain. My people have tried to buy one. Small countries all hoard the ones that they have. Eventually someone might sell me one."

"You're serious? You're trying to purchase a military defense system to protect your house?"

"Wouldn't you if the tennis court on your roof was blown up?"

"Yes."

"I'm doing what I can to make sure this doesn't happen again. Sophie is fine. She got scuffed up from being thrown to the ground by her guards. That's it, though."

"That's it? You don't think she's going to be traumatized by the attacks for months or years to come?"

"We survived and overcame something similar."

"She shouldn't have to deal with this kind of assassination shit!"

"No, she shouldn't. I can't even begin to tell you how angry at myself I am for not protecting her. I didn't need you to come berate me on top of everything else. Yell all you want, but it won't change anything that happened."

"I could ask her if she wants to come home with me and get an annulment. I never should've urged her to marry your worthless ass!" Again, my muscles tense to keep from flinching at his insult. "I don't need your contacts that badly."

"Sophie's not leaving, and we're not getting the marriage annulled."

"That's up to her."

"Look, Dante, it's not even been three weeks. What grounds would she have for an annulment?"

"I don't know. I'll have my attorney look into it. All I know for certain is that I gave you a chance, and you blew it."

"What if she's pregnant?"

"What?"

"You heard me. I doubt she can get an annulment if she's pregnant with my kid."

"Why do you think...never mind. Like I said, I'll have my attorney look into it and contact you or your attorney. I won't make her stay here with you for another second."

"No. She's not leaving. Not today. Not until she bleeds. I won't budge on that, because if she is pregnant then once she's gone, you probably wouldn't let me see her or my son or daughter again."

"Probably not."

"Then give me a little more time with her until we know for sure, then let her decide."

He studies my face like he wants to punch it. Eventually, he grits out, "Fine."

"Thank you," I say in relief. "And you and the rest of her family are free to visit her here whenever you want. Even...Cole." My jaw aches from how tightly it's clenched when I speak blondie's name.

Dante nods. "The penthouse feels empty without her and Madison. I didn't realize how much I would miss them until..."

I start to point out he was probably too busy to notice them, but I swallow those words. "Still no word on Madison?"

"No."

"I'm sorry."

"You should be. It's at least partially your fault that she ran away. If you hadn't been trying to force her into marrying you so soon, then maybe she wouldn't have fled town."

Great, now I'm responsible for Sophie's near death and Madison's disappearance. He's right about the first so maybe he's right about Madison too. I don't bother objecting to his assumption.

"Apologizing won't change anything," I tell him. "And I *was* going to call you today when we got home to set up a meeting to tell you about the drones, give you the blackmail for the contacts you need, and talk to you about another issue."

He looks slightly less furious at the mention of the shit he needs to keep his drug trafficking ring intact. "What issue?"

"Your employee, Eli, he's a master of torture if the rumors are true."

"Trust me, torture is a mild word for what Eli does to my enemies." He says the words like a threat, warning me that if anything happens to Sophie, I'll no doubt be on the other end of Eli's techniques.

"Can I borrow him?"

He arches a black eyebrow. "You want to borrow my torturer?"

"That's what this alliance of ours is about, right? Sharing resources now that we're legally family?"

"For the moment," he mutters as if that has the potential to change at any moment, even though I know he's desperate for my political connections to help him move his product. "And who exactly would you be torturing?" Dante asks.

"No one."

"So you won't fucking tell me but I'm just supposed to instruct Eli to murder, maim, or whatever else you tell him to do?"

"No, I meant that I'm not planning to torture anyone other than the bomber when I find them. I just need Eli to question a few individuals to try and scare the one I'm after into making a move, a mistake. I want everyone to think I'm instructing the infamous Eligor to rip off fingernails or gouge out eyes. What's that nickname about anyway? Is it Eli's full name?"

"No. Eligor is the name of a demonic lord legend says took the souls of warriors in exchange for giving them the secrets they needed to win wars."

"Based on the rumors, I have no doubt my employees will be rightfully concerned by his presence. The innocent as well as the guilty party."

"Why exactly do your employees need to be scared shitless of being tortured? You do know that threatening their families will usually be enough to get them talking, right?"

"Yes, but the threat of torture can be more persuasive. Thanks to your daughter's keen observation that I refused to consider, I'm now certain the casino bomber had to have been someone on the inside. One of my own employees."

"No shit," Salvato says as if it's obvious. Guess he trusts people even less than I do thanks to all the years of experience he has on me. "But how did Sophie come up with that when you couldn't? I know the police interviewed everyone they suspected who worked at the Emerald Paradise. I've even read their reports. But you're telling me you didn't thoroughly investigate your own people? How stupid are you?"

"Fuck you," I snap at him, hating that he's right. "So maybe I've been blinded by my assumed loyalty of all my staff. I was looking for someone out of place. It only makes sense if nobody unfamiliar or suspicious showed up on surveillance feeds. Sophie and I were talking the other day between matches when she pointed out my obvious oversight."

"Matches? Do I even want to know?"

"Tennis matches."

"*You* play tennis?"

"Yes. She seemed equally surprised by my skills on the court. I even beat her. Once."

"I'm glad you two have something to bond over. And yes, I'll have

Eli contact you. He'll be disappointed about the lack of hands-on fun, so pay him well, and give him the person responsible to play with before you kill them."

"I will," I assure him.

"Now, can I see Sophie?"

"Sure. We have dinner at seven, so she'll probably be in the dining room or on her way there."

Glad to have calmed down the mafia daddy, I lead him over to the dining room where Sophie is sitting and waiting for me obediently. At least until she sees her father.

"Daddy?" Sophie exclaims with such affection in her voice that it makes my chest ache. She'll never say my name like that.

Jumping up from her chair, she gives her father a hug while looking at me over her shoulder. "What are you doing here? Did Lochlan tell you about the drones?"

"I heard about them, yes. Are you okay? Do you feel safe staying here?"

"The guards protected me, and Lochlan has snipers on the roof as well as someone at the airport monitoring the skies. That's about all that can be done, right?"

"Right," Dante agrees.

"So, is that all you came for?" she asks as she steps away from him. Seeing her in her white tennis outfit gets me hard so fast I have to take my seat before I pass out or her father sees the front of my tenting pants.

"I've missed you. Vanessa too," Dante says. "Cass..."

"I know Cass doesn't miss me," Sophie scoffs.

"I told your father your family is welcome to come visit whenever you want, even Cole," I remark.

"I doubt Vanessa will let Cole come here until things...settle down," Dante replies. "But I'll let them all know."

Sophie fidgets with her tennis bracelet when she asks quietly, "Do you have to go? Or do you have time to stay and have dinner with us?"

He takes a deep breath, looks to me then back to his daughter. "Sure, if Lochlan doesn't mind."

If he had refused Sophie's offer, I may have stabbed my knife through his back as soon as he turned to leave.

"I'll have the staff put out another place setting. I'm sure they made plenty of food for the three of us," I tell them.

"Great," Dante says, choosing a seat near Sophie's. "Now tell me about how you let Lochlan beat you at tennis."

"He's actually good," Sophie replies with a grin in my direction. "And he beat me fair and square because I was...exhausted."

Exhausted? That's not how I remember it. I think she wanted to say distracted but didn't want to admit her attraction to me.

She obviously wants me; I want her; so why the hell aren't we fucking?

28

Sophie

Being back at Lochlan's house isn't as scary as I thought it would be. My father may not approve, but I feel safe with him here. Mostly. Yes, an enemy may have caught him off-guard once, but I don't think Lochlan, or his security team, will let it happen again.

I got dressed to go play on the newly repaired tennis court, but couldn't find the courage to walk out to it yet. My excuse was that it was too close to dinner so I may as well stay inside.

Seeing my father in the dining room was a good surprise. Although, I am thankful that he left just before dessert. Not that I didn't want him around longer. We're having cheesecake, which makes me think dirty thoughts. *Again.* I can barely go a day without my husband reminding me of that dinner with my family where he had his hand up my skirt.

I eat every last crumb of my slice while Lochlan watches me

silently, hungrily the entire time, as if he didn't have a piece of his own cheesecake sitting right in front of him.

Is that how I look at him when he's shirtless on the tennis court? I still can't believe we have that in common, or how much I want him despite the fact that I'm unable to trust him, to believe he hasn't been with anyone else in months. What is wrong with me? Why can't I have an ugly philandering husband who is easy to resist instead of a gorgeous one? No, I wouldn't wish for that in a million years.

I'm about to get up from the table to tell him goodnight and go to my room when Lochlan blurts out, "What's it going to take, Sophie?"

"Ah, what?" I dab the corner of my lips with a napkin while trying to figure out what exactly he's talking about.

"You know I want you, princess. So, what do I have to do to get inside of you again?"

Oh. That.

My hormones want me to believe him, that he only wants me. My head and my heart are so damn nervous, though. Trusting him doesn't come easy. I want Lochlan, but I don't want him to use me then hurt me.

Actually, I know exactly what I want from him. What I've wanted this entire time.

I don't want to second-guess every little thing, worry about doing something wrong or look embarrassed when my inexperience is obvious like when I got on my knees in the SUV.

Lochlan deserves one more chance, right? Besides, my period is due any day now, so there's no pregnancy concerns for me to worry about if he doesn't use protection.

That's why I tell Lochlan, "There's nothing..."

"There has to be something I can do to change your mind!" he roars, interrupting me. "I'm fucking desperate for you, Sophie. Is that what you want to hear? Do you want me to get on my knees and beg?"

He would get on his knees and beg for me?

"No, Lochlan. I meant there's nothing you need to do to change my mind," I explain to him. "I just...I think I've been waiting for you."

"You've been waiting for me?" he repeats, his brow furrowed.

"Yes, I've been waiting on you to promise to be faithful, which you sort of did, and for you to just...take what you want from me, like you did the first time."

Lochlan's eyes are instantly heavy-lidded, a darker shade of green. "You don't mean that, princess."

"I do," I whisper. "I-I trust you. If you haven't been with anyone else..."

"I haven't and I won't," he promises.

"Then I believe you. That you only want me. I want you too, even if it's complicated."

"Complicated? What does that mean?"

"What I mean is I'm not entirely sure what I want when it comes to sex. I didn't want you to take my virginity that night. I was scared, nervous, but I wanted you. I liked that you took it anyway, that you made the decision for me. One that made me feel good. Is that wrong?"

"No. No, it's not wrong. It's hot as hell," he replies. Shoving his dessert plate away, he gets to his feet and comes toward me. "It's hot for me because I'm the one who will be in control. I'm always in control. I could do anything I wanted to you, and you wouldn't be able to stop me."

"I know that."

"No. If you change your mind in the middle..." His fingers curl around the top of the chair closest to mine, the one my father just vacated, his knuckles white. "If I go too far and don't stop once I have you where I want you, you'll hate me even more than you do now, and you'll never forgive me. And I can't promise not to lose control."

All the reasons he listed for not giving in are what I want from him. So, I try to make that perfectly clear, "There's only one way you'll ever get me in your bed, Lochlan, because I won't ever go willingly."

"Fuck," he mutters a second before he lunges for me. The chair dips backward with me in it, startling me. I don't fall to the floor, though. Lochlan catches me before I finish shrieking, then his lips are on mine. That's when I realize he did it on purpose, to startle me, to get my heart racing. He likes when I'm afraid of him, of what he might do to me. But I haven't been afraid for a while. Not really.

Once he pushes the chair away from the table, he lowers it back to all four legs, grabs my hips, scooping me out of it, and throws me over his shoulder. My hands fly out to grab hold of his suit coat to hold on, which is when he slaps my ass, making me yelp.

"Tell Owen and Flynn to cover my meetings and appointments tomorrow. They fucking owe me. Don't even think about knocking on my bedroom door for anything," Lochlan says to his guards as we pass them on the way up the stairs. One of them replies, "Not a soul will dare disturb you until you say the word, boss."

Then we're in Lochlan's room, the door slamming shut behind us. When I try to squirm down from his shoulder, he smacks my ass again.

My back hits the mattress a moment later, then Lochlan is climbing on top of me, sending a thrill through me, all the way down to my toes. And especially in a certain area between my legs. His mouth covers mine, kissing me hard, his tongue insistent, making all my limbs go slack. I reach up to run my fingers through Lochlan's hair, but he grabs my wrists and stops kissing me to pin them above my head.

He stretches out above me and then wraps a thick, soft cuff around my right wrist, then one on my left.

I try to pull my arms down. They only move a few inches with a rattle of the attached chain. Tilting my head back I see the chains are anchored to the headboard.

My first thought is hell yes, this is so hot, being Lochlan's captive.

The second is...less fun.

"Ah, Lochlan?"

"Yes, princess?" he asks, sitting back on his heels, looking mighty proud of himself as he stares down at me chained to his bed.

"Have you...have you used these before?" I rattle the chains, not sure how I feel about them now knowing the ease at which he restrained me.

"These particular cuffs? No. While I won't deny using plenty of restraints before, I had these installed in here for you the morning of the wedding. Which means, I've had to look at them hanging unused, taunting me every night that you've made me sleep alone. All I could do was fantasize about you in them, completely naked, mine for the taking."

New. For me, he says.

And I believe him.

"There's one little problem," I can't help but point out.

"What's that? Too tight?"

"No. I'm not naked. Might be hard to get my shirt and bra off now that my hands are cuffed."

"Mmm," Lochlan murmurs as he pinches my left nipple and right at the same time through my clothing, making me squeal and squirm away as much as I can in the cuffs. "You're not naked *yet*. Getting there is half the fun."

Grabbing the bottom of my sleeveless top, he shoves it up to my neck. The air is cool on my stomach, revealing my white sports bra, along with the prize tucked down inside the front.

Lochlan doesn't see it at first; he's too busy teasing my nipples with his thumb and finger, pinching, pulling at them through the fabric, making me cry out. Only when he lifts the bottom of the bra up over my breasts does he see the silver knife slide out.

"Oh, what do we have here, dirty girl?" Picking up the weapon, he presses the switch, so the blade pops out. Now he chuckles, "You've been carrying it around inside your bra?"

"I wanted to make sure you couldn't find it," I reply truthfully. "And it made me feel safe."

"Does it? Well, you can have my knife back, after I'm finished with it. I'm going to use it to slice your clothes off your body. Then, I'm going to do something really fucking filthy with it."

As promised, he lifts my shirt in his left hand and rips the knife through the material, cutting through the collar, the right armhole, finally the left, until it's no longer in the way. Next, he works on sawing the knife blade slowly through the center of my sports bra. Both of us are breathing heavier by the time it's done. He doesn't rip the arm holes, leaving it parted, hanging open on either arm.

I expect my horny husband to go right to pulling off my skirt and panties, but he doesn't. No, he leans over me, taking my breast into his mouth. He suckles, licks, nips with his teeth. One side, then the other, taking his time, as if he's got nowhere to go tonight. If he told the guards to have his second and third take his meetings tomorrow, then I guess he doesn't have anywhere to go for a while.

I love that he plans to spend all night and tomorrow in bed with me. Will he keep my wrists cuffed the entire time? I'm nervous and excited all at the same time.

I'm finally dangling over the cliff's edge and it's fucking amazing.

29

Lochlan

How the fuck did I not realize what Sophie wanted from me before now?

All she wanted was for me to take her again. She wasn't waiting for me to buy her more diamonds, or any other shit besides a promise not to fuck around behind her back. My wife wanted my word, my promise to be loyal to her, and then for me to pin her down and take what I need from her.

Which is perfect for me.

For the past eight years, bondage is the only way I ever fucked anyone, and Sophie practically begged me for it.

I want to get my mouth on every inch of her, bury my dick inside of her, taste her, all at the same time, which is unfortunately impossible. After wanting her for so long, I have no choice but to take my time with her, revealing her sexy body to me a little at a time so I don't get overwhelmed and nut on the sheets like a teenager.

Once I've spent quality time with her perky tits, I can't wait any longer to see her pussy again.

Scooting down her body, I grip the sides of her white pleated tennis skirt to yank it off, then change my mind at the last minute. My fingers dive underneath to the waistband of her panties, dragging them, and them alone, down her legs and off.

Now I flip the skirt up to her stomach to admire my wife's pussy.

"Hello again, my lovely wet kitty cat."

"Are you talking to my..." Sophie asks, trying to close her legs self-consciously.

"Yes," I reply while swiping my fingertip down the slit. "So gorgeous." Wondering if she's really as tight as I remember, I slip my middle finger inside of her, curling it.

"Ah!" Sophie cries. Her walls squeeze around my slowly pumping digit, making my balls grow heavy. God, I can't wait to be inside her again. It's actually happening, right here, right now. There's no stopping my dick from sliding home again.

But not yet. I promised her after the first time to lick her, get her soaking wet before I fuck her again.

First, I need to make sure her thighs stay open for me, no matter what I do to her pussy.

Pushing Sophie's knees to her chest, her eyes widen and lips part, curious to know what the hell I'm doing but not objecting.

"You had to know I had cuffs for your ankles too, princess."

"Oh," she whispers. Licking her damp lips, she asks, "At the foot of the bed?"

"Not this time." I reach to the right corner of the headboard to bring the slightly longer chain down, fastening the cuff to her right ankle.

"Wh-what..." Sophie trails off as I quickly fasten her left ankle. Then I sit back and admire my handiwork. Her thighs parted wide, knees nearly pressed to her chest, but unable to lower them or close her legs thanks to the chains.

"Wide open and ready for me," I say as I spread her pussy lips apart with my fingers, then bend down to lick her.

"Oh god. Ohgodohgodohgod," Sophie chants softly as I shove my tongue inside of her and swirl it around.

"You taste so damn good," I tell her as I inhale the scent of her arousal, press my face into it, wriggle my tongue over her clit. The last part makes her hips bounce so I do it again and again, pulling back when she's right on edge.

"Please, Lochlan!" Sophie yells in frustration.

Reaching for my discarded switchblade knife next to her on the mattress, I pick it up and show it to her. "Do you remember what you said about how you would rather fuck yourself with this?"

She nods her head.

I lower the cool steel to her abdomen, sliding it down her pelvis.

"Do you know where it's going?" I ask her.

"Yes." She lifts her head to nod enthusiastically, which is surprising. "I wanted you to put it inside me the first day we met."

Jesus Christ.

"Did you really?"

"Yes. You left me..."

"Left you what?" I ask.

"Hot and aching."

"Hot and aching is exactly how you make me feel every second of the day." I love hearing her say I have the same effect on her, even the first time we met when she was terrified of me.

Retracting the blade on the knife, I swipe the handle through her slit, getting it wet.

"Ah!" Sophie gasps when it's slick enough to ease it inside of her. While she's distracted with the foreign object entering her, I flick my tongue over her clit, teasing, drawing out the building pleasure until she's a panting, sweaty mess. That's when I finally bring her over the edge. I leave the knife handle jutting out of her to watch her pussy spasm around it, slurping it up, trying to pull it deeper, just like I can't wait for it to do to my cock.

I wriggle the knife around before pulling it free and pushing it between Sophie's parted lips. "Clean my knife for me princess," I tell her, sliding it in and out of her mouth. "Did you clean that fucker's blood off of it that night I stabbed his hand?" I ask her and she nods.

"Good girl. Are you ready for my cock?"

"Mmm," she moans around the steel.

"You know I'm going to come inside of you so fucking hard," I warn her.

"Mmm." It sounds like she approves when I leave the knife handle in her mouth to finally get undressed. I shrug out of my suit jacket easy enough. The rest have buttons I rip apart, in too much of a hurry to undo them all.

When I'm finally naked, I kneel between Sophie's spread open thighs. Taking my hard cock in my fist, I rub it through her wetness, making us both groan. I once came just from this the night I spanked her. Not this time.

I line my head up at her entrance and sink right on in. At least the first few inches go in easy. That's when it gets good.

"Fuck, you're so tight," I tell her as I stare down at her raised arms, my knife held between her teeth. I pull the weapon free and toss it on the mattress, wanting to hear every little sound she makes including...

"Yes. More."

I give her what she wants, thrusting all the way in, causing a scream to rip from her throat and a swear from my own. God, she feels so fucking good. I have no doubt that bottoming out so fast hurt her, but I think that's exactly what Sophie wants too—rough, dirty sex.

Stretching out over her with one palm braced beside her head, I press my weight onto her body then give my cock free rein to pump in and out of her deep and fast. Sophie's eyes are squeezed tight, either in pleasure or pain. I wrap my fingers around her throat, and they pop right open.

"There you are," I say with a grin. I tighten my grip on her neck.

"Is this what you had in mind? Being completely at my mercy? I could choke you, fill you with my cum over and over again, do whatever I want, and you can't stop me."

"Yes! *Yesss!*" Sophie makes that mewling sound, then she's squeezing my cock, coming on it and taking me with her. I fuck her impossibly faster through those twitches of pleasure, shoving deep, making sure my seed coats her walls.

Even when the last shudder leaves me and my cock is well sated, I don't want to pull out of her warm body yet.

I hold on to her throat as I press my lips to hers, kissing her like it could be the last time. She gives as good as she gets too. I never gave a shit about kissing anyone before her. It always felt fake during sex, like an obligatory requirement, which is exactly why I stopped doing it.

When I finally pull my lips away so we can both catch our breath, I see the moisture glistening on Sophie's cheek.

Fuck.

"You changed your mind? Bitten off more than you can chew?" I ask, trying not to take out my frustration on her. She shakes her head from side to side again. "You didn't ask me to use protection, and you didn't even take the morning-after pill you demanded, so what's the fucking problem, Sophie?"

I plan to get an answer out of her before I release her.

"You...you knew about the pill?"

"Of course, I knew about the pill. I stole a pair of your satin panties to jerk off on when I threw it in the drawer."

Her shimmering eyes widen in surprise. "Oh."

"I also know you didn't take it. The box is still smushed behind the drawer. Why not?"

"I...I didn't want to get anyone in trouble."

"You thought your guards would disobey me and you wanted to protect them more than you wanted to prevent a pregnancy?"

"Yes."

"And you regret that decision now?"

She shakes her head again. "No."

"Then why the fuck are you crying?"

"I just...I want to touch you. To taste you again."

You've got to be fucking kidding me. Those are tears of longing? Of her inner conflict?

"Oh, princess. We'll have plenty of time for you to taste me later."

She hates that she wants me, that she likes it rough; I fucking know that. Sophie still thinks I'm a disgusting, dirty bastard.

And I am, because I won't be able to resist using her pretty mouth again for much longer. She'll probably beg for mouthwash and a shower any second now, pull away from me like the first time.

At least she's not asking me to release her. I'm not sure I could remove the restraints from her yet, even if she begged me to.

~

Sophie

Sex with Lochlan is better than I remember. Or maybe it's better now because it's not my first time.

There is some soreness after the third round. Lochlan didn't remove the cuffs on my wrists and ankles except for long enough to reposition me, putting me on my hands and knees.

I think that may have been my favorite position if I had been able to see his gorgeous face.

"Jesus, that was good, princess," Lochlan says as he slips around in front of me, leaning his back against the headboard. He's naked and gorgeous, corded muscles covered in ink. And he's already getting hard again, stroking his intimidating length in his fist. Sliding down until he can rub his crown over my lips, he says, "Suck my dick clean, and I'll free you."

I give his slick cock a teasing lick, tasting both of us on him. "Then what? I'm...all yucky."

"I figured you would want a shower. Then maybe I'll even feed you before I chain you up in my bed again."

"Could we maybe cuddle?"

"Cuddle?" He says the word with disgust, as if I asked him to go for a swim with me in a septic pit.

"Uh-huh. Cuddle." I swirl my tongue over his head.

"I don't cuddle. If we're in bed we're either fucking or sleeping. Those are the only two things that are real."

The only two things that are real?

I don't have a chance to ask what he means. Lochlan moves to his knees in front of me, grabs my ponytail that's hanging loose and messy from him constantly pulling it, then presses my lips to him. "Suck me off, Sophie."

His ripped abs and chest are so close I could touch him...if my wrists weren't attached to chains. Since I can't, I take him into my mouth, letting him thrust in and out, over and over again, giving me more than I can take, but not caring. No, he cares. He just likes when I choke, and tears race down my cheeks.

I realize he's not being rough with me because he's mad or because I'm doing something wrong. He's rough because he's right on the edge of that cliff, desperate to go over...

"God, I love owning your sweet mouth," Lochlan groans, hips thrusting, fucking into it faster. "And your pussy. Is my cum still leaking out of your tight cunt?"

"Mmm," I moan around him, hating how much I like the way his hot, thick release feels inside of me, seeping down my thighs, a reminder of our mind-blowing orgasms. I still can't believe it was Lochlan who gave me the emergency contraceptive. The pill I didn't take.

"Fuck, I can't...I can't waste it," he grunts.

Before I can figure out what he means, he's pulling out of my mouth and crawling behind me. I hear the Velcro and a second later my left ankle is free, then the right. I moan in relief as he pulls me off my knees, straightening my legs flat. Lochlan pushes them together, then he's wedging his cock between them...

"Oh!" I exclaim when he penetrates me. His knees on the outsides of my legs keep mine closed as he rocks into me. Rocks, not slams, or thrusts like the times before. He remains deep as if savoring the sensation, his teeth biting into my shoulder to muffle his growl. His weight on top of my back, the angle, the way he slides through me, I love it all. Seconds later, I pulse around him with the mother of all orgasms.

"That's it, baby." With a gruff chuckle, he says, "Your pussy wants me coming in it, even if you don't. Now tilt your hips up so I can give it every single drop."

His weight disappears from my back to lift my hips himself. He gives my ass cheek a slap, then he's swearing, cock swelling inside me before pouring that familiar warmth of his release into me.

Lochlan seems to really love doing that, so I keep letting him without protest. Either my period is about to start, or it won't because I'm already pregnant because I didn't take that pill. If I am, I'll deal with it later.

After our joint shower and breakfast? Lunch? I have no concept of time, but we eat and then I end up back in his bed, lying there restrained and letting his seed soak my flesh over and over again. Until I'm so sore even after him licking me that he only inserts the head of his dick in me to stroke the rest of his shaft through his release. Not a drop goes anywhere else. He's a man on a mission. A man possessed.

I occasionally sleep between rounds. Lochlan mostly leaves my ankles uncuffed, but not my wrists. Never my wrists. The muscles in my arms and shoulders are sore, but I get the feeling that if I ask him to free me, I'll be sent back to my room alone. So, I don't ask. I'm enjoying my husband's rapt attention too much to leave.

30

Lochlan

There may be an extra pep in my step today while striding down to the suite at the end of the fifth floor that's been turned into a torture dungeon. Or so everyone thinks.

Not only did my wife give me this excellent idea, she also gave me her body, over and over again for the past twenty-four hours. Having Sophie chained to my bed in nothing but her tennis skirt or naked, begging for more while I fucked her was even better than I imagined it would be. I lost track of how many times I came inside of her. If she wasn't pregnant before, here's hoping she is now. It was by far the best sex of my life, and I can't wait to have her again when I get home. Hell, leaving her this morning wasn't easy. Knowing she was too sore to go another round is the only reason I was able to walk out the door.

I still can't believe Sophie not only kept my knife, but that she carries it around in her sports bra because she said it makes her feel safe. Even though it's my favorite knife, the only present my mother ever bought for me, I left it with Sophie to keep safely tucked away with her succulent tits.

"What's going on up here, boss?" Wolfe asks.

"Don't worry about it," I reply as we walk down the hallway with Wade. I hate keeping shit from my guards, but Sophie's right. I made the mistake of trusting the wrong person once. Until I find them, everyone is a suspect. "Just watch the door and don't let anyone interrupt."

When we reach the door at the end of the hallway, I add, "Stay here and text if you need me," before I swipe my keycard. Then I slip inside, letting the door slam behind me. As much as I trust Wolfe and Wade, not even my friends or guards need the details of what I'm doing. Or what Eli is doing.

"How's it going?" I ask him.

"Slowly," Eli says, flashing me a grin over his shoulder before turning back to touch the tools spread over the coffee table as if they're his babies. "Just the way I like it."

The sight of the bright red blood splattered over his gauze wrapped hands and rolled up sleeves of his white dress shirt, the handles of his "tools" as well as the plastic covering the floor underneath the single chair are a surprise. Not only because I told him not to actually cut into my employees without my permission, but also because Sherman Young, the security manager here at the casino while paler than usual doesn't have a visible wound on his line-backer-sized body. He's wearing his all-black uniform so maybe I missed something.

"Just waiting for Dante's IT guys to finish reviewing the past years' worth of Sherman's bank accounts and phone records. He has until my phone dings to confess to...well, anything and everything they might dig up. Other than having his team clock in for him on the computer system whenever he's running late, he hasn't admitted to anything of substance."

"I haven't done shit. I wouldn't betray you or the casino, and I would never kill anyone with a bomb. I swear it, boss!" the man exclaims, the whites of his eyes showing. "I'll pay back every penny of time when I was late. Double or triple it."

The few minutes he was running late is nothing. Honestly, I would ask someone to do the same for me if I were expected somewhere and couldn't make it.

"What about your employees?" I move up closer to him. "Any of them doing shady shit that we should know about? Were any acting suspicious before the bombing?"

"No, sir," he replies before he winces. "A couple may fudge their time too. Nothing much, though. A few minutes—"

I cut him off to ask, "You've got a family, right, Sherman? A son and a daughter?"

"Oh, fuck. Now it's getting fun," Eli whispers, as if shit's about to get hardcore. From the corner of my eye, I swear the psycho reaches down to adjust his dick like he's getting too excited by a lap dance in a strip club rather than in a fake torture room. What a freak.

"Y-yes, sir." Sherman's gaze goes to the other man as well for an instant. Noticing Eli's arousal, or more than likely, concerned for his family, his fingers curl around the armrests of the leather chair so hard he's about to rip them off.

"What's fatherhood like?" I ask.

The man looks from me to Eli, then back again. "Well? Answer him!" Eli roars.

"It's...it's the best part of my life. Everything I do is for my kids and my wife."

"Glad to hear that," I tell him just as a ding comes from Eli's side of the room.

"Time's up," the crazy bastard announces. "Any last words?"

Sherman shakes his head.

Eli studies the device in a long, drawn-out silence. Finally, he says, "He's clear."

Clapping my hands together, I say, "Great. Back to work, Sherman. As long as you and your employees aren't clocking in extra hours, I don't give a shit."

"You don't?" he replies.

"Nope. We do have more employees to talk to, some of yours probably. Let's keep this conversation between us, though, yeah?"

"Yes. Yes, sir." He's up and out of his seat a second later. I watch him walk to the door and out of it in a hurry, as if we might change our minds.

"How many have you talked to so far?" I ask Eli. "And where did all this blood come from?"

"Me." He unrolls the gauze I thought were covering bloody knuckles. His knuckles are bleeding, but not as badly as the slit across his palm. "A little blood goes a long way in getting people to talk."

"How...authentic of you," I mutter.

"I don't do anything half-assed," the psycho responds. "And Sherman was the tenth of the day."

I provided Eli with a list of supervisors in and around the casino who could've put a bomb on the cart at some point before the event. If we start at the top and work our way down, it's more likely the employees with better pay and positions will rat out anyone they suspect of, well, anything.

"Keep at it. I know we can't stop them from talking about what's going on in here, which is what I intended. If the one we're looking for overhears and doesn't come when called or suddenly disappears..."

"Then we've got them."

"Exactly."

It's probably going to be a long, tedious process, but it's the best I've got to try and find the fucker responsible. Having someone to put the blame on could go a long way in the civil case too. Which means I need to find the person responsible before the meeting in LA that's just a few days away.

Before the next employee comes in, I get a text from Wolfe.

Something's up, boss. Guards at the estate just reported to me that you've arrived back at home, heading straight into the garage. I told them they're mistaken.

"What the fuck?" I mutter as I read, then reread, his text. I even send back a WTF before heading to the door. At least whatever is up is happening when I know Sophie is safe and sound at the tennis center. I text Lena just to make sure and get her instant confirmation.

"Trouble?" Eli asks.

"Just a mistake, I think. Either way, I have to go figure it out. Keep going down the list and let me know if you find out anything of substance," I tell him before leaving.

31

Sophie

I haven't flown much in my life, despite the fact that my father has his own jet, but the happy, bubbly sensation inside me today makes me feel like I'm floating up there with the clouds.

That's probably just the aftereffects of so many orgasms so close together. I flew high with each one, sometimes soaring again before the first one finished.

Lochlan is...the master of my body. It's like he knows every inch of me better than I do. He's an intimidating businessman walking around in a suit, but when he's naked and has me chained to his bed, he's an insatiable monster.

And I love it.

Every second. Even the restraints, despite the discomfort to my arms and shoulders today.

Swinging the tennis racquet may be painful but I don't care. The ache will just remind me of all the hot moments with Lochlan.

I still haven't played on the repaired court at the estate. Not that I've really had a chance with Lochlan keeping me busy in bed. I've lied to myself saying that it's him and the Vegas heat keeping me from playing, when really it still smells like burning plastic.

But I want to play, and Julia told me I could use the indoor court at the tennis center if there's no class, which is most of the morning when there's only a private lesson or two going on.

"Have fun," Toni says as she takes up her position at the entrance while Lena heads to the one in the back.

"Thanks," I say with a smile over my shoulder.

Since it's early, I head for the office to see if Stacy or one of the other staff want to join me. All four of the women are standing in a huddle, and they stop talking when they see me. It's almost like they were all talking about me.

Crap. Is Julia mad I didn't call to tell her I wouldn't be in while Lochlan and I were in California or during our sex-a-thon yesterday? I've never had a job or volunteered before, but I probably should've notified her.

Maybe I'm just being paranoid, but I don't think so. That's why I begin my greeting with an apology.

"Hey, I'm so sorry I wasn't able to come in the past few days."

"It's fine, Sophie," Julia says. "We all heard about the awful attack on the Dunne estate."

"Right, well, it was a close call, but everyone is fine."

She clutches her palm to her chest. "And we are so relieved to hear that. However, I'm going to have to ask you take a pause in your volunteer work here."

"A pause? Why?"

"We're afraid it's not safe at the moment."

"You don't think I'm safe here? But I always have guards with me."

The four women exchange silent looks before Julia clarifies her statement. "I meant that we don't think it's safe for the children if

276

you're here. It would be terrible if Lochlan's enemies were to try and harm you during a lesson. I'm sure you can understand our concern."

They don't want me to volunteer because they think I'm too much of a risk to the kids.

Wow. I can't believe I didn't even consider that I could be attacked in public, at this place, just because someone hates Lochlan.

"I'm...I'm sorry. I should've realized..." I trail off, swallowing around the burning in my throat and stinging in my eyes.

"We loved having you, Sophie," Julia says with a small smile. Loved. Past tense as in it's over now for good. So much for a pause.

"I appreciate the opportunity," I tell them softly before I turn and hurry out, not wanting anyone to see the tears overflowing from my eyes.

"What's wrong?" Toni asks at my hurried approach toward the door.

I shake my head. "Just take me home."

"Already? You just got here!" She holds open the door for me, then murmurs, "Shit. You're crying. What did those snobby wenches say to you?"

Her cell phone is in her hand, texting Lena that we're leaving.

"I'm no longer welcome here," I explain, followed by a sniffle.

"What? Why not?" Toni asks a moment before it occurs to her. "Oh, fuck. The drone attack?"

"Yep. They think I'm a danger..." Leaning my back against the side of the SUV I cover my face.

"I hate that, Soph."

"Sorry, girly," I hear Lena say when she approaches. "Lochlan and I wouldn't have let you come here if it wasn't safe."

Swiping my knuckles over my cheeks to dry them, I tell her, "Well, it's not his decision. Let's just go home."

"Yes, ma'am," Lena agrees quietly, then we all load up into the SUV.

"Could you not..." I start. "Please don't tell Lochlan," I beg them.

"He might make things worse, and I know he'll blame himself. I'll tell him...later."

"We won't mention it unless he asks directly," Lena agrees.

~

I wish that being dismissed by the tennis center would be the worst part of my day, but as soon as the SUV pulls up to the estate, there's a surprise guest strutting up to the front door.

"Who the hell is that?" Toni asks from the passenger seat.

"What the fuck is she doing here?" Lena grumbles as if she knows the curvy blonde. It's hard to see much of her face yet, but it's impossible to miss the off-the-shoulder, Barbie-pink dress she's wearing. One that is so short it looks like it was actually meant to be a top. It would be a crop-top on me. If she leans even a tiny bit forward, her ass would be out.

Which I realize is the entire purpose of her dress.

"It's one of them, isn't it?" I ask aloud.

"We can drive around until the guards escort her off the premises," Lena suggests without answering my question.

"You mean the guards who are standing there with their tongues hanging out?" Toni asks. "Un-fucking-likely unless it comes from..."

"Lochlan," I finish for her.

I've had a shitty morning and want to curl up in my bed until dinner, so I tell the women, "Just let me out here. I can handle her."

"If you're sure..." Lena says as Toni slows down the SUV.

Throwing my door open before the tires come to a complete stop, I hop out and head to the front door.

"Can I help you?" I ask the woman who is still chatting with the two guards at the front door.

She turns around to answer me, which is when I realize her pretty face looks familiar. I think she was one of the women at the fundraiser who surrounded Lochlan.

Her brown eyes, surrounded by heavy make-up, survey me from head to toe in my tennis outfit.

"You can't help me."

"What the fuck is she doing here?" Toni shouts from behind me to the guards.

"Flynn and Owen said Mr. Dunne approved her visit," one grunts.

Lochlan approved her visit? Before I can take my phone out of my skirt pocket to call him, she mumbles, "You look relatively unscathed," as if she's disappointed. "So awful about the bombing."

"Yes, it was awful," I agree.

Smiling at me smugly she says, "It was hard to hear all the details with my mouth busy, but after we were interrupted, Lochlan looked absolutely devastated when he thought you could be hurt."

"Interrupted?" Did she say her mouth was busy?

No.

She's lying. Lochlan swore to me that he hasn't been with anyone. There's no way he was with *her* during the bombing. He said he had to fire some employees... Unless, the employees were prostitutes.

"Aw. Did you think Loch would wait for you forever? Men like him need rough, dirty sex regularly or they get cranky. If you won't give it to him, then somebody has to."

The night of the bombing...that was definitely before we were having marathon sex. Was he really that desperate that he went to *her?* He told me he hadn't been with anyone in the months before the wedding. Was he lying to me, telling me what he knew I wanted to hear?

Of course, he was.

There's no way an insatiable man like Lochlan goes months without sex.

"What are you doing here, Shana?" Lena asks gruffly.

"What do you think?" Her smile broadens before she strolls up to the door the guard opens for her and saunters inside like she lives here.

Lena, Toni, and I all follow behind her, right up the stairs, then down the hallway into Lochlan's bedroom, like she's been here before. Then the bitch shuts the door behind her.

That...that...son of a bitch!

Lochlan invited her *here* to our house when he thought I would be gone for hours?

He was with *her* when I was attacked? That's why he had to miss dinner with me? For *her*?

Everything he told me was a big, fat lie. I am so done with him that it's not even funny.

"Did she...what..." I try to speak to Lena and Toni but can't form the words.

"I'm looking into it," Lena says, typing away on her phone.

"Come on, let's go..." Toni suggests, nodding her chin to the stairs.

"No."

The three of us stand there in silence for several long heartbeats while the betrayal slowly seeps into my skin. I don't want to believe it. I'm not ready to leave this hallway yet either. I want to confront Lochlan, yell at him, hit him, choke him, stab him in the dick with his own knife. I may as well hear him admit it all, driving the blade into my heart a little deeper.

I take a few steps toward the closed bedroom door, unsure if I should see if it's locked or bang my fist on it demanding he come out and tell me why. Why couldn't he wait a little longer for me? Why after marathon sex does he want *her*?

That's when I hear them, my husband fucking another woman practically in front of my face.

"Soph," Lena says when she lays a hand on my shoulder as if to stop me from going inside.

I haven't decided yet when the door begins to bang rapidly,

repeatedly, much louder than the moans coming from the other side. But still, I hear *her*.

"Hurry! Hurry, Loch! I'm coming! Yes! Oh god, I'm coming!"

Wow. That was fast.

I barely make it past Lena and Toni to get to the nearest bathroom in time to throw up my breakfast. Heave after heave, I try and wrap my head around all the awful shit that's happened today.

It doesn't seem real, any of it, getting fired from being a volunteer or Lochlan cheating on me so...blatantly.

Once the waves of nausea lessen, I get to my feet with a clear purpose. I have my phone in my skirt pocket. That's all I need. The rest of my things can be packed and brought over by someone else later.

"Are you okay?" Toni asks with her brow furrowed when I return to the hallway.

Shaking my head, I tell her, "We're leaving, now." To Lena I say, "Don't even think about telling him I'm leaving. He can find out when his dick is finished with her."

~

Lochlan

Wade sped home even though Wolfe hasn't received any more notifications from the other guards. I'm also relieved to see all is calm at the estate, nothing falling out of the sky when we pull up to the gate.

I have Wade let me out at the front where nothing seems amiss. Still, Wolfe follows me inside.

"Good afternoon, sir. I apologize for Jones mistaking Flynn for you earlier. Owen's in your office waiting for you and your brother somewhere on the estate with your other guest," Dan, one of the guards at the front door informs me.

"Other guest?" I repeat.

"I didn't get any notifications about them being here," Wolfe grumbles from behind me.

"Flynn's his brother and Owen's his second," is all Dan replies with a shrug.

"It's fine. Is Sophie still out?" I ask him.

"She left a few minutes ago."

A few minutes ago? He must not be paying attention if he thought Flynn was me and she just left. I start to tell him she would've left at least an hour or so ago to go to the tennis center to play before classes start but decide it doesn't matter.

"What's going on?" I ask when I stroll into my office and find my second slouching in one of the guest chairs.

"About time," Flynn mutters with a grin when he strolls in right behind me. His dark hair is mussed, and his clothes are even more ratty and askew than usual. "What the hell is this I hear about you torturing your own employees over at Emerald?"

Wow. Word travels faster than I expected.

"The shit I do to my employees at my fucking casino doesn't concern you. Is everything alright? What are you two doing here?" I turn to ask him while Owen gets up to come over.

"We have a surprise for you," my brother says with a smirk.

"A surprise?"

"That's right," Owen agrees. "A stress reliever. You've been a cranky bastard for weeks. More so than usual. We asked your favorite girl to come pay you a visit while the wife's away."

"What the fuck are you talking about?" I ask them slowly.

"Shana is here, waiting in your bedroom for you," Flynn explains.

"She's here?" I look between the two men, wondering if they've been concussed or are high on some shit. Owen looks perfectly fine and sober. But my brother's eyes of course are bloodshot. He's probably high as a kite. "Are you out of your fucking mind?" I ask them. "Get rid of her. Now! If Sophie comes home and finds out…"

"Sophie doesn't want anything to do with you, so why are you still waiting her out?" Flynn asks. "You'll forget all about her rejection after a few times with Shana."

Scrubbing a hand down my face, I mutter, "You stupid son of a bitch."

There is absolutely no way this doesn't bite me in the ass. For days now I've been praying Sophie won't find out the truth about where I was the night of the attack and now…this, gives me something else to lie to her about.

"I don't want Shana or any other whore to step foot in this house again," I turn to tell Wolfe who's lingering in the doorway. "And you two can both get the fuck out," I tell my brother and Owen.

"See. This is what I'm talking about!" Flynn huffs. "You've been a grumpy bastard all because your wife isn't putting out."

"What I do or don't do with my wife is none of your fucking business!" I don't bother to tell him he's wrong, that I've recently spent an entire day and night between Sophie's legs. At least my guards kept their mouth shut about that. "Get the hell out! Now!"

I'm herding them out to the front with Wolfe when Wade runs down the hall, sweat dripping down his forehead. "Ah, boss. We've got a problem."

"What now?"

"I just got a message from Toni. Her and Lena are with Sophie."

"Of course, they're with her at the tennis center."

"No, she's not there anymore, but she's safe."

"Then where is she?"

"Toni won't say. Sophie didn't want…"

"*Where is my wife?*" I bellow.

Wade cringes then goes on to say, "Sophie's asked her to have someone pack up her things and bring them to Dante's because she's not coming back here."

I knew it!

I fucking knew that Shana being here was going to bite me in the ass. I have no clue how Sophie ended up home so early, but she must have seen or talked to her.

Storming to my bedroom, I throw the door open so hard it slams into the wall. The bitch is stretched out naked on my bed. My and Sophie's bed. The comforter and anything else she touched will have to be burned to ash now.

"Finally," she says, as if put out that I made her wait for a visit I didn't even fucking want.

"She saw you here, didn't she?"

"Who?" she asks innocently, finally sitting up.

"My wife!"

"That wasn't my fault. She wasn't supposed to be here."

"What the fuck did you say to her?" I shout across the room. My fists clench with the urge to choke the life out of her, but I don't want to touch her naked body long enough to do that. When she doesn't answer, I roar, "*Answer me!* What did you say to my wife?"

She glances away, then says, "I may have mentioned that you were with me the night of the attack."

"You stupid fucking bitch!" I yell. "Get the fuck out of here. You're done. And if you ever step foot near this house again or any of the brothels, you'll be shot on sight."

32

Sophie

The first place I go when I get home is to my father's office. I barge past his guards, Toni and Lena hot on my heels, and go in without knocking. He's not sitting at his desk but leaning against the front of it looking at his phone. He straightens when he sees me.

"Sophie? What's wrong?"

"Daddy..." That's all I get out before I burst into tears. His arms sweep me into a hug, letting me cry on his chest. "Please don't make me go back. Please..."

"I won't. I won't."

His palm rubs up and down my back, trying to soothe me.

When the sobs finally slow, he leans back to see my face, drying my cheeks with his blue silk handkerchief. Scowling, he asks me calmly, "Do you want me to kill him?"

I immediately shake my head no. Despite how much I'm hurting, I don't want Lochlan dead. That's one of the reasons I didn't tell my father that we had sex the night before the wedding or ask him for an emergency contraceptive pill.

Now, I just want...I don't even know what I want anymore.

There's no apology that can ever fix this. There's absolutely nothing Lochlan can do to make me forgive him.

I stupidly trusted him, believed him when he told me he hadn't been with anyone else. And when I needed him most, he was with *her*.

What I can't wrap my head around is why I'm so surprised and upset. I knew from the beginning, before I married him, that he was a dirty, heartless scoundrel. I fully expected him to cheat on me, especially when he wouldn't promise to be faithful. It's why I tried to keep my distance, why I refused to sleep in his bed with him. And yet, still, somehow, I fell for him, despite knowing the risks.

It's like how the tennis club is scared to have me around. They're smart enough to not take any chances around the kids. I shouldn't have taken any risks with Lochlan, with my heart. I knew better, but did it anyway because...

No. I can't be in love with him. I barely know him! We've only been married a few weeks.

A few weeks that have changed my life, changed me in every possible way. Lochlan was the first person who made me feel like an adult. He made me feel beautiful and special, giving me his undivided attention, like I was the center of his world.

But it was all a lie.

"What do you need me to do, Soph?" my father asks.

I can't help my wince when I ask him, "Could you get me a pregnancy test?"

"I'll get you a dozen just to be sure."

"Thanks, Daddy."

∿

"Well, that didn't take long," Cass gloats when she barges into my room without knocking later that day.

I roll over in my bed to avoid looking at her. "Go away, Cass. I'm not in the mood for your shit today."

"So, the Irishman wasn't your prince charming? How sad."

Of course, he wasn't prince charming. Still, she was attracted to him too.

Without facing her I mutter, "I know you threw yourself at him, and that he didn't want you. Why did you lie to me? Why lie about him wanting you or about refusing to marry him? He never wanted you, so why? Were you jealous of me?"

"He told you about all that?" she asks, sounding surprised.

"Yes, the night I was nearly killed by drones."

"Oh, don't be so dramatic."

Now I sit up to glare at her. Like usual, she's in athletic gear, black leggings, and a black tank top but her hair is straightened and she's wearing makeup for some reason. "I was nearly killed by a horde of exploding drones! One of my guard's head caught on fire. Have you seen her hair?" Toni and Lena are staying at the penthouse with me. After a quick chat with my father, he agreed to hire them both, and pay them more than Lochlan paid them to work for him.

Spinning my computer chair around toward me, Cass lowers herself into it. "He hired female guards for you?"

"Yes."

"Wow. He doesn't want you near *any* other men."

"No, he doesn't, the fucking hypocrite. He flipped out the night of the charity event when I was talking to Cole." Glancing down, my hands fidget with my tennis skirt, my fingertip rubbing over the tiny hole Lochlan made in it with his knife the first time we met. "You wouldn't even believe how mad he got when I simply said his name. Then, when Cole came to play tennis with me, Lochlan showed up all angry and ran him off."

"Cole came over to play tennis with you?"

"Yes. He's decent, better than I expected. Vanessa obviously taught him. She guilted him into coming over." I pause in my rambling, and it occurs to me that it's odd for Cass to ask about our stepbrother. "Why do you even care?"

"I need to know everything there is to know about my enemy."

"Your enemy? Who? Cole?" I ask in confusion.

Shrugging, she says, "Enemy. Competition. Same thing."

"Competition for what?" I ask curiously.

"Who Daddy will choose to take over for him one day."

"You mean...Daddy's going to let *you* take over all the drug trafficking and his businesses?" I ask in disbelief, and a little bit of jealousy.

"Me or Cole. He's going to test us and make a decision in a few months."

"Wow. Why Cole?"

"He's Petrov's grandson. Daddy thinks the pain in the ass Russian holdovers who stayed after he took down Petrov will be more inclined to follow his bloodline."

"Oh. Right. I'm just...I can't believe Vanessa would approve of Cole being part of that sort of thing."

Smirking, Cass says, "Vanessa doesn't approve. She'll let Cole make his own decision, though. She said she's going to try to help me win."

"But I thought...wasn't Lochlan supposed to be Daddy's heir?"

"He was going to be until you came running home a blubbering mess. Daddy just changed his mind, offering me and Cole the chance to become his successor."

"Well, good luck, I guess," I tell her. Our father didn't ask me if I was interested which sort of hurts. But honestly, I have zero interest in running an illegal empire. Or even a legal one. I'd rather be on the tennis court than have to make big, important decisions. "If you're done bragging, you can leave now."

I've just flopped over and laid my head back down on my pillow when Cass says, "So what did Lochlan do that was so bad it sent you running back home?"

"I don't want to talk about it."

When she doesn't speak, I assume she's finally going to get up and leave me alone. But then she says, "I shouldn't have lied, about him flirting with me or wanting to marry me."

"No, you shouldn't have. All this time, I thought I was his third choice."

"And second choice is any better?"

I shrug as much as I can lying down. "A little."

Cass clears her throat. "I heard Daddy tell Vanessa that he was getting you some pregnancy tests."

"Yeah? So?"

"Guess you didn't get a morning-after pill."

"I did. Lochlan gave me one, but I didn't take it."

"Oh," she mutters. I expect her next question to be why not. Instead, she asks, "Do you want me to help you take the tests?"

"Sure," I reply since I don't feel like even reading the directions for them. I just want it to be done, to know for sure either way, so I can curl back up in bed and cry some more.

33

Lochlan

I have my phone to my ear, calling Dante before I even climb into the back of the SUV taking me to his place.

"Don't even think about showing up here," his deep voice rumbles in lieu of a greeting. Not that I expected one.

"Dante, you know I'm coming after her. I thought we had a deal!"

"You and I had a deal, yes. But *this*, whatever you did to send her home bawling her eyes out, doesn't have anything to do with me. I didn't convince her to leave you. She just showed up here and begged me not to make her go back."

Begged. She begged him not to make her come back to me. And she was bawling her eyes out.

"What the fuck did you do to her?" he asks.

"She didn't tell you?"

"Sophie didn't say anything other than she doesn't want you, but

291

she doesn't want me to kill you either. So, I ask again, what did you fucking do, Dunne?"

"It's complicated."

"Bullshit. Tell me. I'll get it out of her eventually."

"It's just a misunderstanding, and a stupid mistake. I swear I can explain everything to her if she'll let me."

"Whatever you did, whatever stupid mistake you made, I honestly don't think she'll ever forgive you."

"Well, I'm not giving up."

"It's no longer your decision."

I know he's about to hang up on me, so I yell, "Dante, wait! Just... give me a chance to come talk to her, to ask her to come back. One chance, that's all I want."

He curses under his breath. "Sophie won't be happy about it but...I gave you ten minutes to convince her to marry your sorry ass, so I'll give you ten minutes to talk her into forgiving you. But that's it. Do you understand me? Whatever Sophie decides, her decision is final."

"Understood. Thank you," I tell him. "I'm on my way there right now."

I have to figure out how to best use what little time I have to explain everything. To explain and beg her to come home with me once and for all.

I'm tired of this bullshit with her and Dante threatening to end our marriage. Either we're going to do this for real or...

Fuck. I don't want to think about any other option.

Sophie may not have been in my life very long, but I can't imagine living without her now.

Even if she won't let me touch her again.

I get why she was hesitant at first. She needed to keep a hold on the power to decide who she shares her body with if nothing else in her life. I understand more than she even realizes how important that decision was for her to make to be with me, and to make it without any manipulation or lies tainting it. She needed to trust me. And when I finally gained that trust, our marriage blows up.

"Got more bad news, boss," Wolfe says from the passenger seat, interrupting my thoughts.

"Great. What is it?" I groan while massaging my aching temples.

"Julia Townsend asked Sophie not to come back to the tennis center."

"What?" I'm so thrown by the sudden change of topic that I don't even realize the significance at first. "Because of the drone bombs?"

"Yes, sir. The center can't take the risk with the children. Toni said Sophie was upset before she even got to the house and..."

"And encountered the stupid whore?"

"Yes, sir."

"Sophie didn't want them to tell you, but Toni thought you should know given...recent events."

My poor heartbroken princess. I can't imagine how disappointed she is about being turned away from the center. She was so excited to be working there, teaching the kids. I thought she may even change her mind about having one someday soon.

Now that plan has gone to shit, and more importantly, it's taken away a newfound purpose in Sophie's life.

I can't even be angry at Julia for making the decision. She's right of course and it's my fault. Until I find out who is behind the drones, and kill them, it's too dangerous for Sophie to be around the children. My enemies want to hurt her to get to me which is so fucking infuriating.

If I can somehow convince Sophie to forgive me, I'll have to figure out a way to find the fuckers responsible for the attack, and make sure she gets that purpose of hers back as soon as possible.

Sophie

. . .

Half an hour later, Cass and I determine that if the three pregnancy tests I peed on are negative, then I'm probably in the clear.

At least for now.

"Exercise and stress can make you late. You could take another test in a few days if your period still hasn't come," Cass says, gathering up the boxes of unopened tests in her arms. "I'll throw the rest of these under the cabinet."

"Okay, thanks," I agree absently as I leave the bathroom to go flop face down on my bed. A moment later, I hear my door open when Cass slips out without a word, leaving me alone with my thoughts. And more tears.

Why am I disappointed in the stupid test results? I don't want a baby, especially not one with Lochlan. I'm free of him now. My father's attorney will figure out a way to get an annulment or a divorce, whatever it takes for the paperwork to be filed. Then, it'll be over. I won't have to ever see him again.

Or so I thought, until my father comes into my room, sits on the foot of my mattress, and says, "Lochlan's on his way over."

I scramble straight up off the bed and to my bare feet. "What? Why? I don't want to see him!" I sob, shaking my head. "Please don't make me see him!"

"He asked me to let him say his piece. I would want the same thing if I fucked up with Vanessa. But I only agreed to give him ten minutes."

"Ten minutes? I don't want to see him for even ten seconds!"

"What happened, Sophie? What did he do to make you this upset? When I asked him, he said there was some misunderstanding and that he made a mistake."

I scoff at that explanation while pacing around my room. What's complicated about him putting his dick in another woman? Multiple times, including the night when he should've been home with me. Yes, it was a mistake, one I'll never forgive him for. And who knows,

294

maybe my dad wouldn't think it's a big deal that my husband has been cheating on me with a whore.

"Did he hurt you?"

I nod since that's a given.

"Physically?"

"No," I quickly answer before he puts a bullet in his head as soon as he steps off the elevator. Yes, Lochlan has physically hurt me before, but I got turned on by it, so I don't think that counts.

"So, he hurt you emotionally?"

"Yes."

"I've never seen you this upset before. Not even when you were about five or six years old, and Cass broke your favorite tennis racquet."

Shrugging, I say, "I knew you would buy me a new one, a better one to make up for her being a bitch."

"And of course, I did. But I can't buy you a new and improved version of Lochlan, unfortunately." When he goes silent, I look over to find his brow furrowed and frown deepening. "If you're this upset, it makes me think that maybe you've already grown to care about him."

Another scoff is my response, but it's not very convincing.

"You don't love him, do you, Soph?" he asks, making it sound as if that would be the worst thing ever.

"No," I blurt out before shaking my head and continuing my pacing, but it sounds like a lie, even to me. Picking up a tennis ball from my desk, one of the few things left in my old bedroom, I dig my nails into the familiar green felt. "I don't know. I wish I had never met him! If Madison hadn't run away, then I wouldn't have had to go through all this!"

"Ah," my dad says. "If you hadn't met him, then he wouldn't have had the power to hurt you." A few silent moments, later, he asks, "So he has some redeeming qualities? I wasn't entirely sure, but I hoped so."

"I don't want to talk about him." I throw the ball against the door, letting it bounce back at me before flopping on the bed, squeezing a pillow to my chest. I definitely don't want to talk about any of Lochlan's "redeeming qualities" with my father since the ones I think of most often are the ones that involve his nakedness and sex.

He also could be kind of sweet, like when he built the tennis court and introduced me to Julia Townsend. Those were a surprise, but both things ultimately turned to shit too. He only did those things to get something in return.

"Well, you don't have to talk to him when he's here, and you don't have to leave with him. Just let him say what he wants to say, then he's gone as soon as his time is up, okay? I'll drag his sorry ass out of here myself if necessary."

I nod since I don't seem to have any other option.

My father stands up from the bed and straightens his suit jacket sleeves as he starts for the door. "Did you, ah, take the tests?"

"Yes. They were negative."

"Good. That's good, right?" he asks.

"I'll know for sure soon, hopefully," I say, meaning when my period comes. If it comes. Which is what I want. Isn't it?

"Right," he agrees sounding relieved. "Vanessa asked if you feel like seeing her."

"Sure," I agree.

"I'll send her in."

A moment later, as if she was waiting outside the door, my stepmother comes in.

"Hey," Vanessa says softly before approaching the bed where I'm curled on my side again. "I know you probably didn't want to talk to your father about what happened between you and Lochlan, but do you want to talk about it with me?"

"No. Not really. It hurts too much," I tell her honestly.

"I understand." She rubs her palm over my upper arm in comfort, like my mother would've done if she hadn't died having me. If she had lived, would her and my father have ended up married? Would she have been a good mother to Cass and Madison too? I have no clue because I don't know anything about her except that she was a masseuse who apparently fooled around with my father until she ended up pregnant.

"Cole's lucky," I tell Vanessa softly. "I wish I had grown up with a mother."

"I wish you had too," she replies. "But at least you girls had a protective father who loves you and would do anything for you."

"Except keep my *husband* away from me, apparently," I grumble. And then I start spilling it all to her. "It's just...I thought he cared about me, so why won't he give up sleeping with other women?"

Vanessa's hand stills on my arm. "Oh, sweetie. I'm so sorry. He doesn't deserve you if he can't see that you are all he'll ever need." She sits on the mattress next to me and gives me a hug.

"Well, I'm obviously not enough," I say when I pull away. "Until very recently, we hadn't, um, had sex since the night before the wedding."

"You mean the night of your wedding?"

"No, the night before, at the club."

"I knew something had happened!" she exclaims. "How did he find you? Why didn't you tell me? Why didn't the guards mention he showed up?"

"I don't know about them, but I was still in shock, I guess. I didn't expect my first time to happen that way."

"Did he...force you?"

"No, not exactly. It's complicated."

"It shouldn't be complicated, Sophie. You either say yes or no and he has to respect your decision. If he doesn't, then your father won't have to kill him because I'll do it first."

"It's not as bad as it sounds. I...I liked it. I liked that he was aggressive."

"Ah, I see. That's okay too. Everyone has their own preferences when it comes to sex," she says. "But...if you liked it then why didn't you want to do it again until recently?"

Because I was waiting for him to slam me against the wall and take me however he wanted.

Then there's the two biggest reasons. "Because he wouldn't promise not to cheat on me once we were married, and he didn't...he didn't use protection the first time."

"Oh."

"On purpose. And I was angry with him. I knew he would do that again and cheat on me."

"That's why you needed the pregnancy tests, obviously."

"Yes. They were negative, but I haven't had my period, so..."

"No wonder Dante agreed to let him come over."

"That's what I don't understand! Why would he agree to let him come over here?"

"Because whether you like it or not, if you are pregnant, Lochlan will still be part of your life and the baby's."

"That's not going to happen," I assure her. "The pregnancy part. No matter what."

"Well, when the time comes, I'm here to help you with whatever you need."

"Thank you, Vanessa."

A knock on the door has her popping up to her feet. "That's probably him. Should I send him in?"

"May as well get this over with," I huff, trying to sound brave even though my heart is already racing. Earlier, I wanted to confront Lochlan, to yell at him, hurt him, stab him even. But now I feel too vulnerable, too weak to deal with him. It's just ten minutes. I can survive anything for ten minutes.

"Good luck," Vanessa whispers. The door opens a moment later and I hear Vanessa say, "This is your last chance to salvage shit with her, buddy. Don't waste it."

34

Sophie

Sitting up so my back is resting against the headboard, knees pulled to my chest, I clutch my pillow to me, as if I need all the buffers I can get between Lochlan and me.

I feel his larger-than-life presence even before I hear my bedroom door shut.

"Sophie," Lochlan says my name softer than he's ever spoken to me before. I rest my chin on my pillow, staring straight ahead at the wall refusing to even look at him. When I don't respond, he says, "I don't have much time, so I'll get right to the point. First, I'm sorry about the tennis center. I heard Julia asked you to leave. I promise we'll figure out a way for you to go back. I'll donate whatever it takes."

I shake my head at that bullshit promise. No amount of money in the world is worth the safety of the center, the kids playing there. It's impossible for me to go back and I hate it. I hate him! And damn Lena or Toni for telling him when I asked them not to!

"I also know why you're angry, why you left."

And just like that, my determination not to speak to him or look at him slips. "Did your whore tell you about our chat between fucks?"

I hate that while I'm a red-faced, puffy-eyed mess, he looks perfectly put together as usual in his custom three-piece suit, not a single auburn hair out of place.

"She's not my whore, and she shouldn't have been at the house or spoken to you."

"So, she was only there to fuck you?"

"What?"

"I heard you!" I yell at him. He looks at me, as if waiting for me to elaborate. "In your room!"

He doesn't even blink, just stares at me blankly as if he has no idea what I'm talking about. "I know you were fucking her in your room, so do Lena and Toni, so don't bother trying to lie about it!"

"Sophie, I swear I haven't...I didn't fuck anyone today or any other day in nearly six fucking months. Only you. I was with Eli at the casino when you ran into her."

It's so aggravating that he's standing there looking calm and unaffected while lying so easily.

"I heard her screaming your name!"

"Sophie, I wasn't with Shana. I'm not saying you didn't hear whatever it was happening, but she must have been with someone else, probably Flynn or Owen. They're the ones who invited her over."

"Right, sure. One of them were with her in *your* bedroom? And she screamed *your* name while fucking one of them?"

"I don't know what you think you heard, but it wasn't me. And I bet I can even prove it to you."

"No, you can't."

"Yes, I can," he says confidently. "There are cameras in my bedroom too."

When understanding dawns on me I become furious. Everything we did, the things he did to me for an entire day and night were all recorded! Anyone could see them, see me naked and him fucking me. My mouth on him. Oh god.

"You fucking pervert!"

"No, Sophie. It's not for that. I swear that no one but me will see the recording of us. Nobody. That's not why the camera was there. Only I have access to the feed, and the reason I had one put in when I did yours was because I..."

"You what?" I snap at him when he pauses.

"I needed to know if you came to me, even if I was gone or asleep."

That makes me scoff. "You put cameras in your bedroom to watch for me? God, you're so full of shit."

"I swear, Sophie. I didn't want to miss my chance if you changed your mind. The motion sensors send me a notification on my phone."

"Well, now I regret changing my mind."

"I fucking know that!" he roars, taking a step closer to the bed and losing the first smidgen of his cool, careful composure. "I know you regret being with me. But we were good. No, we were fucking amazing together, and you know it."

"If we were so amazing then why did you cheat on me, you bastard!"

"I didn't cheat on you." When I don't respond, he says, "You won't believe me even if I show you proof, will you? Because you want to quit on us. But I'm not giving up on you. Not yet."

Shaking my head, I tell him, "I should've known. You made it clear that you were never even going to try to be faithful to me."

"You made your mind up before you met me, so no matter what I say right now, you're not going to listen."

"I wish you would just leave me alone for good."

"What if you're pregnant, Sophie? What then? Will you deny me a chance to know my son or daughter?"

"I'm not."

"Are you certain?"

"The tests were negative, but no, I can't be certain yet."

"Yes or no, Sophie, if you're pregnant with my kid, would you keep them from me?"

"No, because I wouldn't keep it."

"You wouldn't...wow." He strides away toward the door then back, swiping his palm down his face. "You hate me so much you wouldn't have my child?"

"It has nothing to do with you, Lochlan. I never wanted to be a mother! Did you bother asking me that? No. You made the decision to finish inside of me without telling me. So, if you put me in that position, without asking me what I want, then it would be my decision. Not yours or anyone else's."

"What do you want me to say? That I regret coming inside of you the first time we fucked? Every time we fucked? Because that would be a lie. I should've asked you before the first time, I know that. But for whatever reason, you refused to take the goddamn pill you insisted you wanted me to give you. Would you like to tell me why?"

"Because I thought Lena or Toni bought it and would get fired if you found out."

"Fine. Keep lying to yourself all you want," he huffs after my half-ass explanation. "I came to tell you that I know that I've fucked up, so let me try to prove to you that it's not what you think it was today."

"You can't."

"I can prove that I didn't fuck Shana or anyone else in our bed."

"Your bed."

"It's our bed now," he says while typing on his phone. "And trust me, if someone did screw in it, I'll burn the entire room down."

A moment later, voices fill the air, a woman's and...not Lochlan's. They go back and forth but it's hard to understand much of their conversation until the heavy breathing starts, then the man clearly says, "Come here, you dirty little slut."

"Believe me now?" Lochlan asks. Thankfully he lowers the volume before he turns the screen around. On it is a video of a man dressed other than his pants down, banging Shana against the door. It looks like Lochlan except...in casual attire, jeans, and a tee. He's also leaner, with darker hair. It's his brother Flynn fucking the woman against the door so hard it rattles behind them, the same sound I heard so clearly.

I've never been more relieved in all my life.

"Hurry...Hurry...Loch...coming...Yes! Oh god, I'm coming!"

"Huh," Lochlan mutters, looking at the screen again. "So, she did scream my name. I have no clue why. Maybe she wanted to make Flynn angry by calling him by my name or, more likely, she was rushing him to finish before I caught them fucking in my bedroom. Trust me, that shit will *never* happen again."

I feel lighter, but I'm still angry with him when I say, "Fine. Maybe you weren't with her today, but she told me you were with her the night you didn't come home, and I thought I was going to die."

Closing his eyes, Lochlan rubs the bridge of his nose. "Okay, so that much is unfortunately true."

I scoff and bury my face in my pillow.

"No, Sophie. I was in the room with Shana, yes, but so was Owen. I was watching them, her, give him head while only wearing a tennis skirt and no panties."

Hearing him talk about that shit, I want to suffocate myself in my pillow. "That doesn't make any fucking sense! You could've at least tried to make up a more believable lie."

"The truth really is that goddamn shitty. I hated myself for it, for not going straight home, for not being there when you could've been killed. But I swear to you, I never touched her that day or in the past six months. She has never, *ever* laid a finger on me. All I did was watch the two of them. I left Owen there with her when Wolfe came and told me what was going on at the estate," he says in a rush because he knows the clock is ticking down on his ten minutes. "The reason I was there in the first place really was to handle business—a dispute between two girls. I had to fire them both for fighting. Then Flynn was with someone, and Owen wanted to stay and play with Shana. I...I foolishly thought the distraction might be good for me, to try and get my mind off of you and your constant rejection."

Wow. I totally get it now, why Lochlan beat me with a belt for saying another man's name. I hate the sound of hers coming out of his mouth.

Four times.

He's said her name four times in this conversation, and each time is more agonizing than the one before.

I'm still processing my anger caused by that woman's name on his lips along with everything he just told me when Lochlan adds, "Hell, Shana has cameras in her room that I could probably show you. Is that the only way you'll believe me if I get proof from that day?"

"Stop saying her fucking name!" I yell at him.

His eyes widen slightly in surprise at my outburst before he nods. "Never again."

"And you could edit any video to show me only *parts* of what happened."

"I could. You're right. But it should have a date and time stamp on it. Give me a few minutes," he says before he walks to the bedroom door to leave. I want him to go almost as much as I want him to stay. God, I hate him. "If there's a video from that night, I swear I'll show you every second of it."

"Don't bother coming back," I mutter, trying to ignore the part of me that still wants him.

"Oh, I'm coming back. I just need a little time to run this down."

Outside in the hallway, I hear his voice as he makes calls because he leaves my bedroom door cracked open for the next few minutes.

He even growls at my father that he needs five more minutes before he returns, slamming the door shut behind him.

When he offers me his phone playing a second video, I can't resist watching it.

There is a date and time stamp on the bottom right corner. And while Lochlan probably could pay someone to doctor it, I doubt he's had time to do it that quickly, so I just let it play. I watch the three of them walking into the room where Lochlan shuts the door. The curvy blonde is only wearing a short white, pleated skirt when she kneels on the floor, nothing else. Her hands reach up to undo Owen's pants, tugging them down before he takes a seat on the foot of the bed. Across the room, about ten feet away, Lochlan lowers himself into a chair. Slouching as if bored with the side of his head resting on his fist, he watches them. He looks annoyed and angry. The volume is down so I don't have to hear the sounds. A few minutes later, Lochlan jumps up and hurries to the door that he jerks open. I can't see the person on the other side's face, but they look like they're in black clothing, maybe a black suit like the guards all wear.

Lochlan doesn't even glance behind him at the man being pleasured before he leaves.

The woman pulls her mouth off him a second later, the two both look to the door, then each other as if discussing what's going on. Owen stands up, not in a hurry as he strips naked, then he's grabbing her head, kissing her. He picks her up to toss her on the middle of the bed on her stomach where he quickly follows, thankfully blocking most of her perfect, curvy nakedness, other than the skirt, from the camera's view. Then his hips start bucking frantically like he's pumping inside of her.

I keep watching, waiting to see if Lochlan will come back, take his turn with her, but according to the clock on the video, he would've been almost to the airport by the time they finish. I remember the time because I was sitting there in the SUV watching the minutes tick by on the dashboard waiting for him.

I needed him there with me and he was with her and Owen. Even if he didn't touch her, he chose her that night instead of me.

Dropping to his knees beside the bed, Lochlan says, "Sophie, tell me what else I can do to prove to you that I only want you. I'll never touch her again. Ever. I fired her too. Told her she would be shot on sight if she comes to the house again or the brothel."

"I want to be the one who pulls the trigger." I didn't realize I possessed that sort of vindictiveness inside of me, but I know I mean the words as soon as they leave my lips. I would be happy to see that woman's body full of my bullet holes.

"Done," Lochan instantly agrees. "Anything you want, princess, name it. Please just come home with me."

Come home? He just wants me to walk out the door and go home with him like nothing happened? Like he wasn't with another woman when I needed him?

Yes, I want to go, but I also want him to suffer, to hurt like I do right now. Even if he didn't fuck her, he was there with her. I hate her so much. Even thinking about her name is painful.

That's when an idea comes to me, one to also help me work out my anger with Lochlan.

Lowering the pillow to the bed, I tell my husband who is still kneeling on the floor, "Take off your belt."

"My belt? Why?" he asks, but his fingers are already reaching down to pull the leather through the buckle.

"You've earned five lashes."

Both of his hands freeze. His face blanks. "Five lashes? You were keeping count of..."

"Of how many times you said her name? Yes, I was."

The belt snicks through his pant loops as he finally pulls it free. His jaw is tight as he stares down at the leather, then up at me. "Will you come home with me after the five licks?"

"I don't know yet. Take your pants and underwear off, then get on all fours on the bed."

Now he actually winces as he gets to his feet, his green eyes wide in shock. "Damn, princess. You're really going to whip my bare ass with my own belt?"

"Yes. And if you keep delaying, I'll keep adding to the count. Now you're at six."

"Fine. Take a pound of my flesh if you want while you're at it. Whatever you need," he says as he hands the belt to me folded in half. It's still warm from his body heat. While toeing his shoes off he asks, "Can I take all my clothes off?"

"No."

"Being naked just below the belt is weird as fuck."

"Then you're definitely keeping the rest of your clothes on." I want him to feel weird as fuck. Awkward. Embarrassed. And whatever else I can make him feel as punishment. "And that's seven. Don't worry, I'll keep count for you," I assure him, throwing his own words back at him.

"You...you are absolutely ruthless." He says this with a grin, not looking the least bit intimidated by the idea of me swinging the leather belt against his flesh.

Once his shoes and socks are off, he shucks his pants and boxer briefs without delay. His proud cock bobs free, nice, and thick, but not yet as long and hard as I know it can get. Still, he just stands there showing it off.

"On the bed," I tell him, so I'll quit staring at him lengthening. He winks at me like he knows I'm enjoying looking at his big dick.

Watching Lochlan crawl up onto the mattress with the upper half of his body still in business attire and his ass and dick out because I ordered him to is ridiculously hot. So is seeing him waiting on his hands and knees for me.

Getting up, I walk around so I'm behind him at the foot of the bed and get a nice long look at his tight ass.

Without giving him any warning, I use every ounce of strength in my arm and shoulder that are still sore from his restraints to bring the belt down on his flesh as hard as possible.

"Goddamn!" Lochlan shouts.

I don't give him any time to recover, just one lash after another until I lose count. It feels good to punish him, even if it doesn't actually fix anything. Realizing it's probably been at least twelve or so, I finally toss the belt to the floor, my chest still heaving.

Red line after red line appears on his ass cheeks, making me feel proud, but also guilty for hurting him and marking him now that's it done and over.

Lochlan doesn't move, his head hanging when he says, "Jesus, Sophie. No wonder you threatened to kill me if I hit you with a belt again."

He starts to place a foot on the floor, but I push my palm to his left ass cheek that's not as damaged to stop him. "Not yet."

Lochlan gets back into position on his hands and knees, so I run my fingertips over each and every line on both cheeks. He barely even flinches, but it's proof that he's in some pain that has me bending down to place a kiss on each welt. While I'm down there, I'm once again enthralled by his manliness. His heavy balls and his long shaft hanging between his legs.

He's not giving me any instructions this time, so I just do what I want to him.

Kneeling on the floor, I fist his cock and pull it back toward me to swipe the tip of my tongue up his length, from the tip to his heavy sac. That has my husband groaning.

"You don't have to..." he starts. I open my mouth wide enough to apply suction to one of his balls, drawing more grumbled groans from his mouth. "I don't deserve you," he murmurs. I keep teasing him with my mouth, licking the veins up and down his swelling cock, suckling a little on the tip until I taste his salty flavor.

Instead of taking him deep, though, I swipe my tongue up and down, up, and down. When he's nice and wet, I move my tongue higher, licking a path along the crack of his beautiful ass. I do it quickly because Lochlan tenses. Moving my mouth to the right cheek, I kiss and lick the new marks on his skin. Then do the same on the left side before returning my tongue to the crevice between them.

"Damn, Sophie!" he exclaims, making me pause and take my hand off him when he flops to his stomach on the mattress, ass cheeks now clenched tight as he stretches out on my bed.

"Do you want me to stop?" I ask him softly since I can no longer reach him from where I'm still kneeling on the floor.

"Fuck, no. Get up here," is his immediate response. "Just your mouth on my ass. You can do whatever the hell you want with my dick and balls."

"Okay," I agree.

Smiling at his adamant agreement, I climb up on the bed, straddling his legs. His cock is so long that even from this awkward angle I can stroke his steely length in my right hand while lowering my tongue to flutter it lightly over the crown of his cock.

The sounds my husband makes...at least now I know they're good ones as he squirms and barks swear words between gasps and groans.

When the tip of my tongue prods his sac again, he shouts loud enough to rattle the windows in the penthouse. As I suck on it again, I feel his balls draw up tight to his body.

"Fucking hell, baby! *Oh, fuck!*"

I keep sucking them while stroking his length that swells right before the first pulse of his release. I suck harder, jerk him off faster in my tight fist, until the last shudder leaves his body.

"Jesus, Sophie. Jesus," he mutters, the words muffled by his face now buried in my rumpled bedding.

I finally cave and do what I've wanted to since I first saw his amazing ass. I bite my teeth into the fleshiest part gently, hard enough to leave yet another mark but not to break the skin.

Lochlan's chuckle shakes his entire body before he lifts his head, twisting it around to finally look at me kneeling over his legs. His eyes flare with hunger. "What did you do to me, woman? No one has ever whipped my ass or licked my hole..." He trails off as his eyes lower to my breasts, my pointy nipples showing through my shirt and sports bra.

"Was it...okay?" I can't help but ask.

Rolling to his back, Lochlan winces at the bedding rubbing against his sore ass. Then he sits up to grab me under my arms, pulling me up his body until I'm straddling his bare waist. Our chests press together, and it feels natural to wind my arms around his neck even though I've barely had a chance to touch any part of him. Lochlan distracts me from those thoughts by squeezing two handfuls of my bottom underneath my tennis skirt. He presses a kiss to my lips, then repeats my question. "Was it okay? That giant wet spot on your bedding tells you all you need to know, my dirty girl."

I can't help my smile of pride, not only from getting him off so good he roared, but because I like when he calls me his.

"Was I really one of your firsts?"

Between kisses he says, "Yes. First. Last." His fingers on my bottom slip down to press over that forbidden spot through my panties, making me gasp against his lips. "It'll be impossible not to forget how your eager tongue felt right here. I plan to repay the favor sometime."

"Good," I reply, sliding my tongue along the seam of his lips until they part, allowing me access to his magnificent tongue. I hope he thinks about me, us, instead of other memories with other women.

As our kiss deepens, Lochlan's urgent fingers tug the crotch of my panties to the side to enter me from behind.

"So damn wet," he says against my lips. "Did you like whipping my ass, kissing it, and jerking me off?"

"Yes."

"Does this mean you forgive me?"

"No, not yet," I whisper.

He adds a second finger, fucking them slowly in and out of me, making thinking incredibly difficult.

"What will it take, Sophie?"

"I haven't...decided yet." What I don't voice is the fact that I don't think I will ever be able to trust him. I didn't before, but now...

"You haven't decided? There must be something I can do to help convince you, some way to earn a little of your forgiveness even if I can't have it all yet."

"Your tongue between my legs," I blurt out, hating myself for it, but not taking it back. I still want him even if I don't trust him.

"You want my tongue between your legs?" His smile is ridiculously smug, but I don't care because he's so gorgeous it hurts.

"Yes. Every night after dinner."

"Every night, huh? I think that can be arranged."

His fingers curl, hitting that magical spot, making my hips buck until I'm panting in pleasure. "More. Now," I demand.

But instead of more, he withdraws his fingers.

Before I can protest, Lochlan lies back down, his head and body flat on my pillow before he jerks me forward by my hips. One second, I'm straddling his waist, and the next...I'm straddling his face.

His fingers tug my panties aside, and the first lick of his tongue has me falling forward, catching myself on the top of the headboard. I hold on tight with both hands as he penetrates me with his thrashing wet tongue, then licks my slit up and down before finally concentrating on the bundle of nerves.

"Ohhh! *Oh god!*" I exclaim as I bear down on his face, wanting more. His thrusting fingers fill me again, combining with his flicking tongue on my clit to make me cry out in pleasure.

His tongue stops it's prodding, making me whimper in need.

Lochlan chuckles, and says, "Shhh, princess. Daddy's probably listening at the door. You keep screaming like I'm murdering you and he'll bust in here to check on you before I make you come."

"Don't stop," I beg, unable to think of anything but my looming orgasm.

"What do you think he'll say when he sees you riding my face?"

"I don't care, please just keep going!" I order him while rocking my hips seeking out his tongue. I look down at Lochlan but I'm only able to see his eyes and the top of his auburn hair, the bottom of my skirt hiding the rest of his face between my thighs.

A single swipe of his tongue has my eyes closing on a moan.

"You're no longer daddy's little girl are you, princess? You're mine now."

"Please, Lochlan," I beg for him to stop talking and to keep licking me. "I'm so close."

"Am I your daddy now, Sophie?"

What?

"Answer me." Another teasing single swipe of his tongue. "You might whip my ass, but you still belong to me, Sophie. I'm the only one who gets to lick and fuck your tight cunt. You only come for me."

"Yes, only you."

"That's right. Say it."

"I..."

"Say, please let me come, *Daddy*."

I gasp at his audacity, and the swirling tip of his tongue again on my clit.

"Please...please let me come..."

"Say. It."

"Please, please let me...let me come, Daddy. I need to come so bad," I whimper, nearly sobbing.

"Good girl. Now tell Daddy how you like to be licked," he replies before he full on attacks my pussy with lips, teeth, tongue.

And when he hits that perfect spot... "Yes! Right there, Daddy! Oh! Oh! *OH GOD!*"

I have never come so hard, or so loud, in my life as I do with my hips rocking, bouncing on his frantic tongue while his fingers fuck me.

With the white-knuckle grip I have on the headboard, I'm surprised it doesn't crack as I come for him, wave after amazing wave of pleasure rocking through my body. Lochlan licks me through the entire ordeal, drawing it out for as long as possible.

When I float back down from the high, I can't believe the things he just made me say. But I'm not the least bit embarrassed I said them, not when I feel so damn good now because of his tongue.

I'm still straddling Lochlan's head when he grabs the hem of my skirt to wipe off his glistening face, soaked with my arousal.

"I'll eat you out like that every night at the dinner table, on the dining table," my husband promises as he gazes up at me with a smirk full of masculine pride. "But only if you call me Daddy." My panties are back in place, covering me, but that doesn't stop him from running his tongue up the center of the damp fabric, making me shiver.

"W-why?" I ask, unsure why he wants me to call him that or why I think it's sort of hot.

"Because I'm the one taking care of you now, princess, in every way that matters. Only me." Again, his tongue flicks over the drenched crotch of my panties. "And I know you don't want it, but you have no idea how badly I want to put my baby in you." His hands slide up my hips, around to my flat abdomen. "I want you riding my face with a swollen belly, calling me daddy so our kid comes out knowing exactly who makes mommy happy."

Those words of his instantly cool my libido. Or at least they should. They would have before, but now...now there's an ache between my legs that Lochlan's tongue couldn't sate. Only a longer, harder part of his body will suffice, shoving deep, filling me up with... possibilities.

But no. That's not going to happen. No pregnancy. No kids.

"No." I refuse these ideas of his that he's trying to put in my head, dreams he wants to share with me. Dreams that, as much as I hate them, hate him, are quite possibly burrowing into my heart.

"You don't want little Sophies running around the court in diapers chasing tennis balls or jumping into bed with us to wake us up with giggles every morning?"

"I don't want any of that," I tell him flatly. "Ever."

Glancing away toward the door, Lochlan sighs then pats the sides of my thighs. "Message received. But I stand by my stipulation. If you want my tongue, you have to say the word I want to hear."

"Daddy?"

"Yes, princess?" he asks with an arrogant grin.

I roll my eyes at him, even though there's a stupid smile on my face too.

"Are you ready to go home with me now? Or do you want to ride daddy's big cock while your pussy is soaking wet?"

Glancing behind me, I see his shaft long and hard in his fist, eagerly waiting for a tight hole to fuck. The whole time he was talking about getting me pregnant he was ...excited.

Surrendering to him, giving him permission to use my body for the sole purpose of breeding turns him on. He wants me to ride him until he cums inside of me again, increasing the chances of pregnancy. It's probably just a biological instinct for all males to want to reproduce, most likely with as many females as possible. It's hard to feel special knowing he's screwed other women. Lots of other women.

For whatever reason, I do still want him, despite knowing all of that.

And maybe if Lochlan hadn't been with a prostitute the other night when I needed him, I would climb on him and stupidly let him finish inside of me again.

But I'm not his broodmare.

I'm sure as hell not taking those risks if he can't be completely faithful to me, meaning not being in the same room as a mostly naked prostitute, for even a few weeks.

"You weren't there," I remind him before I dismount from his handsome, still glistening face to go clean up in my bathroom.

35

Lochlan

Y*ou weren't there.*

Goddamm it. I'm not sure if Sophie will ever forgive me for not coming home that night. There aren't enough tongue fucks in the world to make her forget I was at a brothel when she was nearly killed by my enemies.

Whoever the hell they are.

I'm still no closer to solving that mystery since every inch of the evidence from the drones went up in flames. None of Eli's threatening Q&As have turned up anything either.

I try not to let that get to me as I stroke my throbbing cock that's hard as fuck again, even after I came from Sophie's punishment. I had no idea I would even like a little pain followed by pleasure. Apparently, anything she does to my body I love. She took her anger and jealousy out on my ass, just like I did to her. Which means...I think she has feelings for me. Ones that go beyond orgasmic bliss.

Sophie doesn't want me near another woman or to even say her name.

Never again. I'll never say that bitch's name in front of her again.

And I have no idea why I told her all that shit about being a father. She's made it clear that she doesn't want to have my children —that she hates me so much she wouldn't keep the baby if I knocked her up.

I know I should stop bringing the topic up with Sophie, it's just, I can't stop thinking about her spreading her legs, begging me to come inside of her until we become a real family. Something I sure as shit never had growing up.

Fuck me. I never had a breeding fetish before Sophie either. Becoming a father from an accidental pregnancy was a risk I always wanted to avoid at all costs. Condoms were a necessity, along with birth control pills. Another benefit of screwing certain women at the brothels was they had their tubes tied to avoid getting pregnant.

I never had a single pregnancy scare despite my promiscuous lifestyle. Never considered going bareback for fear of diseases.

Then suddenly, the night before I'm supposed to marry Sophie, I go all primal and take her raw, unable to get my cum deep enough inside of her, wondering shit like if I should pound her into the floor instead of the wall will gravity give me an assist in shooting my swimmers up to fertilize her egg?

Reproductive terms I hadn't thought about since my sixth-grade sex ed class.

Every moment since that first night, it's been a constant throbbing demand in my dick to lay my wife down and fill her up over and over again until I get the job done.

I have no idea what I would do then. Not be able to keep my hands off her because I love her so damn much and our love created a life together?

In my fucking dreams. Sophie doesn't love me. She barely tolerates me. At least she seems to be willing enough to let me touch her and lick her.

If I learned nothing else from today's close call with my wife, it's that it will take more than a few orgasms to make her happy, to keep her. She needs to trust me, and she needs me to love her. That's what she deserves. I just wish I knew how to do both of those things.

When Sophie comes out of her bathroom, her eyes go right to me still lying in the wet spot in her bed, lazily stroking my cock, thinking stupid family shit. She wets her lips like she wants me in her mouth. But I don't even want a blowjob from her. No, I just want her to come home with me.

I'll do anything to make that happen.

"You should get dressed before my father comes in to drag you out of here," she tells me.

"Are you coming with me?" I ask. Before she can tell me no, I add, "Just until we know for sure."

"It doesn't matter..."

"It matters to me, Sophie. This is my responsibility too. We're in this together whether you like it or not, whatever you decide."

I don't know why I can't just walk away now, knowing she'll probably be coming right back here to Dante in no time. I guess I keep hoping I'll be able to...make her want more. More from me than sex. Which is fucking ridiculous since that's all I have to offer Sophie. She doesn't need money or anything else. I can give her orgasms, sure, but that will never be enough to keep her.

"Fine," she agrees. I let out the breath I was holding, but my relief is short-lived. "Only until we know for sure. I don't...I can't trust you."

She'll be mine, but only for a few days because she doesn't trust me not to fuck around behind her back. Even being in the room with a whore crosses a line for her. And I get it. I wouldn't want her watching some other man go down on a woman.

A few more days with her are better than none.

How long could I keep her chained to my bed before Dante came looking for her? Probably only a few days. I'll take whatever breadcrumbs she'll give me while trying to figure how to prove to her, to myself, that I can be a better man for her.

So, like the pussy-whipped bitch I am, I let go of my dick to stand up and put the other half of my clothes back on. While I dress, I still can't get over how Sophie had me on my hands and knees, only naked from the waist-down. I can't wait to return the favor.

When I'm put back together as much as possible, and her shoes are thankfully on her feet, I reach for the doorknob with one hand and hers with the other. "Ready?"

She looks down at my offered palm a moment before reluctantly taking it. The fact that she'll willingly touch any part of me after everything is still a surprise.

"Wait. Do you...do you think they heard us?" Sophie asks softly, her flushed cheeks darkening.

"Hell, yes. You screamed like a banshee when you were coming on my tongue."

"Shit." Pressing her forehead against my shoulder, she says, "Maybe we can sneak out without running into anyone."

"Doubtful," I reply.

Dante isn't standing in the hallway, but he doesn't look happy leaning against the kitchen counter on the third floor, sipping a glass of what looks like whiskey. Vanessa appears to be trying to calm him down with her palms braced on his chest. Unfortunately, the only way down the stairs is through the kitchen.

Fuck.

As soon as he looks over and sees me, I stop walking, ready to face the music. Sophie remains ducking behind me with her fingers gripping the back of my suit jacket.

"While I'm glad that it sounded like you two have made up, I don't ever want to hear you doing that shit in my house again," Dante grumbles.

Sophie nearly tugs me off balance with her grip on my jacket like she's decided to retreat back to her room and take me with her.

"Whoa," I mutter, having to throw my hand to the wall to catch myself.

"Sorry, Daddy," she whispers.

"It's okay, princess," I reply at the exact same time Dante says, "It wasn't *your* fault, baby girl."

Oh. Fuck.

Dante and I stare at each other as the realization dawns on both of us that we're not entirely sure who she was talking to.

Vanessa is no help at all. She smothers her face in Dante's chest, narrow shoulders shaking as she tries to muffle the sounds of her laughter.

"Get the fuck out of my house," Dante growls, pointing his finger toward the stairs.

I gladly take the offered exit with a little extra pep in my step.

"Sophie, wait," Dante says. "I was talking to him, not you. Never you."

Her grip on my jacket drops. I glance over my shoulder to see her turn to hug her father.

"Are you sure you want to go with him?" he asks her, gripping both of her shoulders while glaring in my direction.

"Yes," she says. I've never loved that one word as much as I do now. Well, maybe the night Sophie used it to agree to marry me.

When she pulls away from Dante's grip, she also hugs Vanessa.

"You are trouble," Dante's wife says to me with a grin. "Be good to her."

"I will," I promise her and Dante both before taking Sophie's hand to lead her down the stairs.

As we make our way to the first floor, I hear Vanessa say to Dante, "Aren't you glad I didn't let you go in to check on them?"

"I'll be eternally grateful that you stopped me," it sounds like he murmurs in response.

"I know you don't like it, but they're married. She's not your baby girl anymore."

"Now she's his *princess.*"

319

"And he's her Da– "

"Don't you dare fucking say it!" Dante growls, making Vanessa giggle.

While we wait for the elevator, I can't help but turn to Sophie and ask, "You were talking to me, weren't you?"

Groaning, she slaps her palm to her forehead and says, "I really wish I hadn't said that."

"Maybe there will be less confusion when he becomes a grandpa."

"Lochlan!"

"I didn't mean because of you, or us necessarily. You have two older sisters, and one is definitely fucking someone."

"You mean...Cass?"

"Uh-huh."

"Really? Who?"

"No idea. You could ask her."

"I could, but she would never tell me. We don't talk like that," she explains. "Although she was sort of nice today. She helped me take the pregnancy test."

"That was nice of her, although she probably had ulterior motives," I reply, unable to help my cynicism when it comes to the redhead.

"I don't know if I can keep calling you that name," Sophie whispers, as if the guards surrounding us, Salvato's and my own, won't hear us.

"What name?" I ask with a smirk, and she slaps my shoulder. "Fine." As much as I hate it, I relent. "You don't have to use that name again unless..."

"Unless what?"

"Unless one day you change your mind, and we have a baby together."

"Okay," she agrees.

And the fact that she didn't say that's never going to happen feels like a win to me.

36

Sophie

Despite our argument, how badly it hurt to know where Lochlan was during the attack, it did absolutely nothing to diminish how great the sex is with him.

I don't remember the walk into the house because my feet didn't touch the floor. Lochlan carried me, our mouths connected, my arms around his neck, legs around his waist until he pried me off of him to throw me on his bed. Once my wrists were cuffed in the usual restraints above my head, he fastened my ankles to the cuffs attached to chains at the very bottom corner of the bed, leaving me spread eagle.

After he promised it was a new mattress, new sheets, and all new pillows on the bed, he licked me and fucked me. Then he tortured me with the vibrating, thrusting dildo, and clit tickler until I came so many times, I lost my voice from screaming.

That's why he's currently pressing a glass of water to my lips, pouring it into my mouth.

"Better?" he asks after the third sip.

"Yes. Thank you. That was..."

"Yeah," he agrees while putting the glass on the table. Then he undoes the cuffs on my ankles so I can bend and move my legs again. Lying on his side next to me, he runs his fingertips over my bare stomach and breasts absently, making circles around my nipples. "I have toys for your ass too. Are you going to let me take that final part of your virginity?" he asks with a raised eyebrow.

"I can't exactly stop you like this, can I?" I reply with a tug on the chains to rattle them, making him smile like the devil.

"Soon, princess. I'm going to pop that cherry very soon. The only reason I haven't..."

"You don't want to waste your cum?" I guess.

"Exactly."

When the silence swells between us, both of us lost in our own thoughts of our conflicting plans for the future, I'm the one to finally break it. "Could I ask you a question and you give me the truth?"

His green eyes with dancing gold flecks lift to mine. "Maybe."

"Did your family have Madison's mother killed?"

Lochlan's fingers still on my belly. "No."

I wait for him to say more, but he doesn't.

"No? That's it? That's all you'll say?"

"I know the rumors spread that my father was behind the drive-by that killed Dante's girlfriend, Madison's mother. I would've been only four or five when it happened, but when I was older, I asked him pointblank if he did it. He denied it, but told me she was one of his...employees at the local brothel. My father said someone set him up to cause problems with the Salvatos after the woman had Madison. The man bragged about every kill he made, so I believed him when he swore he didn't do it."

"So why did everyone think it was your father? Just because she worked for him?"

I wonder if Madison knows her mother was a harlot in the local brothel. I doubt our father would ever tell her that.

"Because he and Dante's father had a falling out around that time. I don't know what it was about, but it happened right before the shooting. Dante and I now believe it was Petrov behind Madison's mother's murder, that he wanted to make it look like it was the Irish to cause a bigger rift between our families so we wouldn't gang up to work against him."

"That makes sense," I reply. "Poor Vanessa. Her father sounds awful."

"Mine was no walk in the park either. But he wasn't one to kill innocent women in front of babies."

"Is that why Madison refused to marry you? Because of your family being accused of the murder?" I can't help but ask. "She never talked to me about it."

"Possibly." He smiles, and it's not smug for once, just pleased. "Although, now I'm grateful things fell through with her."

"If she ever comes home again, I'll make sure she knows it wasn't your family."

"Thank you," Lochlan says, leaning over to press a kiss to my lips. "And I do hope she comes home safe and sound."

"Cass admitted to me that you never flirted with her or asked her to marry you."

"Did she now? Good of her to own up to her lies." Brushing my now loose, damp hair aside to cup my cheek, he presses more kisses to my lips, then says, "She was obviously jealous of you, and rightfully so."

I don't know why Cass would be jealous of me. She just didn't like being Lochlan's third choice.

That reminds me what else Cass told me. I wonder if Lochlan knows his chance of being my father's heir is now zero. If not, I don't want to be the one to tell him. I'm not sure I want to know how he'll react just yet if it'll change everything between us.

Still, I can't help but ask him another question, "Who is your successor? I mean, if something happened to you, who would take over the brothels and casino if you don't have any children and..." I trail off.

"Flynn is my father's only other son. But Owen is blood too, so he's my second. Am I currently rethinking leaving shit to the two of them? Hell, yes. They've both crossed a lot of lines lately. It may be time to make a change and put it in writing, choosing someone outside the Dunne line. They know this life, were raised in it. Owen's father worked with mine. Flynn and Owen help out when I need them to with both businesses. But honestly, I would prefer to leave whatever is left of my legacy to you or my own son or daughter, though. Whatever is left of it..."

Before we can start talking about children again, I ask him another question while he's in a talkative mood. "Will it always be like this, with my wrists in cuffs?"

Now Lochlan seems to avoid my gaze while running a fingertip up the underside of my arm. "I thought you liked to be restrained and at my mercy."

"I do," I agree. "But it would be nice to be able to touch you, to kiss you..."

"No."

"Why not?"

"It's better this way. I'll only have you touch me or put your mouth on me when I'm desperate. I told you that you didn't have to earlier."

Okay, that doesn't sound like just a right now thing, but an always one. I'm never allowed to touch him unless it's his decision?

I try to recall all of our other intimate occasions. Lochlan fingered me under the dinner table, then put my hand on his crotch that I embarrassingly jerked away. He pinned me to a wall and fucked me. I had my hands and fingernails digging into his throat that night, which he allowed and could've stopped. Then I touched his chest, but over his jacket. When I ran my fingers through his hair, he pinned them above my head.

When he came to the dressing room before the wedding and went down on me, I didn't touch him much, mostly because I was still angry with him and didn't want to.

Then, in the SUV after the attack when I got on my knees, I put my mouth on him and took him in my hand easily enough.

He wasn't thrilled with me hitting him with the belt, but I didn't leave him much choice if he wanted my forgiveness.

"When I've touched you before, did I do something wrong?"

"No, but I didn't give you much of a choice, did I? And I don't want to talk about this shit anymore."

"But...I don't understand."

"You don't have to fucking understand; you just have to shut up and leave it alone!"

Wow. Why does he sound so angry at me for asking these questions?

If he's going to yell at me, then I don't want to tolerate the stupid wrists cuffs a second longer.

"Free me," I tell him, biting my lip to keep it from trembling.

"No."

I scoff at his swift refusal. "Let me go now, Lochlan!"

Rather than release my wrists, he climbs on top of me, his green eyes darkening so there's little gold in them. "I'm not ready to let you go yet, and it's my decision, remember? Even if you change your mind..."

Lochlan

"Lochlan..." Sophie's bottom lip quivers before she tries to scramble out from under me. It's no point when I can just grab her hips and drag her body right back under mine or restrain her ankles again. "If you don't let me go..." she starts, then pauses as if trying to figure out what she can fucking do about it. "I'll scream for Lena and Toni."

"After they agreed to work for Salvato, they're lucky I let them keep their jobs. They work for me, and they won't step foot in this bedroom. Besides, they've probably already gone home for the night."

Her lips part with an indignant gasp. Shaking her head, her blue eyes glistening, she says, "So you can do anything you want to me, but I can't touch you?"

"Yes."

"Why?" she exclaims the question just as the first tear tumbles down her cheek.

Seeing her upset torments me, almost more than my past. Sophie hates that I've been with so many other people before her, while she has zero experience with anyone but me and the one stupid boy who grabbed her ass. She's called me a dirty, filthy bastard. She already thinks I'm disgusting. If she knew where and how I learned my way around a woman's body, she wouldn't want to lay a finger on me. Would she ever let me touch her again if I told her?

That's too big of a risk for me to take.

While I'm an asshole for enjoying seeing her tears the first time I fucked her, I don't like them right now when she's hurting in a different way because of my cruelty.

"Please stop crying."

"Let me go or tell me why right now," she demands. I fucking loathe being told what to do, even by her.

"This doesn't have anything to do with you, okay?" I try to explain. "So please just drop it."

"Why can't you just tell me?"

"Because once I do, you will run from me. *Again*," I tell her honestly.

Sophie's head shakes from side to side. "I don't want any secrets between us again. If I can trust you, I won't leave. Tell me. Please?"

She can say those words all she wants, but it still feels like she'll always have one foot out the door. Nothing will ever guarantee she'll trust me or stay with me, not even all the manacles in the world.

Well, maybe my kid...

"It's not a secret. Not really. It's just...fucked up shit that happened years ago. Nothing you need to ever know."

"Then get off me. I don't want *you* touching *me* again, not until you can be honest with me."

I fucking hate her threat of doing exactly what I expected.

"You can't stop me from touching you, though, can you?"

We stare at each other for a long moment before she opens her mouth, and screeches loud enough to temporarily deafen me. "*LENA!*"

I slap my palm over her mouth, muffling her guard's name. "She can't help you. Nobody will save you from me, princess. Especially if my baby is growing inside of you."

Getting her pregnant may be the only fucking way for me to keep her. Not even Dante Salvato could keep me from my son or daughter.

And seeing the angry fire burning in her eyes makes me so fucking hard.

Reaching down with my free hand, I line my cock up, pressing it to her opening. Sophie shakes her head from side to side while my palm muffles her adamant refusal.

Fuck.

My choices are severely limited here. I could take her, likely for the last time, or release her wrists so she can flee, potentially never to come near me again. Or...I could just fucking tell her the truth, knowing she's not going to want me afterwards.

All roads lead to me losing her, which is the last thing I want.

Fuck.

"The only way I'll tell you is if you'll promise on your father's life to stay with me."

She easily nods her head, so I lift my palm from her mouth.

"Say it."

Her tongue wets her lips. "I promise on my father's life that I'll stay, no matter what you say, as long as you promise to be faithful to me. For all of our days."

Fuck. Sophie's finally giving me the words she refused on our wedding day, and within minutes I'll most likely make her a liar. I still wouldn't kill Salvato if she breaks her promise because I know how much it would hurt her.

And while we're talking truths... "And if you're pregnant?"

She bites down hard on her bottom lip. "Once I know for sure, then I'll decide."

I didn't think she had changed her mind, but I still wanted to ask. To hope.

The small chance she's pregnant and will keep it, keep me, is the only reason I decide to tell her. It's better to do it now before I fall even more in love with her and lose her later.

I don't move off her, and I place my palm back over her mouth because I can't bear to hear more insults from her mouth again.

Here goes fucking nothing.

"My father had a sick sense of humor," I start. "He was always giving me 'life lessons' as he called them. Mostly, it was an excuse for him to be cruel. Just stupid shit when I was younger, but when I was sixteen, I was dating this girl, Erma Graves. She wasn't my first, but she was the first girl I had hooked up with more than once and regularly. I liked her. We had fun in bed. Fucked like bunnies. Maybe I wrongly assumed she was my girlfriend. Either way, my father knew I cared for her, and he made sure I caught them together one night when she stayed over with me."

Sophie's blue eyes widen.

"Yes, my father had sex with my underaged girlfriend. I woke up when I heard them in the hall right outside my bedroom. That's how fucking callous he was. And while the bastard was still inside of her, fucking her from behind against the wall, he told me he was just proving to me that she was a gold-digging slut like my mother, like *all* women who would ever want me."

Those pretty blue eyes soften in pity, which I hate, but I don't break her gaze. She needs to trust me, which means I have to tell her everything, even the worst of me. So, I'll trust her with this even if it ruins everything.

"That was only the beginning of my more fucked-up 'lessons' from him," I tell her. "Everyone in the whole city found out he had fucked my girlfriend in front of me because he bragged about it. She was legal, barely, so he wasn't worried about charges. It was embarrassing as hell, but I got over it. And it was *nothing* compared to what he did to me when I turned eighteen. On my birthday, my father dropped me off in one of his, *our*, brothels in Lyon County, about a six-hour drive from Vegas. He told me I had to learn the family business from the inside out. For an entire month, I was to live there, to earn my keep by doing the same thing as all the employees. I wasn't allowed to leave, the guards he left with me would ensure I didn't." I can already see the question in her eyes, so I answer it. "That's right, I had to have sex for money, just like all the other prostitutes."

I can't say for certain, but based on the look on her face, my princess is disgusted and appalled. "I learned a lot, good and bad," I admit. "The first week, I was only allowed to watch, though, with a cage on my cock. A cruel and unusual punishment for a teenage boy who jerked off at least three times a damn day. The second week I received one hell of a sex education from the girls. They treated me like a fucking king. I thought I was living the dream. Until the dream became a nightmare.

"The third week I had to fuck paying customers. There weren't many. The women were all types and sizes. I liked variety, usually. But this was different. It was no longer *my* choice; it was theirs alone. I tried not to think about it too hard the first few times. I fucked like I was a god, not a paid whore. I left them happy and sated, barely able to move a muscle. Whenever I was alone again, I felt hollow, like I had lost a piece of myself every time. The sex was just a simple transaction for money. No emotions. No feelings. It was a release, but it was...empty."

Rolling my neck around to crack it, I take a breather before continuing on. "I made myself keep going. Took pills to zone out and to keep getting hard. There was no way I was going to let my father win. He wanted me to last a month. I could fuck women I didn't want for a month and survive, even if I hated the hands and mouths on me. By five days of that shit, I felt nothing but anger at the customers, contempt for using my body like they owned it for an hour. And they actually did own me for the time they paid for. The worst part was realizing that the women and men who worked at the brothel had to feel the exact same, even the ones I had been with. They, we, were nothing but body parts being used in exchange for a little cash."

Shaking my head, I admit to Sophie, "I honestly don't know why or how the long-term employees do it. Because the money is good, better than a nine-to-five job anywhere else, I guess. Whatever the reason, they do what's required of them night after night. I did what I had to as well. I made it to the end of the third week, day twenty-three to be exact, when my father decided to give me another life lesson.

"An older man came into my room in the middle of the night. By then I had seen and done enough to know I wasn't attracted to men. He made sure I could see the gun in his hip holster when he told me that he could leave me dead or alive, but either way, he was going to fuck me."

All I had with me was the knife my mother gave me for my thirteenth birthday, the only gift she *ever* gave me. It was a week late when she did remember, and pretty fucked up—an illegal switchblade knife on top of that for a teenage boy. Anyway, my father wouldn't let me have a gun while I was living in the brothel. He didn't *want* me to be able to defend myself.

"At first, I just wanted to escape, not kill the intruder. But I knew I couldn't get past him to get out the door. He was huge, taller than me, and had about a hundred pounds of muscle on my eighteen-year-old lanky form. I didn't stand a chance against him.

But I would kill him before I let him touch me. So, I struck first before he could pull his gun, slicing through his thigh with my knife. I must have hit an artery because it gushed like a fountain. When he hunched over to grab it, I slashed the knife across his throat."

Tears now fill and overflow from Sophie's eyes, likely she's hurt and angry I fucked her without her knowing all this shit. Still, I swallow around the knot in my throat and keep going to the end, my palm making sure she can't say a word.

"I had been in plenty of brawls, even dealt out some ass kickings at the direction of my father. But I had never wanted anyone dead like I did that night. While I tried to figure out what the fuck I was going to do with his body and the bloody mess before someone else came into my room, I took out the man's wallet to find out who the hell he was. My father's business card was right there in the front, as if he wanted me to find it, and know he had sent him.

"I left his body lying where it was. Grabbing the cash I had made, I snuck out, running from the guards, then had to beg a cab to drive me to Vegas looking like a walking horror show. It was early in the morning when I strolled into my father's office, blood still staining my hands and pretty much every inch of me since I was only wearing a pair of shorts, all I had on when he woke me up. I told my old man I had killed the guy he sent, then swore to him that I would kill him too before I went back to that hellhole.

"The bastard didn't bat an eye, just told me that it was all a lesson, of course. A test to see if I would take it like a pussy or fight because only a ruthless man could run his empire. He wouldn't give it to a weak pussy who let people fuck him over or couldn't defend himself.

"I was smaller, weaker than that asshole. He would've easily overpowered me if I hadn't had my knife, and there wouldn't have been a damn thing I could do about it.

"That's when I became obsessive about lifting weights, working out constantly because I never wanted to be weaker than anyone else ever again. I swore to myself that I would strike first, ask questions later.

"My father may have looked smug that day, but I could also see the fear in his eyes. He was actually scared of me. He never expected me to come out of that place alive. He had created a monster and wasn't sure if he could control it. At least he never did any fucked-up shit like that to me again, manipulating me like it was all a joke. And I eventually repaid the favor by letting his favorite hooker poison him slowly each night when she was with him. We told everyone he died of natural causes, a heart attack after a hard romp.

"Nobody even questioned his death, either because everyone in law enforcement hated him that much or just didn't care.

"So now you know that every fucking thing you said about me is true. I am a disgusting dirty bastard. I've been used, my dick bought and paid for by the hour like all the whores who work for me. Sex has never been anything more than a transaction. The whores I used to fuck never wanted me. They wanted my money, my power, but never me. At least they were honest about it, unlike the women I dated who were after the exact same things.

"You were different from all of them, though," I tell Sophie. "You grew up with daddy's money and power. Anything you wanted, you could have, except maybe absolute freedom. There's nothing I can give you that he can't except for a good fuck."

Sweeping the hair out of her face, I tell her the final truth, "I'm sorry I didn't tell you before. It's not that I don't want you to touch me, princess. That's not it at all. Yes, I always restrained the whores you rightfully despise after that ordeal because I just wanted to use them rather than have them put their hands on me, pretending like they wanted me. But your hands? I love having your hands on me, even though I stain them. Every inch of me is fucking filthy. Sex and blood have tainted me inside and out for eight years. I knew I was too disgusting to lay a finger on you, but I still selfishly wanted you, so sweet and innocent and good. Everything I'm not and never will be again. I don't blame you for not wanting to keep my baby if you do turn up pregnant. I shouldn't have put you in this position. I fucking know that. What you have to understand is that I would do anything to keep you. You want my word that I'll be faithful for all of our days? I'll give it to you. I'll give you every-fucking-thing I have to give, if you'll just keep your promise and stay with me."

37

Sophie

My tears coat Lochlan's palm that's still covering my mouth when he finishes telling me about his awful past. What his father did to him...I don't even know what I would say even if he would let me speak.

I don't blame him for keeping me quiet. How many times have I insulted him, called him the derogatory things he believes are the worst parts of himself? All I've done is make him think he was right to feel ashamed of himself.

When he eventually removes his palm from my mouth, the first thing I'm able to get out is, "Free me."

Lochlan's jaw clenches, his eyes filled with ire, making me realize I should've said anything else. "You promised me, Sophie."

"I'm not...I'm not going anywhere. Free me, please, so I can prove it to you."

There's still doubt and hurt in his green-gold eyes as he

335

stretches above me to undo the cuff on my right wrist then the left. My arms are heavy, nearly numb from the prolonged stretching above my head. Still, when Lochlan's face is above mine again, I manage to lift my hands to his face, rubbing my fingers over his short, scruffy beard and bringing his lips down to mine for a quick kiss.

"I'm so sorry he did that to you."

That. That is probably what I should've said first, but I just wanted to touch him so badly.

I realize that wasn't the right thing to say either when he pulls away from my grip to grumble, "I don't want your fucking pity, Sophie."

"Lochlan..."

Before I can figure out what he needs me to say, he rolls off me and onto his back scrubbing his palms over his face. "Bet you wish you hadn't asked now, don't you?"

I don't hesitate before climbing on top of him, grasping his wrists to remove his hands from his face, all the while wondering if he'll throw me off.

"Please look at me. Please." The hiccup in my voice alerts me to the fact that I'm still crying.

Lochlan complies, then reaches up to wipe my tears away, before issuing a command, "Stop crying."

"I'm sorry." I'm not apologizing for crying, but everything else.

"I told you I don't want—" Now I place my index finger to his lips to keep him quiet. "I'm sorry about the things I said to you. They were nothing but a way to take my stupid jealousy out on you. I'm jealous of anyone who spent even a second with you before me because I know I'm inexperienced and awkward when it comes to sex. And you...you are the most gorgeous man I've ever seen. I've been so terrified and intimidated by every single part of you since the moment we met, and I love it. If you had been soft or considerate or boring, I wouldn't have wanted to marry you. I love your violent confidence and the swagger that comes from knowing you're a well-endowed, mind-blowing lover. I love you, all of you, but especially the dirty and the bad."

"You think you love me?" Lochlan asks around my finger.

"I know I love you. I have since that night…" I finally remove my finger from his mouth to swipe my knuckles over my cheeks to dry them. "The reason I was so hurt when I found out where you were, it wasn't just jealousy but disappointment because I longed with every fiber of my being to be with you, and you were with someone else."

"That was the biggest mistake of my life," he murmurs. "I'll never forgive myself for not being here to protect you."

"I didn't need you to be here to protect me. Although, I do love how protective you are when it comes to me. I needed you here because I love you and don't want to ever be away from you. I feel safe and…happy when I'm with you."

"You love me." This time when he says it, it's a statement, not a question.

Running my palms up his chest, I tell him, "Touching you will never make me feel dirty. It'll only make me happy because you're mine now, nobody else's. I belong to you, and you belong to me. All of you," I say again. "The good and the bad. There's not a single thing I would change about you even if I could."

"You have no idea how much that means to me," Lochlan replies. "But if I had told you, if you had known from the first day we met…" he trails off, no need to say that he thinks I would've refused to marry him.

And for a moment, I try to think back to that day in my room, what I would've done if we had this same conversation while he ran that knife over my panties.

"Honestly, after you teased me with the knife under my skirt, there's nothing you could've said that would've deterred me."

"Bullshit."

"*Nothing*," I repeat. "I was too turned on to care that you were most likely a dangerous murdering bastard, one who was dead set on taking my virginity. Taking it, not receiving it from me with my permission. And I let you have it even after you stabbed a knife through a man's hand."

Lochlan blinks up at me, then gives me a small grin. "I guess I was far from a saint when we met."

"And yet I still wanted to sin with you."

That makes his grin widen. "If the worst of your sins is sex before marriage, then I think you're still considered a saint."

I start to tell him I'm not that innocent, that I came into the world a murderer. But I push those dark depressing thoughts aside for now.

"Me, a saint? Not after all the fun, filthy things you've done to me." I slide back a few inches until I feel his long hard inches against my bare ass. Of course he's ready for another round. He's always ready. "I don't think saints kiss men's asses. And being fucked with a knife would probably fall under sodomy, wouldn't it?"

"Not if your husband is the one wielding it. I think I get a free pass to put any object I want inside my wife's pussy if she enjoys it. And I do seem to recall you enjoying the hard steel." His fingertips brush my clit, making me gasp and shiver. "I loved watching your pussy grasp it tight. Seeing it protruding from you, bobbing in and out without me touching it was so fucking hot."

"I want you inside me right now," I tell him.

Lochlan sits up, putting us face-to-face, chest-to-chest. "Thank you for not leaving me." He swipes his lips too briefly over mine.

Smiling, I tell him, "I think you love me too. Even if you won't say the words back." His jealousy and possessiveness make me feel like I'm important to him, that I mean something to him, that he cares for me more than anyone else in the world. He helped me find a purpose doing what I love—teaching tennis to kids. While I had no idea that I would love volunteering so much, Lochlan knew. Somehow, within days he had already figured me out. Just like I think I understand him like no one else.

"For all of our days," he says instead of the three words I long to hear. These are almost as good, so I repeat them.

"For all of our days," I agree as my husband fills me.

38

Lochlan

I wake up the next morning with Sophie curled up naked to my side. Most likely curled up to me for warmth since there's not a shred of bedding to be found on the bed. It probably ended up on the floor the last time I went down on her, eager to taste her release and my own combined.

Needing to use the restroom and cleanup, I slip away from Sophie's arms, covering her up with the recovered bedding before I leave her. I quickly shower, brush my teeth, and rake my fingers through my damp hair before returning to bed.

In my absence, Sophie rolled to her stomach. I peel the covers back again to see all of her long, beautiful body. Every inch is mouth-watering, especially the tight rounded globes of her ass I still haven't claimed.

My heart skips a beat remembering what I confided in her last night, and I can't believe she's still here with me.

God, I love this woman so damn much.

Why can't I tell her that? Sophie said she loves me too, but it's so hard to believe, to trust she won't change her wish-washy mind tomorrow...

Still, I want her, despite her fickleness that drives me fucking crazy.

Easing up on the bed, I move between her sprawled open legs. My cock lies long and heavy between her ass cheeks, waking her up.

Wiggling underneath me, she moans, "*Mmm, yes.*"

"Aren't you sore from last night, princess?"

"Uh-huh," she replies in a groggy mumble. "But I still want you inside of me again."

"You need my tongue?" My finger penetrates her from behind slowly, stroking her slick walls.

"Tongue. Fingers. Cock. I want all of you inside of me."

"Your wish is my command," I assure her. Before she can ask what I mean, I withdraw my wet finger to thrust two inside of her, still fucking her slowly. Deeply. Getting them good and wet. Sophie's hips rock in rhythm to them, her moans growing louder. After she comes, she's nice and relaxed so I remove my fingers to push the tip of one fingertip against her virgin asshole.

Sophie jolts forward but doesn't protest. Stretching out over her, I kiss her neck, distracting her while prodding her hole. "Ah!" she cries out, right before, "Wait, hold on."

I remove my finger and sit back on my heels, doing as asked for once. Sophie rolls over to look up at me, so fucking gorgeous. Her hair so messy she'll never get a brush through it, and I love knowing it was because my hands were in it. We stare each other in the eye for a long silent moment before her gaze slides down to my chest, abs, lower. She pops up then, wrapping her arms around my neck, legs straddling my waist, lining up our lower bodies perfectly.

Her teeth nip at my bottom lip, then she says one word. "*Go.*"

Our tongues collide a few seconds before Sophie reaches down to line me up, even though I know she must be aching from all the times I pounded into her last night. Still, she grinds on me until she sinks down those first few inches.

My chuckle at her impatience turns into a groan of pleasure when her walls tighten around me. "Fuck, yes." I love that snug fit made only for my cock, my tongue, my fingers to fill it.

While thrusting upward, forcing my way deeper, I reach around to penetrate her virgin hole again with my fingertip and slide my tongue over hers. I give her exactly what she wanted, all of me I can get inside of her.

Unlike the women before her, Sophie doesn't just use my body parts. She cherishes them, the pleasure I give her, the intimacy. I know because I feel the same about her beautiful body.

Her breath catches just before she cries out, "Oh, god!"

"You think you're full now..." I tell her. "I want to bury myself here one day soon."

"Yes," she agrees, willing to give me anything I want or need from her. She comes so hard and fast, clenching around my finger and shaft.

"God, baby. I love it when you come on me, so tight and wet. Makes me fucking crazy." Before her shudders end, I toss her onto her back to fuck into her harder, faster. I pin her wrists above her head, not just to restrain her but also intertwine our fingers. She's completely at my mercy, and I fucking love it.

I love her.

That whimper escapes her lips, the one I crave, making me growl into her neck. "Come for me again. Use that tight cunt of yours to milk me dry."

She does, and it's...everything.

I erupt, shuddering through waves of pleasure. A pleasure that lingers. It's a kind of euphoria that lasts long after my orgasm ends.

Sex with Sophie somehow gets better every single time. I don't know how that's possible. Fucking has always felt great, at least while it lasts. But with her, it's different. It's like I spent my life having a watered-down, skim milk version of fucking before I met her.

There's one huge difference between my wife and all the other women I've been with. I never loved any of them. Or respected them. Hell, I barely even liked a few. Sophie makes me feel shit I never thought was possible.

As soon as I pull out of her and glance down all those happy endorphins from mind-blowing sex disappear. "Goddamm it," I mutter at the sight of the crimson mixed in with the cream of our mutual releases.

"What?" Sophie asks. She's still lying prone on the bed, boneless from the great sex, her tangled black hair spilling around her in a beautiful puddle.

It's an effort to look away from her, to swallow around the growing boulder lodged in my throat, because despite her claim to love me, this still might change everything. "You're bleeding."

"Bleeding?" she repeats as if she can't comprehend the meaning of the word in her sex haze.

"Either I fucked you too hard or your period just started."

Sophie's brow is furrowed for a long moment as she considers the two possibilities. Maybe it makes me an asshole, but I hope I was just too rough.

Her hand slides down to her lower belly, and she winces as if her pelvis aches before lifting her head to look at the evidence for herself. "I thought...oh god," she whispers before she scrambles off the bed and rushes into the bathroom. The sound of the door slamming shut is more ominous than it should be.

It's her period.

Sophie's not pregnant, which means...I don't know what the fuck it means, and that infuriates me.

39

Sophie

After I take a hot shower, I have to wrap a towel around me to go get clothes and feminine products from my bedroom.

Lochlan's in his closet, an open suitcase on the bed when I start to walk back through. He returns, tossing a hanging wardrobe bag down beside the luggage.

"Are you leaving?" I ask him even though it's obvious he's packing to go somewhere.

He barely glances at me before he gets back to work, unzipping the bag. "Shouldn't I be asking you the same thing?"

I was expecting him to give me a response, not throw the question back at me. Why does he think I would leave now? Last night I told him I loved him, and I meant it. I know he feels the same even though he won't say it. He loves me but...does he not want to be near me if we can't have sex because it's my time of the month? I'm so damn confused, and the awful abdominal cramps don't help me to think clearly.

"Do you want me to leave?" I ask Lochlan softly.

"You can do whatever you want while I'm gone, Sophie."

Wow. He's using my real name as if he's pissed off at me. And I guess he might be disappointed with me, disappointed that I'm not going to have his baby, at least not this month, and we can't have sex.

"Where are you going?"

"I have a meeting in LA early in the morning. I'm going today to prepare with my attorney."

I wait for him to return from the closet again to answer me even though I really need to go get a tampon. "Your attorney? What's the meeting for?"

Bent over with his palms flat on the mattress he says, "I'm being sued by all the families of the people who died or were hurt in my casino. Now that I've settled down and married you, I look like less of a philandering dick. They're finally ready to negotiate a settlement I can actually live with rather than taking every penny I have along with every business, every property I own."

"What does us getting married have to do with the settlement?" I remark before it occurs to me. "Is that why you were in such a rush to marry Madison, to marry me after she ran away? To save your money from...from a lawsuit?"

"Yes. It was my attorney's idea."

"Your attorney's..." I trail off, unable to speak because of my burning throat and eyes.

Lochlan didn't want to marry me. I knew all along that I was just a pawn to be used for my dad and him. But I thought he had started to care about me. Nope. He just needed to look like a besotted husband.

"With a new wife and a baby on the way the lawyers wouldn't leave me broke and homeless, would they?" he asks.

So, he didn't really want to have a family with me. He just wanted me swollen and pregnant in public to gain more sympathy?

Oh, my fucking god.

Lochlan doesn't deserve any sympathy from the families who lost their loved ones.

Does my dad know why he was in a hurry for me to marry him? My father wanted Lochlan's contacts and Lochlan needed a wife.

If my father knew...well, this isn't something I can ask him over the phone. I want to see his face when I ask if he knew the real reason Lochlan insisted on marrying me.

When I reach for the door, Lochlan grumbles behind me, "I knew you would leave me."

"I'm not, that's not..." I start, but I'm too angry at him for using me to reassure him right now. Why should I when everything, our entire marriage, was a fake show I didn't know I was starring in? Deep down, even if Lochlan loves me, he's still a selfish dick.

"You deserve to lose everything," I tell him on the way out the door. I also take a little joy in telling him over my shoulder, "And by the way, don't count on getting a penny from my father either. He changed his mind about making you his heir."

"He what?" Lochlan exclaims before I slam the bedroom door behind me to escape to my own. I need to do something to work off my frustration before my hormones make me attack my bastard husband.

"You're slow today, Soph," Betsy calls out from the other side of the tennis court. The sixty-year-old woman still has more endurance than an eighteen-year-old. Me. She has more endurance than me.

"I'm slow because I'm in pain!" I yell back at her. And it's not just the abdominal pain I'm referring to. My heart aches. My entire body is in agony, all the way down to my soul.

"Why don't you call it good for today?" Lena asks from the other side of the fence. "Go lie down and we'll get you some pain meds and a heating pad."

"Fine," I cave, dropping my racquet right then and there on the court because going back to bed sounds good. "Sorry you came all the way out here," I tell Betsy.

"It's fine. Lochlan makes it worth my time," she says with a smile as we head off the court. I grit my teeth at the reminder of my rich husband who married me to stay rich. "Hope you feel better."

"Thanks," I reply with as much pep as I can muster at the moment.

On the way back to the house with Lena and Toni, I can't decide if I want to see Lochlan or not yet.

I hate that he's leaving, and that we had an argument. But I'm crushed that he had an ulterior motive for marrying me this entire time that he didn't tell me about. Crushed that he cares more about his money than me.

He mentioned the lawsuit several times over the past few weeks, but never that he was worried about losing everything. My father's empire must have been a backup plan. How far would he have gone to get his hands on his money and power?

Lochlan's bedroom is empty by the time I get changed in mine and crawl into the bed that feels empty without him. Toni appears a moment later with a glass of water, a bottle of ibuprofen, and a cordless heating pad.

"Thank you. I could've found all this, though. It's not your job to wait on me," I remind them.

"I don't mind. You're more than a job to us, girly. We're your friends. We're here for you whenever you need us."

"Thank you," I whisper again, unable to express how much their words mean to me.

"And our job is to keep you from all harm, even menstrual cramps," Toni adds.

"I hate them," I mutter as I swallow down two pills. "I can't play tennis and Lochlan is angry..."

"He'll get over it," Lena pipes up from behind Toni. Stepping up beside the other guard, she adds, "The man worships the ground you walk on."

"He only wanted to get married for the lawsuits," I admit to them. "Being a husband looks better than a single philandering brothel owner."

"Perhaps that's how it started, but Lochlan's head over heels in love with you now," Lena tells me.

"Then why hasn't he told me he loves me?"

"Because he's a man, and men can be stupid and stubborn because they hate being vulnerable. Especially men like Lochlan. He probably thinks admitting that he loves you will make him look weak."

"My father isn't weaker since he fell in love with Vanessa," I remark. "He might be slightly less violent, but he would burn the world down for her."

"And Lochlan would do the same for you," Toni says. "That doesn't have anything to do with the lawsuits."

"I don't know what to believe. My dad is coming by later," I tell them as I stare down at my phone that doesn't have any messages from Lochlan. Not that I expected any. "I might sleep until he gets here, so will you have someone wake me when he arrives?"

"Sure thing, girly," Lena agrees. "Get some rest and try not to stress too much about Lochlan's motives. You love him. He loves you. The rest isn't worth worrying about."

40

Lochlan

I knew it was bullshit when Sophie told me she loved me. It was only hours ago and now she's leaving. By the time I finished packing, her room was empty. She may have already left. I refuse to check my phone for notifications. I don't want to know. Because if she left, this time I won't go after her. I'm done chasing Sophie. If she doesn't want to be married to me, then I won't force her to stay for a second longer.

And I can't fucking believe Salvato is already shitting on our agreement. He may have been a long-term backup plan, but being his heir was better than no backup plan whatsoever. My only hope now is to settle with a little something left for me to live on until I figure out a new plan. Honestly, I think I would be relieved if I have to sell the brothels. Fuck them all. And fuck my father's legacy.

I thought I needed to keep the money flowing in to prove my father was wrong about me being a failure. But fuck him. The things people had to do to make him his fortune are fucking disgusting. I know from experience how it feels to be used, bought, and sold. I always thought my failure would result in me going broke and ending up back in the whore house to keep a roof over my head. I thought that was why my asshole father made me spend a month in that hell-hole. But he didn't do it to educate me on the inner working of his brothels or to teach me a lesson. He left me there to break me because he was a sick fuck who just enjoyed inflicting pain on others.

Every time I step foot inside one of the brothels and the smell of sweat, cum, and rubbers assaults me, my father wins. And I'm done letting him screw with me from the grave.

The bombing was my wake-up call to use my second chance at life to be a better man. It took finding a good woman, but I'm finally starting to get there. In fact, I feel damn good about the idea of selling everything my father ever touched. Starting over. I'm just not sure if Sophie will be by my side afterward or not.

First things first, I have to get through this meeting in LA and then I'll figure out what to do about my wife. Maybe Salvato was right, and Sophie was too young to marry. I rushed her into the wedding, knowing I didn't deserve her.

She may not ever believe me, but I always wanted her more than I wanted to be Salvato's successor. Needed her more than I ever needed to save my family's fucked up legacy, even if I didn't realize it until now.

Hopefully, it won't be too late to work things out when I get home. If she needs time, I'll give her time, as much of it as she needs.

Now where the fuck is Wolfe and Wade?

I'm waiting outside for them to bring around the SUV, debating whether or not I should suck up my pride, find Sophie, drop to my knees, and beg her for another chance when a sedan pulls up in the driveway. My brother, dressed in ripped jeans and an inside out shirt climbs out of the back seat with a backpack over his shoulder.

"What are you doing here?" I snap at Flynn as he approaches me, and the car drives off.

"It's my house too. I can't come over and go for a swim in my father's pool?"

"No, it's not your house. Not anymore. I'm on my way out and I don't want you here if I'm not around after that stupid little stunt you pulled the last time you showed up unannounced."

"Come on, bro. You can't be pissed at me for that shit. I know Shana is one of your favorites."

"Was. She was one of my favorite fucks before I got married. I never brought her slutty ass here. If I wanted her, I would've gone to her. I will never bring one of those money-grubbing whores into my home, and you won't either."

"Owen told me you didn't get a chance to screw Shana the night of the drone attack. We were just trying to help you out. I still can't believe Salvato didn't blow your brains out..."

"Well, you didn't help me out," I interrupt him. "You fucked shit up between me and my wife!"

Not that it matters now.

"Trouble with your child bride?" Flynn asks with a grin.

"That's none of your fucking business. Now get lost or I'll have the guards drag you off the property."

"Where are you headed off to?" he asks, fingers gripping the strap of his backpack and ignoring my command as usual.

"LA for a meeting to try and settle the civil suits." Not try. We're going to settle this shit, and I'm resigned to deal with the fallout as it comes.

"You're not gonna actually cave to those greedy clowns, are you?"

"People are dead and it's my fault," I remind him.

You deserve to lose everything.

That's what Sophie thinks, and she's right. "I was supposed to keep them safe in my casino and I didn't," I admit. "Now, you're leaving and I'm informing the guards out here that you're not allowed to step foot on this property again without my permission. And if you fuck shit up again, I'll kick you out of your cozy, rent-free apartment, and toss you out on the street. Do you understand me?"

"God, Loch, you sound just like our asshole father. Remember all the times he told you to stop fucking up? That you wouldn't ever be able to fill his shoes no matter how hard you tried?"

"I remember," I assure him, especially now when I'm on the verge of proving him right. "And he didn't even bother wasting time thinking about the possibility of you taking over shit."

"Fuck you," Flynn mutters just as Wolfe and Wade bring the SUV around.

"Just like our father, I don't have time to waste on you either," I say before I shove past him.

Owen's waiting at the airfield along with Warwick when I get there. Only one of them is flirting with a flight attendant.

"Everything set?" I ask the men while Wolfe loads my luggage.

Owen walks away from the woman without another glance. "Had to grease a few palms to get you off earlier than planned, but Flynn and I managed."

"I don't need to hear that," Warwick says before he climbs the steps to board the plane.

"Let's go then," I mutter before something brings me up short. "Wait. What do you mean you and Flynn greased palms?" I ask my cousin, reversing my steps. My brother was just at the house, asking where I was headed like he didn't have a clue.

"Oh, yeah, Flynn handled getting the pilots and plane ready while I got the control tower to squeeze you into the takeoff schedule."

"Flynn handled the plane and pilots?" I repeat, unable to believe my slacker brother was sober enough to do a goddamn thing worthwhile. Not unless he was asking the pilots to toss my body out the door once they hit thirty-thousand feet.

"That's right. He really came through for once," Owen replies.

"I'm shocked. And surprised he didn't mention it when I saw

him at the house, especially since he doesn't think I should pay the families a dime."

"No shit? That's fucked up. Millions won't bring back a dead family member, but it's the least you can do, right?"

"Right," I agree. I take two more steps toward the stairs of the plane, but something stops me again. I figure my head is just messed up over leaving Sophie, or Sophie possibly leaving me. Everything with her feels like throwing a knife up in the air and waiting for it to come back down. But there's also something else nagging me.

Finally pulling out my phone from my suit pocket, I scroll through the messages looking for the one that says she's left, that she's gone to Dante's, and her things are being packed up as we speak.

But I don't have any messages.

I find Lena's contact and call it.

"Hey, boss," she answers right away.

"Where are you?"

"At the estate."

"With Sophie? She's still there?"

"Yes. She tried to play a match with Betsy, but called it quits after the first set because she was cramping."

"Cramping?"

"It's the time of the month so she took some meds and went back to bed."

I release the breath I had been holding during our entire conversation.

"She said something about Dante coming over later."

"Dante's coming to the estate?"

"Yes. Is that a problem? I thought you didn't mind him visiting."

"I don't. I just thought Sophie would go to him."

After a moment of silence, Lena asks, "Are you on your way to LA?"

"I was about to take off a little earlier than planned, but maybe I shouldn't go."

"Sophie will be fine, sir. There's nothing you can do for her. She's got pain relievers and a heating pad. Toni and I will keep an eye on her."

"No, it's not just Sophie. It's also Flynn."

"What's up? The little prick is still lurking around here somewhere."

"He's still there? Why?"

"I don't know. Want me to go find him and ask?"

"Yes. Don't take your eyes off him. And have one of the guards track down all the brothel surveillance footage from the day of the drone attack. I want to know where he was and what he was doing the entire time."

"Wow. You think your brother could've been behind the attack on Sophie? But why?"

"Because if anything happened to her, Dante would've killed me," I explain. It's so damn obvious. Why didn't I realize it before now? Flynn hates me. Of course he wants me dead because he wants our family's money and thinks that once I'm out of the way, he'll have access. But he would also have to kill Owen since he's third in line. I knew the son of a bitch wasn't trustworthy, but I never expected him to betray me, or try to kill me.

Suddenly, I recall the night before the charity poker tournament. It was so long ago, and so traumatic that I had forgotten everything about the days preceding it. "Flynn was in the event room the night before the bombing," I say aloud, forgetting about the phone at my ear until Lena mutters, "Oh fuck."

The memory comes back to me clear as day. Hell, I had forgotten it before now, maybe because of the concussion or the chaos. Either way, I remember it all now.

"He was begging to come to the event the next day. It was right after his third DWI, he refused to get sober, and I didn't want him to act a fool in front of the celebrities who were there to raise money for charity."

"But Flynn was there long enough to possibly plant the bomb?"

"Yes. He wants me dead and must have been working with

Petrov or Kozlov. He would do anything for a little cash. And he was planning to let Dante finish the job for him when he attacked Sophie because his first plan failed," I tell her. "Put every guard at the estate on Sophie's room right now."

"Yes, sir," Lena agrees. "But she's in your room, not hers."

I'm surprised but relieved. "Good."

Then Lena says, "Hold on. I think I know where he is."

"He had a backpack," I say in a rush when I remember him hefting it up his shoulder like it was heavy. I assumed it was a change of clothes or swimsuit, but who the fuck knows what he was carrying. Everything I thought I knew about my drug-addicted, slack-ass half-brother has gone out the window.

It was strange that Flynn didn't ask me for money for several months after the bombing. I thought it was because he knew I would refuse, but I can't help but wonder if he got a big fat payday from Petrov or Kozlov. We checked casino employees bank accounts but never my brother's. If I had to bet, he probably got cash and kept it under the mattress or some stupid shit to keep anyone from tracing it.

"Cancel the flight!" I shout over to Owen. "Get Warwick and the pilots off the plane and check it for a bomb!"

As if he heard me yelling, the lawyer sticks his head out the door when Owen's halfway up the boarding stairs. "What's going on? Are you leaving?" he asks since I'm already heading back toward the SUV.

"Tell the pilots there could be a bomb and get the hell out of there. I have to go."

"Go where? We can't miss this meeting in LA, Dunne. It could be our last chance to settle. What could possibly be more important than losing your entire fortune?"

"Losing my wife."

"What?" Owen pushes past him to get the pilots out since Warwick's not moving.

"Move it," I tell him. Finally, he jogs down the stairs. When he reaches the bottom I tell him, "Take a commercial flight to get to the meeting. Tell them I'll pay them whatever they fucking want."

"Are you sure?" he asks just as Lena says into my ear, "Found him," Lena says.

"Yes," I reply then strain to hear the muffled conversation through the phone knowing Lena's smart enough not to confront him without her gun out and ready after the recent revelation.

Except, I don't hear anything except a loud pop then the swishing like her phone is moving around.

"Lena?" I shout. She doesn't answer. "Lena!"

When it becomes clear that she's not going to respond and something is wrong, I hang up and call Sophie as I climb into the back of the SUV.

I'd give every penny I have just to know Sophie is safe right now.

Just like before, when Wolfe told me about the drones, all I care about is her safety. She means more to me than anything else.

And I'm an idiot for taking this long to figure that out when it could be too late.

41

Sophie

Unable to sleep, I toss and turn, tears continuously leaking from my eyes. Why does it feel so hard to forgive Lochlan?

Because he refuses to tell me he loves me, to prove to me that he wanted me to be his wife for no other reason?

The past is in the past. I should let it go and talk to him when he gets back, see if he'll finally admit he feels even a little bit of what I feel for him.

I'm just so hurt. And angry, mostly at myself for not realizing our marriage was a necessity for him. The sex is just an added benefit.

The screen of my phone lights up again from the charger on the bedside table with another incoming call from Lochlan. Just like the previous times, I don't answer it. I need to figure out where my head and heart are at before I speak to him again. Hopefully by the time he's home from LA I'll be ready to face him. Not yet, though.

Somewhere in the house, I hear a series of loud pops. Then

several more. It sounds...I think it's gunfire. My father taught me to shoot a few years ago, so I'm almost certain it's a gun. Guns, plural.

I want to charge out into the hallway to see what's going on, but I know that would be stupid if someone's in the house shooting at guards.

And all I have is Lochlan's knife tucked into my sports bra, the cool steel a small comfort but not very effective against bullets.

Walking around the bed, I yank my phone off the charger to text Lena...just as the bedroom door opens.

I can't decide if I'm relieved or frustrated that Lochlan cancelled his trip to come back home. Mostly relieved even if he is a fucking liar and I'm not ready to forgive him.

But it's not Lochlan who strolls into the dim bedroom, shutting the door behind him and locking it. It's just someone who happens to look like him.

"Flynn?" I say in surprise, my eyes instantly lowering to the gun in his hand, pointed right at me.

I stand there frozen, unsure what to do as I stare at him in disbelief. He's wearing a backpack, and over his tee is a thick black vest, like the kind cops wear. Bulletproof. He wore it to shoot the guards. Oh, no. Lena and Toni!

"Did you...did you kill the guards?" All I can think to do is talk, to try and talk to him before he pulls the trigger and then I'm dead like the others may already be.

"After I blew up the guard house, there were only four in the house. Two outside, two in. It was easy as fuck to down them."

Oh god.

"Why? Wh-what are you doing here, Flynn? You know Lochlan would slit your throat if he found you in our room. And killing his guards..."

"Didn't you know? Lochlan and I have shared plenty of women in the past. But that's not what this is about."

"Then wh-what is it about?" I ask, trying to stay calm. He probably knows Lochlan is on a plane headed to LA. If Lena and Toni have been shot, I need to get them help here fast. With a few taps of my finger I could call nine-one-one. I look down at the device and Flynn says, "Drop it."

Shit.

"Now!" His command reminds me of Lochlan's, except it isn't sexy, just terrifying.

I let the phone fall to the floor, landing with a bounce on the carpet. "Why?" I ask him. "Why are you doing this?"

"Loch's gotten too suspicious. I'll be damned if I let that Eligor fucker take out my eyes and fuck the socket."

Holy shit.

The torture rumor worked, just not exactly the way we hoped. In fact, I think it's backfiring.

"You...you're the casino bomber? The one behind the drone attack?" And now he's desperate, determined to avoid being questioned like a regular employee.

"It was nothing personal with the drones, Snow White. I just needed your daddy to get Loch out of the way so I can finally get what's owed to me."

"Owed?" I repeat.

"Our asshole father left everything to Loch when he should've given me half. Now, I'm Loch's next of kin. Well, after you," he says with a grin, wobbling the gun toward me. It hasn't slipped my notice that he doesn't have a steady hand. "It's a shame since I wouldn't have minded keeping you for myself." His dark eyes go to the restraints hanging from the headboard and footboard, the gun lowering a few inches as he examines them. "I like kinky fucks too. Had to get used to them since all the bitches at the local brothel want me to fuck them just like Loch does them."

Of course, he's jealous of his brother that has all the money, power, and all the women he wants. I guess Flynn looks enough like Lochlan for them to pretend. I could've done without the image of my husband fucking them all.

"It's just not as much fun when they're always doped up and

have been fucked so many times that nothing I do ever hurts them. And it's too bad I can't cut them all up, but then we wouldn't make any money off them."

"Kill Lochlan," I blurt out. "I'll give you everything he owns. I was planning to leave him anyway since I'm not pregnant." Of course I don't want him to kill Lochlan. I just need time to talk my way out of this alive so I can call and warn Lochlan. I don't want to have to be the one who kills Lochlan's brother to save myself, even if he deserves it.

"Bullshit. Loch was determined to put a kid in you, and I can't chance letting you leave then have his spawn in a few months."

"I'm not pregnant," I assure him, happy that's the case right now. "I swear. My period came today, so no baby. Loch was disappointed, angry at me even. But trust me, I'm more relieved than anyone."

His eyes narrow. "Prove it."

"What?"

"Prove you're on your period, and maybe I'll consider letting you live."

Since there is no way I'm letting him anywhere near my body, I tell him, "You can look in the bathroom trashcan. All the evidence you need is in there."

And while he's in there, I can grab my phone and run.

"Fine. I'll look but you're coming with me." He keeps his gun at the ready. "Every step I take toward the bathroom, you follow. Keep your palms up too. Understood?"

"Y-yes," I agree. Maybe once he has the proof he wants he'll leave me alone, let me go back home to my father. I could try and convince him that Dante would kill everyone in Lochlan's family if I die. It may not even be an exaggeration. If I could just have time until my father shows up or I can call Lochan or scream for more guards, then they can take Flynn out and I won't have to fight him.

In the bathroom, Flynn peers over into the trash bin and his nose wrinkles at the sight of feminine product wrappers. "All right. I believe you."

"Good. Great. Can I go now? I'll go straight back to Dante's," I say, using his name as a reminder of the man who would avenge me. "We can pretend this never happened. I wanted a divorce anyway."

"No. You'll stay with me. Otherwise, you might try to contact Lochlan and warn him his plane will never make it to LA."

"His plane?"

No. No, no, no.

Oh god. How does he know Lochlan's plane won't make it? What did he do? God, it may already be too late!

I can't lose Lochlan; can't have the last thing I said to him be that he deserved to lose everything. I was angry and hurt and fuck, I love him so much and I may never get to say those words to him again.

"Go back around the bed and kick your phone over to me, Snow White."

It takes me several seconds to realize what he wants me to do because my head is in a panic and my heart feels like it's being ripped down the middle.

"I won't. I won't call him."

"Shut up, Snow White," he says. "Don't lie to me."

I am a horrible liar. I close my mouth, trying to come up with a plan as I walk around the foot of the bed, eager to put more space between us. My bare foot kicks at the device and it easily slides across the carpet to Flynn.

He bends down and picks it up with his gun still in his right hand, not taking his eyes off me. He shoves my phone into his back pocket.

Flynn's gaze sweeps over me for several silent moments. "I am glad I won't have to kill you. You're too pretty to die." Now, he retrieves a huge knife from a leather holster attached to the side of his belt. It's easily twice the size of Lochlan's extended switchblade. The psycho puts the pointed tip of the long, thick blade to his lips. "In fact, I might just keep you for myself. You were a virgin before Loch, right? I bet I could find all sorts of ways to hurt you if you were tied up in my bed."

Flipping the knife over, he lunges forward to stab the mattress between us, dragging the blade through the bedding, easily ripping it. Unlike when Lochlan threatened me with a knife, I'm not turned on by Flynn's violent demonstration.

Why is he even bothering to threaten me with the knife when he has a gun?

Unless the knife is for carving into skin, for his enjoyment. Not to kill but to viciously injure.

He's a jealous asshole and apparently a psychopath who likes hurting women.

My stomach rolls and I'm certain I'm going to throw up all over the bed in front of me I'm using as a necessary buffer between us. Would vomiting even deter the crazy bastard? Probably not.

"We can use Loch's bed since he won't be sleeping in it again and it's already got the restraints built into the headboard and footboard."

"How will you...how do you plan to kill him?" I ask to keep him talking rather than attacking me. "Is...is there a bomb? On the plane? Did you, were you really the one who bombed the casino and sent the drones after me?"

"I missed Loch, then missed you. I won't miss this time. A dozen kamikaze drones are locked on the plane, all set to hit it right at noon. They won't miss, no matter where in the sky it is or if it's still on the ground at the airport."

"That's...I'm glad," I lie. I need to get my phone back, to try and call him. Maybe he's taking a different plane or...or...I can't fucking think! I have to talk about something, anything while figuring out my next step.

"I tried to choke Loch the first time he fucked me," I admit just to try and convince Flynn that I hate him.

"Really?" Flynn asks, sounding surprised.

"Yes."

"Too bad you didn't kill him then. Now get on the bed."

"What?"

"I want you in those cuffs. You'll forget all about him when I'm

362

making you scream, carving this knife into your flawless flesh. I can tell just by looking at you that you've got a low pain tolerance. I bet Daddy never let anyone hurt you before, which will make it even more fun for me to slice you up."

"Someone...more guards will come when they hear me," I say in a rush. "They'll see the guards you...the guards you shot."

"Anyone who tries to come through that door will get their head blown off. I've got more bullets than Loch has guards." Gesturing to the bed with the gun he says, "Now quit stalling and get the fuck on the bed, Snow White. Convince me you'll do what I say, so I won't have to kill you too."

No, I'll just wish I were dead while he drags that blade across my skin. I bet he'll keep the gun in his dominant right hand and the knife in the shaky left to do maximum damage.

"Wait," I say, my head spinning as I try to figure out how to keep him talking until my dad shows up or guards get to the bedroom. Someone has to come! I have to believe that, or I'll fall to pieces. "Will you tell me about the drones? The ones that came after me?"

"They were pre-programmed to the time and destination—your face. Once the first one found you outside, the rest were sent to kill you. I controlled them from the brothel."

"That's...that's impressive," I say to try and stroke his ego.

"Get up there on the bed and fasten your left wrist to the cuff. I'll do the rest," he orders me as he shrugs off the straps of his backpack.

Glancing at the closed and locked door, I consider screaming for help now. Would Flynn try to kill me for that? He's already said he would kill anyone who tries to come into the room. I don't want anyone's death on my hands. So, with shaky hands of my own, I turn my back to Flynn to crawl up on the bed. While reaching for the cuff, I quickly remove the knife from my bra and free the blade with my other hand.

I can do this. I can protect myself and kill him if I have to in order to keep everyone else safe. I need my phone back to call Lochlan, and there's only one way I'm going to get it back—over Flynn's dead body.

"Hurry up," he says from behind me, still having no clue that I'm armed. Lochlan's naughty little switchblade going up against Flynn's gun and giant blade. The odds are horrible, but it's all I have. "You better have that cuff fastened before I get my dick out."

Yes, Flynn. Pull your dick out. That's the first place I'll aim because I refuse to let it anywhere near my body.

42

Lochlan

The smoke from the guard house fire could be seen for miles. Firetrucks had already arrived when the SUV skids to a stop at the front of the house. Two guards lie dead at the doorway right where I left them standing earlier. There's not a gun to be found in either of their hands, as if they were ambushed by someone they thought wasn't a threat.

And inside, the house is way too quiet. Or it was until I hear the screams coming from upstairs sending me running toward the staircase as fast as my legs will go because it sounded like Sophie. If she's screaming she's still alive which is a relief, but I'm terrified to find out what he's doing to make her scream like that. And why it sounds like it was coming from the direction of my bedroom.

There's blood splattered all over the foyer, a trail of it leading up the stairs.

"Jesus," I mutter at the scene before me as Wolfe and Wade run past me. I knew shit was bad when I saw the blood loss, but I still wasn't prepared to see Toni and Lena lying on the staircase. That's when I realize that the stains were left behind by them. Both are severely injured, but still trying to get up the flight of stairs to Sophie.

"Help...coming," Lena says as I approach her. She's holding a phone in her left hand and gun in the right that's hanging awkwardly. I feel like I'm in a nightmare. Lena's a sharpshooter with a hell of a shot. If Flynn took her down, Sophie won't stand a chance. Wolfe's jacket is shrugged off, and he's kneeling down, pressing it to Lena's abdomen while Wade tends to Toni who is thankfully also moving.

"Nine-one-one?" I ask as I remove her fingers from the gun in her hand and make sure the safety is off and there's a bullet in the chamber. There's another scream, making my heart drop to my stomach.

"Yes. Go," Lena urges me on.

"Loch wait!" Wolfe calls out, using my first name in his urgency to stop me.

"I've got this, stay with them!" I call back to him, then hear his footsteps and Wade's following me to the bedroom despite my orders. It barely registers at the same time my phone is ringing from somewhere on my body.

I try the doorknob first which is locked. I consider shooting it open, but if Sophie's on the other side trying to escape, I could hit her. Lena's gun at the ready in my hand, I lift my foot, slamming my heel into the wood near the knob to punch through. As soon as I'm inside, I lift my gun to aim it at Flynn just as he lets out another shrill scream.

"Jesus Christ," Wolfe mutters when he shoulders past me.

Neither Flynn nor Sophie seem to notice we're in the room pointing the muzzles of our guns at the son of a bitch. He's too busy writhing around the floor in a puddle of blood. Rolling from side to side, he screeches at the top of his lungs. His bloody hands are clutching at the gushing coming from his crotch.

Realizing it was him screaming and not Sophie, that he's no longer a threat, I turn my attention to my wife. She's kneeling on the bed in her cotton shorts and tee, her back to the door, holding a bloody knife in her left hand, my knife, and a gun that must be Flynn's pointed at the fucker as if ready to strike him again if necessary. Her phone is lying on the mattress in front of her, the screen lit up like...she was calling me. There's blood on the device and the torn bedding like she used her thumb or knuckles to dial while refusing to put down the dripping knife.

I quickly search her body for injuries as I continue listening to my voicemail message coming from the phone. Other than Sophie's hands, there's a light splatter of crimson on her arms, but that's it. She's looks miraculously unharmed.

"Princess," I say in relief. Her head finally turns toward the door as if she hadn't heard us bust through because Flynn was screaming so loudly.

"Lochlan?" Her blue eyes blink at me then the phone before staring at me again, her cheeks glistening. "Your plane didn't explode?"

"I'm so sorry I left you, baby," I tell her as I go to her and peel the weapons from her shaking hands. "Are you okay? Did he touch you? Hurt you?"

She shakes her head. "I'm sorry I...he wanted to kill you. I thought I was too late," she says. "He wanted to kill me at first. I convinced him not to and-and he decided he wanted to put me in the cuffs and cut me up instead."

My gun is raised and aimed at Flynn's head again, but Sophie quickly drops her weapons to the mattress in a clatter, then her bloody right hand covers the arm of my suit and lowers it.

"Not yet," she says softly.

Turning to look at her, I roar, "He killed all those people in the bombing! He sent the fucking drones after you, killed my guards, and was going to blow up my plane!"

Sophie winces then stares at Flynn on the floor but continues clutching my arm. "I know. I know. Just...let him suffer a little longer. He can't hurt us anymore."

God, I love this woman.

"Get him out of here and go help the women," I tell my guards. "Let the paramedics keep him alive, but don't let them take him to the hospital."

"Yes, sir," Wolfe agrees as he and Wade grab either of Flynn's arms to drag him out of the bedroom squalling.

Once they're gone, I lower my gun, putting it down on the bed to cradle Sophie's damp face in my hands, pressings my lips to hers.

She's here, she's alive. Flynn didn't hurt her, and fuck, I hope she's going to stay.

The fact that Sophie kisses me back gives me hope that she's not going to leave me. Still, I need to know for sure. How could she want to stay in this house another second when she's nearly been killed here twice?

Pulling away first, Sophie says, "Toni? Lena? Are they..."

"Alive but badly injured. They tried to crawl up the steps to protect you."

She nods and then throws her arms around my neck, pulling me to her. "I thought you were dead. That the plane left...and I would be too late."

"I didn't want to leave you after our fight. Then I finally figured out the bomber was Flynn. It was my own damn brother all along."

"I'm sorry," she whispers against my neck.

"You don't have anything to apologize for. I'm the one who is sorry. I keep failing you, and I'm terrified of losing you. I'd give anything to keep you, princess. Anything. Everything."

Her bloody fingers clutch the back of my suit jacket tighter. "Do you love me or—"

"Yes," I assure her. Pulling back to see her face, I cup her chin to lift her glistening eyes to mine. "Of course, I love you. Last night you said you knew I did even if I didn't say it."

"But this morning, I thought you just married me to have a family, to save your money. Then I...I just mutilated your brother..."

"Fuck the lawsuit and fuck Flynn," I grumble as I wrap my arms around her again. "He had it coming, and I'll pay every penny they want from me. All I care about is you, princess. Only you."

∼

The rest of the afternoon and into the next day is a shitshow of telling cops who want to talk to Sophie to fuck off until the smoke literally clears, then convincing Dante that his daughter is safe and unharmed, capable of taking care of herself since I let her down again. The easiest part was lying to hospital staff, telling them Sophie and I were family so we could see Lena and Toni.

Both of the guards suffered serious injuries. Lena's right arm was all shot up, and it could take months of physical therapy to get full use back in it. She also needed surgery to repair the damage.

Toni took a bullet through her inner shoulder, just missing her heart, and two in her leg. She lost a lot of blood, but the surgeons say she should also make a full recovery.

Sophie and I then spent the rest of the night going house to house to break the news to the families of the deceased estate guards. It feels like their blood is soaking my hands, even though it was Flynn who killed them.

I should've figured out he was behind the bombing, the drones, and killed him before he hurt anyone else.

I'll never forgive myself for that failure.

For nearly losing Sophie. For the fate worse than death she could've endured if I hadn't come back home.

"What a fucking day and a half," I groan when Sophie and I finally make it to her old bedroom since ours still looks like a crime scene.

"Worst day ever," Sophie agrees as she flops onto the bed on her stomach.

"At least Lena and Toni will be okay. I'll make sure the two of them and all of the families of the fallen guards are paid first from the sale of the brothels. The rest will go to the bombing victims. And fuck, I hope I'm not responsible for killing anyone else except Flynn."

As the cherry on top of the past twenty-four hours, Warwick called to tell me he's settled the civil case to the tune of three-hundred million dollars.

When I climb into bed, too tired to take off anything except my shoes, Sophie reaches over to cover the top of my hand with hers.

"If you're worried about paying the settlement, I could...I could ask my father to reconsider making you his heir."

Rather than get upset at the reminder like I did yesterday morning I just chuckle. Or try to make a similar sound. It feels like a year has passed rather than a single day. "That's what you're thinking about right now?"

Sophie nods. "Aren't you?"

"Yes, but not how you think," I promise her, finding the strength to lift the back of her hand to my mouth to kiss it. "You know, after you called me daddy in front of Dante, I shouldn't be surprised he doesn't want me to be his successor. Still absolutely worth it, though."

"It wasn't that that made him change his mind. When I came home upset, he told Cass and Cole that he would choose one of them." I don't even flinch when she says the other man's name, which seems like progress.

"Oh, yeah? Poor Cole. I actually pity that blond bastard."

"Why?"

"Because I think your sister can be a vicious little bitch when provoked. I bet she'll do whatever it takes to beat Cole, even if it's just for spite. He should watch his back, or she'll stab him in it."

"So, you think my father will choose her?" she asks. "And you're...okay with that?"

"I don't know. Cole *is* Petrov's grandson. Blood, family, means more to the old Russians than most other mafias." I pause then add,

"At first, yes, Dante's money and power was my backup plan because of the civil case threatening to leave me bankrupt. But lately, I think I just wanted to make sure I could give you the kind of life you deserve."

"For richer or poorer," she says softly. "I *never* cared about how much money you had."

"I know. I cared, though, even though money never brought me happiness. Only you ever did that."

Biting her bottom lip, she asks, "So do you still want a family even if you won't be Dante's heir and the civil case is settled?"

I tell her the honest to god truth. "Yes. Fuck yes, I want to have babies with you. Lots of them. But if you don't want to be a mother..."

"I don't know if I would be a good mother. I never had one before my dad married Vanessa."

"I didn't have one that stuck around," I remind her. "But I know you and I could figure out how to be good parents together if you wanted to."

"I wasn't sure I could even take care of myself until yesterday. I didn't want anyone to die trying to save me."

"I knew you could protect yourself if you had to, princess."

"Flynn deserves to die slowly now that he's confessed to all the horrible things he did," Sophie says. "Does that make me a bad person, to want him to suffer? To like that he's suffering?" she asks.

"No, baby. You're my ruthless mafia princess, and you're fucking perfect. I love everything about you, but especially that side."

"I love you too," she replies followed by a yawn.

"Try to get some sleep, baby. I know you're exhausted."

"Okay," she agrees. Pulling our clasped hands toward her, she rests her cheek on them and closes her eyes.

I slide closer, until I can wrap my arm around her, tucking her against my chest.

Before either of us drift off, Sophie says softly, "Your knife saved my life too."

"*You* saved your life," I tell her, placing a kiss on the top of her head.

"Yeah, maybe. But I want it back."

"It's yours, princess," I assure her. "And so am I. For all of our days."

EPILOGUE

Lochlan

One year later...

F lynn lived long enough for the District Attorney to gather enough evidence to arrest him and charge him for the casino bombing, the drone attack on the estate, killing the guards, and attacking my plane that was destroyed at the airport. At least everyone had been evacuated before the drones blew it up.

My idiot brother also confessed that he had some help from Shana, and that there was Russian dissent in the ranks following Salvato's takeover. They purchased the drones and shit and even taught him how to operate them. Dante intends to find each and every one of the culprits and make them pay. I'm guessing he'll let Eli have a little fun with them as well.

For his assistance in questioning casino employees, I gave Eli an hour with Flynn and Shana before I finished both off myself.

They were begging for death by the time that crazy bastard was done.

I offered to let Sophie put the final bullet in the whore, but she declined, saying she had seen enough violence to last a lifetime.

I sold every brothel in every country throughout the world to pay off the settlement with all of the bombing victims, guards, and their families.

My casino and family's estate are all that's left, but it's all my wife and I need.

Well, Sophie also needs tennis. Thankfully the tennis center welcomed her back once the news spread of Flynn being responsible for all the shit that went down.

And while I usually stay away from the center, knowing Julia Townsend doesn't want to be associated with a lowlife like me, Julia actually invited me today.

I slip in with Wade and Wolfe, Lena, and Toni, well, as much as the five of us can slip in anywhere, at the end of the day's lessons. We watch from afar as Julia and the other three women approach Sophie and offer her a piece of paper. A teaching certificate granted following the completion of her twelve months of part-time, supervised instruction.

Sophie reads the paper, then slaps her palm over her gaping mouth. She lunges forward as if to hug the women before catching herself. They offer their congratulations, then point in our direction.

As soon as Sophie sees us, she runs over and jumps into my arms.

"I did it! I'm a certified teacher!" she says as I lift her off the floor. Reminding myself there are kids around is the only thing that keeps my hand from going up her tennis skirt.

"You earned it, princess. Congratulations."

I let her down, still clutching the paper in her hand when she hugs her guards who are almost as good as new. Toni has a slight limp and Lena isn't a consistent perfect shot, but I wouldn't want anyone else protecting my wife.

Facing us all, clutching the certificate to her chest she says, "Julia offered me a full-time teaching position."

"That's great, baby."

Lena says, "Congrats, girly."

"Yeah, Sophie. You deserve it," Toni agrees.

"Thank you all. I really appreciate it," Sophie says. She sinks her bottom teeth into her lip like she wants to say more but stops herself as she leads the way out into the parking lot.

"Everything okay, princess?" I ask her when we're standing next to one of the SUVs.

She nods and glances over toward the tennis center before facing me again with an odd combination of something like hope and fear in her wide blue eyes. "I was just wondering if Julia will be upset when I tell her I'll need to take a few months off next spring."

"Why would you need time off?" Grinning at her, I lower my gaze to her long legs and working my way up before reaching for her waist to pull her closer. "Are you planning on us taking a trip around the world?" Fucking my Snow White in every major city in Europe could be fun.

As if knowing exactly where my thoughts went, Sophie's palms flatten against my chest as she says, "Sorry, but no, I'm not planning a trip."

Then she blinks up at me rapidly, as if she's about to burst into tears. My gorgeous wife starts chewing on her lip again, knowing what that does to me. If she bites down any harder, it's going to start bleeding. When that happens, I'll have no choice but to put her on her knees and wrap her sore lips around my cock. But first, I feel like I'm missing something here, and not knowing is driving me crazy. "So then why won't you be able to teach for a few months?"

Finally, she gives me an explanation. Her voice is so soft, I nearly miss it. "Because I'll be on maternity leave."

"Maternity leave?" I repeat, turning the phrase over a few times in my head before it hits me, nearly knocking me on my ass. I actually do stumble back the few inches into the side panel of the SUV. "Maternity...you're...really?" My eyes lower to her smooth, flat stomach that doesn't look any different yet. I had my hands on every inch of my wife this morning, especially her pelvis. I had to hold it down when I licked her pussy, and it didn't feel different. Then I came inside of her, wanting to put a baby in her, even though she's been taking birth control pills since the first month we were married. Sophie wanted to focus on her certificate that we knew would take a year since she only volunteered on a part-time basis.

"Pills?" I say, unable to speak in complete sentences as I watch her lower belly as if it'll suddenly pop while we're talking. And where the hell are her guards? Did they know? They've apparently stepped back to give us privacy.

"I stopped my birth control last month. I didn't know it would happen this soon. I...I wanted to surprise you."

I'm fucking speechless. This is the last thing I expected to happen today.

"Are you...are you happy?" she asks, as if I could be anything other than thrilled after spending the past thirteen months coming inside her, wishing for this very thing, even knowing it wasn't feasible because of her damn pills.

Reaching for her face, I slam my mouth over hers, showing her how damn happy I am with the stroke of my tongue along hers. Over and over again as I wrap my arms around her down her back to the cock-teasing skirt.

Reaching behind me, I fumble for the door handle of the SUV opening the door. Spinning us around, I lift Sophie onto the seat, following her inside as she scoots backward on the black leather.

After I slam the door behind me, I climb on top of her. Even in the dark interior, I can see Sophie's pale face, blue eyes widening. "You...you still want me, even though I'm...?"

"God, yes," I tell her as I run my hand up her skirt to pull down her panties just far enough to rub her pussy. "I've never wanted you more than I do right fucking now. There's a part of me living and growing inside of you. You have no idea how much I love that."

Sophie's eyes close on a moan as my finger drags down her folds, pressing right into her pussy.

"Look at me, Sophie," I command her as I add a finger, in a hurry to get her ready for me. Based on how wet she's getting already, that won't be a problem. Beautiful blue eyes blink open, shining up at me with tears. Happy ones or at least they will be. "I love you and I'll always want you, any way I can have you. Now, can I fuck your brains out without it fucking up our baby?"

She smiles and nods enthusiastically, her hips squirming toward my hand, teeth nearly piercing her lip. "But what if someone sees us?"

"That's what the guards and tinted windows are for, princess."

Moaning my name when I press my thumb to her clit, her back arches, and eyes close again.

"Yes! Uh! Please, Lochlan!" Sophie's hand covers mine, pressing it into her body even harder until her thighs tremble and the walls of her cunt squeeze my fingers. While Sophie's hips ride out the pleasure on my hand, I use my free one to undo my pants. Getting my dick out in record time, I remove my fingers and shove inside before her pussy stops spasming.

"Oh, fuck yes, baby," I groan as I fuck into her tight heat with quick thrusts, needing to come hard and fast before my balls explode.

As if she's been underwater and is just now coming up for air, Sophie's eyes fly open on a gasp. Her legs wrap around my waist, and her hips lift to meet mine. Grabbing onto my back, she holds on tight, as if she's getting close again already.

"Are you going to come on my cock, princess?"

"Mmm," she hums. Her lips and tongue kiss my neck, making me shiver. "I'm so close...I need...I..."

Pulling back to see her face, I say, "Tell me what you need to come, baby."

"I need you. Just you." Sophie looks up and kills me with four little words, "Fuck me harder, *Daddy*."

The End

COMING SOON!

Thank you so much for reading *Ruthless Little Games*! If you enjoyed it, please take a moment to leave a review.

Vicious Little Games is coming soon!

Order your copy now!

ALSO BY LANE HART

While you wait for the next book, read the <u>complete</u> Savage Kings MC series!

"The rugged men of the Savage Kings Motorcycle Club are hardened and ruthless — especially when it comes to protecting the women they love! A sizzling series featuring a brother's best friend, a sexy second chance, a determined single dad, and more."

https://mybook.to/SKChase

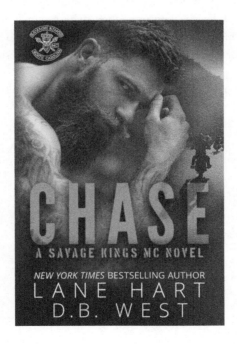

Chase Fury, the VP of the Savage Kings MC has dealt with his fair share of tragedy over the years. He never wanted the responsibility that comes with being at the head of the table, preferring to leave that to his brother, Torin.

But after an unexpected attack on the Kings sends his brothers on a path of vengeance, Chase will have no choice but to take on the burden of being the man in charge.

Reporter Sasha Sheridan has steered clear of any and all bad boy bikers wearing the bearded skull for the last ten years. While investigating a story, she suddenly finds herself back in the crosshairs of the Savage Kings. Uncovering the secrets that the club's president is trying to keep hidden may very well put her life in danger. She may be able to handle the threat, but she can't escape the man who broke her heart.

Chase hasn't forgiven himself for hurting Sasha and causing her an unbelievable amount of pain. He still wears her name on his chest, a reminder of the night that he wrecked his bike and everything the two of them had together. Now, with secrets, lies, bloodshed, and violence causing chaos in the club, Chase is determined to use his second chance with Sasha to keep her safe. He never imagined that the best way to do that would be to get her as far away from him and the MC as possible.

Read now: https://mybook.to/SKChase

ABOUT THE AUTHOR

New York Times bestselling author Lane Hart lives in North Carolina with her husband, author D.B. West, and their two children. She enjoys spending the summers on the beach and watching football in the fall.

Connect with Lane:

Author Store: https://www.authorlanehart.com/
Tiktok: https://www.tiktok.com/@hartandwestbooks
Facebook: http://www.facebook.com/lanehartbooks
Instagram: https://www.instagram.com/authorlanehart/
Website: http://www.lanehartbooks.com
Email: lane.hart@hotmail.com

Find all of Lane's books on her Amazon author page!

Sign up for Lane and DB's newsletter to get updates on new releases and freebies!

Join Lane's Facebook group to read books before they're released, help choose covers, character names, and titles of books! https://www.facebook.com/groups/bookboyfriendswanted/

Made in United States
Orlando, FL
28 September 2024

52057048R00215